BLOOD ON THE BRIDGE

Christopher H. Meehan

ISBN 1-882376-59-5

Cover photography and illustration by Aaron Phipps

Thunder Bay Press
Holt, Michigan

To Mary,
for her many ways of helping.

Other Novels by Christopher H. Meehan

Deadly Waters
Murder on the Grand

CHAPTER 1
ARLY

Out of breath from running through damp woods, across a cornfield and around the gravel pit, Arly stopped in the driveway of the hillbilly singer's doublewide and felt for the Colt knife at his side. He could not damned believe how this had gone down, how Lonnie had screwed him but royal.

Looking either way down the road and seeing no one, he started walking, a stealth soldier on a mission. The trailer was mostly dark. Soft light in there someplace. Go slow, he warned himself. Don't spook them again. But goddamnitoshit, they had fucked him, after he had cut them in and was planning to give them their share. He didn't need them beyond the robbery. Not at all. So why do this?

Still catching his breath, Arly wondered only for a moment what he would do. As for the particulars, he didn't know. But one thing for sure: he was getting his money.

Just thinking about the slut singer and how she'd jerked him around made Arly's head squirm. The bastard archangels began to stir.

Outside the bar, less than an hour ago, he had overheard Lonnie and the singer plotting to take all of the money the three of them had stolen from the gook picnic. Christ, he was pissed. He had scared them when he stepped out of the shadows—which was a mistake. Too many people around; the joint was busy with drunks on Friday night. The both of them had split and come back here. To get to them, Arly had parked his cycle on the other side of Blanchard's Bluff and slipped in from the back.

He dug his hands through his hair and yanked fingers through his beard, then stopped again in the driveway. Man, this was why he didn't trust anyone, not even in the movement. Straight out greed got you every time, whether you were a white power freak or a goon for the government. He should have known, should never have gotten his worthless cousin Lonnie or that sleazebag bitch involved.

All that time in the cinderblock cell at Milan, he had made his plans. Careful plans, down to the smallest details. How he would make them pay, especially that politician. How to use the bomb to free his father's bones. And now here he was, just starting, and the thing was botched. Time was ticking. He had to get north, give the fat kraut his money, and grab his payload.

Inside, behind the front curtain, he saw quick movement. A flutter, there and gone. Standing in a stream of moonlight, Arly knew they'd seen him; he could feel a film on him from their looking.

He leaped forward and headed for the front door, planning to burst through. But then behind the trailer he heard metal pop and feet on wooden stairs. Then voices, trying to sound hushed, but not succeeding. They wanted to escape, out the back. To bust him one more time.

Damn. Godfuckingdamn them, he thought as he started running, knife in his fist. He raced for the two of them taking the coward's way out. They were scared of him. Probably had the money with them in the Army pouch.

Now Arly's brain exploded with familiar flames, like the transformers on telephone poles crackling. Connections snapped. Fast wings flapped. "Cocksuckersfuckingshit," he growled.

Arly could see she had a blanket wrapped around her and damned if she didn't drop it and keep running stark white naked next to Lonnie as the backstabber stumbled through the yard, toward the gravel pit. Arly wanted to call out clear words, but they wouldn't come now. Not when the funnel clouds spread open in his head. "Fuckingassholeshitheads!"

Across the yard he ran, boiling like a furnace, stepping on the blanket, watching them run toward the pit. When he caught them, he wouldn't stop. If they were lucky, they'd drown first.

Otherwise, he'd ream them to shreds. Tear them apart without stopping. Crush them to bits. Smite them with his weapon, like in the Bible. He was an ascending storm and they were going to pay.

CHAPTER 2
GANNON

Squatted on his heels, Police Chief Cable Gannon stared at the clean, six-inch slice just above the singer's sternum. Blood clotted in the gap. The wound made him think of a small mouth, showing muscle, speaking silent words.

Ignoring the tight feeling in his throat, Gannon looked into the stunned, half-open green eyes, mostly swallowed by dilated pupils. Her mouth was twisted, as if paralyzed by sudden, devastating strokes. Her belly sagged, legs twisted under her. A thatch of hair showed, making him think of the gawkers, behind the yellow tape, by the road. He'd been out here for a half hour and had checked her from every possible angle. The county evidence tech had already taken pictures of her lying against the tree, her nude body on view for the world.

"Larry," said Gannon over his shoulder.

The sheriff's detective detached from the police officers searching the scene, their heads bent, studiously, even calmly, at work. "Chief?"

"Get a blanket, could you? Let's cover her."

"You don't want to wait for Perry?"

Frank Perry, the medical examiner, might not show for another hour, given his weekend habits. If he got mad about blanket fibers on skin, tough. This women's dead nakedness didn't need to be further displayed. "No."

Larry Lee shrugged.

"Bring some bags, too, for her hands."

Lee moved off toward the cops searching the edge of the nearby gravel pit.

Gannon pinched his chin with two fingers. His eyes settled on the breasts. Small as plums. Nipples bumped and purple. Then he checked the wound again. Fairly clean, a straight up and down swipe. It took someone with a hell of a lot of strength to do this, he knew.

A deputy returned with Lee, who gave Gannon the paper bags. He bent and carefully slipped them on, noticing grit around the nails, and wrapped them tightly with black tape. He hoped Perry'd find something. Then Lee and the deputy spread a tan blanket over her. Softly, almost with reverence. Not the same blanket they'd found in the yard. The one with the big footprint.

The Chief kept trying to imagine her death. Out here, naked, under the night sky, the swift sawing of the knife.

Gannon stood and looked to the singer's trailer on the other side of the pit. They had searched it earlier and it didn't make sense. An open suitcase sat on her bed. On the dresser were two half-empty beers and an ashtray with a half-smoked joint.

Looked like she was with someone and getting ready to go on a trip, when she and maybe he came out here. A man's jacket, shiny silk with a dragon on the back, and a matchbook from the local bar, had been on a chair in the kitchen. Neighbors said they'd seen a pickup about midnight. Gannon had a good description of it, plus an idea whose it was. As for the death scene, the ground was clay and gravel; no footprints showed.

"Bad way to die," Lee said.

Gannon didn't answer. He had just arrived at his office when the call came. A couple kids, on their way to fish the Belle River, found the body. "She's the singer at the bar, isn't she?" asked Lee.

Gannon nodded, noticing soft brown freckles around her nose and upper chest. They looked like dabs of brown dust. Or blood.

"One who ran with Lonnie Fleck?"

"God knows what she saw in him," the Chief said.

Although Gannon was the village's only full-time cop, he had an arrangement with the Macomb County Sheriff Department for regular patrol and backup on heavy things like this. Didn't need it often. Thank God.

"He wear a silk jacket with a dragon?" asked Lee.

"We'll find out soon enough."

Lonnie Fleck was a mean little bastard who fancied himself the next Garth Brooks. More than that, he'd been marginally involved in the local militia. In this neck of Michigan, with its flat fields of beans and sugar beets, groups of these nuts were big. Most made more sound than fury, but some were damned dangerous. Fact was, that guy who helped make the bomb that blew up the federal building in Oklahoma hailed from not too far down the road. It made Gannon sick, and a little scared, to think the anti-government scud might be to blame. He kept hoping it was a lover's spat. But then there was what he had learned about the victim, whose name was Brenda Scott.

"She was a pretty woman," said Lee. The detective's large brown eyes gazed impassively at the body. He had two daughters, much younger than the singer.

Gannon's daughter, Cully, was older. In fact, he expected she'd be along shortly, if she wasn't already snooping. She'd stumbled in late last night, half looped after a date with God knew who. His middle-aged, chronically unhappy only child. She had decided to stay with him after his wife died and ended up being more hardship than help. "Say Larry?"

The detective averted his eyes from the lumpy blanket. "You hear about the Vietnamese picnic that got robbed Sunday?" Gannon asked.

"The family reunion in Port Huron?" asked Lee.

It made the local papers. Two masked robbers showed up. They took jewelry and a wad of cash from the immigrants.

"You think there's a connection?" Lee said.

Gannon looked at Brenda's corpse. He had heard her sing a couple times. She was good, had a clean country voice. "There might be."

The sky rolled sluggishly above, a mass of humid clouds. The temperature hung in the upper eighties, hot for Labor Day weekend. The last getaway of the summer. Gannon looked beyond Lee to the road and saw a flurry of activity: a TV truck with satellite dish, plus more vehicles arriving. One carried the sheriff. A circus in the making. Gannon suspected the state would be here soon. Not long after that, they'd nudge him to the sides of the investigation. He knew how things like this worked, killings that made headlines. Especially if this turned out as he feared.

"State cops made a visit this week," said Gannon. "They think maybe this woman, plus Fleck and someone else, might have been in on the deal."

"Robbed the picnic?"

"From what I hear."

Gannon saw Sheriff Ray Fallows, stocky and gray-haired, talking in front of a TV camera. Jawboning, and he hadn't even visited the scene yet. Up for election, he took every chance to stick his mug before voters. Mr. Law and Order.

"You say someone else was with them?"

The Chief was thinking ahead. If he stayed here, sifting through the spilled blood, he would be stuffed away for sure. If he was going to play a part, he had to get away. If nothing else, he knew the locals. Hardscrabble but generally decent. Not everyone in town was a militia freak, not by a long shot. If he was going to put this together, it wouldn't be here. "They aren't sure who."

"You have any ideas?"

"Some." Gannon had stopped by the bar the other night to ask a few questions about the picnic. Between sets, the singer sat at a table, nervous as a firefly, smoking and glancing at Lonnie playing pool. The State Police had told Gannon they thought she drove the getaway car, a rusty red Buick dumped on a back road. They didn't have much of a description on the other two, but Gannon had an idea. As for Lonnie, he had stopped speaking English and shook his head dumbly when Gannon talked to him. He didn't know anything about a picnic.

Fallows started their way, striding like MacArthur storming the Philippines.

Gannon looked down again. The singer's face was turned to the side, the skin pale and doll-like. He knew she'd be out here for another couple hours as the county and state people swarmed. The Chief thought he'd leave them to it. He'd keep what edge he had, which was knowing how to beat the bushes in his town and find Fleck. "Larry, I'm going to stop by the bar," he said.

"You're not waiting for an audience with his highness?"

Gannon saw the sheriff had been waylaid already. He was talking to a few of his deputies, back by where they had found the footprint on the blanket. A huge footprint, made by boots with cork treads, the type of military-style boot the militia loved to wear. "I'll stop and give him my regards."

Gannon started toward the sheriff, pondering the size of that boot. The State Police had told him someone at the picnic had recognized the singer from the bar, but the other two were masked.

Gannon paused when Lee called, "Chief, you sure you don't want any company?"

Without turning, his eyes settling on Brenda's doublewide trailer, Gannon answered: "Thanks, but this part I can handle."

CHAPTER 3
CULLY

Turning onto Durfee Road, Cully Gannon noticed a handful of sheriff's cruisers, an ambulance, a fire truck, and lots of bystanders. She guided her rattletrap Horizon to within a couple hundred feet of the activity, then pulled onto the side of the road by a path she knew wound through the woods and came out on a bluff overlooking the gravel pit. Digging through her glovebox for a pen, Cully tried to decide: should she sneak along the path toward Miller's Pond, the pit, and see what she could, or wander down and ask questions? Seeing TV trucks, she figured she better join the pack.

"Crap!" she said, unable to find a pen in the clutter of her glovebox. Rooting through papers, a hairy comb, a repair manual, rubber bands, gum wrappers, a waterlogged Sue Grafton novel, and whatever-the-hell else, she found one. Wiggling it out, she ignored the dropping junk and slammed the glove box shut with the heel of her hand. It popped back open. She shoved it again. It didn't stick. "Screw it," she said and yanked open her door.

Outside she took a couple breaths to steady herself. She felt a horrible tickling in her chest. Last night, after an awful date at a Detroit jazz bar with a not-quite-divorced copy editor for the *Macomb*

Daily, the rag for which she now freelanced, Cully had vowed never to smoke again. She had smoked two Slims on awakening and was hoping to avoid a third when she heard traffic on the police monitor in her dad's kitchen. Someone had a found a body. She called the metro desk at the *Daily* in Mount Clemens and told them she'd check it out. Normally cop stuff got left to other stringers, since the Chief was her father. But this was Saturday of Labor Day weekend. The paper was short staffed and the editor said get what she could.

Pad and pen in hand, Cully started toward the scene, angrily ignoring the plea for nicotine pouring from her lungs. Aware of the damage smoking did her, Cully loved it nonetheless. She shoved that obsession aside by replacing it with another: the adrenaline rush of breaking news, particularly when it involved murder. These were the stories that got the chemicals coursing through the blood. She felt guilty at the way it quickened her, but that didn't stop her from wanting to get at what happened.

"He haw," Cully said to no one in particular.

Up ahead, she spotted a familiar figure wobble her way on a bike. Noah Potts, the town idiot. Or, as the politically correct mind police would call him, an exceptionally challenged adult.

"Noah!" she said when it was clear he was making a bullseye out of her with his bike.

He bumped to a stop, a stupid grin on his pumpkin face. "Hi, Cully!" A newspaper sack was looped over a shoulder. He had a *Daily* route in this part of town. Cully imagined her story tomorrow. Front page, maybe. For a second, she thought of the comedown. A year ago she was a general assignment reporter for the *Philadelphia Bulletin.* It went defunct, and then so did she, for many reasons, including two terrible deaths. "What's happening back there?" she asked.

Noah's head moved like a searchlight to the people and cars and trucks. "You see the TV?"

"Right." She made a smiley face with bad teeth on her pad. "What happened?"

"Woman got killed."

"Who?"

"One who lives in that house."

"Which?

"The singer, I think." He smiled brightly as he looked back at her.

She had met the woman, Brenda, a time or two. Cully knew her as a tough woman with a wispy smile and desperate eyes. They'd gotten drunk at the local bar a few weeks back. Or rather, the singer had joined Cully as she slugged down a few after a bad week in which her proposed series on the local militia movement got deep-sixed by the faggy features editor. Now the singer was dead. Cully wasn't sure how she felt about that. "How was she killed, Noah? Did you see anything?"

He stared dumbly at her, as if trying to read Latin on her brow. "You going to put it in the paper?" he asked.

"Might."

His head bounced, as if on a spring. "You going to use my name?"

Cully frowned. "If you saw something."

He leaned up on his toes and swung his head side to side. "Like if I knew who stabbed her?"

"She was stabbed?"

"Right in the throat," he said solemnly.

"By who?"

"I guess I don't know."

"Do you know who does?"

"Tommy might."

"Who's he?"

"He was going fishing when he saw her. Lives right there." Noah pointed to the house across from the singer's.

This was a start. She wrote the boy's name in her pad.

"You putting in what I said?" asked Noah.

Cully tried to smile, placating him. "You might need to give me a little more than that if I'm going to use your name."

Noah leaned up on his toes, legs straddling his bike. "Maybe I'll see something later."

"That would be good." She started off, skirting Noah and his bike.

"If I do, want me to tell you?"

Cully turned and noticed the keen, hopeful look on his face. "Sounds like a plan."

His smile grew. "Because, there's lots happens around here some-times, like what happened to that woman."

Cully stared at him. Crazy as a bedbug, but who knew what he might spot? "Just look me up."

"Then I'll be in the paper?"

"Right."

He puffed out his chest, his mouth ropy with pride. "My picture, too?"

"Who knows?" With that, she turned and started for the action.

CHAPTER 4

THE COLONEL

The ferry from Drummond Island rumbled across the rolling waters of DeTour Channel on its way to the mainland, where Colonel Huntz Burger could see a few cars and trucks waiting to take the return trip.

Standing at the rail, feeling cool air swipe his face, the Colonel let his eyes wander from the boat landing to the high pale sky. It was a fine day in Michigan's Upper Peninsula. A solid breakfast of pork sausage, hash browns, eggs, and thick coffee with cream sloshed in Burger's belly.

Patting his gut, the Colonel checked the swirling, barely visible clouds for signs of bad weather. This far eastern edge of the Upper Peninsula, not far from the rugged rim of Canada, was known for unpredictable storms. It wasn't too far north, in Lake Superior, that the *Edmund Fitzgerald,* an ore freighter, went down in a November gale several years before. He once heard it wasn't weather that did it in. It was a government patrol boat. The Colonel wasn't sure what to think about that, although he certainly wouldn't dismiss it out of hand. In fact, push coming to shove, he believed it.

Whatever had happened back then, patrol boats or not, the sky today was a vast covering of blue. The radio station out of St. Ignace said only sun and temperate winds for the second day of the Labor Day weekend.

Taking in a big belt of air, the Colonel dropped his gaze to the emerald water stretching far to his right and curving toward the mouth of the St. Mary's River, where ships inbound or outbound from Lake Superior constantly shuttled. Far out there, outlined by early morning haze, he spotted the flat bow of a big boat chugging toward them, carrying goods to fuel a dying economy.

"Everything stored and ready, Winston?" the Colonel asked, drawn back to the reality of the day's mission by the sound of boot steps shuffling to the rail.

"Done."

Winston Groom was a small, bug-eyed man. The Colonel's second-in-command, Groom went by the nickname Rat. They had worked together at the assembly plant in Wixom. Rat had followed the Colonel a half dozen years back when, encouraged by an early out from the car factory, Burger moved north. "We don't want to run into any trouble if we are stopped," the Colonel said.

Slipping next to him, Rat sniffed the air with flared, flicking nostrils, as if smelling for cheese. "Did it like you said."

The ferry had reached the halfway point, the water churning underneath. Only three other vehicles were on board. "The weapons?"

"Right where you said."

The Colonel checked behind him to make sure none of the islanders—those intruders on his paradise—were listening. No one else had gotten out of their cars for this ten-minute crossing. Feeling the boat bob, the Colonel figured they wouldn't need much firepower for what they were planning. But they needed some. Plus, the money.

"You think this'll work?" said Rat.

The Colonel looked at him, feeling the glorious swell of his breakfast wobble from the waves. "Why wouldn't it?"

They were closing in on the landing. The day, and all that was to transpire, held such promise. Agents for the government awaited them in St. Ignace. "Lots could happen," Rat grumbled.

The Colonel was tempted to be curt, to snap at his partner. But not today. Not on this mission that he was convinced would win him a long-term lease on the island and the chance to build the world he knew God had ordained him to create. An Anglo-Saxon camp, for the chosen, to prepare a defense against the coming one world union. The enemy was the Zionist Occupation Group with its military patrol boats and roving bands that fired at will, hunting down people like him. It was an enemy he had to deal with on this matter, to get his lease, but it was worth it. "We have laid some powerful plans, Mr. Groom."

Rat looked a little sick, his face turned to the frothy water.

"What?" the Colonel asked, patting Rat on the shoulder of his gray jacket. For today, they'd forgone the uniforms of their cause. They wore drab street clothes, the covering of the mud people. They looked like any other sheep. "What could go wrong?"

Rat shook his head, looking at the Colonel with a sick, hangdog expression. "For one thing, we're dealing with Arly. "

True. Arly Fleck was a shotgun with too many shells. If he lived a little closer to the right side of the moon, he would be a solid soldier. As it was, he had moxie but little wisdom. When it came down to it, he was committed to one cause—his own. And his latest scheme was the wildest of them all. It had flair and a sense of genius. Nonetheless, it wouldn't work. Even if he was allowed to give it a try, which wasn't going to happen, it was too grand, too technical, and far too crazy for anyone to ever pull off.

"Arly Fleck, when all is said and done, is a stupid man," Burger said.

Rat wasn't convinced. "You really think the damned governor is going to listen?"

The Colonel didn't want to argue or explain. "Please, Winston. He has so far."

More grumbling.

The Colonel, feeling a bad shift in his mood, said, "The Lord is with us."

Rat sighed. "If Arly doesn't fuck us, the ATF will for sure."

Burger wanted to gently lift the tip of Rat's chin and slap his cheek. "All ducks are in a row, mein friend."

Rat shrugged, unconvinced, backed off from the rail, and returned to the Cherokee. The Colonel watched him climb into the passenger seat. For a brief moment he wondered if he should have entrusted this mission to someone else. To one of the others. He hoped Rat would come through.

Stretching arms over his head, the Colonel let his eyes fill with the full sweep of Drummond Island behind them. But the feeling of hope, the expansiveness of only a few minutes before, had started to slip. The Colonel couldn't stop his mind from wandering. Damned Rat had left doubts, like bad odor, in his wake.

For one, Arly.

Arly had come to him, wanting a bomb, and the Colonel agreed to deliver. But in the meantime, he was working his own double-cross so he could get what he wanted. For a moment, Burger wondered if he should have pressed Arly to explain his deeper reasoning, if there was any. But even if he had asked, what would that gibbering ape have said? Probably nothing.

The real wild card, in the Colonel's estimation, was Cody Burke, the bomber. He was the hardest to read and ultimately the most dangerous. The Colonel had wanted to deal with someone else who wasn't available. Since this had to happen so fast, the choice had fallen to Burke.

As the boat bumped the tires lining the dock to the mainland, the Colonel stopped thinking about the bomber and Arly. He worked hard to calm the anxiety that had begun to pound him, beating like tiny demon fists in his belly. Once loosed, fear was a formidable foe.

Even so, he found himself still able to take comfort in his cause, in the rightness of what he wanted and had planned. For that matter, this was something he absolutely needed to do. Because it wouldn't be long until the united armies of the one world order started their final push for total control and power. Right around the corner was an Armageddon that the Colonel wanted to be prepared for. There were so many signs: the Jews stronger than ever; the stock market on a relentless spiral; the year 2000 on its way. The only answer: secure his piece of island and fortify it to the gills. No, Arly's request had been a petition from God, a way for the Colonel to bolster his path to protection. All was as it should be.

Stepping from the rail, he returned to his Cherokee. He told himself he was ready. Through some sign, the Lord on High would tell him if it was going to be any other way.

CHAPTER 5
BONES

Jock Piersma scissored a neatly pressed blue jeans leg over a knee, smoothed a hand across the legal pad in his lap, and fixed Governor Franklin W. Bones with an expectant, should-I-start-with-things look.

Situated in the firmly padded, turn-of-the-century cherrywood chair, the governor of Michigan nodded. He was ready to dive into his day, having just come in from a long jog, shower, and late breakfast. Even though this was vacation, he had business to handle.

"You have a lunch meeting with Fritz Walters, the speechwriter from Baton Rouge," said Piersma.

"Tell me again, what he's looking to do?" asked Bones.

"Last year in Washington . . . "

The governor leaned back. He could still feel blood pumping from his run an hour earlier around Mackinac Island and couldn't help tuning out Piersma's ramblings. He thought of his feet pounding the path along the water, of the fresh air, of Big Mac itself, the huge steel, concrete, and cable structure that joined the state's two peninsulas. He had admired it again during his run at sunrise. The towers stood tall and sturdy, the asphalt connecting three miles of water. Its power stretched out and beyond him, fueling his run. This was the structure he would honor on Labor Day.

Almost a year's worth of negotiations had led to this Monday's event. They were going to close the bridge to traffic and throw a party. For only a couple hours, but long enough to get things done right. Because Bones was going to celebrate his father, his real blood father, Rolly Walls, whose body was still buried in the cement of the bridge. He was killed during construction in 1954 and lay under Pier 20. It would be a banner day. Nothing was going to mess it up. As he ran this morning, he had glanced out, as always, at the final resting spot, a pillar of concrete half-hidden by mist.

"What do you want me to tell them, then, sir?"

The governor blinked, as if trying to focus underwater, and saw Piersma leaning forward in his chair and giving Bones a squinty-eyed once-over. Closer in, the governor saw tributaries of veins skimming the spin doctor's nose. "What?" asked Bones.

"The road commission workers."

He half recalled Piersma finishing with the speechwriter and launching into this. Bones sat up straighter, scolding himself for day-dreaming. "What about them?"

"They're demanding double time, for all of them, for the entire weekend." A small army of road workers had been assigned to get the bridge ready for the bash. It had been a problem bringing some of them on board because of a few loudmouths in the union. If Bones wasn't mistaken, they'd been over this before, several times.

"I thought this was resolved."

"Apparently not."

"What're they saying now?" the governor asked.

"They'll strike if the whole crew doesn't get paid the full shot through midnight Monday."

"Dammit, we already hashed this out."

"I think they're trying to make some hay," said Piersma.

"Is it the union or Haroldson?"

"Both."

Bones's adoptive father, Preston, had been director of the Michigan Department of Transportation—in fact, had been on a state road crew during bridge construction—for many years. He'd been an icon.

Now that someone else was ruling that roost, there were problems. "This is fly shit."

"I essentially said that this morning to Haroldson."

Ben Haroldson, MDOT director for the last year, was a Democrat, but dressed and acted Republican. Among other things, he was mad that Bones had refused to name his girlfriend deputy director of Community Health. "Send him an e-mail. Tell him he's got a contract to honor. Tell him I don't want to hear anything more about this. As for the union . . . shit, Jock, just work it out."

Piersma scribbled on his pad. Bones felt his heart pump fast, hammering in and out, the blood filling his face. Just as it did in the courtroom, where for so many years he had defended the little people who were raped by big business. Sometimes he defended unions, but they were often as corrupt as the companies they fought.

With effort, Bones reined himself back. This is what he hated about the job—handling the million and one petty grievances. Normally he'd let a lot of it slide, but not when it involved this event. He figured Haroldson was being picky about the overtime as a ploy to gain favor . . . hell, it didn't matter. Bones didn't want to think about it now. "What else?" he asked as a tap came on the door. "Yes?" he called.

The door opened and his wife peered in. "Honey?"

"We're almost done," he told her.

Charlotte, his wife, actually his second, hovered in the massive doorway. Zeke and Travis, the twins, sat in a large stroller, both sucking rattles. "We're going to take a walk," she said.

Two rolling acres stretched beyond the pillared back porch, dipping into the woods and edging toward the lake. If he turned to his window now, he could see the manicured lawn, the tops of trees, and the water beyond. To the left, he could spot the roofs of downtown Mackinac Island. Farther out, the bridge. On this very public of islands, a place with a hotel as grand as any in this country, the governor's summer getaway was pretty darned secluded. "We're about done here," said Bones.

He had a good couple hours before the Louisiana speech writer arrived, a boozy old hound who liked to quote William Faulkner. He had a couple phone calls to make and then could pop out with Char.

But then he noticed Piersma giving him a Nervous Nellie look. "We're not done?"

Piersma checked over his shoulder, where the boys and Bones's better half stood. His wife took the hint and backed out, dragging the stroller with her. "We won't be far," she said.

Nettled, Bones folded his hands on the desktop. Piles of paper, much of it the workings of next year's budget, sat on one side. On the other was a stack of letters he had answered late into last night. He'd been hoping to get a little hooky in this morning, other than the five-mile run, which he didn't consider goofing off. "There's another problem?" Bones asked.

"Possibly."

Piersma had a long, angular face with a wide nose and the deep, dark eyes of an aging, over-the-hill movie star. The governor, on the recommendation of his father, had hired Piersma's PR firm out of Lansing to handle his campaign.

"Recall the man I spoke to a week ago. The assembly line worker turned militia leader."

Bones felt a slight chill sift through him. "Refresh my memory."

"The one who wants the lease on the land on the island. Drummond Island. The one with the supposed tip about a bombing."

Bones twisted around in his chair, wishing it had wheels, this antique, and glanced outside at the sweep of bright green lawn, the brilliant beds of flowers lining the sides of the grounds, the trees, the slender form of his wife and kids, all wearing bright white outfits. The lake sparkled out there; the bluff on which they were positioned allowed for a wide vista. To the left, in a blue haze, stretched Big Mac. A graveyard of sorts that he was going to have a priest bless. As part of the deal, they were going to hold the service his real dad never had. Part of last year's campaign promises. He was a new governor with big plans. Goddamn these little people with their little lies to leak, their pathetic agendas to push, their fights over double time and talk about militia. "What about it?" he asked.

"Sir?"

The governor turned back from the window, no longer reflective. "This auto worker. You told me he was full of it."

Piersma frowned and looked in his lap.

Bones stared hard, his eyes shooting tacks at Piersma, whose pleasant but boozy features had become grave, a little elongated. His hand tapped his pen nervously on the legal pad. Since they were supposed to be on vacation, Piersma wore a canary yellow polo shirt with the speck of a green alligator sewn to the chest. The alligator seemed to be smirking at the governor. Bones had the brief urge to rip it off. "What was his name again?"

"Huntz Burger."

Stupid name, sort of like his own, the governor thought. "The FBI said he was a crackpot."

Piersma covered his mouth with a large hand. His fingernails were buffed and shiny. The brown eyes, filmy and brooding, revealed the barest hint of calculation. "We had thought so."

"What's changed?" Bones snapped.

"I got a call from Major Barnes who says possibly this Burger isn't blowing hot air."

"They just decided that?"

"Apparently."

Bones carefully placed the palms of his hands on the polished top of the desk. The room was lined with leather-bound books and decorated with paintings depicting eras of his state's history. Major Carl Barnes, head of State Police intelligence, was a moron. The governor didn't like this. "Is there a real threat?"

"I wouldn't go that far."

"How far will you go?"

"Major Barnes simply wanted you made aware. But everything is in hand. Mr. Burger is probably this very moment in custody of the State Police."

"Exactly what has this man done?"

"It's not him. It's one of his associates." Piersma flushed, checking his lap again and looking back.

"And what has this associate been planning?"

"We're not sure."

"You said a bombing."

"That's the rumor."

Bones felt his irritation burst into smoldering rage. "Bomb what?"

"We're not sure."

"What the hell *are* you sure of?"

Piersma shook his head. "Like I say, there's every reason to believe it's an idle threat."

"This Burger, he has a bomb?"

"Who knows, sir? It sounds complicated."

The fact he had been trying to avoid suddenly rammed into him, forcing him to face one of his nightmares. "Is this connected to the ceremony on Monday?"

Piersma said nothing.

Bones felt the rage bubble and burn. His body clenched. He had sworn to himself many times that he would have this event. He would talk to the people of his state; he would honor one of the greatest engineering accomplishments in Michigan; and he would remember his blood father who gave his life to the cause. Bones slapped the desk with a hand, as if it were a jury box, and leaned toward his aide. "Get Barnes on the phone. I want to talk to him now. We have to cut through this bullshit. If there's a problem, I want it solved."

"As I said, Frank, I think it has been."

"Goddamnit, Jock, call him!" Bones took in a breath and let it singe his lungs. He let it out and added: "Then get that cocksucker Haroldson on the phone. I want to talk to him, too."

CHAPTER 6

GANNON

Smoky light stung Cable Gannon's eyes when he stepped into the Roadhouse Tavern. A twanging country song played in the background and a few heads turned as he walked toward the bar.

A quick glance down the row of stools assured him he knew everyone. He acknowledged a few nods, trying to drive from his mind the confrontation he'd just had with his daughter before leaving the murder scene. Cully had burst out of nowhere, her reporter's pad in hand, wanting a comment on what had happened. He couldn't believe it; his own damned daughter, pushing him like that. He didn't like journalists to begin with. She had never done that before. She always kept a distance. Which of course had been easier when she worked at the big shot paper in Philly. Anyhow, he goddamned well ignored her and got in his car.

Gannon now took a seat at the end of the bar, directly across from the bandstand. Red drums; "Country Lovin' " on the face of the bass; two guitars in stands; a couple speakers; a microphone on top of a flexible pipe: the place for Brenda. The image of her lying by the tree, so gruesomely dead, replaced thoughts of his pushy offspring.

"Hear we got a bad one." Rabbi Cole, the Jewish bar owner, stood in front of him. He wore a cowboy hat, a pearl button shirt, and jeans.

"What can you tell me about her?" asked the Chief.

Rabbi's eyes narrowed under the brim of the ten-gallon monstrosity. He twisted his neck, as if crunching a nagging vertebrate. "Nice girl."

Replica guitars hung from lights over tables throughout the large room. A Conway Twitty song warbled from the rainbow juke. Something about poetry and a father. A son's ode. Made Gannon a little twitchy, him being such a bastard of an old man. "You work last night?"

"My night off."

"Who was on?"

"Maggie. A couple others. But you might want to check with Baxter there. He's been spouting off what he saw." Rabbi nodded at the booth behind the Chief.

Gannon turned. Beer bottle in hand, Doug Baxter's scarecrow figure slouched in the booth, alone. He was a good old boy from Doyle, a few miles down the road, and Gannon had nailed him twice for drunk driving in the last five years. Both times during the day. He must've been in the john when Gannon came in. Either that, or he had blended into the darkness of the booth, nondescript yahoo that he was. Another would-be patriot, a weekend militia warrior who liked to march at the county fairgrounds in an all-black uniform. Baxter frowned and looked away as Gannon gave him the twice-over.

"Rabbi?" the Chief asked, keeping Baxter locked in his gaze. "What kind of jacket does Lonnie Fleck wear?"

"Come again."

"Any idea what he might've been wearing last night?"

"Like I say, Cable. I wasn't here."

"How about you, Doug? You see what he had on?"

A glower, a twist of the head. Baxter slumped into the shadows. "Wasn't paying attention."

"Rabbi here says you were."

"Not to what he had on." A salt-stained baseball cap covered Baxter's mop of stringy hair. With cigarette in one hand and a Pabst Blue in the other, he leaned into the light, his eyes droopy. Among other things, he was a pal of Lonnie Fleck's cousin Arly, or at least Arly had been renting a room from him lately at his dairy farm, the way Gannon heard it. Once Arly had gotten out of the joint for burning IRS forms, quite a bonfire really, he had shown up and started marching around with a few of the local militia types. But then he had gotten low key the last little while. Gannon hadn't seen the bearded bugger around lately. "C'mon up, Doug. I'll buy you a drink."

Baxter drained his bottle, set it down, scooped money from the table, and slid out of the booth. He wore a red hooded sweatshirt, jeans, and knee-high milking boots splattered with shitty straw. "I got to get back."

"Sit!"

Baxter ducked his head as if in shame. Reluctantly he looped a leg over a stool and settled his bony butt next to Gannon. He smelled like manure and booze. "No rest for the wicked," he groused.

Gannon turned slightly away from the rotten waft of him. "Arly still living with you?"

Baxter gave him a funny look, as if wondering how Gannon knew. "He comes and goes."

"Is he there now?"

Baxter shrugged. "Didn't see his cycle when I left."

"Was he there last night?"

"I didn't check."

Gannon noticed Rabbi fiddling with beer glasses down the bar, pretending not to listen. "So what'd you see, Baxter?"

Baxter squinted bleary-eyed at Rabbi. Licked his lips, sniffed. "Hey, Hebe, Chief says he's buying," he called.

Rabbi glowered and tickled his beard, but opened the cooler.

"Make it coffee," said Gannon.

Baxter didn't like that. He turned to face the Chief, sending out more stink fumes.

"You've had enough," Gannon said.

Baxter's stringy face swiveled away. He sucked wetly and hungrily on his cigarette, his mouth pinching in a kiss of pleasure. With one eye shut, as if squinting into the sun, he pouted.

"You saw what?" Gannon prodded.

Rabbi set down a mug. Baxter looked like he wanted to gob in it but instead ignored the steamy brew. "Wasn't much." He smacked his lips.

"What was it?" Gannon demanded.

"On the rag, Chief?"

Gannon twirled, leaning into the force field of farmyard stink. He stuck his face close. "I'm not going to kiss your ass."

Baxter tilted back, out of easy grabbing range, fear flickering in his eyes. The bar got quiet. The Chief glared, as if daring anyone to give him grief. The daytime boozers, hunched over beers and smokes, weren't up for it. They knew about his temper. In all his years as a cop, he'd had a half dozen homicides and double that number of people who offed themselves. Gannon didn't like any of it and always made it his business to find out why it happened and who did what to whom. Unless it was self-inflicted, and even then, he hungered to get it straight and answer all questions. And if it took getting a little pushy, so be it.

"You want to talk about this at the station?" Gannon said.

Baxter's shoulders pushed up and pinched his neck. "Probably nothing, like I say."

"Let me judge that."

Baxter nodded glumly. Sighed. Stared blankly at the row of bottles behind the bar. He rubbed his eyes with one hand, mashed out his cigarette with the other, and checked his buddies at the bar. "They got in a fight in the parking lot."

"Who?"

"Lonnie and the singer."

"How'd you come across this?"

"I was heading home, stopped to whiz by the bushes."

"What were they fighting about?"

Baxter's eyes looked like trapped ferrets. He sawed a finger under his nose with one hand. The other chiropracted the back of his neck. "I think over money."

"What money?"

"Think they had it from somewhere and didn't want to give it back."

"From where?"

"Don't know."

"Anyone else there?"

Baxter slopped some coffee into his mouth and rubbed at his chin with the back of his hand. "Arly showed up."

"When they were fighting?"

"After."

"What did he say?"

"About that time I split."

"You didn't hear anything else?"

"Nothin'."

Gannon laid his hands on the slimy bar and thought it over a bit. Arguing over money. Maybe the money stolen from the Vietnamese picnic. Maybe Brenda wanted to keep it. Or turn it in. Who knew? Probably keep it. A robbery like this sounded right up Arly's alley.

"Rabbi," he called. The barkeep turned from a conversation he was having next to the register. "Did Brenda say anything to you about leaving town?"

He shook his head, eyes shadowed by the huge hat.

Gannon turned back to Baxter. "Was Arly angry when he was talking to them?"

"You know, Arly. He always looks pissed. He was telling them they were traitors."

"About what?"

"You know, the movement."

The movement was a raunchy bunch of whiners as far as Gannon was concerned. But beyond that, he doubted that Arly was having a political discussion with them. "Was Arly in the bar earlier?"

"He just showed out of nowhere. Sort of like always."

The Chief thought it over some more, especially about the bootprint on the robe. Then he stood and slapped a couple ones on the counter. He told Baxter he might get back to him with more questions and started out of the bar.

Halfway to the door, the Chief paused. "Baxter, last night, what was Arly wearing?"

Slumped over his coffee, the dairy farmer spoke without turning. "Don't recall."

"How about Lonnie?"

Baxter sighed. "Maybe some kind of Chink jacket. I think."

CHAPTER 7
CULLY

Cully stood in the woods above Blanchard's Bluff, looking at the scarred land left from gravel mining. She was trying not to seethe. She needed to forget her father and do this herself.

Head cocked to one side, she made herself listen, for what, she wasn't sure. Directly below, down the sheer sandy slope, she saw movement in Miller's Pond: a man in a slick rubber suit holding a rope. The line stretched taut and disappeared in the glassy green water. Divers, searching the murky bottom for evidence, a weapon, maybe. Or another body.

She had spent an hour or so interviewing folks around the singer's trailer, getting background on Brenda, learning the singer liked to bring guys back at night. As best she could, Cully tried to ignore the TV numbnuts sticking their blow-dried faces into everybody's business. Then she'd used a neighbor's phone to call the *Daily,* mentioning what she'd come across, the basics of who died.

The editor, not her dreary date, had said, "Hey, we're hearing this thing's connected to militia. We got a photog en route and another reporter. Hit this hard."

"Even with my dad?"

"Well, don't get in his way."

"You sure?"

"Hell yes. Story like this breaks all the rules. Plus, you know some of these militia goons."

There you go, she thought, they didn't want militia stuff until something like this happened.

"Maybe they're tied in to that guy over by Port Huron, what's his name Nichols, the one who helped out in Oklahoma. Find out. This could be great! Shit, talk to your dad. Maybe he'll tell you something."

So that was what she did soon after hanging up. Spying him leaving the scene, ducking under the tape, and heading for his car, she buttonholed her old man. The look he flashed her, which as much as said get out of my way, girl, made her bold. Take no prisoners was her attitude as she blocked his way to his fancy Caprice. A car Cully's had mom called a ritzy hearse.

The militia tie, if there was one, got her hot for the story. Not too long before they had squelched her proposal for a series on the movement. Now they wanted it, and she wanted to give it to them. Build some clips and get back on full time. The job market was tight. It was time for her to return to the real world.

She hoped her dad would at least confirm a connection. The least he could do, if only out of flesh and blood decency, was give her a quote. But she had hardly got a word out before the bastard blasted by, nudging her aside to get to his car. God, how she hated him. "Can't you tell me anything?" she had sputtered as he climbed behind the wheel.

"Go home."

"Go to hell."

His blocky face flushed. He looked a little hurt and she felt bad. Without another word, he jammed down the gearstick and left.

After that, Cully decided to come at it another way. She hustled down the road, parked her car on the shoulder, and headed straight up the path that took her to this spot above the bluff. Now she was sucking on a cigarette, hoping no one down there spotted the smoke.

"Damn him," she said, her eyes hot, recalling so many times when her cop father shoved her aside, not so much literally, but he did it. The hurt was deep. For a moment, she felt a hot resentment. She had come back from Philly, jobless to be sure, for her mom's dying, and stayed on, partly to look after him. The jerk. He had ignored her the whole time, acted like she was the burden, not him and his own mooning, which turned terrible the night of the fire three months before. She had tried to hold him then, give him comfort, since she knew the pangs of grief, too, but he'd frozen her out and just stood there, a block of pain.

"Fuck him. Fuck him in the head," she said, dropping the stub of her cigarette and digging it in deep with her boot.

Then, she thought, not good to leave a butt full of fingerprints, above a crime scene. So she picked it up and stuck it in her pocket.

Still blazing over how he had treated her, she tried to figure how to handle this. Maybe go down and talk to the divers. Possibly she could soft-soap them into telling her about this militia business. Because she was a damned good reporter. She could get the goods. Always had. She'd done it around the U.S. and in Central America. When David died she crashed and burned. She had thought for a time that all of the real writing had been wrung out of her. But she knew it hadn't; it was still there, anxious to get out. She'd done that magazine piece on the militia and got good response from it. But not enough for the halfwits at the paper to give her a green light.

Cully started along the ridge to the path that led down. The worst the cops could do was slap her hand and give her the no comment routine. As she walked, she thought of her heroine, Edna Buchanan, the former cop reporter for the *Miami Herald.* A woman who never took no for an answer, a reporter who believed yellow crime scene tape was not meant to keep her out. A writer Cully had tried to emulate, hard edges and all, for many years.

Partway along the path, Cully felt an odd burning at the back of her neck, a crisp prickling. She told herself she was feeling paranoid; just get down there and ask questions.

Planning how she'd approach the cops, something snagged her attention: a wad of color. Exactly why she glanced once and then again, she couldn't say. Even before anything registered, anxiety somersaulted in her chest.

Wedged in the elbow of a tree trunk, a couple of feet away, was a small olive-green pouch. She bent closer. It was a military sack of some kind, with faded black lettering she couldn't quite make out. She wanted to touch it, but didn't. Angling her head around, she detected faint purplish blotches on one portion. Blood? A taste of hot wax coated her tongue.

Cully looked down the path, which cut between two steam-shoveled portions of the ridge to the area around the pit. She saw cops moving and a diver sliding into the pond. She thought of calling out but instead lowered to her knees and leaned in, memorizing every inch of it. As she did, her nape itched again, like a low current of power being applied. Her pulse beat fast. She reached out, held back.

Behind her, a rustle. She turned quickly. Nothing. She told herself to get a grip; maybe it was the remains of her nicotine frenzy, the result of her hour-long bout of quitting. Except she'd just had a smoke.

Taking a breath, she stood, feeling a flush move all the way up her spine. She turned slowly, as if trying to catch herself in a mirror. Again, zip.

She rechecked the pouch from an upside-down vantage and now made out faint lettering: Army. Black stencils, faded. Hadn't the cops combed this area? Maybe not this far up, or maybe they didn't see it. Cully nodded, sure this was important. David always told her that good reporters go with their instincts. As if he, a photographer, would know so much about those who made a living knocking together words. But he had been right, with that as with many things. Damn the baseball player's illness that made his body stop working.

She had to tell the cops, if for no other reason than it could be information to trade for an insider lowdown on the killing. Quickly Cully turned toward the pit and rammed right into a wall of flesh, bumping hard against an unforgiving belly. Jesus!

She only got a glimpse of the huge beard and those eyes—familiar eyes. Christ, it was . . . Arly Fleck. Who wouldn't recognize him, the smelly beast. He was one of those she interviewed for the magazine, if his grunted responses could be considered answers. She was going to say something, anything, but got no chance. He jerked her around, sprayed fire in her face and began to squeeze so hard she was sure she was on her way to heaven or hell, or both, but nowhere in between.

CHAPTER 8
GANNON

Parked in the street in front of Lonnie Fleck's house, Cable Gannon sat for a couple minutes looking through the stand of trees at the rundown bungalow. It tilted slightly to one side, a hillbilly joint. Fleck's pickup was parked in the drive. With the weedy lawn, a pole barn in the back, and sun on the leaves, it seemed so still, so calm, almost eerie. Getting on the radio, he told the county dispatcher where he was. He thought of giving Lee or someone at the murder scene a call but figured he'd let that go. Likely he was on a much hotter track than they were. Plus, he didn't want anyone else out here. Not yet. Keep the natives from getting restless, if any were in there.

Making sure his .35 millimeter Glock Special was safe at his side, he climbed out, planning to waltz up and engage in a nice talk with Lonnie, let him give his lying side of the story. If necessary, he'd hightail it back to his cruiser and call Judge Baker for a warrant.

Just as he took his first steps for the house, a county cruiser bounced along North Maple Road toward him. "Shit," Gannon grumbled.

Eustace Patterson rolled to a stop in a small cloud of road dust a few feet from him. She was one of the three deputies regularly assigned to patrol their neck of the woods. Of them, she was the best.

That she was black and doing a bang-up job in their redneck town surprised everyone but Gannon.

"Heard you calling in, Chief, and was nearby." She hauled herself out and leaned on the open door for support.

"How are things back at the pit?"

"Divers are there but haven't found anything yet."

Gannon joined her in front of their cars, hers ticking under the hood. The Chief noticed perspiration on her brow, reminding him the temperature was over eighty. He hardly felt it, not now; he felt icy. They spoke a minute or so about the scene at the gravel pit and what had happened, and then Eustace said, "Saw your daughter out there."

Gannon suddenly started to feel the heat. He wiped an arm over his brow and dug hands through his bristly hair. "You didn't tell her anything, did you?"

Eustace frowned.

"She was pumping me for information," he stammered. "She oughta know better than that."

More frowning. "You ought to cut her some slack."

Gannon felt the urge to defend himself. He was probably too curt with Cully earlier. But, damnit, she was in the way. "I didn't know you and Cully were such good friends."

"From what I hear, the stories she writes are fair.

"As long as they aren't about me."

Eustace, fifteen years younger than the Chief, gave him the stern, motherly treatment with her eyes. She shook her head, then changed the subject. "This horsefly involved in the murder?" Her expression turned official and moved in the direction of the house.

"Might be."

"You think he's there?"

"He's probably still sleeping."

"Or waiting behind the door with a gun. I heard this might be militia." Eustace had a broad, square face, firm around the lips and nose.

The Chief thought most of these two-bit weekend paper soldiers were harmless blowhards. Malcontents who liked headlines but backed off from anything real. "I'm going to check."

"Why don't we call first?"

"You think then he'll invite us in?"

Eustace scowled. He shrugged, figuring she was right. Give him fair warning. Maybe Lonnie the wanna-be country star was looking for himself on TNT the Superstation and didn't want to be disturbed. He slipped back in his cruiser, got Lonnie's number, dialed it, waited through twenty or so rings, hung up, and got back out. "No answer."

"He's probably not in there."

"That's what I wanted to see in the first place." He started off.

"Not wise, Chief."

Maybe not, but this was his territory, more or less, and his particular brand of slime. Plus, there was what someone, possibly Lonnie, did to that girl. "Wait here, Eustace."

She caught up with him, her boots crunching gravel on the drive. "He sees my black face, he'll probably break right down and confess."

"Oh, he's too smart for that."

She snickered.

Gannon led the way. They stopped and looked in the pickup. Didn't see much. They stood there a second; heat swelled around them.

"I heard Fleck was maybe involved in that robbery in Port Huron," Eustace said.

"Could be."

"Also heard someone else was involved."

"Who said that?"

"I forgot. But we need to be careful."

They walked to the rickety wood porch and took the four steps to the top. With Eustace facing the road and checking the sides of the house, the Chief pounded on the dented screen door a couple times. Even from the porch, the place stank. He slipped out the Glock for good measure.

Eustace shook her head, probably noticing the half buried engine parts in weeds, a broken lawn chair, a pile of tires. None of it was visible from the road. "White trash," she observed.

Gannon knocked again. They waited. No sounds inside. He heard scratching insects out here and a truck grinding gears along the cross street a quarter mile to the north. Gannon tried the knob of the screen; it moved. The front door was slightly ajar. He looked at her, well aware of what he was about to pull. "I think he said come in."

Eustace gave him wary eyes.

"He needs help," said Gannon.

Clouds massed in those eyes. "We don't have a warrant, Chief."

"But he's asking."

"We need to call in."

She was right.

But Gannon didn't budge. He waited a half minute more on the porch, straining hard to listen. His gut told him to chance it. The image of the singer, sprawled and naked and dead under that tree mingled with the mental picture of his nosy daughter, who damned well looked like her mom, the wild red hair, the freckles. Fleck, you know something, don't you? he said to himself.

Gannon spent a few seconds thinking Lonnie could be cooking up a welcome. Especially if it was militia related. Gannon knew if he were any other cop, and not someone who knew this town and the people in it, there would be no door knocking without the backup of a SWAT team. "I'm sure of it, he's calling."

Eustace shook her head. "My hearing's off."

"Wait here."

But she slipped in behind him. "Fleck, you here?" she called, stepping into an alcove leading into the dark living room. Everything mostly dark. No TNT on the tube. A chill in the place and a bad odor.

"Shit, what's that?"

Gannon stepped next to her and spotted a small lump, curled and furry on the floor. He bent and got a better look. Squashed head, mashed eyes. "Cat," he said.

She squeezed her nostrils between two fingers. "Hey, Fleck!"

Gannon looked at the couch and saw a balled blanket, squashed pillows, beer cans, stubbed-out cigarettes, a sopping magazine spread across the glass top of the coffee table. The cat had stiff hair. Red oozed from the eyes. The skull was sloped and flat, as if stomped. The sight bothered him, made him think of all those kids he'd grabbed over the years for torturing animals. Then, although Gannon tried not to, he recalled the night not too many months before: soft wind, lots of stars, the flames dancing, the gas can in his hand. Their show horse, his dead wife's pride and joy. Nearly cost him his job.

"Chief, best get back here."

Deep in the house, Eustace's voice. Damn, when'd she get away? He'd let her go without him, not even noticing, lost in his own past and his mistakes. He hurried in her direction, through the kitchen, down a dank, skinny hallway, and into a bedroom with the shades drawn. Inside, he stopped and peered over the deputy's shoulder. There was another lump, this one much bigger, on the bed.

"Dead?"

"I ain't touching him to see."

Gannon fumbled along the wall, found and flicked a switch. The overhead light dropped an unfriendly glare. A drab green blanket covered Fleck's legs and ass. Twisted on his side, his bare back revealed buckshot scars, nibbled gouges. Gannon recalled the farmer, now dead, who took potshots at three kids stealing pumpkins. No reason to be shooting, but the irritable old coot did. Mostly blind, he'd been aiming at the dark and said later he was hoping to scare the thieves. He got Fleck, who wasn't hurt badly.

This time Fleck wasn't so lucky. A tiny pool of dried brains, buckled with blood, lay on the bed next to his head. Already a few flies buzzed. One arm hung stiffly from the side of the bed. A small handgun, looked like a .22, lay on the floor. Gannon stepped around Eustace, whose breath came as a guzzling wheeze, making sure not to disturb the gun. A small hole, the size of a dime, showed at Lonnie's left temple. A mottle of blood froze there, ringing the hole in the skull. Circling it, just visible, were powder burns, and closer in, a backwash of smudged gases. Gannon touched clammy skin on Fleck's bare, pitted back.

"How you figure this, Chief?"

He didn't respond, trying to imagine it: a fight with his girlfriend in the bedroom of the trailer by the gravel pit. She was leaving with money from the robbery. He threatened her; she ran. He chased her outside and slit her throat. Ran. Came back here distraught. Stomped his cat. Went to bed. Stuck the gun to his head. Pulled the trigger. Some of it figured. Some of it didn't.

Fumes of booze, a swizzle of urine, and the dried odor of sweat and feces filled the hot air. Still, Gannon wasn't sweating much. He bent and peered at the gun, then the tip of the barrel, and thought he saw tissue there. Brain matter, which also made him wonder. Most suicides pulled away at the last moment, no matter how stoned they were. Very few had the desperation or guts to aim true at the end. Plus, the powder burns on the skull. Like an execution.

Leaning back up, Gannon realized he felt relieved. He had been more anxious than he'd thought. He cursed himself again for letting Eustace go first while memories gripped him, especially in the middle of his job. He knew they had trespassed, but that didn't matter as much now. That is, if it was a suicide. His suspicions were taking a familiar form. A familiar fear.

"Check out the candy." Eustace pointed at a split rock of what had to be crack on a bedside stand. A blackened pipe lay next to it. A tumble of beer cans were scattered on the floor at the foot of the bed.

On the mattress, Fleck's long face was sullen-looking as always, even in death. Above him on the wall hung a tattered American flag, tacked in with penny nails. To one side was a glossy photo, its edges curled: two men in Army fatigues, berets on their heads, M-16s slung Davy Crockett-style in the crooks of their arms.

Lonnie and his cousin, big bad Arly. Lonnie had a shit-eating grin in the picture, the look of a model citizen. You couldn't tell what expression hid behind Arly's beard. But in his burning rabid eyes the fierce zealot's look was there, piercing out for all to see. He wore shiny military boots, maybe the kind with the large cork wedges. The Chief had been thinking about Arly without really thinking about him. Like cancer, like the tumor that took his wife, he had been there all along.

Gannon shivered a little, wondering where Arly was. He had the sense that Arly would know all about this. A shadow seemed to fall across the room, bringing with it a chill. "Eustace, call the state. Get the crime lab out here, too."

"You're thinking he didn't do himself?"

"Might be hard to prove, but yes."

"Than who?"

Gannon's eyes hadn't left the photo, those eyes, that mad warrior's stance. Those boots. Again he thought about that footprint on the blanket.

CHAPTER 9
SMEREAS

ATF Agent Herb Smereas held his hands under the hot air machine and rubbed skin against skin. He wanted to take a few moments before heading back to the table and the pair he still couldn't figure. Colonel Burger and his scrawny sidekick. Their exact angle, their reasoning, eluded him. Smereas shook his head, feeling the water drops dripping away. Even though his hands were dry, he remained.

Tell the truth, Smereas still couldn't decide how to play it. Should he go in hard, hold back, or dismiss the whole deal? Even as he stood in the john at the Denny's Restaurant, he wondered if he should have taken it this far. Because, shit, he was climbing out on a limb here. He had wrangled long and hard with Gambrini in Detroit to keep the troops at bay and not blast this thing wide open. At the same time, there had been questions, especially from the State Police, as to whether this thing was even real. After all, there were dozens of these yahoos out there, cooking up plans, offering half-ass deals, and rarely were they taken seriously.

Before going back into the restaurant, he detoured to the back door held open on a chain. It led out on the parking lot to the green Cherokee that Burger and his scrawny buddy had arrived in. Parked on the far end of the lot, luckily out of sight of the dining area, it likely now had the tracking beeper attached to the underbody. A homing device that neither Burger nor the other one knew about, put up by a state trooper in plain clothes. The two militia nuts had refused a wire and were damned adamant about anyone tracking too closely. Their argument was that any scent of a double-cross and the thing would not go down. If anything was going to happen anyhow. Smereas just didn't know.

Watching sun flash on the roof of the Jeep, Smereas knew his ass was in a wringer if this got out of hand. Hell, he was probably up a creek if nothing happened. Either way he was fixed. His best hope was to allow things to unfold without too much fanfare and stop whatever it was before it started.

Burger was well known as a blowhard, but maybe he was feeding them some real juice this time. And a big part of it involved Cody Burke, the Motor City Bomber.

Smereas rubbed the back of his head. He didn't like being away from home over Labor Day, and he didn't like the position he was playing: middle of the road. As lately as yesterday, he had been arguing his case for an even hand, for letting Burger call the shots, to an extent. "We have to do it his way," Smereas had said over the phone to Gambrini.

"Dammit, Herb, if this does end up being something and we aren't inches from his ass the whole time, we're screwed. You're screwed."

"Like I say, it might play out to be nothing."

"Then fuck him."

"Or it could be something."

"Herb, I'm giving you some slack. Only some. You know these people, so go your way. But keep on him. Don't let this blow up in our faces." In an agency still reeling from Waco, from going in too hard and too fast, Smereas's suggestion about being low-key had found support. For now.

Checking his watch, knowing he'd been away too long already, he turned. His gut wormed with worry. The beeper and a State Police chopper in the air were all the recon they had. Maybe he could make a final plea for a wire. Maybe Burger would relent. Probably not. The fat kraut seemed to have his mind made up.

Walking down the hall, Smereas recalled briefly the horrible image from the TV. More than a dozen ATF agents, some of them his friends, hauling the limp body of one of their own away from that Waco compound. The picture unfolded in slow motion, the men climbing away from the carnage, their jackets displaying their agency colors. Smereas was deathly afraid of messing up like that again.

At the same time, Herb Smereas did not want Cody Burke, the cowardly bombing son of a bitch, to get away. That is, if he was out there. If he had indeed made a bomb, set to go off somewhere around here to disrupt a Labor Day weekend that was already turning into a mess, something involving the flashy foolish governor and a shitload of other politicians, a couple of whom Smereas had already had to deal with. One of them, the governor's aide, had as much as laughed in Smereas's face when he told him what Burger wanted in trade.

In the doorway, he saw Burger shoveling in grub. The skinny one sat there, smoking, head twisting this way and that. Detective Lieutenant Colin Parker, the State Police terrorism guy with whom Smereas had been saddled, was sipping coffee.

It didn't look like anyone was having a very good time. Well, except for Burger. Get him around food and he was usually happy as a pig in mud.

Smereas took in a breath and started toward them. He felt like he was freeflying through the air, parachuting toward a haystack full of broken glass.

CHAPTER 10
THE COLONEL

Curling through the thick woods in the Cherokee with Rat at the wheel, the Colonel liked thinking about his scheme. It would take precision planning. As best he could tell, he had it figured. Still, you never knew what could botch it. At that thought, his gut burbled a bit, now full with the remains of brunch at Denny's, and he patted it as if trying to calm a nervous dog.

He needed to set his mind on other things, not on what could foul the air. He stared straight ahead, out the windshield, at the two-track curving up Crow Mountain.

"I don't trust those cops," Rat said.

Damned griper. The Colonel shifted his bulk in the passenger's seat and faced Rat, who had to sit on a foam pad to see clearly over the steering wheel. "Why's that, Winston?"

Rat nibbled his lips and shook his head. Shadows from the trees rolled over his face. "Gave me the heebie-jeebies."

The Colonel nodded, thinking of the two government men in the corner booth, looking arrogant as the four of them talked over coffee and omelets. Actually, the Colonel had done most of the talking while Rat sat there, scowling in his cup and slopping toast through eggs.

More or less, the Colonel had asked Smereas, the ATF man, if he'd upheld his end of the bargain. Had he recontacted the governor's people? The agent assured him he had and the governor was waiting for final word. The state cop, dark-haired and a little chubby, kept his trap shut, but made sure to let the Colonel know, by the flinty glint in his eyes, that he considered the Colonel as well as Rat to be no better than snail droppings. Once again, the cops had mentioned a wiretap and trailing them in cars. And he had refused. Burger had to do this alone. Too many eyes in these woods. Any suspicion of police involvement would wreck everything.

"What made you nervous?" the Colonel asked.

"Lots of things."

"Such as?"

Rat turned, flushed and angry. "They smelled."

"Of what?"

"Lies and mud!" Rat's teeth showed through his lips.

"Winston. We need them for now."

"They'll stick it in our ass first chance they get."

The Colonel forced down his irritation. Settling back and staring out the windshield again, he tried not to be grim. He cradled his belly. "They simply have to uphold their end."

"They won't. I'll bet they're coming after us now."

The Colonel turned. "Have you seen someone?"

"Don't need to. They're out there, all right."

"Do you have evidence of that?" The Colonel looked behind them into trees, mildly wondering if Rat's paranoia had a basis.

"I heard a helicopter earlier."

"When?"

He shrugged.

"Why didn't you say so?"

"I thought you heard it, too."

The Colonel wasn't sure what to make of this. On the way here, he had insisted Rat take a complicated route and make sure no one was following. Until now, it seemed they were in the clear.

"Your opinion is we should abort?"

Rat didn't respond for a few moments. Then he said, "Doesn't matter, they'll bust us any way we play it now."

The Colonel frowned at his underling. He realized it was far too late to turn back. Even if someone was out there, he would make this work. He had to. It was in the greater plan. "Ye of little faith," he said.

"Isn't anything about that."

The Colonel shook his head, not wanting to argue. He forced back the belly bubbles. "You'll see, Winston."

"I wish it was over," groused Rat.

Once again Burger wanted to reach over, grab Rat by the throat, and pinch thumb and forefinger till his voicebox broke. Damned little whiner, the Colonel thought.

"Why do you trust them, Burger?"

"What have they got to lose?"

"Why would they help us?"

"Winston, shut up." For a moment he thought he heard helicopter blades, the sound of a blue machine peering into them with infrared cameras. But he shoved those thoughts away. Finally his insides settled, until he heard Rat say, "Looks like Cody's here."

The Colonel opened his eyes as they rounded a bend on the two-track. They were at the hunting lodge already. He saw Burke's station wagon, and then Burke sitting on the front porch. But no Arly. "He's alone," observed the Colonel, not liking this.

"Looks like." Rat pulled into a spot by a row of jack pines and killed the engine.

"Arly is supposed to be here."

Rat tapped the steering wheel with his hands and glanced over, his eyes slit. "Maybe he's inside."

"I don't see his motorcycle." Burger leaned up to check the entire area around the cabin.

"Probably around back."

The Colonel shook his head. "He'd better not screw this up."

"Or what?"

When the Colonel looked over, Rat had his handgun pointed at Burger's belly. The Colonel glanced for a moment at the place where the bullet would enter, should Winston choose to shoot, then back at Rat. "Lord, Winston. What are you doing?"

Rat sniffed and jerked his head. "That's what I been wondering about you."

CHAPTER 11
GANNON

At the desk in his storefront office of the Village of Memphis Police Department, the Chief felt weariness flood through him. Eyes still closed, he knuckled the tense muscles at his temples. Digging in the soft tissue, he made it hurt with relief.

The monitor crackled occasionally behind him. The soft rush of traffic on the main drag washed against the large window at his left. Wiping his face with rough palms, Gannon could see starry flames dim to sparks behind his lids, falling like the trailing chain of a spent bottle rocket. Blackness moved in for a moment, but then the image of Sally, his cancer-killed wife, appeared. He saw her crossing a lava field of bones.

Gannon shook his head and slapped his palms on the top of his desk, flesh pounding wood on either side of the phone. "Shit!" He said it more to get himself back to policing and away from the bad places where recollections of his wife, and also the time after, especially in the barn, brought him.

As if in answer to his curse, the phone rang. He grabbed it. "Yeah, Gannon."

"This is Garth Adams at the *Macomb Daily*."

He waited.

"I just talked to the sheriff's department, and they said they're mostly handling the case on the singer's murder and the other guy's death, but you might have a comment or two."

Still, he didn't answer.

"Is that true?"

Gannon noticed a shadow move past his window, a familiar form sliding by on a bike. Beyond, he saw the mostly empty street, the failing light of dusk, the movement of customers inside the diner across the way. His town, his world, so different these last couple years. "What's it you want?"

"Are you assuming that Brenda Scott was killed by the man whose body you turned up outside town?"

After they'd found Lonnie, the world sped up and seemed to cave in. It was true, by the letter of the law, that Lonnie lived on the edge of the village limits, just in the jurisdiction of the township. Rarely had there ever been any real turf battles, at least that close to town, over who would handle a situation. But this time Sheriff Fallows pulled rank, probably because he didn't like it that Gannon barged in without a warrant. The Chief and Fallows got into a donnybrook of an argument behind Lonnie's house as State Police evidence guys filled the place and deputies scouted the grounds for whatever they could find. Basically the Sheriff was grabbing the deal for himself, forcing Gannon into the wings.

Cable went nose to nose with him for a bit, but then, resolve leaking out of him, he backed off. He wasn't exactly sure why, but he did. He drifted off, figuring maybe he did need the help, after all, what with two deaths to probe. He hoped it panned out to be a murder-suicide, a clean and neat double dipper that everyone could wrap up long before the picnics on Monday. But then there was Arly, a wild card he had yet to play. Those boots, that picture. He still didn't know what to make of it. "Chief?" the reporter said.

Gannon used his free hand to grab a pencil and doodle on a pad handed out free by the local funeral director, a chubby old dunderhead from Saginaw. "What?"

"Is it true these things are connected?"

"How's that?"

"You know, Wolverine Militia?"

"Ask the Sheriff."

"Or is it a lover's spat?"

He fiddled with the pencil and closed his eyes. Sally stood there, a survivor in a field of burning rocks. He kept his attention on the ghost in his brain, as if encouraging her to talk, but she vanished. In a way he wished he could too. He was well aware he ought to be searching for more reasons for these deaths, but somehow the Sheriff had taken it out of him. He'd seen this reporter out there earlier, ranging along the street in cowboy boots, looking for the life of him like a rabid dog. But reporters always looked like that, frothing and snarly. Which made him remember that his daughter hadn't been at the second scene. He wondered if she had wised up and gone home. If so, it would have been the first time. "I've got to go."

"Is this a militia hit?"

Gannon smiled, opening his eyes. "Sheriff says that?"

"More or less."

"Then quote him."

"It is?"

"I didn't say that."

"But ..."

"Or talk to my daughter," he added, feeling a little fatherly pride at her accomplishments. She was a pro, not like this guy, whom Gannon had dealt with before and who never got it straight.

"That's another question. We got a call from her earlier, but then she was gone. She said she was going to write up all she had and send it in. The boss said her stuff never got here."

"You call her at home?"

"Couple times. No answer."

"Was she supposed to be writing this story?"

"Mostly helping out."

Gannon shook his head. Too bad. But that's probably why she took off. Just handed it over to the amateurs. As much as he disliked journalists, he had read with interest all of the stories she'd sent him over the years from far-flung locations. Far as he could tell, she was damned good. Which is why he never wanted to tangle with her over information. "Are you using the right number?" Gannon asked.

The reporter rattled it off. It was right. "I'm going to stop by home," he said. "I'll see if she's there." Then he hung up and looked at the phone. He picked it back up and dialed, first their house and then the number she used for work. Answering machines at both ends. Maybe she was on a lead; that is, if she was staying with this story. He didn't know. Maybe she had another dead-end date.

Truth was, he didn't quite understand what she was doing these days. When she had returned for her mother's funeral, Gannon never envisioned her staying. But she set up shop in the attic and refurbished a place to do her writing. It had been nine months now. Far as he could tell, she didn't have a hell of a lot to show for it.

The Chief figured he'd better check at home. Then he had a couple more folks he wanted to talk to.

For a few moments he went over the scene at the gravel pit in his head. The way the body lay, the gutted throat, the clothes inside the house. The jacket by the back door. The footprint ground into the blanket. Then there was Lonnie in his bed, in that twisted, off-kilter position, the delicate but lethal hole in his skull. Brains on the gun barrel, likely a sign someone stuck it to his head. The picture of the two men on the wall. The two of them grinning. Arly in his beard. Arly the troubled kid and the wild teen and the even more explosive adult.

Suddenly he heard tapping on the window and turned to see goggle-shaped fingers ringing raccoon eyes, a mashed mouth and nose smashed flat to the glass. Gannon flipped a hand. "Noah, go home."

Noah shook his head and grunted something. Then he stood back and put his hands to the sides of his mouth and said what sounded like, "Cully."

Gannon stood, pressing closer to the window. Noah Potts stared back at him, an expression of stark, stupid fear on his face.

CHAPTER 12
CULLY

Arly's swampy dead fish odor bothered her the most. Even the wire, biting into her neck, wasn't as bad. Hands rigid on the wheel of her flunky Horizon, Cully wanted to puke. She pictured him as slimy backwater, oozing onto the floor of the back seat. "Which way on Davis?" she asked.

She felt a tug on the wire, just enough to make her heart thud, as he shoved himself up. She caught his reflection in the rearview mirror and winced.

"Left."

Coming to the intersection, she slowed and edged the wheel in the direction he'd ordered. Farm fields, starting to take on late summer rustiness, stretched on both sides. "Where are we going?" she asked. She checked the mirror; he'd disappeared. But he was there, down under, keeping the wire on her neck.

"Just drive." Another tug for good measure.

"I'd do a lot better without a friggin' coat hanger around my throat."

"Shut up."

Not two months before, she had interviewed this rank-smelling weirdo for the magazine piece. But Cully knew him from way back, when they were in high school and he was one of the sulky, even then dangerous-looking goons on the fringes of her more normal and far more popular world. He'd had quite a history since she'd moved away to journalism school at Michigan State and then to various newspaper jobs around the country.

In her recent article, she had sketched how he'd spent a year behind bars at the federal prison in Milan for burning IRS forms when he was a mailman outside Detroit. Plus, there were other skirmishes with the law, like the time he led the cops in Monroe on a twenty-mile chase. One cop collided with a school bus, not seriously injuring anyone. And that had been over a bad muffler.

Arly had never been much one for authority. Once, in school, he had shoved a history teacher against a locker when the teacher asked to see his hall pass. For her article, he'd given her a quick, mostly useless interview. She got most of what she had on him from other sources. He wasn't the main focus of the article anyway—just one of the short sidebars.

Watching a double-bottom diesel bear down on her along the lumpy two-lane blacktop, Cully felt an odd inkling of resolve. It was something that came on her sometimes when she was reporting, a notion to push head-first into the story. David often told her she was the type of person who could never keep her finger out of the fan. Even with a wire at her throat, she had an idea and some questions. "You killed that singer, didn't you?" Her heart thumped; her brain told her be very careful. Still she went on. "Why?"

Nothing.

"When I get you to where you want, you'll kill me, too?"

She felt her seat jiggle and looked in the mirror to see him sitting in the seat behind her. A massive, bearded hulk, still holding the ends of the wire.

"You shouldn't have been there," he said.

She pressed the gas as they rode a hill that curved between fenced pasture. "I'm going to need gas soon," she said.

"Drive."

"Where are we headed?"

His hairy face, along with the tar pit eyes, remained passive.

"Why don't you let me out here?" she asked.

For a second, Cully thought: the singer was weak. She couldn't hold up in the face of someone like Arly. But then she also thought with a shiver: if he killed once, and who's to say it was his first time, he'd do it again, in a flash of his huge hands on wire. "What do you want from me?" she wondered.

"No more bullshit."

"Besides that."

"Drive."

They were taking back roads, many of which she recognized from years before when she ran them with high school friends, Arly not among them. As far as she could tell, they were wandering northeast. "What's this about?" she asked.

A hot, stinging slice in her throat. Not too deep, but her eyes stung. She gave up the wheel for a moment and her car swerved across the center line. No one was there. She felt a warm slender sliver of pain that she suspected meant the bastard had drawn blood. Enraged, she reached for the wire, wanting to rip it loose. The car tires spit gravel.

"Don't!" he said.

"You prick!"

This cowed him for some reason. But he didn't let go of the wire.

The car, almost by itself, righted onto the road, as if nothing had happened. Cully grabbed the wheel gratefully and drove. "You're crazy," she said.

"Shut up."

Through pinches of pain, if for no other reason than to calm her fear, she forced herself to think of something else.

But nothing came for a while. She merely drove, the wheels spinning underneath them. Then her mind drifted to that night in the bare burning hills outside Managua when she and David and their missionary-turned-interpreter spent the better part of the evening with a group of barely teenage Contras.

One of them, Emilio, had been a burning bush of hate. He wanted the communists out of Nicaragua at all costs. He gestured wildly around their small campfire, taunting her, waving his weapon. He was skinnier but had the same personality as Arly. Back then she felt surprisingly in control. Somehow danger soothed her nerves, grabbed her gut and gave her mind powerful focus. Emilio had warmed up when it became clear he wasn't scaring her and she wanted to tell his story, his side of the war. He thought she was interested in him, and she was.

Thinking about that time, Cully shoved aside her fear and ignored the pain at her throat. "Arly," she said, "why don't you tell me what this is all about?"

He hardly moved, his thick arms holding the tips of the wire as if they were reins. But he seemed to be listening.

Up ahead she saw a stand of apple trees, a green-painted farm-house, a sagging barn and a couple of kids flipping a football under the drooping arms of a willow. She felt her chest grow tight; her neck tingled and ached. For a moment, she thought of wheeling in there, braking to a stop, and screaming for help. Because she knew right now she was taking a big gamble. "I mean, you must have some rea-son for what you're doing."

"Why?"

I want to get away from you, she thought. But I also would like to write about what really goes on inside a brain such as yours. Emilio had been tortured as a child by the leftists, hot coals pressed to his balls. His story got her a Pulitzer nomination. "You probably have something worthwhile to say," she told him, feeling as if she was reaching in the dark.

"What you wrote before?" he said.

She waited.

"Lies."

Great, she thought, there goes that idea. Still, she tried: "Then tell the truth."

"Why?"

"Don't you want it out?"

"Even if I did, you'd get it wrong."

"Try me."

For several seconds she drove, aware she'd reached a place where things could go either way.

After a time, the wire dropped. Still there, but loose. The relief she felt was enormous. The only problem, she thought: what's next?

CHAPTER 13
GANNON

Sheriff Ray Fallows directed the flashlight beam along the two-track that disappeared up the side of the hill into the trees. The cone of light paused along the edges of the dirt path, touching tire marks, one on each side of the two-track.

"Go through it for me again, Chief."

Gannon took the light from Fallows, which was his anyway, and trained it on the ground by their feet. The telltale studded pattern formed in the soft clay looked like the prints from his daughter's Horizon. He had put the snow tires on the front last January. So far she hadn't asked him to take them off, and knowing her, she hadn't had it done by anyone else.

Turning around and gazing down the hill they'd just climbed, Gannon saw three cars parked—his, the Sheriff's and Larry Lee's. Noah, the dome light dropping a stark glow on his idiot face, sat with Lee in the front of his cruiser. Neither was talking. Noah looked scared to death. Lee looked tired.

"Noah saw Arly Fleck carrying Cully down," Gannon said. "He put her in a car, looks like hers, and had her drive off."

"She didn't fight it?"

"Sounds like Fleck had her pretty good."

"But she's the one who drove?"

"What Noah said."

The Sheriff cleared his throat as he stepped next to Gannon. Both faced the cars below. Usually outgoing, Fallows seemed subdued now. Probably he was tired, too. Gannon had called and got him just as he was clearing the scene at Lonnie's. "What do suppose your daughter was doing up there, Cable?"

The night was damp and chilly, the sky speckled with stars. A truck rumbled, leaving the grain elevator on the other side of town. "I suppose doing her job."

"Which is?"

Gannon swung the light up, illuminating Fallows's soft round face. "Ray, don't yank my chain."

The Sheriff stared into the light, a cagey man whose bland features showed no emotion. "I'm trying to understand what happened."

Gannon stepped away and swooped the light through the hemlocks and scattered chokecherry bushes. The air smelled so familiar: a mixture of dust on tar, mossy ground, and faint late summer flowers.

In his office, Noah had got out in short bursts what he had seen. Cable suspected he had been wanting to tell someone for hours, but couldn't figure who until he rode by the building and saw Cully's dad inside. Once Cable had driven here and found the tracks, he called Fallows. "Cully must've seen something," he said, addressing the trees.

"Such as?"

Gannon snapped off the light, bringing on dark. Suddenly, the crickets began a racket again, drowning out the frogs. "That I don't know," the Chief said.

Fallows scraped something in his hands. A match flared and a smoldering circle appeared. Pipe smoke, the odor of chestnuts, floated between them. "Humor me a minute, Cable. Why was she up there?"

Gannon thought of her standing in his way outside the singer's trailer. How he'd slammed the door on her. "As far as I know, she was doing a story."

The bowl of the pipe glowed; the scented smoke rose skyward. "Didn't she do that piece a while back, on the militia, in that magazine?"

"I don't recall," Gannon lied, but remembering well. He told her she had romanticized the scum. She took this as a compliment.

"You think maybe she was meeting Arly up there?"

"What for?"

"Just conjecturing, Cable, trying to get this straight."

"There's nothing to get straight, Ray. He's got my girl." Gannon was surprised, although he wasn't sure why he should be, by the depth of emotion he felt. Given the lousy nature of their relationship the last months, he had all but forgotten how much he loved her.

More pipe sucking and smoking. Gannon recalled the determined reporter's expression on her face. She had wanted the story, come hell or high water.

"You believe Potts?" asked the Sheriff.

Gannon had wondered until he had searched farther up, before the Sheriff arrived, and confirmed his suspicions. "There's large boot prints coming down from the hill right to the car tracks. Same prints as we found on that blanket."

"Fleck's?"

"Who else?"

"Lots of people wear boots, Cable."

The pipe bowl burned embers; the smell drifted down wind toward the crickets belting out a high tempo nocturnal tune. Gannon felt his body turning into a fist. To an extent, he understood why the militia types got so angry with authority figures.

"How does Arly fit in?" An edge in the Sheriff's voice now.

"I suspect he's the one we're looking for," said Gannon.

"For what?"

"Killing the singer and his cousin both."

Fallows coughed. The pipe, cupped in a hand, dropped to his side. "This the first you've thought of this?"

"Mostly."

The Sheriff made a fuss out of sighing. Gannon, his eyes adjusted to the dark, noticed the look of concern on Fallow's face. "If you thought this earlier, Cable, why the hell didn't you say so?"

Fallows was right. By holding back, he might have damned well put his daughter in hotter water.

Fallows puffed, stoking his thoughts. "I still don't get it. If he killed the singer and faked the suicide, why wasn't he hell-bent somewhere by now? Why take hostages?"

"I don't know," said the Chief, not liking the word hostage.

A pickup truck rolled to a stop on the street, just behind Lee's cruiser. Gannon saw a guy he recognized, a local part-time farmer and insurance salesman, Kurt Brady, get out and approach Lee's window.

The Sheriff scratched his chin, probably to expand his thinking. "What's your theory on why he snatched your daughter?"

Gannon shook his head, exasperated, noticing that Lee had climbed out and was talking to Brady. "Lots of questions here yet, Ray."

"Are we sure it's Arly?"

"Noah says it was him. I don't see any reason not to believe it."

The Sheriff tucked the hand with the pipe under one arm. "Christ!"

Gannon saw Lee get out of his cruiser, step away from Brady and approach the hill. Fallows meanwhile shifted to the side, gazing up the hill, as if looking for Arly's ghost. "Cable," Lee called. "You ought to come down."

"What's up?"

"Fella says he come across a motorcycle a while ago when he was cutting his weeds. Maybe Arly Fleck's."

Gannon nodded, noticing the Sheriff firing up his pipe again. As he did, shadows touched his face. The Chief thought about hell and Arly as the devil, alive in the flames. But this confirmed it. Now he needed to go after his daughter.

CHAPTER 14
THE COLONEL

Cody Burke sat on the front of the wrap-around logpole porch, boots on a rail, hands crooked behind his neck, and noncommittally watched them cross the parking lot. He hardly moved.

"What the hell is this, Burke?" blustered the Colonel as Rat jammed the gun barrel into his side, nuzzling his ribs and shoving him forward.

Burke smiled.

They stopped just below Burke's cowboy boots. Rat wheezed next to him. The Colonel couldn't believe this betrayal. It had to be a mistake. "Winston," he said. "Take the gun away."

Rat looked to Burke for a sign. The bomber from Detroit took off his New England Patriots baseball cap, revealing a shiny bald dome. He ran a hand over his skinhead and shrugged. "Grab a brewski, Rat."

"You sure?"

"Benedict Arnold isn't going anywhere."

It slammed into him: Burke knew. Rat told him. The Colonel had been sold down the river. As Rat scurried for a beer, the Colonel's mind did what it did best: made quick calculations. If Burke was letting Rat go, maybe he had room to do some fast talking. How much did the bombmaker know? Maybe not everything.

Stretching and twisting the kinks that had settled during the long drive here, the Colonel got a grip on himself and tried to act calm so he could make some fast decisions.

"So, Burger, how's it hanging?"

Hands on his wide hips, the Colonel gazed quickly around the parking area and asked, "Where's Fleck?" Always best to try diversionary tactics.

Cody dropped his chin on the chest of his maize and blue University of Michigan sweatshirt, cut off at the sleeves, and resettled his hands behind his head. "Not here."

"Has he left any messages?" The Colonel stepped closer, nodding at the cabin whose slatted wood sides shone in the shafts of sun slicing through pointy pines.

"Not for you."

The Colonel tapped his fingertips together, trying to give off a commanding presence. "What's that supposed to mean?" he demanded in a voice that came out wrong.

"You figure it out, kraut."

The Colonel was still thinking, his gut roiling. He tried to read Burke's expression, which wasn't easy. Cody's hands were shoved in the pockets of his jeans, his shoulders turned up around his ears. He wore eggshell glasses perched on a slender nose. Ice-blue eyes stared down at the Colonel. Cody told everyone he had experience as a demolitions expert in the Marines, but the Colonel knew his knowledge came from books. His father was a physics professor at Wayne State University. Cody taught himself his lethal concoctions, but what he learned on his own, he learned well. He had a history of making bombs for the movement, a mercenary mixer of explosives.

Sticking a foot on the second step leading up the porch, the Colonel tried to give Cody a brass-tacks stare, but the man with the slender white scar crisscrossing his brow and those steady, steely eyes wasn't easy to handle. And that was why he hadn't been the Colonel's first choice. "You've got me very confused here," said Burger. "With the enemy."

"Because you are," Burke said softly, hardly moving in his chair. His body had the coiled stillness of a snake.

The Colonel's hand moved toward his holster, hidden under his bulky sports jacket.

Burke raised one finger and wiggled it. "Not smart."

Rat appeared at the door and shoved it open, beer in one hand, pistol in the other.

"Winston, what have you told him?" the Colonel asked.

Rat didn't reply. Just sipped his beer.

"Your friend doesn't like the company you keep," Cody explained.

The Colonel had the feeling of things cracking open and breaking away. He'd been had, and he needed to up the ante by telling some truth. "This really has nothing to do with you."

"Don't bullshit me."

"Let me explain."

"Tell me how you plan to feed Arly to the fuckin' dogs?"

"That's not it at all," lied the Colonel.

Burke rose slowly, stuck a hand under his sweatshirt and rubbed his belly. His steady eyes crept beyond the Colonel and drifted into the trees. The Colonel thought of turning and asking what the hell he was looking at. But he was a man fumbling for the controls; he didn't want to be popping his cork, at least not yet. Even so, it was getting late. Maybe he should make a break for it.

"Couple days back," said Cody idly, "the rodent gave me a call. Told me between him and you, I was supposed to get a hot one in the back of the head. Then you were going to turn the jackals lose on Arly."

"Hey, wait a second," said the Colonel, heart whacking in his chest. Damn Rat, damn him to hell. "There was nothing in this about you." Which was true; he didn't plan to shoot Burke. Not if he didn't have to.

"No, you wait, Burger," replied Burke, getting very serious. Those eyes were still steady behind the glasses. "You're a coward and a whore."

The Colonel had to beat back his fear and think this through. "Look, I've got my part of the money in the truck. Take it. Leave Arly to me."

"What about his share?"

"I'll send it to you."

"You're fucking me," Cody said.

The Colonel swallowed fear, even as it made his chest quake.

"Tell me, Burger, who was going to scratch me? You or Ratso."

The Colonel was feeling boxed in. He realized his grip on the situation was pretty flabby. His only chance to get on top was to put Rat on the spot. "Why would you believe Rat? He's the one who didn't want any part of this in the first place."

"Oh?" He glanced at Rat, who had his nose in his beer. "That right, pinhead?"

Winston didn't respond, just eyed them both, nervously, as if wondering who was going to slap him first.

Cody sat on the rail and leaned his back against a pole. He spoke in Rat's direction: "Who was it going to off me, shit for brains or you?"

Rat sipped the beer, his face pinched. "Him."

"What the hell," the Colonel blustered. This was a lie. If anyone was going to do it, it was Rat. He had said he wouldn't mind. Said he thought Burke was a stuck-up jackoff who was only in it for the cash. "He's lying."

In one smooth move, Cody reached behind the back of his jeans and brought out an awfully big handgun, shiny black and lethal.

The Colonel looked to Rat, who seemed more interested in this turn of events than alarmed. The Colonel's hand twitched up toward his own firepower. "Cody, watch where you're pointing."

The bomb maker slowly leveled the barrel at the Colonel's mid-section. Inside, the Colonel's belly went on red alert, firing it up but good, making an ulcer in no time flat. "Turn around and take off your pants," said Cody.

"What?"

"You heard him, dumplin'."

From around the left side of the cabin ambled a woman with black hair, leather jacket, face the color of a ripe peach. "You better listen to Cody, honey," she said. She, too, carried a weapon, a small machine gun. Even in the best of times, the Colonel wasn't much on recognizing weapons. But this was Israeli issue, a smart little Uzi.

The Colonel swept around between them, noticing Rat had sidled closer to Cody, his hand caressing the butt of his pistol. The woman had very red lips. Burger knew it was now or forget it. They weren't going to let him go. The time for talking was over. But they had him. There was no way out. Stupidly, he reached for his gun.

Cody fired a shot, exploding it not far over the Colonel's head.

"Dammit!" Burger tried to roar.

Then he felt a cold prod in his back, brought in on a whiff of deadly perfume, a flowery scent that made him think of fingernails raking his spine. "Down and dirty, dear," she puffed into his ear, jamming the gun into his gut, as if searching for his liver.

He elbowed her away and turned to smash her with his fist. But a powerful force spun him back and drove him to the ground. Eyes closed, he saw a torch-toting crowd, heard it roaring, felt himself heave, wanting to get to the front, to bow at the feet of his leader. But his mind sputtered. If he wasn't mistaken, he'd been shot.

CHAPTER 15
CULLY

Cully wiped a hand across the rusty, dusty face of the mirror and rolled a smudged circle with her palm. If she bent her head back, she could catch a cone of sun sneaking through a crack in the plywood over the window. Moving closer to the mirror, she eyed down the ridge of her nose, trying to get a good glance of the damage the son of a bitch did with his wire. Dark as it was in this bathroom, there was enough light to make out the slit, shaped like a bloody smile, just above her collarbone. It stung but didn't look deep. She wanted a smoke, but had none. What she wanted more was to escape. Short of that, she wanted to get clean.

Aware of Arly murmuring not too far beyond the door, she switched on the tap and heard the water groan from down deep. She didn't care if he heard as it coursed through old pipes, swam up from the floor into the spigot, and slurped out the faucet. She waited as it filled the sink, then cupped some of the liquid and splashed it on her face. A circle of pain, sharp as the prick of a dozen needles, shot around her neck as water dripped down her chin.

Ignoring it as best she could, Cully scooped more and cleansed herself again, trying to scour Arly's odor from any place even remotely close to her nose.

The pipes clanged as she washed. She figured Arly wouldn't like that. But he didn't yell or come pounding on the door. So she poured the water on and doused herself good, moving from her face to neck and dabbing blood and grit from the wire wound.

Just as she was finishing, there was sound at the door. She heard the scraping of the chair or whatever he'd used to block her in. Swinging open the door, he stood glowering, the blocky bearded force of him taking up the empty space. "You done?" he asked. He wore a dark T-shirt, blue jeans and Army boots. She tried to ignore the coiled snake tattoo on his right forearm.

She glared at him.

He blinked, as if she'd slapped him softly somewhere in the beard. "Turn it off!" He shouldered in, shoving her to the side, twisted the faucet off with a vengeance, and turned to her, his chest swelling.

Standing inches from him, Cully suddenly believed she had a good chance of survival if she gave him back as good as he threw her way. Show weakness and he'd lash out. "I was dirty," she told him, not mentioning he was to blame.

If she wasn't mistaken, she saw anger and maybe a sliver of confusion in his coal-pit eyes. Then he turned to go.

"Wait!"

He paused, his broad lumpy back to her, dipping a shoulder, like a dog, to show he was listening.

"What're you planning to do . . . with me?"

Part of his face, a chunk of hairy cheekbone, a probing eye, showed over the shoulder. "Still thinking about it."

"What's to think?"

He had turned to face her, smelling of root cellars and dank caves. His T-shirt expanded along the sides of his chest. "You want to know something," he said.

She waited and watched him carefully.

"That singer, I slit her throat like a melon."

She knew he was watching her very intently, those eyes taking in her reaction. Exactly why she wasn't sure, but she suspected this was a test. Fail it and she was history. "Why are you telling me this?"

Arly looked behind him into a spacious room at rows of boxes, as if looking for the answer to her question. He had made her drive to a warehouse section along the St. Clair River in downtown Port Huron. She gathered he knew whoever owned this place. He gazed away from her for a good thirty seconds, his body swaying like an oak in the breeze. His head was tilted to one side, as if he was listening for radio waves. "You're a cunt," he then said in a low voice.

The word hit her like a blackjack. She winced. "What else?"

"You're like the rest of them."

"Who?"

Facing her full on, his face grew blank. Suddenly, his eyes popped and he jerked his head to the side, as if someone had popped him in the noggin with a ballpeen hammer. "Dammit!"

The head jerked again and again, some sort of spasm. "Sonofabitch, goddamn, motherfuckers!" His face snarled; his body grew rigid, then twitched again. He just stood there, in spasms. Contorted, but controlled.

Cully thought of making a run for it, but she'd have to barrel through him to do it. Watching him move, she forced herself away from her own emotions, the stark, shivering fear. She knew this was a time to be steady. Like a surgeon. Arly was her patient, her story. She wondered about Tourette syndrome, the brain disease that made its victims twitch and curse. She'd once done a story on a lawyer in Allentown who had it. This maniac had all the signs. Did he have it back in high school? She didn't recall. "Arly?" she said.

He stepped back, pushing out his hands. "Cunt, fucking cunt. Stay there." He slammed the door, his head still twisting. A few seconds later, she heard heavy footsteps shuffle across the wooden floor. The swear words followed in his wake.

CHAPTER 16
GANNON

Mud slopped at Gannon's pants as he stood in the doorway of the milking barn. A large shadow moved on the far wall beyond the row of munching cows. Pinching his nose to ward off the stink, the Chief sloshed in the shadow's direction. "Baxter!"

"What?"

"Need to talk to you.

"I'm busy."

Bits of hay and chunks of crap stuck in the wet dirt. Milk sluiced through tubes clamped to drooping udders and flowed into a central pipe, which ran along the floor under the bellies of the dumb beasts. The liquid ebbed toward the shiny silver tank Doug Baxter now tended.

"This won't take long." Gannon rounded the last Guernsey who, along with the rest, champed pulverized grain from a half-filled chute.

Baxter stopped fiddling with a dial, wiped his hands on his bibs, and turned his blurry eyes to the Chief. A beer can sat on a slab of cement by Baxter's shit-blotted boots. "Not a good time to talk," he said, sliding the back of his hand over his mouth.

Gannon heard liquid burbling in the tank. He decided to try to be nice. "Little late to be milking, isn't it?"

"Been a long day." Baxter stuck his hands in the pockets of his overalls and gave Gannon a strained smile.

"Doing what?"

Baxter looked away, as if turning from a bad breeze. "The usual bullshit."

"You talk to Arly today?"

"What am I supposed to know about him?"

"He's your roommate, isn't he?"

Baxter probably had to decide how much of a lie to tell. "He stays here once in a while."

"You mind if I see his room?"

"He crashes on the couch."

"Did he leave any of his belongings?"

"I'd have to check."

Soft slurping came from the tank; milky cottage cheese residue swirled out a bottom spout and bubbled into a drain. "You hear about Lonnie?"

Baxter's red-sweatshirted shoulders collapsed in a shrug. "Don't know anything about that."

A couple of cows made low, moaning sounds, ready to get the contraption that sucked on their teats the hell off. A radio faintly playing country music hung lopsidedly from a nail on a rafter over Baxter's head. The farmer's face looked blotted and weary, small lumps of flesh swelling at the crest of his cheekbones under indistinct eyes.

"Look, Doug, I've had a long day, too. I don't want to go around the maypole. I need your help. Looks like Arly's got my daughter."

"Cully?" Baxter blinked slowly, then took off his seed cap. He had a wife and three young kids.

"It looks that way."

In high school, for a few weeks, Baxter and Cully had dated. Gannon never knew why it ended, but he suspected it had to do with his daughter's ultimate ability to make good decisions for herself, more or less. Gannon had to admit he had liked David, her husband, a lot. Damned shamed the way he died, strapped in a wheelchair, his muscles gone haywire.

"Why'd he do that?" asked Baxter.

"You tell me."

Baxter swiped a forearm over his oily hair, replaced the cap, and patted the dome, as if arranging it for a newspaper picture showing him as drunk dairy farmer of the year. Baxter was in a fix, Gannon figured. He liked Cully, and truth be told was a decent enough man. But Arly was one of his friends, too, and also the kind of guy who wouldn't take kindly to anyone telling tales about him, either in or out of school. And Baxter knew for that matter that the Chief could make his life miserable in any number of ways if he didn't cooperate. Besides the boozing, Baxter liked to smoke dope—weed he grew out back, not much, but enough to get him time. Gannon had hinted to him a couple times in the past that he knew it was there. He didn't bust him because he didn't sell it, as far as Gannon could tell. Plus, it gave the Chief an inside edge in times such as this.

"I told you, Chief, I don't really know anything."

"Let me be the judge of that." Gannon leaned close.

Baxter's face registered a little fear, as if he could see the Chief was about to back him into a corner of the barn and do convincing of the bare-knuckled nature. Which wasn't far off. For a second, the image of that other barn at home flashed in Gannon's mind. The gasoline. Bashful Blue, their show horse, on the ground. Himself, mad with grief. Another time he had crossed the line. "Look, Baxter, it's my girl we're talking about here."

The farmer's face looked sick, drained, as if sucked dry by one of those metal teat cups. "Wish I could help."

"Don't wish. Do it. Else I'll break your ass, Baxter, for the dope and God knows whatever the hell else. Being an accessory." Gannon leaned in closer, smelling the mixture of cow crap and breathalyzed hops.

"Accessory to what?"

"We're looking at two murders and a kidnapping."

"Shit, Chief, I ain't involved in none of that."

"We can let Haney Mills decide." Mills, the prosecutor, had already been called twice, had even shown up at the scene at Lonnie's, eager to get his teeth into anything that stank of militia.

"I can't be going to jail," Baxter said, looking at the cows, as if they would tear the place up if he was behind bars.

"Then help me out."

Baxter's father, who worked this farm for forty years, had been a friend of the Chief's. But he, too, had a sour streak in him and consorted with the local malcontents.

"Why would he take your girl?" Baxter asked.

"That's what I'm trying to find out."

"You're sure he's got her?"

"It's not Peter Pan."

They faced off for a few seconds. Baxter's face softened, took on a shade of kindness. "Whyn't you wait in the office?" Baxter flung a thumb over his shoulder. "Lemme finish up."

Gannon nodded and swiveled his eyes in the direction of the office. His nose watered, a reaction to the foul odor filling the place. "How come this barn stinks so bad?" he asked.

"The cows for chrissakes!"

"Why don't you clean up after them?"

They stood a few inches apart. Baxter's mouth had twisted into a sickly frown. "Chief, give me a break, OK? I didn't kill anyone."

"Did Arly?"

Baxter licked his lips, as if tasting for salt. He sighed. "Give me a few minutes, would you?"

Gannon sat in the hard-backed chair in a room big enough for a desk, another chair and a coat rack. Hands behind his neck, he looked through the door and watched as Baxter unhooked the cows and shooed them outdoors. He thought of the motorcycle in the ditch. Arly's all right. One tire flat. He must've dumped it there and grabbed Cully and her car to get away.

Back at the ditch, the Sheriff had ordered the cycle impounded and asked Gannon if he wanted to call out lights and generators, and maybe the posse on horses, to search the woods. The Chief said wait until morning. He was convinced Noah had seen what he said. And yet, what if Noah messed up? What if Cully was in the woods? Gannon had mulled it over a minute or so and decided the best bet was to somehow pick up Arly's trail right then and not waste time dragging through the trees. He had radioed the State Police to look for Cully's car and had given them a complete description of the kidnapper and his hostage.

"You want coffee?" Baxter yanked on the back of his stringy hair as he stood in the doorway.

Gannon didn't.

Baxter stepped in and dropped into the chair on the other side of the desk. Looking half boiled and potted, he shoved aside a stack of papers, magazines and fast food wrappers and leaned forward on his elbows. "Got a couple heifers acting like they got that thing from England," he said.

"What?"

"That fucks up your brain. Man, they're ornery tonight." Baxter's head lolled as he laughed, his voicebox clucking up and down. "Kind of like my old lady."

"I didn't know you kept up so well on current events."

The goofy smile dimmed. Taped on the wall behind Baxter was a calendar showing a naked woman holding a puppy to her face. The month was April. The year was right.

"Look, Doug, anything you can tell me will help."

Baxter sat back, making a pucker with his mouth, possibly pleased the Chief was kissing his behind. "You sure he's got Cully?"

"That's what I've been telling you."

Baxter slid a can of chaw out of the pile of papers. Examined it as if it was made of gold. Twisted off the top, dug ground tobacco onto a forefinger, stuffed a tarry chunk behind his lower lip. He waited a couple moments, gazing into the container, before replacing the top and returning the can to the debris on his desk. "How'd he get her?"

Gannon told him.

"You believe Potts?"

"I saw the tracks from her car and boot marks. Looked like he dragged her in."

"Suppose if anyone sees something around here, it's that kid," replied Baxter.

Gannon shifted in his seat, anxiety gripping him out of the blue, as if a jolt of electricity had slapped from on high. He needed information; otherwise his daughter could be left under a tree by a gravel pit as well. If she hadn't been already. "When's the last time you talked to Arly?" he asked.

Baxter's jaw swiveled, adjusting the lumpy plug. He sniffed. He sighed. He twisted his neck.

"Doug?"

"This afternoon."

"He was here?"

Baxter picked at a Burger King wrapper. Heat blew down from the vent, softly rattling the paper. "He called."

"From where, for what?"

"You figure he's going to hurt your girl?"

"Doug, why'd he call?"

"He ever hears I talked to you, I'm fucking French toast."

"If you don't talk to me, it's a sure thing, sooner than you think."

Baxter nodded. "He needed a couple phone numbers."

"For where?"

Baxter leaned back, scraped open the drawer, pulled out a phone bill, and flipped the papers toward Gannon. The Chief stared at the line of numbers, noticing a mustard splotch obscuring a few.

"I got them marked there."

"Are these places you call?"

"He did, when he stayed here."

One number was to an exchange in Gaylord, up north; the other to Grand Rapids. "Who're these to?"

Pain flushed across the dairy farmer's already rosy face. "I don't know anything more than that."

"You know, Doug, playing around with these militia is going to get your nuts in a wringer."

Baxter frowned and folded his arms over his chest, looking like his balls already hurt.

Gannon picked up the bill and ran a finger down a row. Gaylord was near militia territory. Grand Rapids was a city that the Chief had visited a time or two. His former MP partner in Vietnam, Chang, lived there. "Who was he calling, Baxter?"

Baxter held up his hands, as if he'd just burned both palms on a stove. "I don't know, Chief. Honest. Arly didn't tell me nothing else. He sure as shit didn't say anything about Cully."

"He made calls from here?"

Baxter shrugged, a sick look on his face. "Like I said before."

Gannon leaned forward, his chest over the desk, and squelched the urged to grab and shake Baxter. He was about to hit the farmer with another question when suddenly a dumb-eyed cow appeared in the doorway, a green tag stapled to its ear.

"Dammit, Bruce," said Baxter, waving an arm at his wandering cow. "Get outta here. Get some sleep!" The cow stared at its milker, as if trying to interpret his words.

"Whad I tell ya?" Baxter glanced at the Chief. "It's that crazy disease. Next thing that heifer's gonna be foaming at the mouth."

"Bruce?" said Gannon.

"Yeah," said Baxter. "I think she's gay."

CHAPTER 17
CULLY

Cully stood at the bathroom door, stuck her ear against the wood, and tried to hear. Nothing. No curses, no muffled talking, no stalking on the creaking floor. Maybe he'd gone and left her here, which would be very much to her liking. She quietly tried the knob. It didn't budge. She thought of slamming her shoulder against it. But that wouldn't work; it wouldn't break her free. And even if it did, he'd probably be out there nearby waiting.

Cully sat on the toilet seat lid. She thought of calling out, screaming for help. But she didn't want to stir him up. If he was there and she made more noise, who knew what he'd do? To an extent, she felt relief. He could easily have ripped through her neck with his wire, or gone after her when he'd come in to complain about the water.

Idly touching the cut and pressing fingers to the pulses at the sides of her throat, she thought of Brenda Scott and shuddered. If Arly had killed the singer, and he doubtless had, what was to stop him from doing the same to her? She was crazy to think he wouldn't just burst back in and fix her good.

As if prodded by that damned wire again, Cully turned and gazed at the boarded window. No sun cut through the cracks now. Leaning down, she felt the tank for sturdiness, wobbled the top, and decided it would probably hold.

Climbing up, Cully reached for the first slat of plywood and slid her fingers between soggy pulp and the window frame. Then she raised herself as far as she could go, stretched her arms, tugged on the wood, and felt a sloppy tearing of material. Her heart bumped in her chest, excited now, pumping chemicals into her blood with the hope she could rip free.

She looked behind her at the door, balls of tendon and muscle tight in her calves. Seeing and hearing nothing to stop her, she pulled at the wood covering the window. She had to tilt her head away as wet chunks dropped. One landed in her mouth; she spit it out as quietly as she could. With not too much ripping and little sound, she removed enough soaked wood to allow a foot-sized gap of light to show through. Hands reaching up, she felt a whiff of wind. No glass. Just empty space, leading to freedom, beyond the wood.

Air puckering her face, she thought of her father. For a second she felt this was his fault. If he'd been forthright; hell, if he'd just talked to her, this wouldn't have happened. She wouldn't have had to sneak up the hill.

But she doubted anything he could have said would have kept her from the bluff. Once she started sniffing a story, she kept at it until she got it. That part was good, David had said. She was tenacious. Many times she had put herself in jeopardy to get the interview. She had walked through crack neighborhoods, visited inmates in jail, and once met an anonymous caller who wanted to talk to her about a bank robbery. Not long ago, she had helped chase down a rapist who burst through the side door of a bakery. He had been barricaded inside and took the chance to run just as she circled around back in hopes of getting a better bead on the scene. When it came to things of journalism, she was fearless. Almost a sickness. Just like Edna. Except now she wanted out of this story. She didn't want to write her own obit.

On her tiptoes, Cully grabbed the upper half of the window wood. More sodden chunks came free as she tore. She let them drop, working more furiously until a shoulder-size space appeared. Enough to squeeze through.

Even better, she saw an iron bar running widthwise across the window frame. She hoped it would hold her weight. She wiped mulchy, termite-chomped debris from her hands and took a couple seconds to get her breath. Then, vaguely aware of shuffling movement outside the bathroom, she flexed her legs, rocked back and jumped. Her right hand caught the bar; the other grazed it, cartwheeling the left side of her body down toward the floor.

Hanging from one arm, the rotator cuff wrenched and ready to rip, she swung up and snagged the bar with her free hand. She didn't wait to rest or gather strength. Stepping her toes against the wall, she climbed quickly and awkwardly, using her arms to draw her into the window well. Shoving her head through the opening, she tried to see what she could. She wiggled the rest of the way up and jiggled her shoulders further through the space as she took in the sights.

A hint of dusk lay in the sky. Pausing for breath, she saw a boxy, warehouse-looking structure across the way. Just beyond, through an opening in the bricks, there was fluid movement, light flashing on water. The St. Clair River.

To the right, she saw an alley curving toward an even taller building. Left and below, she spotted a white van, motor running, parking lights on, a string of colored lights blinking along the edge of the roof, and a figure behind the wheel, flaring up a cigarette, it looked like.

Glancing directly in front of her and down, she saw the slight slope of a roof ending at the metal frame of what looked like a fire escape. Cully pushed herself up into the place between the bar and the sill, wondering if she should call out to the driver of the van. She felt vulnerable from behind, as if a dog was about to bite.

The driver's door of the van opened A small, black-haired kid, Oriental-looking, stepped out. Cully cleared her throat to call, thought better of it and used all of her strength to wedge her head and shoulders through. The rest of her was about to follow. But then, behind her, the door exploded open.

"Help!" she croaked. The Asian peered up, hooding his eyes with an open hand, the cigarette pointing in her direction.

"Help me," she called again.

He raised a hand and waved tentatively, as if he'd recognized her from the dim past.

Cully twisted hard, corkscrewing her head and shoulders out. Her upper body, caught between the bar and sill, felt heavy. Ribs crunched. She wanted to cry out, it hurt so much. She kept shoving, trying to missile through. But she was stuck; she couldn't go any farther. She knew Arly was back there.

"Call the police," she said to the guy two stories below. He kept squinting up. "Please?"

From behind she heard: "His name's Pham."

"Pham, get help." Stupid, she thought. And then she felt the tug. Arly was yanking her legs. But she wouldn't budge either way. She was stuck. "Shove back," she heard him say.

She did, with all her might, her shoes making contact. She hoped she slammed him good and hard and maybe even mortally in the bearded kisser.

CHAPTER 18
THE COLONEL

The Colonel felt fire race through his upper portions, piercing like shrapnel. The wet ground was moving as the voices grew louder, more distinct. Closer in, one of them was calling his name.

"C'mon, wake up."

A stink blew into his face, blasting his nose, jerking open his eyes. He tried to wave the horrible odor away, but only felt terrible pain. His shoulder, he wasn't sure which one, couldn't move.

"You with us?"

He tried to make out the face behind the voice. A blurry shape, slender and enticing, worked at him, demanding recognition. The woman.

"We need to talk."

His eyes flipped shut. He searched for a way out, to escape down a path to the voices calling from a distant room illuminated by a thousand torches. But the rotten stink kept him here, made him pay attention. His eyes opened again. Things were more clear now.

Cody stood next to the woman, his arm around her shoulders. Her hips were slung to one side; she flung back her hair. He saw the heavy weight of breasts inside her blouse and thought of Eve, the first woman, the tramp, screwing the snake. For an apple. Like all women.

"Listen up, Burger," said the bomber. He stepped closer and dropped to one knee. He was smoking a small cigar, its red tip flaring. The Colonel felt chilly. "We need to know some things."

The Colonel wondered what time it was. For that matter, he wondered where he was. He saw tall trees above him, faint sunlight. He wondered if they had been through this before, hours ago. He felt damp on the ground. His eyes drooped as the hall of his forefathers called to him. But he felt a tug on his chin, drawing him up, face to face with the bomber. Looking this close, the Colonel could see the smooth pale skin, the round glasses, the baby's butt of a head and that twisted scar on the forehead, a wiggling line of white. "You with me, Colonel?" Cody asked.

The Colonel smiled to think of the beauty of explosions when they were done right. The bomber had a couple videos of his work that he liked to show in training sessions. The Colonel particularly recalled the suburban home, it must have been in Maryland somewhere, that he blew to smithereens. Quite a sight—like the big bang the liberals said started the world. "Colonel?"

The woman appeared again, next to the bomber. "Don't make yourself suffer."

The Colonel nodded, thinking about suffering. Which made him recall his mother, Helga, stout and crabby and full of stories about the farm the family once had, before the big war, before the world caved in around them, before the Fuehrer raised them up. It was Helga who lied and cheated and bribed their way into America. Then she died, pulp mill press rollers grabbing her hair and then the rest of her in the plant in Albany. Helga. He had once watched as she hiked her billowing skirt and let his father's brother, Rudolph, climb underneath.

"Exactly how much do the mud police know?" asked Cody.

The Colonel tried to focus on the answer. "Not sure."

Cody shook his head sadly. "This is how it is." He slipped the cigar from his mouth and stuffed it out of sight into the Colonel's cheek. For a second, nothing registered. Then he felt a vast cable of hurt rip the side of his face. He knew he screamed but didn't hear it.

"You see?" said Cody after what seemed an ocean's worth of time.

The Colonel certainly did see. He just wished he could talk about it. Even so, he nodded his head. Or tried to.

"Good," said the bomber. "Because we have work to do."

The woman had backed away. She stood to the side, arms folded over her chest.

"First, you were short on money. About eight grand worth." The bomber was leaning close again.

"Cody, just ask him what he knows."

The bomber turned around. "Honey, shut the fuck up."

She turned away.

"Women. Can't live with 'em, can't live without 'em, ain't that right, Burger?"

The Colonel wasn't sure what he thought about anything. But he did think: no, all the money had been in the case. Rat probably helped himself.

"Colonel?"

His eyes wouldn't open. He tried hard to hear those voices in the other room. Would his father be there? A mousy man who had run a shoe store before the war. The war that should have cleansed the world of Jews and others whose genes were bad. His father always said that, sounding like a Jew himself.

Again, that smell and burning. He fought to keep his eyes closed, but they rolled up, like a garage door. He found himself facing the skinless head, the sharp nose, the thin mouth, Cody. Maker of vast flames. "Semper Fi."

Burger blinked.

"Your friends at the restaurant, how much do they know?"

He shook his head.

"Do they know about me?"

"No."

"You're sure?"

"I never told them."

"You're sure about that?"

He nodded.

"Do they know you were coming here?"

The Colonel had to think. His plan. How he and Rat were going to roll in, give Arly what he needed. Get him on his way. Then tell the cops where Arly had gone to get his bomb. He thought he heard the sound of helicopter blades, a black helicopter from the hypocritical United Nations. The Zionist Occupation Group, come to do them in, carry them away. Maybe save him. But the sound was only in his ears, he knew.

"Burger! Did you know they stuck a beeper on your truck?"

He wished he had the energy to fight them off. Even so, they were farther away now. He felt something hard and hot and hurting on the balls of his feet, like someone carving and peeling. Oddly, he didn't care. Let them cut. For a second he wondered about the man with the Greek name. The ATF agent. What would he think, waiting in his motel for a message that would never come? The Colonel wondered if he should tell Cody and the woman about the two cops. But they already knew, didn't they? Or did they? If they did, why were they hurting him so much more now?

CHAPTER 19
SMEREAS

Fingering open the blinds, ATF Agent Herb Smereas watched traffic shoot by on Old U.S.-27. A few vehicles had lights on already. No doubt they were headed for a last fling at summer, while he was holed up in this lousy motel outside of Gaylord, a place called the Bear Claw Inn.

Smereas had taken the room after the meeting with Burger. He wanted to keep out of sight here on the edge of militia territory. He also wanted to avoid using his cellular phone unless absolutely necessary, in case someone unfriendly up here knew how to tap in. He had been on the motel room line on and off for hours, keeping everyone abreast of developments, of which there had been precious few. He had hoped to be wrapped up by this time and have grabbed the guy with the bomb, as well as its maker. But, now, hell, look at the mess.

It had been his job for the last eight years, five of them undercover, to track the various factions of militia. When Burger had come to him a couple weeks before with a story about bomb in the making, he had to listen. And then when he figured who the bomb builder was, he had to act, if for no other reason than to arrest the zit who had been on the agency's most wanted roster for a while. Cody Burke, the Motor

City Bomber, who mixed all kinds of munitions for whoever paid the most. A bastard whose work Smereas had seen up close and personal. Twice. Blood on walls, twisted bodies. A child's fingers, a woman's arm.

Behind him the phone rang. He scooped up the receiver. "Smereas."

"This is Piersma."

Smereas felt anger flicker through him. The governor's stooge had been hounding them since morning. Understandably he was interested, but a major pest. "What's going on down there?"

"Nothing new." Smereas slipped the photo from his breast pocket and stared at the bald head, beady eyes and square jaw of Burke. A booking shot, taken in 1992, shortly after he had sold four cases of dynamite and fancy remote detonator to two agents disguised as members of the Freeman group in Idaho. Burke only spent a year in prison on that one. Since then he'd been busy.

"Where's your man?"

Smereas hated having so many noses stuck in this business. He strongly suspected Burger's vanishing act had something to do with the fact that everyone, from the FBI on down, wanted a piece of this action. Smereas, with backing from his bosses in Detroit and Lansing, had been able to keep most of them at bay. Until now.

"We're working on it, sir," he said.

"With little progress."

A dripping dinosaur of an air conditioner rattled next to the window, pushing in stale, hardly chilled air. To keep something fresh moving through, Herb had left the door open when his partner from the State Police left to buy dinner. He noticed Colin Parker's nondescript Corsica pull into the lot now, headlights on, the so-called militia expert a boxy hump behind the wheel.

"Do you need the governor to send more help?" asked Piersma.

"Not yet."

"Why the hell not?"

The agent thought about his wife and kids home in Lansing, probably already done with their barbecue with the neighbor couple, both professors at Michigan State. His wife hadn't been happy when he told her he had to be gone. But she accepted it; it went with the job. "We've got a handle on it, sir."

"That translates into you have no idea?"

Parker edged open the door with one shiny-shoed foot, holding Wendy's bags in each hand and frowning.

"We're doing our best," Smereas said.

"Giving yourselves handjobs."

The roly-poly State Police captain set his booty on the table by the bathroom and began to root inside. Parker was second in command of the Michigan State Police Anti-Terrorism Unit. Unlike most of the State Police, he was pretty out of shape. He had got involved earlier in the week and had been a pain in the ass since. He'd talked with his boss, Major Barnes, after lunch, got his ass chewed, and then gave Smereas dirty looks as the day went on with no word from Burger. "Is there anything else, sir?"

"Yes, goddammit, we want this resolved. Stop farting around."

Parker sat in a chair, unfoiling his sandwich. He had been the one who coordinated having a State Police helicopter in the air this morning when Burger and the other one shoved off from Denny's in the Cherokee. It had tracked the pair to a dirt road outside Wolverine that led into deeply forested territory. Tree cover prevented them from seeing anything more, and the beeper apparently had malfunctioned.

"I'll call you as soon as we have something," Smereas said into the phone.

"You've been saying that since noon."

Smereas had argued all along that they had to play this close to the vest. No storm trooping at any juncture. There had been a few who wanted to force the wire on Burger and then proposed swooping in with all they had once he met with Burke and whoever wanted this bomb. Make it another Waco.

Knowing the local militia and the wilderness area as he did, Smereas had wanted to string the rope out as far as it would go. But he now had the sinking feeling in his gut that he had given Burger too much slack.

"Agent Smereas?"

He shook himself back into the moment.

"Do you have enough people looking for this Burger?" asked Piersma.

The agent checked his watch and saw it was nearly eight. "Three sheriff's deputies are likely on the island right now talking to the Colonel's friends."

"What else?"

"There are some places we're checking."

"That is it?"

"Right now, that's our plan."

Silence on the other end of the phone. Parker slurped on a straw stuck in his cup. "This is unacceptable, Herb."

"Sir?"

"Excuse me, but we've apparently got some scary shit going down and now we have no fucking idea what to do about it."

Smereas had not liked this guy from the start. A gladhander with a boozer's pug. But he was right to be worried. "We're holding up our end, sir."

"Pissing your pants, you mean."

Smereas stood again and squeezed the phone hard. "Look, Mr. Piersma, I have to go."

"Let me get this straight. You call us with a cockamamie story about the Michigan Militia run amok. Get us to make some concessions. And now say your informant has failed to live up to his end of the bargain?"

"Not the militia, only a couple members of it."

"What-the-hell-ever. We can't keep stopping our work because of rumors."

Parker stuffed fries in his mouth, his cheeks bunched out like a squirrel. Smereas scratched his neck. "These are more than rumors."

"If there's a threat, stop it. If not, get off the fucking phone!"

Smereas took a deep breath and made his voice level. "Sir, I would seriously reconsider the celebration on the bridge," he said.

"Cancel the bridge walk and alarm everyone in the entire state, you mean, about something that still sounds like a lot of horseshit?"

"I'm saying don't write this off."

"Then give us something besides hot air."

Smereas, because he was trained to put manners before emotion, let Piersma do the phone slamming.

Keeping himself in check, the ATF agent then gently placed the receiver in its cradle. Almost immediately the phone rang again.

Smereas stared at it through three rings, then grabbed it. It was a dispatcher for the Gaylord State Police post. "Herb, I've got a guy from downstate on the line. Says he has a lead on a militia nut who's been making calls to a number up here."

"Does he sound on the level? I've talked to enough crackpots already today."

"He says he's a cop."

Smereas didn't let his voice betray the faint surge of hope he was feeling. "Put him on." The line clicked. "This is Herb Smereas," he said.

The voice on the other end sounded frazzled. "Cable Gannon. I'm chief of police in Memphis, Michigan. We have a suspect in two murders down here who might be headed your way."

"Who?"

"Arly Fleck. He's a militia sympathizer. I found some calls to a number near Gaylord on his roommate's phone bill."

Smereas took a deep breath. "I'd like to help you with your murder cases, Chief, but right now I'm tied up with other matters."

"There's one other thing," Gannon said. "He has a hostage."

"Who?"

"My daughter."

Smereas nodded. In his mind he framed possibilities. Logically he had no reason to think this was important, but his instincts were telling him otherwise. He gave Gannon his beeper number and told him to buzz back at midnight. "I'm waiting on an important call right now, Chief," he said. "Can't talk. But I want the lowdown on this Fleck."

As soon as Smereas hung up, the phone rang a third time. It was the dispatcher again, calling to tell him that a DNR officer had spotted a Jeep Cherokee on a back road in Pigeon River State Forest, the heart of militia country.

CHAPTER 20
SOFTSHOE

His ears were alive, probably more so than the rest of him, to the dark that felt familiar even when it wasn't. In his many years in the north woods, Donnie Mumberto, also known as Softshoe, had grown to know the wilderness well. He was paid to memorize the hills, valleys, swamps, bogs, paths, streams, lakes, and fields. Among other things, he did search and rescue when the civilians got lost or into trouble.

The DNR conservation officer was blessed to do what he loved most, which was to be outdoors, patrolling the still mostly wild places in northern Michigan. He had been making his rounds in Pigeon River country earlier this afternoon when the Cherokee drove past him. He recognized the passengers. They'd been part of a band of militia he had to chase out of a federally protected bog last spring. Dressed up in their soldier gear, they were staggering through the brambles, getting torn and ripped. They had actually been happy he arrived; they were lost, they said, and looked it. He had led them to a feeder road.

Mostly he viewed these militia men as bothersome but not particularly dangerous. He sort of even liked their philosophy of how the government liked to stick it to folks. Witness Wounded Knee, for one example. Unfortunately, there had been more of these militia in recent years, infesting the woods, shooting off guns, and setting up camps in places they had no business to be.

Softshoe had been driving home from Gaylord when he heard the be-on-the-out for the Cherokee on the scanner. Actually he'd been to town for food and an AA meeting. Remembering the two men he saw on the road earlier, he radioed the State Police post in Gaylord and then made the drive back into the state forest.

Before the cops showed up, he thought of driving in the direction the Jeep had been headed to see if it was still around. But he waited, figuring if they were looking for the two men, he'd better not spook anyone. The ATF agent, guy with the Greek name whom Mumberto knew, had met him down on the dirt road where he had passed the Cherokee. A stumpy state cop whose name he had already forgotten had tagged along. Smereas had told Mumberto to stalk his way up toward the hunting lodge at the end of the road and take a look.

Moving quietly across a carpet of jack pine needles, Softshoe heard a few frogs croaking in the background, maybe the same kind he had seen from the canoe this afternoon. They sounded angry, probably complaining about the bad soil from acid rain killing so many of them these days. Luckily he hadn't spotted any mutant frogs. But one of his partners, south of here, recently came across four with extra legs. Two had only one eye. The cycle had been disrupted. Damned world was poisoning itself. Just what Softshoe's grandfather had predicted.

Listening to sounds, Mumberto crested the final knob leading to the paper birches and pin cherries that surrounded this side of the hunting lodge atop Crow Mountain. No mountain really, just a big hill. Not many crows either, to tell the truth.

Leaning forward, his senses tuned to the night life around him, Mumberto thought for a moment of his father, Henry, who never went into the woods. He made refrigerators in Benton Harbor and preached against native Chippewa ways. Softshoe thought about his sad father a lot these days. How he grew fat and lazy in his chair at night, and how he hiked with stooped shoulders every morning out the door on his way to the plant. How he liked Stroh's beer in forty-ounce bottles, which he put on the kitchen table when they were done and his mother threw out. Always his father was an inspiration to him, not in a good way. More a lesson in failure.

Holding out a hand, as if trying to catch words or some better idea of what lay ahead, Mumberto started forward. The whiff of last night at the bar came to him. Beer and smoke in the air, Donna swaying to a Travis Tritt cheating song. Their marriage had ended last year, partly because of his drinking. But he was getting over that. The dream he had during his afternoon in the canoe had helped. The dream of the bear, the notion of rescue, came to him again. He often had these dreams before he set off to find someone. Mystical bullshit, he knew, but he believed in it. Look where he was now. The bear had replaced Donna, who in the dream was naked on a floor, and brought him to this place.

Stepping carefully forward, he touched the revolver buttoned to his belt but didn't take it out. He relied on his nose, ears and eyes to be his weapons. His grandfather, who had been a trapper near Mt. Pleasant, always told him that his best protection was to understand the world around him and to adapt to it when necessary. But not to give in the way Henry did.

As he thought of his grandfather, the bear dream coiled against him, nuzzling his memory. Donna was gone. The bear was lost in the woods. He chased it, wanting to protect it. A manitou, a dream spirit. And here he was, on some strange quest, not for a lost bear, but a fancy sport utility vehicle.

Up ahead he heard a snap and soft ruffling. Then he spotted swift, certain movement: whitetail deer, smarter and keener than him, protecting themselves by skedaddling. He hoped they didn't alert whoever might be in the lodge. Thinking this, he waited a while, knowing animals carried wisdom in their blood. He heard the hooting of a horned owl, its sharp hunter's eyes tuned to the night. After a time the sounds dimmed and the steady beating of his heart took over like a soft river in his ears.

Pinpointing the path before him, Softshoe forced himself to be smart to the dark that could so easily deceive and cause confusion. He had deliberately chosen this route through the trees, not wanting to use the road in case any of the militia were watching it. Exactly what these silly soldiers were up to had not been shared with him on the road with Smereas and the State Police trooper. It was made clear to him, though, that a show of force of any kind was not yet necessary. They had to know, they told him, if the men they were chasing were in the lodge. If so, more police would come.

His nose picked up the smells of gasoline and the sap from the pines. He made his eyes see into the dark ahead, through the straight trunks of the pines and birches, into the clearing. Everything kept to itself, except where splashed by the moon. He saw a darker shape that was the lodge.

On his way up he had been careful with his feet to avoid humps of leaves or too-soft ground. The militia was known to plant booby traps, though mostly they were not done very well.

Softshoe had the feeling he was not alone. He had a second sense of these things. Always, whenever hunters, campers, hikers or one of these militia were lost, he was the one called. The DNR was smart that way; they knew what they had in him, which was probably why they gave him the choice: stop drinking or lose the job.

As he moved forward, he saw the Jeep. Buffed metal shimmered in a shaft of moonglow. He waited, his legs ready to spring away or in, depending on the danger. But there was none. No one appeared or made a sound. No muffled coughs, no scratches, no shuffles, no tell-tale hums. He wasn't surprised. He was not alone, but there was no danger.

Remaining firm as a statue, Softshoe let his eyes gather what light they could so that he was able to clearly see all of the Cherokee, an-other Indian name gone bad by being stuck onto an expensive toy. As best he could tell, no one was in the cabin. As for the Cherokee, Mumberto wasn't so sure. Something about it bugged him. A hint of shadow behind the wheel. A slumping, maybe.

The vehicle's windows reflected moonlight. Yes, thought Softshoe, there was a form inside, in the driver's seat. A person waiting for the right time to turn the key. Except this person wasn't moving.

He stepped into the parking lot, suddenly feeling a gentle chill scratch against his arms. He thought of his dog at home, Jim, waiting patiently for his dinner. Not moving, staring down the road for his bachelor master. In a way, Mumberto was that dog, suddenly catching the scent of something bad, not of dinner coming at all, and he edged across the packed dirt.

His nose twitched, picking up the nature of the odor—something wet and clogged and smelling of copper. It was blood, no doubt.

Picking up his pace, hand idling to his gun, Mumberto approached the Cherokee. Closing in, he thought he saw dark dabs on the ground, a path of bodily fluid, leading his way. But he wasn't sure. Then his right boot slipped slightly, twisting to the side, on something slick. He bent, touched it, brought it to his nose. Definitely blood.

He rose and crept forward. Two feet from the vehicle, he still couldn't quite see through the smoky glass. The reflection of moonlight on the window threw back his own vague shape. Before going on, he looked at the cabin again and unsnapped his Smith and Wesson, but didn't take it out. He had to decide: should he leave fingerprints? Possibly this person wasn't dead and needed help. He wasn't sure. He leaned close and tapped the window. No stirring.

He used the tips of two fingers to lift the latch. A dome light flashed, spilling down enough bulb power for him to make out the big body slumped against the wheel and blood everywhere. Although the head was partly blown away, he knew it was the large man who had been riding shotgun a few hours before. One of those the police were looking for.

CHAPTER 21
CULLY

Cully tried to ignore the way the road rushed under her. The Vietnamese kid in his souped-up van was trying to pass every car on I-69. Arly, on the carpeted floor across from her, had already twice knocked Pham's shoulder and snarled to slow down. Nodding, smiling and spouting unintelligible words, he did, for a bit. Now he was again trying to break the sound barrier.

Cully figured it was about time for Arly to order him again to cool it. But Arly was too intent, it seemed, on his garbled story to pay the Southeast Asian speed demon much mind.

Sitting behind him in the back of the van, her feet duct-taped together, Cully took notes on the legal pad he had provided. After dragging her from the window, he hadn't taken much time to give her grief. He shoved the paper and pens at her and edged her out of the bathroom, down some stairs, through another storage area, and into the alley, where Pham, grinning like a car salesman on speed, shook her hand profusely, smoke from his randy cigarette swirling between them.

Quickly enough, Arly had explained that Pham was going to take them on a drive. Somehow the debate over what to do with her had been determined in his mind. Or so it seemed. Since it apparently meant he wasn't going to kill her, for now, she went along. Not that she had much choice.

Nearing Flint from what she could tell, Arly had grown excited, his neck jerking slightly, his depthless black eyes shining with intensity. He rambled on about the system, the need for a united white nation, the usual paranoid BS.

"What you're telling me," she said, cutting in, "is basically what you said when I wrote that magazine article."

Arly paused a moment and craned his head, as if trying to see her better. He looked like an agitated, oversized child, with embers for eyes and a barrel for a chest. "Thing you wrote before was garbage."

The van bounced and jerked to one side. Their speed troubled her. On the other hand, maybe it would attract attention.

"Slow down!" Arly barked.

The Vietnamese driver gabbed words she didn't understand, but he did ease up the lead foot. Meanwhile he switched on the radio, blasting hard rock through the speakers. Arly snapped at him again. The sound dimmed a couple decibels. The outline of two naked women, lit by a string of lights, showed in the back windows.

"So tell me something different," Cully prodded. She was thinking of him as a kid, when he first came to town. Distant and angry, even then. Her first real memory of him was Arly getting in a fistfight with the undertaker's son over a stolen base in a pickup baseball game. Cully had been walking by with friends and stopped to watch Arly whip the guy's butt. Since she had disliked the mortician's spawn, she had been halfway pleased. Even when the blood flew, she watched, fascinated. Her friends didn't like it. It made them sick. Not Cully.

Arly folded his ham forearms over his chest. "Like what?" His face had turned to granite, the eyes brackish probes. His legs, crossed at the ankles, seemed to swell inside his jeans.

Arly had moved to town somewhere around eighth grade, from what Cully recalled. When she'd spoken with him for the magazine article, on the infield of the county fairgrounds, he'd talked a little about his past. How he'd been in foster homes after his mother died in a fire. Or maybe she read that part in one of the news articles after he torched the IRS forms.

"More about your childhood. What about that?" Cully asked, feeling the van rock again.

Arly stared, a hand scratching through his beard at a hunk of chin.

"If I'm going to write this, you have to fill in the blanks," she said, tapping the pen on the legal pad. She wondered what she would ever write. This disjointed story. She felt trapped and yet curious as to what drove him.

"Don't mess with my mind," he replied.

If only you had one to mess with, she thought. She looked around the inside of the van. In the very back was a bed, covered with a silk bedspread decorated with butt-rumping dragons. Pham's mobile sex machine.

"Then write about my parents," Arly said.

"What about them?"

Suddenly, Pham started to babble, quick harsh words and turned with a frightened face, his Buggs Bunny teeth flashing.

Arly shot him a glance.

Pham spoke again. "Police." At the same moment, blue lights flashed through the back window, above the sodomizing dragons.

Arly's head swung to the lights and back. He grabbed behind him and pulled out a thick-handled black handgun. "Drive!" he commanded.

Pham flapped his jaws, sounding a protest.

Arly pointed the gun at Pham. "Do it!"

The van bucked forward; the engine roared, kicking into full throttle. Cully tried to twist around so she could see better. On her knees, tape pinching her ankles, she glimpsed a large factory on the side of the expressway. But that was all. Arly leaned forward to peer out the mirror. Cully heard a siren whoop and saw the lights circle madly. Pham had his foot firmly planted to the floor.

God, she prayed. Pull us over. Stop this man before he hurts anyone else.

CHAPTER 22
ARLY

Far as he could tell, it was only one cruiser, at least for now, a county dick if he wasn't mistaken. Looking in the side mirror, Arly set it up in his mind: if stopped, they'd go through the van. They'd find Cully, who would make no bones about what she knew, which still wasn't much, but definitely enough.

No, Arly decided, they'd have to keep running. At that very moment, the van started to slow, as if the gook wanted to throw in the towel here in the middle of the expressway with cars jamming all sides. "No!" Arly shouted. "Keep going."

Pham looked scared, damn him. Arly considered grabbing the wheel but realized that would be too dangerous, unless they could get someplace for a quick switch. He glanced ahead, a quarter mile up, and saw the Hill Road exit. Ten years before, when he first started with the Postal Service, Arly had run mail from the sectional center in Lansing to little burgs and larger offices out this way. He knew the lay of the land. East of where they were lay the scrubby burb of Burton, which had a large substation where he dumped mail at about four o'clock every morning, on his way into Flint. "Get off there!" He pointed with the hand holding his Browning P38.

Pham started flapping his jaws, pushing out words Arly couldn't for the life of him understand. "Talk English," he snapped, his neck starting to twitch.

The cop was flashing his lights. Traffic kept right up with the van and the cruiser. These Flint factory rats weren't going to let a little chase hold them back.

"Police," said Pham.

"No shit," replied Arly, scooting to the edge of his seat. Over his left shoulder, he saw the Gannon girl poking her nose where it wasn't wanted. He wanted to backhand her with the gun barrel, but she kept her mouth shut, so he paid attention to the business at hand.

The green-painted exit sign approached under the gut-ugly light from the freeway overheads. "There," said Arly, leaning over and wrenching the wheel right when it was obvious Pham was half-frozen in place. Arly smacked the gook's shoulder, trying to beat life into him, and got only another frightened, open-mouthed gape. Christ, he was nothing like his cousin, Tong, the guy who came up with the picnic scene. Arly's bunkmate at Milan, his inspiration. Arly had tried to hire him for the ride north but he was busy with some damned thing and instead sent Pham, this runt.

The van swerved onto the ramp, cutting in front of a white car trying to exit. Shooting up the concrete, Pham's bugged-up buggy tilted hard to the left, as if it wanted to tip. Arly kept a hard hand on the wheel, wrestling it straight, and an eye on the mirror, which told him the cop had made a wide sweeping turn at the last minute and careened onto the ramp as well.

"You're going to kill us," said the girl. Now he did clip back with his elbow, jabbing at her jaw. That didn't help, because she started whopping at him with her arms. He swirled around with the gun and shoved it in her nose. A large part of him wanted to pull the trigger. But her eyes narrowed and she sat out of the way.

Arly reached over again and returned in time to see the street approach. A green light gave them the go ahead. Pham had let the van climb into the ass end of a BMW, ramming it hard in the bumper, making it spin to the left.

Arly jerked the wheel right. Tires squealed and the van slid toward the curb and a chain-link fence, then veered back.

The cop pulled next to the them just as they reached the intersection. A dumb move if he ever saw it. The pig had the passenger window down and was waving a gun in their direction. Arly wanted to smile, but he didn't have the time. Leaving his seat, he grabbed the wheel from Pham and turned it to the right, forcing the van around the curve, the back end wobbling, the engine sounding like Arly's head just before it erupted in a holy storm of curses.

Sweetass Jesus, he thought, realizing the van was heading straight for a gas station parking lot. He cut the wheel back, noticing Pham transfixed in his seat, so unlike Tong, who would have handled this chase like it was a waltz down a summer lane. Just in time, he bounced them away from the lot and onto pavement. Arly wasn't sure, but he suspected the cop had blown through the intersection and would have to U-turn to get back on track, which might give them a half minute or so of lead time.

The van slowed to a crawl in the middle of the road. Arly grabbed at Pham and yanked him out of the way. Slipping into the captain's seat, Arly felt bad angels astir in his brain, flapping wings, scratching with long fingernails inside his lobes. He punched down on the gas, thinking of how many things had just gone up in smoke, starting with Lonnie and the greedy hillbilly bitch who put the extra dollar signs in his eyes. But there was no time for complaining. Then there was the reporter. He felt the need to tell her, but she would lie in the end anyway.

He checked the rearview, saw highway and car lights stretched far back on the fast food hellway south of Flint. He didn't see blue flashers, but that didn't mean much. He figured if they weren't behind, they'd be coming from the front soon. A whole army of them, in their uniforms, with their pasty white faces and burp gun pistols and rules. Cops never worked alone, like Arly. To have power, they needed to be flies. They worked best in a messy mass.

"Arly?"

He looked over to see Pham holding the P38, pointing it in his direction, wondering when he had dropped it. The chink now wore a sick, scared smile on his face; oily black hair dripped in his face. He was skinny and smelled like rancid rice. Arly slapped the gun away. "Keep it on her," he said, his head swinging to the back.

Pham smiled wider, in a better mood now, and did as he was told.

Another traffic light was coming up. Arly gauged it as best he could, working for control, feeling the power currents starting in his ears. He suddenly realized he had them beat; he knew he could pilot the gook's van to freedom, away from the bugs who wanted to feast on his flesh.

He took it all in—the gaudy signs showing golden arches and little girls in short dresses holding hamburgers—and felt his mind pulse. He breathed deeply, the twitches buried, his mind making split-second decisions. Years back, when he was early on his mail route and needed to pass time, he would catch a few winks in a huge cemetery nearby. He had always loved graveyards, visited them often, felt forces in the stones, the wonderful murky silence. He slept in them, walked in them, sometimes dug through them. Like the one in Detroit, where they buried his crazy mother.

Even as he thought and calculated their chances, Arly blasted through the busy intersection just as the light turned red, twisting the wheel to avoid a car, the back end of a bus, and a helmeted biker.

Once through, he didn't even look back. He had to slow a moment, but not too much, to jam the wheel right. On two wheels, his body sagging toward the Asian, Arly guided straight down the middle of a two-lane road that almost immediately turned residential. Almost as quickly, he snapped off the lights and began looking for the graveyard, remembering it on the left, through a bricked arch. A hidden hilly place, looking out on Flint in the distance.

Stomping the accelerator, he rounded a curve, the sides of the road lined with trees. He wondered for a moment what he'd find when he finally made it up north. He was late. On the phone, Cody had been pissed he was giving the cops a place to trace, and even madder that Arly was making him wait. But, screw him. Things came up. Burke was getting big bucks out of this anyhow.

Racing along, his mind trying to keep up, Arly spotted a sign: Crestwood Memorial Gardens. The side mirror showed no pursuit, at least not yet. He wondered if he should just drive on, but decided not to. He'd been careful enough so far. He didn't need to blow it now. He punched the brake, jerking them forward as he half-circled in under the arch and motored down a winding road toward the back.

Slowing now, he heard Pham blubbering an angry undercurrent. It sounded like he was chewing his words before spitting them out. Pham's cousin Tong always spoke English when they were bunkmates at Milan. He taught Arly a lot.

"Shut up, man!" Arly ordered.

The van was dark now. Nothing to give definition to Pham, still turned around, yapping. The words forced movement in Arly's brain, making the snake angels twist. Pham turned to Arly and said, "She's not listen."

Arly took the van past a couple bulky mausoleums and the blunt, toothy shapes of tombstones. The place, even years back, had been pleasant and peaceful for him. These were places that brought comfort. His heart ached, as always, when he thought of how his father still had no decent place to rest.

Pham wouldn't let up. Goddamn him, he wouldn't let up in his chopped up language, the words cut to shreds with his teeth, coming out of his harelip nose. Tired of asking, Arly swung over at him just as a horrible explosion sounded in the van. A noise that slammed the eardrums, releasing the snakes.

Arly stomped the brake, the van screeching to a stop, revving him into the steering wheel. "What the hell! Goddamnit to shit you fuckingpisshead!" Arly yelled through the shattering aftermath of the gun's bursting.

"She cut tape."

By the time Arly got it, the side door in the back had flown open and the girl, who had been minding her own business as he had asked, leaped into the night.

CHAPTER 23
CULLY

Pushing through the doors of the van and jumping into the grave-yard night, Cully crushed her ankle. The stupid thing twisted, its liga-ments weak as rubber bands from many years of injuries. She stumbled and fell once, then forced herself to head for higher ground and, she hoped, a way out.

Hopping painfully, she heard footfalls and heavy breathing, the source of which she had no desire to stop and face. She ran around a tall marble gravestone. As she hobbled up, she wondered for the first time if she had been shot. All she had done was react, her legs free of the tape, as soon as Pham pointed that thing.

"Sonofabitchingcocksuckershitdamn," she heard behind her as Arly, she suspected, took a tumble.

Cully labored around another set of markers, limped quickly around trees, and dead-ended at a tall fence. Shit!

A quick glance down the hill beyond the chain link showed a street. A couple cars moved in the glare of one another's headlights. She thought of calling out, realized how stupid that would be, grabbed metal and boosted herself up. For a moment, every sense was keen, sharp, clear. She was in control and hoped she could get away. But then the lousy foot had a hard time taking a hold, and her neck felt as if it had been bitten by a thousand crazy ants, those jungle bugs that eat everything in their path.

Still she shoved up, just as she had not long before in the bath-room. The fence sagged as she hauled her weight toward the top. Even so, she hoisted hard, spearing up, a wild recollection of those crazy ants, coming from a Discovery Channel documentary, scurrying in her head. The image of them swimming voraciously over a plump rain forest rodent. Eating everything down to the bone. Cully shook her head hard, as if trying to dump out the ants.

Meanwhile, she climbed, fighting the fence. But she'd gotten only a couple feet when it happened again: Arly. Grabbing hold of her ankles, clamping on, fingers hard as pliers, arriving from his own jungle. Grumbling.

She yelped, bad ankle feeling like he had pinched the bone to its marrow. She looked down. "You idiot, lay off!"

For a second, Arly backed off. "Then climb down."

"So that asshole can shoot me again?"

"You're hurt?"

"Not from that."

Arly opened his arms, offering help.

Out of the pot, into the fire, Cully thought, shaking her head. "Thanks, but I really think it's time for me to go." Her hands dug into the metal, ready to yank her up.

Arly started at her again. Cully scrambled, one hand reaching for the top of the fence. As she did, she noticed what waited an inch or so beyond: swirls of barbed wire. Glittering, sharp as teeth, ready to gnaw. Peachy, she thought, wanting to spew her own Tourette syndrome diatribe.

Arly gripped the back of her knees. He said something, but she couldn't make it out.

"I'm sick of this," she said.

"What you wanted."

Cully's face dropped against the fence. Through hexagonal holes she saw the tops of trees and, further out, a spattering of lights and the hulking gap-toothed shape of buildings. Downtown Flint, probably. A dirty, dying car-making city. She wanted to stay where she was forever, to give up, to cry, to die. To will Arly away, into a hole, where ants could feast on his stinking skin.

Defeat, rich as a rank pastry, filled her mouth. Tears marched into her eyes, ready to stream out in a flurry. But she swallowed them back and forced herself into the moment. She didn't know why, but she saw in her mind the flash of flames, the barn ablaze. Her father weaving just outside, yelling at the crackling timber, raging at the loss of his wife and her mother. She had approached him, wanting to wrap him in her arms, give herself comfort by helping him. But the bastard didn't want it. He became a clamshell, threw out a force field of grief that drove her away.

For some reason that recollection gave her a burst of strength, hope even. The awareness that she was far from giving up surged in her. Even as she let go of the fence, flopping back to the ground, she thought she wanted to stay around as much to get Arly's story as to piss off her dad. As long as that kid kept his gun to himself, she thought, she'd be all right. For the next little while anyway.

CHAPTER 24
JOY

Slapping one foot in front of the other, Joy Williams reluctantly gave herself over to the movement of the sixteen-hundred-dollar treadmill. The machine had sat for months, since Christmas actually, and beckoned like a scolding parent every time she walked by.

Joy had ignored it, shunned it, actually flipped it more than a few birds as she made her way up and down the stairs and back and forth from the big-screen TV and the laundry room. Arranged in a corner of their finished basement, angled so she could look out the glass doors as she exercised, if she ever exercised, she had given the drippy yuppified home jogging machine a solid brush-off. Until the last couple weeks, that is. With the bridge event day after tomorrow, she had been trying to get in at least marginal shape. After all, she was supposed to be up there, on the platform, showing her support to Frank. And so far, her bod had been responding halfway favorably. Combining a diet with exercise, she'd dropped five or so pounds.

Tonight, after returning from the movie with Ralph, her rail-thin, fireman, smokes-like-a-chimney, ball-and-chain hubby, she had marched straight down here. She disrobed eagerly by the washer, slipped into some sweats, hustled over, flipped the switch and climbed aboard. She had surprised herself with her dedication, but she wanted to put in a good appearance. After all, she had been part of Frank's election committee. Frank, her half-brother's son, and in many ways her adopted boy. She had been so pleased when he had returned to Michigan and then was delighted, more or less, when he ran for governor.

Huffing along on the belt, Joy made plans for the next couple days, ticking off her duties, home and otherwise. She was packed and so was Ralph. Dog would go to the neighbor's. Car had its oil changed. Most everything in order. Except . . . and this wasn't a task, really. It was anxiety left over from speaking briefly this morning with Piersma, the little weenie whom Frank kept on as his spokesman. A smoothie and, if she was to tell it like it is, not a man to be trusted. She had tried a couple times to warn Frank off him, but Preston, as always, had his way. He liked Piersma.

Anyway, Jock wanted to ask her again about that situation a month or so ago at the mall in Novi. About the man who appeared out of nowhere, a bearded man who sent shivers through Joy. A man who made claims that rang terrible bells for her and brought back possibilities she had hoped had been left behind.

"What do you remember about him, Joy?" Jock had pressed. "You said you recognized him."

But she didn't give Piersma anything. "Why do you want to know this now?"

He had hemmed and hawed and didn't tell her, although he alluded to some situation he had to handle.

"What situation?"

He didn't say and hung up.

Probably nothing, she told herself. But it didn't exactly sound like nothing. For a moment she thought of that lug with a beard appearing out of nowhere, then vanishing. Piersma did make her remember. But she wondered if that was good. The past, especially as it involved Frank, could be a swirling sewer, full of questions.

Joy decided to bend her mind back to the moment, to getting her body smoother.

"Hey, mind if I catch the end of the Tigers game?"

She turned and saw the gaunt figure of the love of her life, according to him, standing at the bottom of the stairs behind her. "Have at it," she called over her shoulder.

"Olympics are over, sugarplum," Ralph reported as he padded past in his fuzzy slippers, his striped bathrobe pulled tight over the washboard he called a stomach. In his hands he carried a steaming plate of chips and cheese. A sixteen-ouncer, no light brew, sagged in the side pocket of the robe.

"Drop dead!" she shot back.

He smiled his shy grin and scratched the top of his bald head. "Hey, *you're* gonna kill yourself. Take it easy."

She shoved harder into her stationary run, her eyes burning, sweat dripping. She ignored him and closed her eyes, trying to imagine herself, maybe eight pounds thinner, on the stage. Behind Frank, maybe next to Preston. Honoring a story that was only half told, she was afraid.

The TV burst to life. Ernie Harwell was reporting on a ground ball to third as Detroit's Tigers battled for a place in the basement of the American League East. "You know," said Ralph, no doubt positioned comfortable as apple pie in his corner of the sectional, "doing that this late in the game is counterproductive."

What did he, the couch potato bar none, know about productive? Chin forward, arms swiveling, feet making a valiant effort to keep up, Joy ignored her better half. Maybe he did get some exercise fighting fires, she gave him that, but otherwise he was a slug. Cute, but a slug.

"Anyhow, that bridge deal's, what, a four-mile walk, tops, out and back. A piece of cake, long as the both of us poke along at our normal pace."

Ernie was blathering about a fly ball to center as Joy slowed, snapped off the machine, and turned to her husband. She had to wait a few seconds for her lungs to catch up with her need for oxygen. Looking at him, she was well aware her face was probably as red as the fire engines he rode when he really did have to work, which wasn't often, not in their part of Manistee with its newer homes and strict fire codes. "We're walking in the governor's group," she huffed.

"That mean we're supposed to run?"

Joy could catch only the top of Ralph's shiny white head over the padded plaid rim of the couch. Her airways heaved; sweat streamed

down her face. She smudged it with the sleeve of her sweatshirt, decorated on the chest with a macramé robin. For a moment she felt a
wave of sadness to think of what the governor wanted to commemorate on that bridge. But beyond that was what the handsome, square-
jawed politician didn't know. "We don't need to run, but we have to
keep up."

Ralph's head turned, and an eye poked up at her. Someone was
racing the bases, with hardly any effort, the lucky dork. "Why's that?"

"If you remember, I'm going to help introduce him."

The eye hung there, not too far below the capitol dome of the
curved bone enclosing her husband's bird brain. "What did Piersma
want earlier?" Ralph, of all people, had helped hook Piersma up with
Preston first, and then ultimately to Frank.

"He wasn't saying. He wanted to talk about the weirdo who accosted us at the mall that day."

"Why?"

"Beats me."

Ralph nodded, then turned back to baseball.

Joy could smell the chips and cheese. But she didn't give in. She
returned to the machine, got it running again, on turtle speed, and
poked along. Preston was her older half-brother, a politician to the
core. If it hadn't been for Frank, Preston's adopted son, Joy would
probably have drifted away from him years ago.

"Hey."

She paused.

"Look at that."

Joy saw the TV screen filled with a talking head, a news broad-
cast. Ralph turned up the sound.

"We have just learned from an anonymous source that a militia
group is plotting to disrupt the festivities planned on Labor Day at the
Mackinac Bridge."

She flinched. Shook her head. Felt something grab her chest. A
shadow moved across a parking lot. She took a long, steadying breath.

"You believe that?" asked Ralph.

The TV guy was spouting more words. Her husband was looking
at her. "Honey? You going to be all right?"

"No," she said, wanting to fall on the floor in a heap. "I'm not."

CHAPTER 25
BONES

One of the last passenger ferries had pulled away from the Mackinac Island docks and started its quick trip across the darkly burnished waters of the straits toward St. Ignace. It was a small, illuminated dot, cutting across a surface that lolled and heaved with majestic indifference.

Standing on the small balcony outside his bedroom, Frank Bones turned, as he always did, to the bridge. Illuminated by lights strung from shore to shore, it rose like a staunch apparition. Cars crossed its surface, their sound muffled by the distance. Even from this distance, the bridge spanned the water with authority and purpose. It was a stupendous testament to engineering, the work of some ten thousand ironworkers, among them his dad. For a second he imagined the boom towns that sprang up on both sides of the bridge during its making. Busy wild west places. Hookers and con men galore.

So much of his day had been wrapped up with roadblocks to his plans for the celebration, not forty-eight hours away. It shouldn't have surprised him. A deal as big as this was going to draw many last-minute bonfires. He had handled the bulk of it. He would never have gotten this far in life, from the University of Michigan law school to a successful law practice as a consumer attorney and then to the governorship, without having developed some darned good crisis management skills. But this damned would-be bomber business was something more.

He'd been assured, over and again, that it was nothing. Just malcontents kicking up dust. But the answers weren't coming. Last he heard, the rumormonger, a guy with a German name, was nowhere to be seen.

He heard the phone ring somewhere inside. Bones turned, cocked an ear, and heard a muffled voice. His wife. Probably for her.

The governor turned back to the view, offering a wide vista of the northern shore of the Lower Peninsula. The lights of Mackinaw City were almost directly across the straits; the smudged glow of Alpena to the east; to the west a sheer bluish dark, specked by stars, around the rim of Wilderness State Park.

Watching it all, Bones felt his chest expand with pride. His state. Such a large, diverse place. From end to end, it was his to supervise and lead. He couldn't help but feel lucky that even a kid such as himself, an orphan really, could rise so far in its political life. That he was able to take down Governor John Engler, a rich Republican, and sit in his place of power.

Bones thought of his real father, whom he never knew, buried in the bridge standing firm in its bedrock, spanning land that linked the world he governed. What would Rolly Walls think about his boy?

Without much effort, he could make out the area of the pillar in which his dad was buried. Day after tomorrow, Bones would offer him a fitting memorial. And his stepdad, Preston, former state road czar, would be at his side. Preston and Rolly had been pals. Preston had been one of the construction bosses for the bridge project. He had been one of those who had seen Rolly slip and plunge into tons of still-liquid concrete. Preston, the man who truly made Franklin who he was. Sometimes Frank resented the way Preston pushed, but he had to admit it was the old man's fire that had brought him this far.

Strong, slender arms snaked around him. He hadn't consciously expected them, but wasn't surprised when they hugged him from behind. He could smell his wife's perfumed soap. "Jock was on the phone."

He turned. His wife's face was strong-browed and high-chinned. Her hair hung softly on her shoulders. Her breasts, outlined by lace, hung inside the fabric. For a second, he thought of one of his biggest cases ever, the silicone breast implant deal. Got him and a lot of women big bucks from Dow. As for Char, hers were the real deal. "He say what he wants?"

"Only that it's important."

The governor frowned. "I was right out here."

Char said nothing at first, no doubt catching the tone in his voice. "I thought you were in the shower."

"Did he leave a number?"

"He said he'll call back in a few minutes. He was between places."

Which probably meant bars, the governor thought grimly.

"Frank, what's this about?"

Char's full lips had opened partway, as if trapped between words and diplomatic silence. "I've heard you talking on and off about this all day." She watched him carefully.

"Did he say something to you right now?"

"His voice sounded upset."

"Or blitzed."

Char crossed her arms over her breasts, as if protecting them from him. Even now, in the mild heat of a marital discussion, he thought of sucking them, the milky taste. She was his second wife, a would-be attorney who had clerked in his Detroit office. "Is there a problem?" she asked.

Bones felt his back grow stiff. Prying or eavesdropping was not her normal approach. He didn't like to involve her in his job. She was there for other things, not this. "What kind of problem, honey?"

"I heard Jock say something about a terrorist."

"Just now?"

"Earlier."

Bones laughed. It came out louder and more sarcastic than he had wished.

"What's that supposed to mean, Frank?" Her eyes narrowed and she held her chin higher, getting miffed now.

"There's no terrorist." He reached out and touched her shoulder, felt the bump of bone under the slippery fabric. She kept her chin up and the arms folded. "Just another mental case making noise."

"And that's been bothering you since morning?"

"There's the road commission idiots, too."

This type of talking really was out of the ordinary for them. One of the building blocks of their relationship had been her ability to step aside, not to butt in and ask too much. To let him build his career. He decided to offer a little more explanation and leave it at that. Plus, the way she looked in that nightgown in the shimmer of the balcony gave him an idea. A sure stress reducer. "I'm all wound up."

But she made a slightly pained face and didn't melt into sexy. Which didn't help his mood. To tell the truth, she was making him feel trapped. What he had liked best about juries is that they didn't talk back.

"Frank, is something bad starting to happen?"

"Between us?" He wasn't sure why he said that.

Char sighed angrily and turned her attention to the water. So did he. For a few moments he tried to let it suck out the tension. But it didn't work.

Shaking his head and grinding his molars, the governor made a note to talk to Piersma about keeping his mouth shut when his wife was around. She didn't need to hear about terrorists, especially when there were none.

They stood in silence for a few minutes. The breeze notched up to an easy late summer wind, bringing in the smell of water and fish. The governor leaned his groin against the rail. He wasn't ready to give up on sex, at least not yet.

He had been a couple months old when his dad died on the bridge, that sturdy monster. Bones never knew him. He'd seen pictures. He didn't know his mother, either. She went crazy after the accident and moved to New York, where she drank her way into a mental institution and eventual death. A terrible story that still dug at his insides. A story he learned only late in high school, when the only real parents he had ever known sat him down to talk. The newspapers had replayed it, even nationally, this year, recounting that past, only touching on his real mother. That part had been glossed over, with Jock's help.

Bones thought of how grateful he was that his parents had intervened and took him from his distraught birth mother. He had been protected. But that didn't mean he was going to forget them. Not at all. Come Monday, much of it would be made right. For his father, at least. His mother had been cremated and her ashes dumped somewhere. He had vowed to make it right, no matter what, because he needed it, his family needed it, his state needed it and because, hell, it would help him get reelected.

He heard his wife sniffle. Startled, he looked over. "Honey?" he said, reaching out with a worried hand.

Char shook her head, warding him off.

His mind scrambled for what he had done. Even after all this time, a previous wife, headline court cases, a meteoric rise to the top office in Michigan, a life in which he rubbed elbows with the cream of the crop's cream, he still let the woman he loved and needed gnaw into him at the drop of a hat. Then he recalled the crack he had made moments before. "Char, I didn't mean anything by that, about us."

She kept at the tears, palming them away as they fell.

Bones was absolutely astounded, but not surprised, at how helpless he felt. He wanted to outright order her to stop. But he remained where he was as she let the emotion take its turn. Like a dog waiting for some sign that he could eat his dinner, the governor watched, his hands at his sides. He was angry that he cared so much what this woman, fifteen years his junior, had to say. Strangely, he thought of Preston. The old man wouldn't stand for a woman's tears. Never had, never would. "What is it?"

She shook her head, closing up, drawing away.

"What, Char?"

Finally, wiping the last of the tears with her forearms, she spoke: "I never told you."

"Told me what?"

She looked away, as if gathering strength, or maybe wondering if she should get into this. "About the man who approached me in the mall."

One of the governor's gifts was an uncanny ability to spot troubled waters long before they burst to the surface, or so he liked to tell himself. A tone in her voice and the taut lines in her face put Bones on red alert even more than the tears. Char would not get so overwhelmed, or bring up something such as this, without reason. He forced himself to pay attention, the lawyer in him aware that important evidence, hidden until now, was about to show its face. "What man, which mall?"

"In Novi, earlier this summer."

He waited, sensing the ground under him sift, the first stirrings of a cave-in. Why did he feel this? It was silly.

"Remember when you gave that speech for the Children First conference?" she said.

He nodded.

Char touched a hand to her chin. "It was at Twelve Oaks Mall. You left early to go to Dearborn or someplace."

To meet with the top brass at Ford, about tax break legislation. Afterward, he and Char had quite a party. That time he didn't have to beg and kiss ass to get some relief.

"This man," said Char. "He came up to me in the parking lot when I was leaving. He looked angry and mean. I was frightened."

"You were alone?" This had been an ongoing battle. His wife refused to have the State Police security detail tag along with her. They'd been around and around on it.

"Jock was there, too. So was Joy Williams."

"They were with you when you were accosted?"

"Right behind." Her eyes glistened.

Bones stepped closer, forcing his voice to soften. "What happened?"

She took a few level breaths and returned her attention to the water. The night was growing cool. He thought they should go in. But he waited for her to talk. "He didn't force himself on me exactly," she said. "But it's how he looked and then what he said."

Bones noticed a freighter, a sliding, light-bedecked form, had started to move under the span of Big Mac. "He said, Frank, he was going to make you pay. He said you ended up with so much and he got nothing."

Bones looked at her curiously, a deep part of himself twisting in confusion. "What?"

She shook her head. "He had this bushy beard and wore a black outfit, ratty jeans and a sweatshirt. He looked like a mechanic or something."

"Did Jock step in?"

"Joy did."

A loud screech, like a cat being hung, sounded below, making the governor flinch. "What about Piersma?"

"He was there. But Joy did the talking. She blew her top, you know her."

The cat moaned, long, low, and languid. Probably hadn't been hurt at all. Bones looked at the sky, searching for one flickering star to blame. Tightly, his lips stretched thin, he asked: "What then?"

"The man walked away. But not before he wanted to know where you were."

Bones was irate, feeling betrayed. Joy, if anyone, should have said something. "Why didn't anyone tell me this before?"

"We didn't want to upset you."

The freighter's rear end rode under the bridge. Traffic rolled on the roadway itself, suspended several hundred feet from the water. The governor felt the chill of the evening flow through him, as if someone had shot cold dye through his blood. "Damnit, Char, at least you should have said something."

"I'm sorry."

Bones swung his head around, taking in the dark trees, the town below, the water, the bridge. With effort, he squelched the discomfort swaying inside. It was a trick that had always served him well, in court, in politics, in college, in relationships. Something Preston had taught. He told himself this was nothing, not related to anything. And probably it was nothing, just another weirdo, which was why he didn't want his wife walking alone. "Why bring it up now?"

She didn't answer.

He turned to her. "Why?"

Still, nothing. But he had an idea. "Did Jock say something about this on the phone?"

"No." He heard a skirl of fear in her voice, rising, moving up and away, as if taking on a life of its own. Bones wanted to know more, to offer her comfort, to scold her for not telling him, to hold her, to crush her fear. To have her grab him. But he didn't get to do any of that. Because the phone rang. And it was Jock. And the world was about ready to turn inside out.

CHAPTER 26
SOFTSHOE

Black Bear, his grandfather, often said white men were crazy. They were like nervous women, always fussing about how they looked and if they were doing the right thing. Of course, they acted this way just before they stuck a gun into your guts and demanded your land, your wife and your money.

Donnie Mumberto watched a small army of cops scurry around the brightly lit area surrounding the hunting lodge at Crow Mountain. Arms crossed over his chest, his back against a balsam fir, he thought much of what he was seeing and overhearing wasn't making sense.

For the last couple hours, vehicles of all official shapes and sizes had rumbled up the twisting road. Several were still parked at all angles across the bare ground parking lot. One of the most recent arrivals, an ambulance out of Gaylord, was backing up to the Jeep Cherokee. A couple cops had lifted the dead fat man out and into a body bag a few minutes before. The bagged body sprawled on the ground; no one seeming willing or able to haul it from there.

State Police, county cops, a couple FBI, and a few local firefighters had spread through the woods. Softshoe's boss from the DNR was wandering around somewhere as well. All in all, quite a party.

"Hey, Don."

Mumberto glanced over. He recognized Tony DeHoop, a county volunteer firefighter from Wolverine. Tony wore black hip boots that hung by yellow suspenders from his wide shoulders. He and his boys had been at a car fire when the call went out for all available personnel to help search the grounds. His square face was sweaty from slogging in the brush.

"Looks like the motherlode, down the other side of the hill," said Tony.

"What's that?"

"Shitload of guns, some dynamite and who knows what else."

Softshoe wasn't surprised. He suspected the militia who used this area probably stored some of their crap nearby.

"Looks like the guy got shot not far from here. We came across some blood," said DeHoop.

Mumberto stepped away from the tree, reached back, and tugged on his ponytail. Two county sheriffs, both as wide in the rear as upright freezers, lumbered past, hungrily smoking cigarettes. Thunder rolled to the south.

Softshoe noticed the Greek ATF agent striding through the crowd, headed toward the hunting lodge. Mumberto had detected tension between him and the burly State Police captain. Matter of fact, the whole scene bristled with bad feelings.

"Do you think this guy dragged himself up here and died trying to get away?" The young man's face was flushed and excited.

"Hear the State Police tell it, it's suicide."

DeHoop scowled, shook his head There was an avid, almost fevered expression in the kid's eyes. Stalking around murder scenes did that to you, Softshoe knew. He did it firsthand a few times in his three years on the police force in Muskegon. Before getting canned for boozing. Before landing the job with the state. Affirmative action really was a wonderful thing, long as you were the one in on the action.

"Suicide?"

"That's what I heard."

DeHoop spat on the ground, rubbed it with his boot. "You believe that?"

Given the remote location of this killing, Softshoe was surprised at how busy it was. Almost as if someone had been expecting this. "I suppose he could have shot himself in his shoulder, cut holes in his feet with a knife, and then strolled on up here to shoot himself in his truck."

"His feet were cut?"

Softshoe nodded. He had seen the marks almost as soon as the first cops on the scene popped the door and began peering inside. Slashed, gouged, awful-looking.

"So, what the hell's going on, you think?"

Softshoe pulled his silent Indian routine, which usually went over pretty well. Folks liked to think of him as inscrutable.

"Damned militia," Tony said.

Softshoe had the same sentiments. But he thought this was a little much, even for them. No, things didn't compute.

"Smoke?"

Softshoe passed, thinking a cold Bud, maybe a dozen of them, sounded good. "You know, Tony, any chance of finding anyone to talk about this is long gone."

Whipping out a match, and sucking in smoke, the fireman nodded. "Tell me about it. Like a fart in a henhouse."

Earlier, Smereas and the state cop got into an argument. The Greek wanted to keep a lid on for a while so as not to spook anyone who might be in hearing distance. He wanted to check it over on the sly and then make some plans. Normal ATF procedure. But not the chubby one. Nope. He was high on the hog to bring in the storm troopers. From what Softshoe could tell, they took it to their respective bosses and even to higher-ups in the state, and Smereas came up short. Within an hour, the place exploded with activity.

"Who's the guy in the Jeep anyhow?" asked Tony, blowing whiffs of cottony smoke out of his wide farmboy's nostrils.

"He's from the U.P., I hear."

"What's his tie-in?"

The million dollar question. For a moment, Softshoe wondered if his dream of the bear was about finding the dead man. He thought not. Across the parking lot, the Greek was in another intense discussion, this time with Chip Hurley, Softshoe's boss. Both glanced over at him. Very sweet, he thought. What do they have in the cooking pot?

"I knew this would happen sooner or later."

Mumberto waited a beat before looking over at DeHoop.

"Way these yahoos been showing off last couple years. I knew they'd pull something like this."

Whatever it was they had pulled, thought Mumberto.

The paramedics from Gaylord climbed out of their rig, stepped over, and loomed above the body-bagged form by the driver's door of the Cherokee. An evidence technician was nearby, on his knees, plaster casting a footprint. After a moment, both medics got on their knees and tugged around for a grip on the body.

"So who's trying to bugger who with the suicide story?" asked DeHoop.

Mumberto shrugged.

"You're thinking there's more to it?"

"Has to be."

Even in the bag, the German was big, and his stomach made a bubble in the middle. Counting to three, the medics lifted, but the bundle sagged, as if fastened to the ground. One of the guys, a Hispanic who grew up in Saginaw named Frank Vega, looked over his shoulder, directly at Softshoe and Tony.

"What's the matter, fellas, blob's too heavy?" called Tony.

Vega gently raised a middle finger and scowled.

Softshoe wiped his hands on his pants and sauntered over. He could still taste beer in the back of his mind. The AA meeting had been on acceptance. He was thinking, I can accept having one more go at it. Boozing, that is. But then he realized his thinking was going into the shitter. He told himself to forget it. The suds would kill him for sure this time around. He almost laughed to think of it—now that would be suicide.

Rubbing his palms together, Softshoe said: "I'd like you to know, Frank, I'm officially off the clock."

"Suck my cherry, Redman."

Softshoe shook his head. The two of them liked to fish for browns in the spring along the streams north of Dog Lake. Ethnic slurs were their stock in trade. "Way I hear it, Frank, you Latinos have dicks the size of dead shrimp."

Vega, still on his knees, his hands buried in body bag leather, snarled and shook his head. "I can't believe this, an Injun with a sense of humor."

Thinking of the assaults his father bore with good will until he got home and beat his children, Softshoe bent, without kneeling, and got a good chunk of the sack in his hands. "When the Lone Ranger, meaning me, counts three, let's haul ass," said Vega, who smelled like peppermint schnapps.

Tony took a side. The other medic fisted up his portion. At the end of Vega's count, they lifted. For a second it seemed as if the body was boulders, big ones, from the Continental Divide. But with all of them grunting, it rose, a heavy toad of a load. Feet shuffling, they swung the blubbery bastard over and onto a gurney, which creaked in protest and momentarily threatened collapse. "Never knew turds weighed so much," said Vega.

"You ever get on the scale?" asked Softshoe.

Vega liked that. He laughed as he helped shove the mobile bed to the back doors of the ambulance. Giving it another one-two-three, they lifted and rolled it inside for the trip to the regional morgue in Petoskey.

Vega shook his head. "Who is this, bozo, Don?"

"General Custer's gay grandson."

"Right."

The medic Softshoe didn't recognize climbed aboard to batten down the hatches. Vega slipped out a flask and took a good long pull, his eyes closed as he chugged. Finished, he stuck it in Softshoe's direction. Softshoe shook his head, although he was tempted. "Prince Valiant," said Vega.

"I'll have some," said Tony, reaching.

"So?" Vega asked Softshoe, handing off the liquor.

"You better ask the cops, Frank."

Behind them, Softshoe heard wheels churning gravel. Another arrival. He turned. A white Town Car. It pulled to a stop and a lanky, flushed-faced man in a pink golf sweater and gold chains around his neck and wrists climbed out and strode directly to the chubby state cop who was now in charge. "Who's that?" asked Frank. "Looks like Arnold Palmer."

"The governor's right-hand man," said a nearby cop, his face lit pale by the glare of the searchlights.

"What's he doing here?"

"This is big news, fellas." It was the Greek ATF man, appearing at Softshoe's side. Softshoe liked him well enough. From time to time during the past couple of years, Smereas had called and asked him to do some unobtrusive checking on militia activities as he made his rounds in Pigeon River country.

"Hey, Herb, what the hell is this circus all about anyhow?" asked Vega, slipping the flask from view.

Smereas peered hard at him, his bushy eyebrows bunching together into one hairy line. "Do me a favor."

Vega waited.

"Do your job."

The medic shrugged sullenly and got in the ambulance.

Smereas approached Mumberto. "You have a second?" The ATF agent had a long bony face, eyes sunk in hollows, scrubby black hair. Cheeks full of pits, the remains of acne. He was tall, stoop-shouldered, and had large shovel-shaped hands.

Softshoe followed Smereas to a fairly quiet spot in the pines behind the lodge. Not too far down the path was the killing site. Mumberto sniffed the air and noticed the branches wave above them, picking up a quick coursing of wind. Once again, the rumbling of bad weather to the south. The governor's man, thought Mumberto. This was big.

"I need a favor," said Smereas.

Shadows moved down the hill from them, investigators humping toward the barn and the booty it contained. "What's that?"

"I need you to check a place over by Big Swede Lake."

"What's there?"

The Greek's face was swaddled by the dark under the trees. Softshoe couldn't make much of it out. Their eyes met. Information was exchanged in silence. "It wasn't a suicide, was it?" asked Softshoe.

The Greek stared straight and hard at Softshoe. "No, Don," replied Smereas, "it wasn't."

"Then who killed him?"

"That's what I'm hoping you'll help me find out."

CHAPTER 27
ARLY

Shooting north on bumpy back roads, Arly was glad he'd spent so much time over the years learning how to get from here to there and avoid freeways and highways. In jobs, in his free time, in militia maneuvers or back in prison, he'd memorized maps. He loved looking at them, their lines and symbols. He knew the alternate routes throughout most of Lower Michigan.

As rain slashed from a cracked and thundering sky, he pointed the van toward Pigeon River in the most obscure way possible. He would have preferred grabbing another vehicle, since the gook's van was no doubt on the government's hot list for the time being. Only thing, he knew he had to get to the spot that Cody had described over the phone not a half hour before. Cody wasn't bullcrapping: if Arly didn't show before dawn, he was gone, and with him he'd take what Arly needed for his holiday splash. Also on the horn, the bomb maker alluded to some problems with Burger. Exactly what, Arly didn't get and hardly cared, as long as the fat blowhard brought along his chunk of the juice.

All along Arly had not been able to figure why Burger was being so nice anyhow. He kept saying he wanted a piece of any action that splattered egg on the ZOG's face. If that was his deal, fine. Still, Burger had been especially accommodating. Arly had met him the same weekend he got out of Milan. Burger had been at a Klan rally outside Howell and invited him to his island for some soldiering. Arly went, for two days, liked it all right, and left. But first he had mentioned his need of a bomb. Burger had said he'd see what he could do. Which led to Cody.

Shoving down the gas, he squinted through the slapping wipers to check the dreary road ahead. They were skirting through the Au Sable State Forest and would pick up a dirt road that ran into M-33 north of West Branch. It was past midnight now; he'd get them there by three at latest, he hoped.

"You were saying?"

Arly's mind was racing almost as fast as the gook's van. He forgot that he'd been spouting off to the Gannon girl. He shot her a glance, noticing how she scrunched there in the seat, the tape securely around her ankles again. He'd thought he should mummy her good and dump her in a ditch in the forest. But he didn't. At least for now. She got him on his story again. And he had to tell it. It kept coming out, like a snake seeking the sun's warmth. Anyway, how he had it planned, he wouldn't be around for any interviews after the fact.

Pham sat in the back, stiff as a stone, his arms folded, glaring at Arly as if he was ready to burn up or blow apart. Probably that was because Arly had clipped him good on the side of the face with the butt of his gun after he hauled the girl back from the fence. Likely that wasn't smart, but the damned Oriental dope had shot off the gun in the van and caused all kinds of uncalled for grief. For that matter, he'd been busting balls so fast along the expressway that he almost got them locked up or worse. Should have stuck a bullet in his brain and shut him up for good, Arly thought.

"You're finished?"

She was facing him. Her face was puffy, hair stringy. Had to hand it to her, she hung in there, which is why he'd put up with her so far. She didn't bend; she had gonads. Plus, she had a wholesome body, the sort Arly tried not to ponder too much. Getting twisted with women, even for a little while, had never been wise for him. There was Connie, his wife for a short time, the one who really got him hooked up with the anti-government freaks. Shrink one time said Arly didn't do too well with women probably because of his relationship, what there was of it, with his now dead mother. Another place he didn't let his mind go.

"What?" he said to Cully.

"You were talking about getting adopted," she said.

Was that true? Arly didn't recall. He knew his mouth had been motoring, but his thoughts were elsewhere. Like, why had Cody had to move the spot of their meeting? And what about Burger? Then there was his stupid dead cousin, Lonnie, and his slut girl friend, the one whose throat he'd given a new smile. She had whimpered when he grabbed her, no longer so keen on busting his ass.

The violence, once it started, really couldn't be stopped, he knew. Even so, he was trying to keep a lid on himself. He had a date with destiny, he liked to think. The fulfillment of something that had started in his cell at Milan, reading the article about the governor claiming Rolly Walls was his father. This man with the spoon in his mouth, the one who didn't know him, the one who was taking credit for what wasn't his.

"I what?" he said, feeling his shoulders jerk. Words were bubbling up there in his soupy brain. Curses. Demon dragons wanting to spew. Dark angels getting hot in the ass. "Goddammit, why didn't you fuckin' say that I didn't shitass know?" he heard himself say. Or did he? Was it him?

This bothered her; he could tell by the way she looked out the window and stuck her hands on top of the pad. Part of him wanted to apologize, but the pot was starting to boil. Seething. Too much stimulation causes you to get twisted up and cussing, the fag counselor in the pen had said.

Arly's head broiled, his body fired up in a big way. All that had happened in the last twenty-four hours had put him over the line and he couldn't quite get back. He watched the wipers wash away the water. The road ahead was slick and treacherous. The hamsters in that first family's house. Why he thought this now, who knows? How he stuffed them down the garbage disposal. Couldn't say now how he, only four or five, found the switch and got them screaming. "I wasn't adopted, at least not then," he told her, getting a grip.

She wasn't looking.

"What I remember, my mother said both of us were born during thunderstorms. Sons of thunder, she called us." Did that answer her question? If he wasn't mistaken, he heard sonic booms of it overhead, drumming down the rain.

"Both of who?"

She wanted to know about him. Which he liked, which was another reason he hadn't dropped her off yet. He liked that she asked questions and didn't seem scared about it. He knew that was what it would take for someone to write his story. His true story. "Him and me."

A sheet of water, thousands of tiny drops acting as one, blasted the road. He saw the pellets bounce once they hit. Arly checked the rearview and saw only the outline of the gook, those eyes, white-rimmed and steady, staring his way. "Pham, cool it," he snapped. No response from the peanut gallery.

"Who's him?"

The road curved to the right, rolling uphill, along a deeply forested corner. Desolation up ahead; a couple more miles of empty. Soon enough, he knew, they'd blast onto a state main drag and have to be real careful not to get chucked by another ZOGlydite. His mind felt like a nest of spiders that had just been brought to life by a blow torch. His hands worked nervously on the wheel. He thought of how unfair it was; how the rich got together to get their stories straight. How they ruled the roost in their fancy suits and hundred dollar haircuts, screwing women left and right and making rules to suit themselves. Rules that filled their pockets and left other people dead and crazy. How they came in the middle of the night and poured gas in your lungs.

He didn't want to talk anymore. Except he had to. He calculated the time, thinking ahead to Monday, working it out some more, wondering about Burger, mistrusting Cody, wanting to get his story out, because that was important, before it was too late. But there was too much up there, so many thoughts, defeating his purpose. He had to make it smaller in his mind, to nail his attention on the bridge, the steel nightmare that imprisoned his father.

"Was he was adopted, too?"

"Who?"

"This other one?"

Arly wished he could see farther in the rain, so he could better prepare for what lurked ahead. Not too long ago, in prison and on the couch at Baxter's, he had mulled it over and over and scratched out schemes and formulated time tables and studied and restudied maps. He wanted to prepare for anything that could go wrong. He had been up there three times, checking the structure in person from all angles. Cody had made the big one and was supposed to give him plums and pineapples to launch as well.

The picnic caper with the rich slopes went off like greased lightening. But then, once the hillbilly bitch got her hooks going, it started to turn rotten. He had begun improvising after he slit her and that wasn't good. Too much going with the flow usually led straight into the crapper. Plus, Cody. Did he have it right; would it work? Crap. His stomach rushed, too fat, I'm too fat, he thought, as his brain bubbled.

"Is this important?" she asked.

Her voice, it grated on him. It had a knobby edge to it; not soft, not kind. He suddenly had the urge to give her a hard forearm. The gook, for example, had gotten the picture. He was lying down, playing with himself no doubt. He remembered his real mother. How he slept in bed with her, in that small house by the lake, in that time of all the activity, with her belly so big, and his dad gone working on the bridge. How she'd describe wild plans for them all, as soon as the new baby was born and Big Mac was built. They were going to move to Florida, she would say, where the sun always shone and the beaches were filled with sand that made your feet feel so good. He wasn't much more than three, but he remembered it. He also recalled the tall ghost who came late and took his place in bed. Stealing his air. "It's part of the story," he said, noticing a sign for West Branch.

"What is?"

Arly sped along, the van tires spinning off slurping slicks of water, his eyes riveted to the horizon, where he saw suspended light. Like phantoms dancing, twirling like cows in ballet outfits. "He got lucky. I got shit."

The hovering lights, appearing and vanishing and returning only to be gone again, came from I-75. Concrete pillars, paltry compared to the one in which his old man's bones were buried, held up the freeway. Arly cruised the van underneath. The pelting rain stopped for a few seconds. He was the good humor man, or would be soon.

"Lucky how?"

Emerging onto a wider, better asphalt road, Arly moved them straight toward the hazy, pulsating sky that marked West Branch. He spun them onto the first road leading east to bypass the town, then braked back to about forty and heard the wipers squeak against dry tempered glass.

The rain had stopped, although the road held puddles, pothole mouths, through which he splashed without slowing. For a second he recalled how nuts his mom went when the red-faced cop came to their door with the bad news about the bridge accident. She started pounding on his chest and then kicked the cop's shins. That's when the guy got pissed and pushed her away. The ghost came later and took the kid. Basically, his mother never got better again. The death snapped her into a bunch of Humpty Dumpty pieces. He thought of it that way because he'd been reading that stupid nursery rhyme poem just before the cop came with word of his dad's death in all of that murky cement. "I got the shaft," Arly replied.

They scooted past a few doublewides, stationed not far off the road, and farm fields with corn stalks looking slippery in the light of the moon that had just appeared. The windows in the van fogged, and he clicked the air conditioning on.

They rode a couple miles without her asking questions. The quieter she got, the more he wondered why she'd stopped pestering him for details. He wondered if she figured she had what she needed. Which he doubted. He gave her a quick once over, seeing that her face looked blank and sad and still a little scared. Hers was a heavy lipped face, with eyes that never stopped taking in the scenery. He thought of her mother, a teacher who had helped Arly. A good woman, really. "So what are you planning to do?" she finally asked.

"You'll see, on Monday." Arly followed the road as it bent northwest, along another field. The shadow of dead men stood in a ragtag file across the top of a small hill. Or maybe they were deer waiting to be shot.

"What's Monday?" she wondered.

"You'll see."

"Arly, what're you going to do?"

"I just said," he replied.

"Then I don't get it," she replied, sounding mad.

He shoved a hand in her direction. "Not now." Fire crackled in his head, the neurons snapping together in wrong ways, bullwhip sparks. He twisted his shoulders, stretched his neck. "I'll do it if I want, fuckingdamnitshit!"

She shut up. He wanted to apologize again but realized it wouldn't help. He wouldn't really mean it a few minutes from now. Connie once told him never to say he was sorry, since he never meant it anyway. Before she left; before she went to Waco. He needed to just drive.

CHAPTER 28
CULLY

Imprisoned in another bathroom, Cully sat on the toilet. Her head hurt, her neck ached, her ankle throbbed. As best she could, she tried to ignore where she was and thought of the first time she'd seen David.

She had been interviewing, through an interpreter, a leftist Sandinista captain on a dusty roadway in the boonies of Nicaragua when she saw a man shuffling along the road toward them. Trucks rolled past in clouds of dust, carrying troops to stop an incursion of Contras, the "freedom fighters" the U.S. was bankrolling. Around one of the trucks appeared an Anglo man. He had cameras slung every which way over his stained, many-pocketed vest. He was wiping hair off his forehead, looked flushed and a little frazzled. The commie captain immediately broke off the interview and beckoned the photographer over for a chat.

Pissed off that she'd been shunned, Cully glared and huffed and puffed as the two men exchanged excited words in Spanish. Within a minute, the captain began barking orders at the soldiers standing on the side of the road awaiting their turn in the trucks. Soon enough, the officer had rounded everyone up, climbed aboard a truck himself, and headed away, without as much as a glance at her. The interview was over. Cully's interpreter didn't need to tell her that.

As the cameraman snapped pictures of the convoy bouncing off, she barreled over, stuck her face in the lens and demanded to know what the hell was what.

David, of course, got her picture, which in later years graced several apartments, her eyes, nose and open mouth blown up to triple their real size and matted on poster board.

Outside the bathroom, Cully heard Arly talking to someone. Her heart picked up its pace. Should she call out?

When they had pulled into this godawful Mobil station for gas, she insisted she had to use the bathroom. Arly was disgusted, but didn't want her crapping her pants, so he had cut the ankle tape, took the keys for the van, and led her to the unisex. She didn't really have to perform any bodily functions, other than to think. She had hoped for another window or some chance to call out for help. But Arly had made sure there was no escape route when he let her in.

Plus, the bearded reprobate had told her if she made any trouble he wouldn't hesitate to hurt anyone. Meaning, she figured, he'd probably shoot or smack or somehow quiet any would-be savior. Such as the guy who was yakking out there now in a high-pitched, wavering voice. An old guy. Still, Cully thought she ought to try. Standing, she stepped to the door and listened.

"Mackinaw City," Arly was saying.

"Gonna walk the bridge?"

"No." Arly, the conversationalist.

"I done it once. Ought to give it a try," replied the geezer-sounding man.

Arly grunted a response, rapped on the door.

"Little woman in there?" asked the geezer.

No response this time.

Cully opened her mouth, almost as she had for that picture on the road in Central America. That day David had just come from a nearby bridge over which the two sides had gotten in a fierce firefight. He'd been on patrol with some of the left-wingers when all hell erupted. Fearless as always, he'd shot away with his Nikon, getting, as it turned out, a prizewinner showing a Contra solider, a woman, falling as she charged across the small bridge with a bandanna on her head and an M16 blazing at the enemy. She'd been stitched with gunfire in her belly. The photo ran the next day in newspapers all over the world. Among other things, it showed that the Contras were busy as little beavers and using American weaponry in the process.

"Just come from Houghton Lake, raining to beat hell over there," said the geezer.

Arly knocked again.

Tapping her brow on the closed door, smelling urine and disinfectant and feeling a slurry of sand and water under her feet, Cully thought about David that first day. He had hitched into the village with her. After sending his photos, they drank warm Schlitz beer at an outdoor dive. Two cans of the tepid brew brought a rosy color to his face and got him talking excitedly about journalism in a war zone. Later, when she knew him better, she realized how unusual it was for him to open up like that. Which is maybe why she recalled so thoroughly the moment when he pounded a fist on the table, leaned toward her and said: "If you don't take chances, you never get the story. We're lucky, writers and shooters. We crawl right into the belly of these beasts and get paid to tell about it."

Cully straightened as she faced the door. She didn't want to kid herself; this was a dangerous spot she was in. Arly, with his tics and violent impulses, could decide at any time to waste her. Even so, she knew this was a story unlike any she'd ever been close to. She was getting a firsthand glimpse into a vastly criminal and chaotic mind. Plus, he had some big plan that she strongly suspected was going to make news, one way or another.

Another knock.

She remembered the story of Edna Buchanan staring down a robber in a hallway. Another one in which she traveled into a seething Miami ghetto with no weapon but her notebook to get the goods on a machete-wielding drug dealer.

Cully grabbed the handle and yanked the door open, startling Arly and the old guy. Both stepped back. The geezer had on a T-shirt that said "AARP is for the Snowbirds." Arly looked like a linebacker in biker duds. "Ready?" she said to him. Arly grabbed her arm and pulled her toward the van.

The geezer looked at Arly, a little surprised. "You don't need the facilities, buster?"

Arly shook his head.

The geezer had a droopy-eyed puss with chunks of gray beard growing from the nubs of his cheeks. He nodded at Cully. She was just about to risk both of their lives and ask him for help.

"Miss," the old guy said by way of greeting and slipped in. That fast and gone.

They had just started for the pumps where the van was parked, when it happened. The van's engine started to roar and the chassis bucked. Pham must have climbed behind the wheel, revving it up, ready to roll. Behind them was parked a big boat of a car, probably the geezer's. The van lurched back and rocked on its wheels, the motor exploding with noise. The outline of the naked women glowed in the back windows again, signaling that Mr. Pham the Man was back in business.

"Slope's got another key," said Arly as the van jerked forward and spun onto the two-lane they'd driven in on. Tires screeching, the back end swaying, the van quickly got up a full head of steam and blasted south, returning toward West Branch. Its tail lights winked at them in the dark.

Arly cursed a gobful.

Meanwhile, the geezer was filling the bowl with a loud stream, mumbling something in what sounded like pig Latin. He'd left the door partly open.

Caught between the old man's piss sounds and Arly's neurological disorder, Cully thought of breaking for the trees behind the station. Ugly yellow light from a tall telephone pole street lamp showed on brambly bushes, skinny poplars and what looked like a small brick wall. But even as she turned to check on an escape route, Arly returned and grabbed her arm.

Already the van was a blur of motion. Cully tried to dig in her feet to stop Arly, but he started dragging. "Where are we . . . ?'

"Shut up!" he growled, getting behind her and shoving her forward in the direction of the gas pumps. "Get!" he ordered, pressing his pistol to the back of her neck and running her toward the older Grand Marquis, the geezer's gas guzzler.

Arly opened the door and pushed her inside. Cully ducked but was unable to avoid smashing her skull on the frame. Pain shot down her neck and halfway into her spine. Her eyes filled with water. Shaking it off as best she could, she turned just as Arly slammed the door shut.

She reached for the handle, wanting out now, wishing this was over, thinking to hell with the story. But she couldn't find the knob or whatever it was, or maybe her hand wasn't working. Sooner than she expected, Arly was beside her, ramming the stick into drive and screeching them out and away.

Looking back through throbbing eyes, Cully caught a glimpse of a fat woman lumbering from inside the small store. Her stomach seemed to carry her out and her pudgy arms waved, as if she was trying to get the attention of a husband who had left his lunch pail on the counter. The geezer showed up, too, his hands rummaging around by his crotch, probably getting it zipped. Scared out of her wits, Cully wondered if he would remember to flush.

CHAPTER 29
GANNON

After his visit to Baxter at the dairy barn and the call to Smereas, the Chief made a decision. He hadn't even realized at the time that it was a decision, exhausted as he was from all the bad things he had seen during the day. Gannon simply got in his car, drove to the entrance ramp on the edge of town, and headed north on I-75 to find Cully. If she was still alive.

He drove at a steady 80 MPH, locked in a red-eyed trance, too tired to think or remember, which was probably a blessing. He focused what little remained of his energy toward staying on the road and looking for Cully's Plymouth Horizon among the cars streaming north in the dark.

After three hours on the freeway, he realized it was almost midnight and time to call Smereas, the ATF agent, again. At the same time it dawned on him that he had only the vaguest idea of where he might find his daughter. Pigeon River was a big place, and Gannon didn't know the lay of the land or the people in it the way he knew his own back yard. It pained him to admit it: he needed help.

The closest State Police post was in West Branch. Gannon thought of calling them on his radio but realized he was too exhausted to explain who he was and what he wanted. In the end he decided to go in and ask for a cup of coffee. He got off on the M-55 exit and drove to the boxy, red brick building in the edge of town.

After his first dose of coffee, Gannon started making phone calls. He beeped Smereas exactly at midnight and the ATF agent had called him back on the police radio. Gannon described the two murders, his daughter's kidnapping, and Arly's sordid history. He heard voices in the background on the other end of the line, but Smereas wasn't giving away any information. When Gannon asked him where Arly might have taken Cully, the agent had told him to sit tight and wait until something turned up.

This didn't sit well with Gannon. The caffeine was kicking in and he wanted to get moving again. He tried the other number from Baxter's phone bill, the one in Grand Rapids, but got no answer. Dead end.

Then he remembered that he had a connection in Grand Rapids. It had been three years since Gannon had visited Chang, his former partner in the MPs from his tour in Vietnam. Gannon had helped sponsor Chang into the U.S. after the war. He dug out Chang's number and was about to dial when the babble on the two-way in the other room was interrupted by an alert.

Gannon listened intently for some news of Cully's Horizon. Instead the vehicle in question was a white van that the police out of Flint had been chasing north. The Chief had just picked up the phone again to call Chang when the radio announced that one of the passengers was a man with a heavy black beard. The driver was an Asian. There was no mention of a woman.

Gannon put the receiver down. Two surly, T-shirted teens shuffled into the small squad room of the State Police post, with a trooper following closely behind them. The first kid, who had a purple berry of a cut under one eye, gave the Chief a hard-guy glare. His hands were cuffed in front of him. He wore a cut-off blue jean jacket over bare arms, jeans, and boots. His hair was mostly shaved, just stubbed on his head. The second one, smaller, with a baseball cap turned backward on stringy blonde hair, looked bored. He too wore wrist bracelets compliments of the citizens of the Great Lakes state. He had on an oversized plaid shirt and the front of his black cap said "White Power."

The trooper guided them to wooden chairs in front of a metal desk in a far corner by a plant whose long leaves looked like parched tongues. "Sit!" the cop commanded.

Both did, slumping in unison. "I need to call my lawyer," said the kid with the busted face.

"Legal aid doesn't work weekends," replied the trooper, smiling at Gannon.

"You got to read us our rights, right?" asked the same teen, twisting his head around, presenting Gannon with another view of the oozing slice of open skin. It looked as if he had some kind of tattoo numbering above his upper lip. His eyes flashed with an off-kilter strangeness.

"Pack it in for a couple minutes."

"We weren't painting on that store."

The state trooper, on his way toward Gannon, turned back to the prisoners. Both struck the Chief as tougher looking than most lawbreakers their age, skirting on the edge of something. "Zip it," the cop said.

Both glowered.

"I'm Ted Goulding," the trooper said, approaching the desk where Gannon sat with his second cup of coffee.

Gannon stood and shook Goulding's hand. The trooper looked about thirty. He was in good shape, his form-fitting uniform shirt showing the results of many hours in a gym.

"Hey, officer, this place smells like you had niggers in it," said the blonde one, giggling. His buddy bumped his shoulder.

Goulding's jaw clenched and his eyes narrowed. His fingers went reflexively to the side of his Sam Browne, just checking that the revolver was in handy reach. Gannon knew the drill. Always prepared to act, but at the same time you had to keep your cool, even when kids were jerking you off. And there was something about this pair that put Gannon on alert. "What's it you need?" Goulding asked.

The Chief turned and flicked a hand at the five-county map pasted on the wall above him. He worked hard to keep his anxiety under control. These were cops, and if he showed them too much emotion, they'd back off, wondering about his motives. Still, feelings were pretty damned universal when they were about your daughter in a situation like this.

"You know anything more on the van they're looking for out of Flint?" he said to Goulding.

Goulding checked the other room, looking a little confused. "That why you wanted to talk to me?" He turned back to the Chief. "I was on my way to the county lockup with these dipshits when they said you were here."

Gannon sat up straighter. Keep your story clear, don't bend off just yet, he told himself, wondering if he looked as frazzled as he felt. Other cops might sympathize with his plight, but that didn't mean they would warm up to him if he was showing signs of flying off the stick.

"I need someone to help me find a murder suspect. We think he's hiding out in Pigeon River State Forest."

"This involve militia?" asked the trooper.

"Maybe."

Goulding glanced over at his prisoners. They had grown alert. "Mind clueing me in?"

"I have a guy downstate who killed two people and headed north with a hostage. My daughter."

They exchanged quick stares. "You think your man is in this van?"

"It could be." Gannon was torn. The guy in the van sounded like Arly, but it could be his own wishful thinking. Should he stay here and see if the cops picked the van up, or keep driving north? He figured keeping on the move was best. "Look, Ted, I'm in a hurry. Just give me directions into Pigeon River."

Goulding nodded, his face full of questions. At the same time, he didn't seem to want to say much with the surly little hatemongers in chairs across the room.

Returning to the map, the trooper stuck a finger on M-33 leading north and ran it up toward the skimpy burg of Atlanta. He tapped one place, then another, scratched his chin. "Carl?" he said over his shoulder.

The tall one straightened, leaning away from his pal with whom he'd been whispering.

"Is the bridge still out over the Tea?"

"How'm I supposed to know?"

The trooper turned. "Answer the question."

Carl looked at his buddy, as if for confirmation. "Don't remember."

The trooper stuck his finger on a curving, gray-lined road that ran east of Higgins Lake. County Road 32. "I think it is open," he said. "You take this, you can shave some time off. Plus it gets you right into where're you're headed."

Gannon memorized the route. The trooper watched him doing it. "Some lower life forms live up that way," said Goulding.

The Chief nodded.

"I wouldn't be turning over any logs by myself if I were you," the trooper advised.

"I'll be all right."

Goulding shifted his weight from one foot to the other. "I heard on the way in that there was a shooting, maybe militia connected, near there." He gazed hard at the Chief. Again, the teens were all ears.

Gannon wobbled, wanting to fall back onto the chair, but held himself steady. "Who was shot?"

"Not sure, but not a woman."

Now Gannon did sit, relief flooding in. The dispatcher appeared in the doorway. "Chief, just heard more about that van."

"What?"

"With the Oriental driving and some lights in the back window."

Gannon stepped anxiously up and away from the glass-covered map. "What've you got?"

"County's chasing what sounds like could be your man"

CHAPTER 30
BONES

He knew reporters and others called him Boner, sometimes damned close to his face, to hell with behind the back. But what could he do, that's what it was. All his life it had been there; he learned to live with it. Tough as elephant's hide, he liked to think of himself when it came to things like this. Even in his lawyering days, the name Bones was a reason for a carnival of puns.

Now in the dark of his bedroom in the mansion, with his wife asleep behind him, the governor thought about his real name. Walls. Son of Rolly "Spud" Walls. The man buried in that bridge out there. Under Pier 20, one of the two tall towers through which Big Mac's miles of suspension cable was spun.

Taking in deep even breaths, Bones forced his mind away from the conversation he just had with Piersma about a murdered militia man in some hunting lodge. Piersma said the situation was stable; the dead man was the bomber and the threat was ended. Good to know, but Bones told Piersma to drive down there anyway, get a firsthand account, and call back. Which he had failed to do so far.

If dead militia men were all he had to worry about, Bones might not be as stoked as he was. But then there were the images from the

eleven o'clock news, at a highway department garage outside Gray-
ling, the blowhards talking about their strike. It sure sounded like
they were going to do it, just up and refuse to work on the bridge
detail. Bones had made a few calls to a couple aides who said they
were hoping, at this last minute, to enlist support of some county road
commissioners up this way. A damned last minute screwup that the
governor had not planned very well for. But it might work; he offered
to find some funds in the road budget to help support a couple of pet
county projects up this way. All he really needed were some folks to
put up barrels and, especially, put the last minute touches on the bridge
itself.

He thought about his earliest days and what he'd been told. They
said he was a couple of months old when his real dad died. Not too
long afterward, he was taken in by Preston and Maureen. He had no
idea, even after a clandestine year seeing a shrink in Ann Arbor, if he
had any real recollections of his mother or not. He had been too young,
he knew. Still, a couple of mental pictures clung to him, buried as
deeply as his father's body, maybe. He went back to them sometimes
when he was daydreaming or, like now, trying not to ponder other,
weightier matters.

Eyes closed, there she was. His real mother. Holding him, pointing at a man on the tinkertoy bridge with other workers, looking like
an ant. Bones knew he couldn't remember back that far. Still, it was
clear as a picture stuffed at the bottom of a shoe box. She bounced
him in her arms, her hair whipped in the wind, flicking his face, getting in his eyes. She was a strong beauty, with dark hair and full of
fever. Not like his wry, soft-spoken, former swimming champion
stepmom, now dead and replaced by a socialite named Martha. A
woman who more than once had made a play for him, Preston's adopted
son. Only once did he give in to the come-on, in a bathroom at a
campaign dinner. For a second, Bones recalled that time: Martha on
the floor of the massive shower stall, him over her. Preston coming in
unannounced and seeing them. Stunned but not surprised, it seemed.
Preston had finally turned and left, as if he hadn't seen a thing. Bones
had felt oddly powerful. The shame had fueled him and he had settled
in to complete what he had started.

He looked now at his wife, who curled toward him, a spill of hair covering a cheek, her hands folded prayer-like under her chin. Probably drawn so heavily into sleep by her nightly pills. He did feel inklings of regret at how he had been unable to rein in his needs, but she wasn't stupid. She knew he was a man of strong appetites when they met.

Earlier that evening she'd told him of the phantom man, burly and bearded, who bullied her in the mall parking lot. More often than he cared to think, his job put him and his family into the path of loony birds with one agenda or another to push. Most likely this was just one more. But he wished Char had told him sooner. On the phone he had mentioned the incident to Piersma and asked him why he hadn't said anything. Jock said he forgot, but he had the man checked out, and he was a drunken blowhard. But then, Joy had been there, too. It was unusual that at least she, perhaps the only bottom line trustworthy person in his life, didn't tell him. He had called her, too, earlier, but the line was busy. Only now did he think of calling back. He checked the clock; going on two. He'd wait until morning.

As for himself, he knew for sure by now he wasn't going to sleep. He pushed himself up and out of bed. His feet hit the cold marble floor with a muted slap. Two sounds, first one and then the other.

Quietly he stepped to the sliders, pushed aside the gauzy curtain, and took a look at the lights outlining the massive girders of the bridge. Far out, the cables stretched like huge cobwebs, barely visible in the dark. They hung above the passage of water, a crossroads for hundreds of years, first for the Indians and now pleasure boaters and freighters. Water shimmered below, the structure reflecting a quiet majesty. The second largest suspension bridge in the world. His gaze went quickly to the spot, the burial area, the area where he would talk. Where he would praise his father and workers like him. Where he would give a speech about uniting the two peninsulas of his state, bringing them together in one purpose for them all. A message of healing, in the wake of a Republican administration that raped the little people, the working class stiffs who built the structure.

Looking out, another image from the past flashed in his mind. He was there, with his mother, but there was someone else along. Wasn't there? Another kid, tugging at her, demanding her attention. Bones caught this mental picture out of the corner of his eye. When he tried to look at it full on, it evaporated. He shook his head. What was that about?

Bones turned from the glass, took his silk bathrobe off the chair by his dresser, slipped it on, and left for the room next door. He stood in the doorway staring at his sons, their dark-haired heads on opposite ends of two large cribs set side by side. His first children; sometimes they seemed almost like toys to him. Fatherly feelings were fleeting for him. He wished it were different, but that's how it was.

At home they had an intercom connecting their room with the nursery. Throughout the night he could hear his boys burble and gurgle and even giggle in their sleep. Char demanded it; it bugged him to no end, this incessant childish chatter. But he grew used to it, like rocks being polished in a machine. He knew they were his flesh and blood and he had big plans for them, but right now, as babies, they were basically useless to him. Again, he was aware of his selfishness but he shook it away. He suspected he was a little sociopathic when it came to child rearing. But, given his past, why would that be so odd?

He heard a creak behind him and turned to see his wife, hands rubbing her arms. "What's wrong?"

Damnit, he thought. Stop following me. Then, he thought, no, she loves me. And I love her. Most of the time. "Nothing."

She stopped inches from him, her face tilted around his shoulder, getting her own look at the twins. "Were they fussing?"

"No," he replied. "I was."

Concern wrinkled her face. He knew he should watch his tongue. He touched her elbow, feeling a scaly chill. He tried gently but firmly to edge her away from the door and back to bed. Her pajamas shimmered in the creamy light streaming down the hallway from a Toy Story night lamp in the bathroom. He felt silly in domestic situations such as this. He was much more himself in his suit, riding herd on others. Speaking to juries. Being governor. Living out Preston's dreams, which were certainly now his own.

His wife's mouth made for a smile but didn't quite get there before veering off into a faint frown. "You have a lot going on."

Early on, he had told Char his tale of woe. Of course, she could have read it in the papers anyhow. Of how his father died, fell off a strut into a caisson filled with wet cement. How his mother left and how he was placed with Preston and Maureen Bones. How that child-less couple became the best and truest kin anyone could ever want. How they helped him get through school, how they always supported him, how they were kind enough to never, ever mention his mother or dead father at all. Of how they let him be his own boy and then his own man. How Preston kept encouraging him to one day think about politics as a career as he climbed through the hierarchy in the state. Bones had told his wife everything.

He and Char turned from the boys. But his wife stopped in the middle of the hall. He nearly bumped into her. She spoke without turning. "The reason I woke up was a dream."

Here she was confiding in him again. He didn't have the emo-tional room for it. Not now. He wanted to get her back in bed so he could slide down to the office and beep Piersma. Find out what the hell was happening. When he didn't respond, she looked over her shoulder. "It was about that man in the mall parking lot."

Bones thought she sounded melodramatic. Despite himself, he shivered, as if a clammy hand had touched his cheek.

"He was coming after us, Frank, down a long road, in some truck that was right out of the Rocky Horror Picture Show."

"I never saw that one," he replied, trying for levity.

Char turned and faced him. They stood in the long, high-ceilinged hallway. This summer home suddenly seemed way too big for them, and, he had to admit, a little haunted. "It was awful, Frank, it really was."

He tried to chuckle.

"I mean, who was he, do you think?"

"Jock had him checked out. Nobody. C'mon, let's go back to bed."

"Frank, this scares me."

He was grappling for something to say, something glib or stern, he wasn't sure which, when the phone in their room buzzed. He grate-fully slipped around his wife, went in and picked it up.

It was his father. Preston. Wanting to know what he knew about the shooting in the woods.

"Frank, this doesn't sound good," said his adoptive father.

"Dad, it's two in the morning."

"It's not good."

For the life of him, he had the sudden childish urge to tell Preston about his wife's dream. To ask him for comfort. Because her mood was starting to infect him. It was crazy, but it sure did feel as if there was something out there. A big angry bird, maybe, about to fly in the window and peck out their hearts. Like in a Poe story.

But Preston didn't seem to be of any help either. He sounded upset. Once again, for what seemed like the hundredth time in the last twenty-four hours, Frank Bones rose to the occasion. He started, even if hollowly, to reassure Preston. Everything was on track; nothing to worry about.

"But, Jock," interrupted Preston.

"What about him?"

"Jock called. With questions."

"About what?"

"This man, some man, Frank, that they saw at the mall."

CHAPTER 31
GANNON

Bouncing in the seat next to Ted Goulding, Gannon leaned toward the windshield and peered down the road. They'd roared out of the post and were now speeding west on M-55 at 85 MPH. Goulding switched on his light, its broad red beam sweeping out ahead and along the sides of the road. Voices kept up a steady chatter on the trooper's two-way.

Back at the post, the dispatcher said the driver of the van was a failure to pay at a gas station south of town. There had been other traffic from the same station, about a possible stolen vehicle, and reports of a bearded man and a woman. That car had disappeared, but the county had the white van in pursuit. Goulding, after sticking his prisoners in a holding cell, told the Chief to climb aboard and he'd lead him to the action.

"What'd you get those two kids for?" Gannon asked, his stomach churning as the cruiser shot along a rolling stretch of pavement.

"Spray painting the front of a party store."

"They sound like regulars."

"You hear of the National Alliance?"

Gannon shook his head, leaning forward in his seat.

"Nasty bunch of bigots. They're part of it. They targeted the store because it's owned by an old black guy."

"Seems to be lot of that up this way."

"Christ, world's crawling with them these days."

They blasted past trees, a couple farmhouses, the chained entrance to a landfill. The voices on the radio paused for a moment, then returned. Gannon heard plans being made for a roadblock.

Goulding was talking into a hand-held mike, getting a better location on the fleeing van. "Why a Vietnamese kid?" the trooper asked.

The Chief shook his head. "No idea."

A large semi, its lights bearing down hard, appeared on the road ahead. Goulding kept both hands on the wheel. As they rushed by the truck, an echoing vacuum of air sucking between them, the trooper punched down hard on the pedal. Gannon noticed they were pushing ninety. A very dangerous speed. "You don't need to put yourself on the line here," he said.

"If it were my daughter, I'd haul ass," the trooper responded, grim-faced, his teeth nibbling the lower lip.

On the radio he heard a quick jumbling of words. There seemed to be some confusion as to where the van had gone. "You think the Vietnamese kid killed that woman they found in that gravel pit?" asked the trooper.

"More likely the guy who was riding with him." If Arly still was, thought Gannon.

"This Arly, he's militia?"

"More a one-man band."

Goulding shook his head. "Damn," he said.

Gannon tried to sit still. He wished he was driving now. Images of his daughter, moving through his mind like fast shuffled cards, made him think of how much distance had always been between them. Even from day one. Gannon never knew how to be a dad, particularly to a headstrong little girl. He remembered her on her first hobby horse, then in her communion dress, and then with the red spots from measles. At her wedding to the photographer, held in their back yard. On the bed at home with her mother, his wife, wiping her brow as the cancer did its dirty business. A child he could never control. Impulsive. Look at her now.

"Kid sounds crazy," said Goulding.

Gannon hadn't been paying attention. "Who?"

"The Vietnamese. Ran a roadblock."

"Why don't you slow it down," said the Chief. "No need for us to make things worse."

"Why'd he take your girl?"

"I'm not sure."

Goulding was into it now. He'd crashed through that threshold, that place where caution and restraint were on one side and all-out get-that-bastard fury on the other. Gannon had been there a few times himself. All stops pulled, you became a threat yourself.

They took a winding curve at fifty, tires screeching, the gum machine light tendrilling the fields. Rain began to spatter the windshield. Not good.

From around the curve Gannon saw headlights coming their way, head on. A huge bat out of hell. A vehicle with lights as wide as mountains. Fierce and cutting right at them.

His stomach leaped high, trying to grapple into his windpipe and out his throat. He held up a hand to protect himself from the sharp sweeping stab of lights. Goulding, maintaining more control than Gannon would have predicted, cut the wheel at a clean angle away from the approaching vehicle.

Absolutely sure he was going to get broadsided, Gannon tried to get a look at the driver blasting down on them. It was hard to tell with the spinning, reeling motion of the cruiser, but it looked as if the guy behind the wheel, caught there for a second by the twirling red lights, was Vietnamese. But no others, he thought.

That image, if none other, slammed deep into the Chief's bank of bad memories. He had no time, however, to ponder anything. Because in a sudden shuddering second the cruiser had been clipped in the rear and started a tumble and turn from the road and into a dark wall of trees.

CHAPTER 32
ARLY

He couldn't stop talking. As he drove the words raged out, blasting across the front seat at her. Arly knew she couldn't keep up, but he didn't give a damn anymore. All parts of his brain were firing at once, huge explosions of electricity bursting like transformers on poles. With his eyes on the road ahead, sucking them into the wilderness, he talked.

How it came out he didn't know. It jerked from him in spurts, pieces here and chunks of it there. Green lights from the dashboard glowed into his face as he spoke. He wanted to hammer them out so he could drive these final miles in as much dark as possible. A couple times he wanted to blame her for the ugly way the lit-up cockpit of the stolen car kept getting in his face. Another time he might have, but not now. He was rolling, telling her about the apartment above the freeway, with the stink of oil everywhere, and how it went up in flames. The way gas got poured all through the room; the way it happened; how he escaped.

He thought of telling her about the nightmare, the one that had gripped him for so long. The dream of his dad in the deep cement of the bridge, locked in by tons of terrible concrete, his bones rigid, his mouth open in horror, his bridge-maker's clothes still preserved by the massive fall-out of muck that turned so hard, his fingers clawing to get out, to punish who did it to him. The hair on his head growing, growing even in the cement, expanding like seaweed.

Even as he spoke and she wrote things on her pad, he wasn't sure how much of it he spoke and how much of it tumbled wordlessly in his head. He felt more fractured then ever, split open, like a beehive leaking honey. He tried to explain how he had to release his father from that grave, how his dad could find no eternal peace until he was broken from his prison. Down in the pillar of the bridge, his father had been calling out to him for years, his voice a vast hollow echo, asking for help, informing his son, his true son, of the necessary task. He thought of telling her how so much of it came to a head in prison, Milan, where the real plans were laid. How he was part of the movement, but the movement itself was really too small to contain his plans. The movement, though, tied right in with what he had to do. In prison he had talked about this once, got in a fight, and was stuck in the hole.

Not too long ago, when he took that medication the doctor in prison gave him, the animal would go to sleep and other parts of him would calm as well. Problem was with that stuff, it didn't give him the fire to do his job, particularly since his father never really stopped calling. When Arly didn't hear it, he just wasn't paying attention.

Arly was within a few miles of his destination, the cabin Cody had told him about, when his throat got to hurting. It felt like claws were grabbing it, as if insects were in there, trying to get out. Noticing that she wasn't writing and was just staring out the window, her hair in her face, her chin hanging, her mouth dumb and half open, he wanted to hit her. To smash her skull against the window, to see her brains smudged there, to get her attention.

But, he didn't do that. Because she had a purpose; he saw it now. She needed to tell the world about the forces of evil that had killed his father and his mother and who were now dogging him. Forces that showed up in newspapers, on TV, in movies, even carried themselves through phone wires. He needed her to talk about the beast that was loose, running this land, this state, his very own flesh. The god of hate had been turned loose, eating itself, ripping everyone apart with its terrible greed-lust.

So he got himself calm. He had to if he was going to complete his mission. Watching the road, he tried to talk to her about the evil one, the Democrat politician, the ZOG dog, who was planning to put that plaque on the bridge, a memorial that wouldn't free the man buried below. It would only lock him down forever. A fancy lying politician who made noise that everyone believed. The one he had wanted to find at that mall. But then they stopped him, caught him, stuck him in a room. He told them nothing and knew then that the only answer was to act on the bridge.

This part, though, got garbled and jumbled. He knew what he meant to tell and all of the reasons were abundantly clear. But he knew he wasn't getting it right when she stopped gaping and day-dreaming and turned to him.

"Let me get this straight." She didn't say anything for a couple seconds, like she had said enough. Then she went on: "Your dad died building the Mackinac Bridge. Your mom, who had two kids, went nuts. She left the one kid for adoption. This kid's the governor now."

He guided the wheel with one hand and rubbed his crotch with the other. He was humming inside. He didn't like her tone, but he did like the fact that she had been following along. He thought of how that fire from so long ago kept burning in him. He escaped, but not before watching his mother in flames. Or was that in his memory, from what others said? Even so, even if it wasn't him, the fire scarred his chest and part of his neck, hidden by the beard, but marking him like the beast in the Bible. He realized that more fire was about to explode, to rage wild and bring about true freedom. For his father; for himself. Except, he had to follow the plans. He had to get to Cody. He had to stop jack-in-the-boxing.

"She tried to burn herself up and got stuck in a mental institution. You were sent off to foster homes, and ended up with the Flecks, in Memphis, who were distant cousins of yours. You got sent away to prison for burning IRS forms, found your true destiny in life, and now . . . what?"

She had some of it, but not all.

"Correct?"

Arly slowed for a stop sign. It suddenly hit him with a powerful force that she didn't understand. He could tell by her stuck-up expression. Here he'd been kind to her. He hadn't truly hurt her, hoping she, if someone, would understand. That she would see the forces, the dark currents, like bad electricity, that ate away at all that was good, in his soul and in this country. How the powerful people kept everyone else as their slaves. How everyone was on an assembly line, without names or real reason for living. Arly remembered Connie, in bed with the minister from Chesaning. Pastor Jack. A fraud. Another Judas. Before she left Arly.

What was that part in Revelation, about the wind and the fire and earth ripping asunder? No, it was that other part, about the woman. It said, right there in the Bible, to give her back what she has given. He recalled it: give her as much torture and grief as she deserved. Something like that. He knew that no matter how hard he tried, she would betray him. Her story would make him the villain. Not the ghost. Not the liberator. "Harlot," he said.

"What?"

Arly gunned through the intersection, his mind racing ahead to all he needed to do. The fire crackled, the force of what he had become was loose. He thought of the truck, of the massive destruction it was his to bring. "You see this?" he said. He glanced at her. She was leaning as far from him as possible, looking wet and dragged out and uppity. He yanked down his T-shirt, showing her his throat, part of his chest. He gave her a good look, revealing the clumped, gouged flesh. He could rip the shirt away and show her it all. "This," he said

"What is it?"

"What they did"

Her eyes flicked back and forth, staring at it, maybe seeing the scars in the glow from the dashboard. "Who's they?"

He looked outside. It was dark. He thought of how that politician thought he could take credit for everything. How he wanted to make the accident on the bridge his. Arly thought of the man's wife, the bitch he had scared at the mall. How he wanted to crush her, too. But that was before his true plan and mission had started. Lord, how his mind was racing, his heart pounding, the hatred burning in his veins.

"Can you tell me that, Arly? Who's they? What are you planning to do?"

It slapped into him, again. She was stupid. A traitor. She would spread her legs for anyone with a story to tell. Why had he trusted her? Another quote came to him: "She will be consumed by fire, for mighty is the Lord God who judges her." He thought of his mother, in that bed, in that whore's town by the bridge, growing the seed that would set the fire and destroy her. Or was it she who set the fire? The shrink in prison said that Arly had made most of it up.

He swung the wheel to the right onto a rutted two-track that he'd seen without even paying attention. He had made a decision. She had heard enough. Her smell and her heavy body, with its breasts and smoldering cunt, made him so sick he wanted to scream. She was only in the way now.

"Arly," she said. "Why not stop it now, before it gets worse?"

The car bumped on ruts. He realized his left hand was touching his scar. He remembered his mother, drunk and wearing her pink slip, spilling gas on him as he lay in his bed, her only remaining son. She wanted to use the fire to stop her pain and to take him with her. He had leaped from the bed and ran to the door just as she flicked her lighter. The explosion made him fly down the hallway. But no one came. No one ever came. He had left her in her fire. That happened, didn't it? He didn't dream it.

Jerking the car left to right to avoid potholes, Arly sped another hundred yards or so into the dense trees. He jammed down on the brakes and slammed the car into park. "Get out!"

Her face lost that arrogant expression. She knew he meant business. Finally. He shoved her toward the door. She swung out at him. Batting her off, he cranked the handle, heaved himself out, and ran around the front to her side. She had locked her door. Arly reached in the back of his pants and pulled out the .38. He aimed it down and pulled the trigger. Empty. Pham had used up all of the bullets. He had spares in his pockets.

She was crying. Returning to his side, he smashed on the window with the butt, twice, as hard as he could and broke the glass. He reached in, unlocked his door, and told her to unlock her door and do as he said. "I'm not fooling," he told her.

"Fuck you," she said through sobs.

"You're worse than the rest." He thought of Jesus, a savior who had been turned into a faggot by most churches. Arly leaned around her and popped the lock. When he circled around this time, she didn't resist. He dragged her out.

"Goddamnit," she whimpered. The whore. Making her face the car, he pushed her shoulders, jamming her head against the roof. For a second, he thought of tearing off her jeans and taking her. Ramming her. But he didn't want that. She turned around and started swinging at him, her knee moving into his lower belly.

Arly grabbed her wrists and flung her on the ground. Standing over her, he saw her eyes glint up at him. For a second, she lay there. He smelled damp earth and a cotton candy sweetness, which was maybe her sweating fear. His mother had swayed in the room, the only room of the apartment and sprinkled the place with fluid, splashing it like holy water. Or was that him?

"You goddamn loser," she said.

Again, the dare. The resistance. He thought of the knife slicing easily through the singer's neck. Of the .22 against his cousin's head. Arly dropped to his knees and began working on his pants. His mother had slept with him a few times, comforting him, before sending him away, giving him to her drinking friends.

As he knelt, she began to scream and started to wiggle away. The sound cut into him, reminding him again that he didn't have time for this. It made him think of his mother with her lighter, the hoarse sound of her voice, the way she swigged booze from a bottle.

Feeling rain, or was it sweat, on his forehead, Arly swung out and hit her on the side of the head. He dug the gun out of his waistband again. "Stop!"

Her face was mean, but still superior looking. His mother had twirled, as if dancing, before flicking the lighter and turning the world into a firecracker. Or, no, it was him, wasn't it, who made the fire. "Fuck you," she said.

In one swoop, Arly caught her on the cheek with the pistol butt. Blood burst and her awful sounds stopped. Her head flopped to one side, loose-necked, at peace, or so it looked.

CHAPTER 33

SOFTSHOE

Mumberto climbed hand over hand up the rusty rungs of the oil company water tower. Rain spattered his face and dripped down his neck. Heavy clouds kept a blanket of dark over almost everything. His shirt sopped and sticking to his back, Softshoe could feel the weight of the Remington 30.06 sniper scope rifle hanging along his right side. His longtime companion, this rifle. A pair of binoculars dangled below his chin.

Halfway up, he paused and squinted into the pelting water. By the steady fall, he had a pretty good idea this rain would be around a while. The thickness of the sky, the dark blotchy swirls and billows, and the loud thunder told him the worst might be ahead.

Taking a deep breath, he continued his ascent, lifting himself up the backside of the green monster tower that stood in a clearing in the pines. The tower had been built twenty-five years before by a gas exploration company out of Texas and still served a scattering of cabins and cottages on Big Swede Lake.

He was careful not to lose his footing on the slick metal. The ladder hung straight down from the lower ledge of the catwalk surrounding the belly of the water tank. It wobbled as he made his way up. He figured it might swing loose and go caterwauling to the side, like a door swung open into a gale, at any moment. But it held.

Near the opening in the metal floor leading onto the walkway, Softshoe stopped to unsling the rifle. He wiggled it through, settled it to the side, then hoisted himself onto the firm flooring. The rain smacked down harder. He wiped some away with his forearm, grabbed the gun, stood, and quickly stepped around to the area facing the lake, which was only visible by the rise and fall of liquid movement. He'd visited this perching place twice before, both times to get a lowdown on the movement of fire. Once it had crackled in from the southeast, out toward Atlanta. The other time it had hopscotched its way from the west. Each had been contained, both times with the help of water drained by fire trucks from his very tank.

Sticking the glasses to his eyes, Softshoe tried to focus on the cabin in question. He knew which one it was. Fortunately, it was the closest in, down a small hill through the brush, not too far from the rutted road running from the highway. In the dark, he could make out only the outline of the building, a bulkiness beyond the trees. A pale yellowing in one corner could have been a light inside.

Softshoe took a minute to lay down his weapon and glasses and to unbelt the pack from his waist. Once he had it open, he dug out a poncho and dragged it as quietly as he could over his head. He hadn't worn it on the way up because of the sound it would have made as he moved, and because it would have made the climb harder. Settling into it now, he picked his field glasses from the floor, leaned against the rail and tried to force his eyes into a better view of the world below.

Rain pecked the rubber, too loudly, he thought. But no one would hear it up here. He hoped. Letting the glasses hang, he hunched up, shouldered the rifle, and snapped on the scope, which gave the world a hazy purplish glow. But he could see much better. He trained the sight, which magnified things about tenfold, toward the cabin. Bullseyeing in, the scene took shape. He made out a roofline, a chimney, and a square of light in the front facing the lake. Closer in, pushed into a clearing by some bushes, was a station wagon. He couldn't make out the license.

Before Mumberto left Crow Mountain, Smereas had told him who to look for at this cabin. There was Cody Burke, the baldheaded militia bomb-builder. There was Winston Groom, the skinny, ratlike guy who had been driving with the murder victim at the lodge. As an afterthought, the Greek had mentioned a murder suspect from downstate, a burly man with a black beard who had taken a woman as hostage. The woman's father, a police chief, thought her kidnapper might have dragged her up here. As for this cabin, Softshoe had learned it was owned by a defrocked urologist out of Flint. Smereas had mentioned that this weenie doctor headed up his own viscous little militia faction. Quite the rogues' gallery. Softshoe had no idea if any of them were down there now.

Softshoe's right eye ached from peering through the scope in the rain. Switching eyes, he made his head and heart slow to a crawl. He was narrowing into a comfortable but keen hunter's awareness. He cleared his mind of clutter, one of the things his grandfather had taught him.

As far as he could tell, no one was awake down there. He thought he should climb back down, call Smereas, and tell him that not much was happening at Big Swede Lake. But he waited, and soon enough he noticed movement. A shape passed behind the curtain window at one end of the cabin. Then another shape. Two people pacing. Might be something; might not. He thought if he went down now he could possibly get closer to write down the license plate number from the parked vehicle. Then head out.

But he saw someone walking up the side of the hill from the cabin. He crouched down on the catwalk and trained the scope on the form of a skinny man in a dark jacket. The guy had a rifle stuck under one arm, the barrel pointed down. A weird looking rifle, fancy, a bolt action of some kind.

Shit, thought Mumberto, taking in a slow steady breath, wondering if he could be spotted if someone looked in his direction. It was a little foggy, the trees dripping water as the rain slacked off to a drizzle. In the murk, Softshoe figured he wasn't too visible. Even so, it was hard to tell. For the first time in the couple hours, he thought of drinking. How many times in years gone by, as he waited in the woods to hunt, had he nipped on booze? Always seemed to give him a fine edge, until near the end, when it made things much worse, which is what it would do now, he knew. And anyway, there was his dream. The bear, the power of it. Softshoe blinked once, shifting his mind back to the present.

Down below, the man had stepped onto the road, smoking a cigarette. Softshoe tried to scour the man's features with the scope, hoping to recognize him. In the flare of his cigarette he was visible in the rifle's built-in bull's eye: long face, pulled down at the chin, with deep-set eyes. Something about him seemed terribly nervous. He sure looked like that other one in the Cherokee, the skinny driver. The man was facing the road, as if he expected company. Softshoe checked his watch. It was four-thirty. Later than he thought. Birds had started to make noise.

The lake caught a few stray rays of dawning light. Man, thought Mumberto, he'd sure be happier bobbing out there for bass or bluegills, instead of hiding a hundred and fifty feet up on the catwalk of the tower. Who was that back in that cabin? He wanted to get down and call for help. But no time for that now. His hair sopped to the roots, he kept careful aim with his rifle. He used this scope for shooting competitions and to stalk sick or dangerous wildlife. He had never used it on a man.

CHAPTER 34
CODY

The doctor's cabin smelled like it had whiskey rubbed into its wood walls. Overlaying that was a lingering cigar stink. Normally, Cody didn't pay much attention to such minutiae. He prided himself on being able to blend into almost any environment and to learn to live within it, all the while, of course, keeping his wits and notions about him, planning bombs, crafting schemes, using his mind as his laboratory. Years ago, as a kid, he had learned from books he found in his father's library, building his smarts alone.

But things had been bothering him the last few hours as he waited for Arly. Smells, sounds, the whole shit bucket. Rita, for one, the hot bitch, two-timing on him with Gregor Pauls and pretending not to, at a time like this. He would deal with her later.

For now, Ratso had gone outside to cover the road and she was crashed on the sagging couch. Cody could finally grab a few minutes for himself to start making better plans. He had to get his mood back on track, empty out the jitters and start figuring his next move. If Arly didn't show, he had to contemplate who to punish, in what way, and when. Revenge for him was always a subtle geometry, a delicate form of math meted out slowly, usually after he was no longer around.

Stepping into the bathroom, an ear cocked for the return phone call from the guy he'd just beeped, or for the rodent coming back in the door, Cody took a good long look at himself in the mirror. Hands on the sink, he leaned in close and twisted his shiny head this way and that. He didn't like what he saw: stubs poking through, a few wisps bearding out behind the ears. He had felt them the last few hours as he walked around the cabin. His hands rubbed, touching the faint bristles.

He popped open the medicine cabinet, hoping to find some shaving cream and a razor so he could lather up and rake his skull smooth, keep his dome sharp and sure. His statement of cleanliness and power. Skinhead perfect, a sign of his true place in the world. But, wouldn't you know, nothing. Hardly a bottle of aspirin on the shelves.

Cody slapped the door shut, breathing deeply. He knew shaving, scraping the crud from his head, could have put him in a much better mood. He had to settle for looking at the rest of himself. He stood straight in front of the mirror. He presented a neat enough appearance. Except he knew the tiny stubs would soon be much longer than they already were. But there he went, worrying about his head again. Cody forced himself to look away from that part of his anatomy.

Pale blue eyes locked to the mirror, Cody turned his torso this way and that, checking out the definition. The tattoo of the fiery cross burned on his upper biceps. On his chest, which he didn't bare for his own looking, bled the permanent sword and shield symbol of his particular branch of the Aryan Brotherhood. He didn't have to peel his shirt to look; he knew it was there. He could feel it burning. It was a symbol he took to show his allegiance to a power he sometimes felt only he truly understood. A wonderful darkness, better than any benevolent God, a god of knuckle-splitting swiftness and strength.

Watching himself, his body pounded into muscle for times such as this, Cody smiled, a cruel twisting smile. In his teens he had been pudgy, buried in his books, but that had changed. So much of him had changed.

Running a hand toward his crotch, Cody thought of Rita putting the pistol to the fat hamburger's brow and triggering in the final bullet that split open his German skull. The traitor, the lousy Kraut turncoat. Cody expected as much from the mud people in the world, but not from one who was supposedly a brother. As for Rita, it was her initiation. Plus, payback for how she'd been screwing around with Gregor back at the barn, Gregor. Whom Cody should have killed outright and would have if he didn't need him and his land while he built the bomb for Arly. Later, maybe later.

Thinking back to when he first plugged Burger in the shoulder, Cody recalled how strongly right it had been. It had been commanded. Blast away anyone who tried to block the righteous path to the white order. Blow them up, explode them all. Of course, the fact that Burger wanted to scratch Cody's business deal mattered, too, in the accounting of his reasons for waxing him.

As he thought this, Cody faced himself full on again, his sharp pale features reflecting back the fierce determination of his will. He knew it would have been wise to have packed up and left for home with Rita, the two-timing bitch, after it became clear Burger had tried to sell them out.

But he had worked so hard for so long building this business for Arly Fleck. Sure, he had crafted many other explosives. He'd booby trapped a synagogue in Tampa and maimed a rabbi and his wife in the process. He'd wired a home in Montana that erupted when the tax goon stepped onto the porch and was blown into the bushes. He'd blown up a county bus garage in Tennessee, a pile of post office boxes in Denver, a small government office in Ogden, Utah. Never, though, had Cody Burke had a chance at something so fine and strong and potentially world-changing as this. This was on the scale of what the Arabs did at the Trade Center and McVeigh did in Oklahoma City. The thing was so right, and the Lord had confirmed it in prayer at the church near Fort Bragg, where Cody got his materials to begin with. No, he believed that Arly Fleck had been chosen to be the instrument of retribution. Plus, the money. Always that. Cody didn't work for free.

At first Fleck had seemed to him merely nuts, but later, after they had met three times, Cody was convinced this man was true and proper for the deed. Even if Arly didn't really understand the crusade, he was willing to be part of its final justification. He was volatile, especially when he started that swearing routine, but he had the true anger of a holy servant. He was for real. Except he was unpredictable. For example, where was he now? Cody was pretty sure that Arly was not in on it with Burger. But if he was, Cody was a sitting duck in this damned cabin.

Cody dug dried skin from his chin and felt the mugginess of the new day seep through a window by the shower. He recalled the first white power freak he had met, the chubby maintenance guy at the University of Michigan. He filled Cody with the right words and pushed him in the right direction. Cody had learned much from his computer, then set up his own station on the wirewaves, which brought in requests, mostly through the Net, and then he began offering hands-on service, here and there, for the brethren. And, except for that one bit behind bars, look where it had led: to the opportunity of a lifetime. As long as Arly didn't blow it.

Cody felt like he was floating in a barrel toward Niagara Falls. He either had to bail out soon, or decide to ride it over into the massive froth, come what may. Never before had he, the maker, taken it to the end. But this time he wasn't sure.

If flaky Fleck didn't show soon, Cody would have to make a choice: either abandon the mission and leave his weapon hidden away where it was, or become the bringer of necessary doom himself. Which he had not been planning. He was tugged every which way. Wisdom and precaution told him to split. Deeper urges—and they included the desire for his payday—kept him where he was. All those hours in Gregor's barn north of here had to come to something. Building his explosive, wrapping it in the beer barrel, getting the truck, piling up the other explosives; the charges should not be wasted. Everything counted: getting the permit to take their disguised weapon onto the bridge during the governor's ceremony, agonizing hours of making sure the vehicle was rigged just so. Cody didn't want to abandon it now.

The phone rang in the other room, startling Cody at the mirror.

He didn't turn immediately. Which made him feel very good. Anxious as he was for a call, his trained body, his well-controlled reactions, kept him calm. He always told people he had learned in the Marine Corps in San Diego, in a crucible of a time that put him on the shining path as one of the few and the proud, until he was dishonorably discharged for smarting off to and then cold cocking the nigger captain. But that was all lies, a colorful cover-up. He had never joined the Corps. He taught himself what he knew, through many hours of trial and error, and eventually with the maintenance man's help.

On the third ring, Cody turned and stepped out into the living room. Rita had sat up, her long hair bunched to her hard, sexy face, lips still etched with the blood red lipstick he liked. Her eyes, sultry and mean and weary all at once, met his as he picked up and grunted into the receiver.

"Buster Bragg, this is Charlie Tuna."

Code words were necessary, particularly at times like this. "Tuna, I need your help," said Cody.

"Does it involve the Brew Meister?" The caller meant Burger.

Rita uncoiled, arms over her head, breasts swelling inside the dark pullover. She swung her head to furl out her hair. Cody turned away, feeling anger at how he'd let sex creep into his thoughts and boil over into trouble, even when he was engaged in the mission of a lifetime. Sex had nearly derailed them at the barn. "Mr. Meister poured beer all over our plans."

"Your party is off?"

Tuna was actually Perry Smith, brigade commander for the Scorpion cell of the Wolverine Militia out of Atlanta, one of the few groups that truly understood and had dedicated themselves to the cause. A friend of Gregor's. Cody had alerted him a week ago of a possible operation, although he didn't give him the total story. Even then, Cody had his suspicions that Burger was about to turncoat. Burke had sketched for Smith some basics of the plan. Now he was glad he had. He was also pleased he had made Smith buy the beeper so he could be contacted anywhere at any time. His concern was that Smith was a pal of Gregor's. "I'm not sure," said Cody. "I'm waiting for Porky Pig."

"Pig's not there?"

"Not yet." Where the hell was Arly?

"What do you need from us, Bragg?"

His tag came from the Army ammunitions depot from which the C-4 explosive, grenades, and other goodies had been stolen. "I was hoping you might want to play a part in the party."

Something sharp tickled the back of his neck and spidered up the back of his smooth skull. He crunched his shoulders but didn't drive her away. He felt tingling in his groin. Hadn't she had enough when they first got here after midnight and they'd sent the Rat out to walk the perimeter? Cody had often wondered what her reaction would be to killing someone. Now he knew. She had done Burger. The awareness both appalled and excited him. Either way, it was getting him off the path.

"What sort of part?" asked Tuna.

"Party this big, now that it's getting attention, needs security."

Her hand cupped a buttock and squeezed. He turned and slung her away with his eyes. This was her problem, with everyone. She gave him a haughty glance even as she backed off, pretending to pout. He put a hand over the phone. "Check on Rat. He's outside." For a moment he wondered if the mud soldiers were out there, in the woods, ready to make them a Waco. God, this was getting too tight. He had to get moving.

Rita straightened haughtily and saluted him, turned on her boots and made for the door. Cody had needed her as he built the Two-Ton Popsicle. She was able to wheedle parts and goods and information out of an amazing array of crackers down south and then again up here. She had given sex to the guy who came up with the permit to get the truck where it needed to be. He didn't mind that; it was the other thing, with Gregor, that scorched him. And now she was starting to remind him of how dangerous it was to rely on women for anything other than blow jobs or cooking. True, she'd wasted Burger, but he suspected the power was going to her head.

"You mean, security to keep out gate crashers?"

Cody doubted anyone had tapped the prostate doctor's phone. Yet, who knew? They had to keep to the silly talk. "Something like that."

Out the window in front of him he saw a small motor boat curving through the green-gray water, rustling up a wake. A little bit of light showed dawn coming. Cody definitely did not like this cabin as a meeting place. But he needed communications. By the clock on the wall, set in a pair of deer antlers, he saw it was just about five.

"Where's the party?"

"Strawberry Fields is close enough."

"Not a bad place for a blow-out."

Cody couldn't help adding: "Blow-out's not there."

Tuna didn't reply.

"Look, Charlie, can you get a few of the faithful together as soon as possible for this?" Cody had debated letting anyone else in on the particulars of the deal. But he decided he had to. After all, he might have to be the one doing the special delivery, if Arly didn't show. War meant taking terrible chances. He realized now that he was pushing ahead, regardless. He was in too deep. Maybe he could dump out later, after securing the popsicle.

"You think Porky Pig's going two-faced, too?"

Cody had thought of it, until he had gotten the call from Arly in which he had sketched some of his own problems. "I'm just being careful."

"Well anyhow, Bragg, the crew was meeting for Sunday services. We'll just hold them in a different place."

"Make it as soon as you can."

"Will do. And, hey, Bragg . . . ?"

Cody waited, hearing something outside now, through the screen door, the crunch of heavy footsteps.

"Can't you tell me who this party's for?"

Rat appeared first and grabbed open the door, followed by Rita who slipped in with a somber, chastened expression on her face. Then, almost filling the door space from jam to jam, was Mr. Porky Pig himself. Big-bearded and looking mean as a hungry snake: Arly.

"I have to go." He had wanted to mention one more thing, but now he forgot what as he stared at Arly. "I'll explain later," he told Tuna. "See you in the fields."

CHAPTER 35
GANNON

The Vietnamese kid started to flail, smacked an arm across an IV pole, and then convulsed. Sitting on the bench of the chopper, Gannon watched as the two medics worked to tie the patient's arms to the sides of the bolted-down gurney. The thumping of the helicopter's rotors drowned all sounds, so the Chief had no idea what either of the paramedics were saying to the kid whose name was Pham Nguyen, according to his license. His home address was in Grand Rapids, where this air ambulance was now headed, and this destination was why Gannon had decided to go along for the ride.

The kid continued to struggle even though he was mostly out of it, verging on a coma and in need of delicate brain surgery to treat a ballooning clot. Hence the need to airlift him to the nearest neuro-surgeon available on this busy holiday weekend.

Gannon closed his eyes as one medic blocked his view of Pham. His own head throbbed from a hard bump into the windshield when the trooper's cruiser had spun off the road and into a swamp full of weeds, muck and grasses that luckily cushioned their tumble.

In his mind he saw flashes of the collision, of them flying into the mud. Of him shouldering open his door and climbing into knee-high murk. Goulding, too, got out under his own power. Blood dripping from his head, Gannon had run for the van, which had spun off the other side of the road into a tree. He didn't remember much, only that he ripped open the side door, looking for his daughter. Instead, he found Pham sprawled on his side, thrown back from the driver's seat. On his knees, Gannon had tried to talk to Pham, demanding to know about Cully, his own blood flooding his eyes. He got no response and soon enough found himself being dragged from the van and laid on the highway as a small army of vehicles arrived.

"Hold him tight!"

Gannon opened his eyes. One of the medics was yelling over the roar. Pham looked terrified, jaw twitching, a thick bandage covering one ear. Gannon knew the kid was the key to learning about Cully. Or he sure hoped so, since he'd bet it all on him. Back in the emergency room in the midst of the chaos that led to this flight in the air ambulance, Gannon had abandoned his plan to go north, at least for now, since there was no sign of Fleck or Cully anywhere.

The medic checked over his shoulder, seeing if the Chief could lend them a hand. He wasn't up to it. Even though this kid might be able to fill him in on Cully if he came back around, the Chief wanted no part in helping. He closed his eyes again, feeling the helicopter sway under him. He wondered if he might be in need of a neuro-surgeon himself.

From the highway he'd been rushed to the ER at the hospital in Gladwin. Pham was also shipped there. Ted Goulding, Gannon later learned, got shipped to Saginaw for surgery to repair a badly shat-tered leg. They had stitched the Chief's head wound under bright lights. A young doctor told him that he ought to have a CT scan of the head injury, but the hospital's CT machine was on the blink.

Once he'd been patched up, Gannon got on the horn, trying to track down Smereas. Problem was, the ER was swarming with cops who all wanted to know his role. A detective out of somewhere made it clear that as soon as Gannon's head settled, he had a shitload of questions to ask. Which is when Gannon realized he could easily be detained in Gladwin for the day and longer. He wanted to get another vehicle and head to Pigeon River. Except another cop, this one a state trooper, pretty much told him there was nothing up there. The bearded man and the stolen vehicle had disappeared, or so Gannon was led to believe. Smereas wasn't answering his beeper. No one knew about Cully except Pham, and he was in no condition to say. The hospital was swirling with activity and rumors and no assistance to him at all.

When the Chief learned they were choppering Pham to Grand Rapids for surgery, he made another call to Chang and this time his friend answered. Chang said he would be available to talk to Pham, and would ask his friends in town how Pham got involved with Arly.

So in wee hours of the morning, with cops everywhere asking questions, the Chief decided his best chance at learning anything was to ride down to Grand Rapids with Pham. With no car and no real allies, he could be stuck in Gladwin forever.

A State Police sergeant had agreed to let Gannon fly along in the helicopter while he and another guy drove the hundred and fifty miles to Grand Rapids. They, too, wanted to talk to Pham if he became conscious.

"How you doing, sir?"

Gannon blinked and noticed a medic, this one with red hair, sitting next to him on the bench. Pham lay still, inert under a thin green blanket. "Is he dead?"

The medic smiled and raked fingers through his hair. He wore a white uniform. "Back in la-la-ville."

"He going to make it?" Gannon asked over the thump and grind of the helicopter.

The medic shrugged, rubbing his freckled upper arms. "Sounds like he could stroke at any time."

Gannon wondered vaguely if the same was true, if more mildly, inside his own brain. It felt like it. But so far he'd been showing no real signs of a cranial bleed. He'd played up his medical condition, but only slightly, so that he could tag along with Pham. Still he wondered if he should have stayed and worked on this with the cops in Gladwin. In his mind he saw the white power punks on the chairs in the squad room. The one with the hat; the other with the tattooed lip. He wondered: why so much hate; what drove these people? "How long till we're there?"

The medic checked the shiny face of his watch. "Twenty minutes." He went over to help his partner keep an eye on Pham.

Gannon leaned his head back and let the thwomping chop and rhythm of the helicopter lull him around the edges. It had been years since he'd ridden in a chopper. Last time had been in Vietnam. If he wasn't mistaken, that time Chang had been right next to him in the seat. His partner on the streets of Saigon, and now his best hope of finding his daughter.

Cutting above U.S.-131 near Big Rapids, the helicopter broke through a bank of soupy clouds and sped for a moment into the full glare of the rising sun. Gannon, facing toward the open door of the craft, reared back and blinked. They'd been battling low-slung rain clouds the whole trip. Faced with the bright ball before him, the Chief felt a swift surge of pessimism shoot through him. Strange how a break in the weather made him feel like lead dropping in an empty bucket. His head banged with pain. Down below on the snaking highways, probably much farther north, Arly was still at it, full-speeding ahead. Going somewhere, with Cully, and he was helpless up in the air.

He felt someone sit next to him. The red-haired medic again. He pointed to the hilly horizon. "Grand Rapids," he explained, leaning close to Gannon's ear.

The Chief saw a few buildings poking up, a scattering of houses and plowed fields leading into the city. This part of the state rolled with hills, spreading off toward Lake Michigan.

"You ever been in one of these?" the medic asked, meaning the chopper.

"A few times."

"Vietnam?"

The Chief nodded. He'd worked a detail for several months after the Tet Offensive at Long Bihn Air Base, north of Saigon. The Cobra gunships and other Hueys were always blasting in and out. Gannon had ridden in a few, a couple times to transport prisoners, twice for R&R up to Nha Trang. He remembered they always made so much noise, churning up dust in the summer and slapping around water in the rainy season. Guys who drove them had balls bigger than their brains, Gannon always figured. "They going to get some pictures of you at the hospital?" asked the medic.

Gannon wasn't sure what he meant.

The medic tapped his forehead.

"Not if I can help it."

The guy gave him a funny look.

"You think our buddy there is going to be able to talk soon?" Gannon asked.

The other medic had stood and was getting the gurney and support equipment ready to transfer into the hospital.

"Hard to say. He's got blood coming from his ears."

Christ, thought Gannon, he probably did make a mistake. This kid was going to die on him and leave him stranded miles from where he wanted to be. For a moment, he thought of leaping up and trying to force Pham to talk before he died. But somehow he didn't have it in him. The Chief felt a heavy weight fall in his stomach, forcing him to double over. He was ready to puke but he wanted to cry.

CHAPTER 36
JOY

Funny how easy it was to go right back to smoking. Three years without a puff and here she was in the middle of the night in her kitchen sucking hard on a cigarette. Outside, through the window, she saw the fast quick glint of the Manistee River, curling through the woods in the back yard of their home. On the east edge of town, not too far from the abandoned pulp mill, they lived with all the privacy of the country, with deer often wandering through, and yet were not five minutes from downtown. If you could call that clump of stores, on either side of the new riverwalk, downtown.

Joy filled her lungs with the nicotine, grabbing for relief from the worry that had been with her ever since she had seen the news and then made a few calls to friends in the Democratic party. She had even tried to get through to Frank, but his line was busy. Then he had called her back, but she was on another line. They hadn't been able to connect.

She did not have a good feeling about what was happening. Not at all. The person she needed to call, and the one she was holding off from talking to, was Preston. She wanted to ask him—no, tell him—that it was way past time to tell the truth. Frank needed to know it, or at least part of it. To keep it from him for so long was terrible and probably dangerous.

Joy stubbed out the cigarette she was smoking and looked at her dead coffee, festering in the cup she bought when they visited the Soo locks last summer. They had seen the big boats come through and waved at the deckhands from so many foreign countries. She had gone up there for Ralph, who crafted model freighters in the garage in his spare time.

She thought of Ralph, sleeping the sleep of the innocent in the other room. Her heart turned into a prune full of pits to think about the real story. That is, about Preston. There were things not even Ralph knew.

Exactly why it was time for it to come out, she didn't know. But all along, ever since Frank stepped straight into the spotlight, and especially when he got it into his head to celebrate the bridge, she knew it was going to emerge. The dripping, bloody, awful truth.

Joy stood, stuck her coffee in the microwave and zapped it on for a half minute. She stood there looking at the phone on the wall. So long ago, working late. That woman, the wife of the dead bridge builder, in Preston's office, distraught, with the other child, the one no one mentioned. The wild card all these years, it seemed to her. Demanding money, she was, raging against Preston. Already Preston had Frank with him. His child. The other, the woman took, or did for a while.

On that night, as Joy had pressed her ear in horror to the door of her half-brother's office, she heard more than she ever wanted to know. But it had driven her in powerful ways to care about Frank. To mother him in a fashion that his stepmother, the swimmer, and his real mother, the madwoman, could not.

"Honey?"

Joy turned to see Ralph in his terrycloth robe in the dim doorway. Skinny Ralph. They weren't married back then, not yet. She was single, building her life. Neither Preston nor anyone else knew that she knew so much. She had returned to the office that night to pick up some ledgers, for work on the bridge, to take home and get done by a deadline for the state. She came in, opened her files, and heard them in Preston's office. Their voices had been loud, hard to ignore. The true story bounced back and forth between them. And there it was, not six months after the argument, the death in the big tube of cement. She wished now she had confided in Ralph, but then that could lead to other things, among them the way Preston had helped to seal her mouth, even though he didn't know all that she had learned.

"Hi," she said.

"What's wrong?" She noticed his nose twitch slightly, picking up the smoke and knowing what that meant.

She sighed and stuck her arms over her chest. The microwave beeped. She ignored it. On TV, the reporter had talked about militia wanting to make some sort of statement about the bridge. Maybe there was no connection. After all, no one was really even hinting at the truth yet. But it was a truth, the whole of it, that could destroy Frank if it got out. Then there was the man at the mall. Neither Frank's wife nor Jock seemed to sense the real danger in him. She hadn't spoken to either of them after it happened, just buried it inside her. She found a place for it deep in her belly, that barren place that she tried to fill as a surrogate mother to Frank. "Can't sleep."

"The news?"

"More or less," Joy said.

"It sounds like that's done. I don't think there'll be more problems."

Joy loved the look of him in the dark, his lined face mostly hidden by the poor light. If only they could have had children. Probably it was shame, she knew, that kept her secrets hidden. "Ralph?" she said.

He waited, hovering. One of his hands rose, as if to touch her words.

"There's some things . . . " She leaned against the wall and closed her eyes. Preston had been her boss for so many years, several before she ever married this fireman. Ralph was on his second go around, with two kids who were now in California with his ex. So, there had been times, lonely ones where . . .

The phone rang next to her ear, the noise drilling down into her. She slid out of the way, telling herself to calm down. It was all right. No need to worry. Things weren't twisting beyond her control. They weren't. "Ralph," she said, reaching for a cigarette. "You take it."

CHAPTER 37
CODY

Sitting on the picnic table bench on the enclosed deck overlooking the water, Cody felt the ragged early morning warmth wrap around him like a scratchy blanket. Muggy already and it smelled like fish out here. But he ignored everything except the sack at his feet. Arly's chunk of change.

Controlling his thoughts and counting his heartbeats, he bent and unsnapped the olive drab bag, actually a small munitions container that in the service often held cylinders of dynamite. He had given it to Arly a while back, after their second meeting, when it became clear this bug-eyed wild man was the real McCoy.

"It's all there."

Cody looked from the stacks of bills. Arly was turned, arms folded over his chest, to face the water. Pale sunlight sneaked through ugly looking clouds. Too early in the day for a tornado, but the barometric pressure was definitely in transit. Cody could feel different weather fronts at work. Churning, boiling rain, mixed with Caribbean-style heat and promises of ice was about how he'd predict it. He figured they shouldn't be out here in the open, but Arly said he needed air. Other than that, he hadn't said squat about his adventures. Just made like, hey I'm here, let's get down to it. And all the while he seemed like a boiler about to blow. "Arly, man, chill. I just want to make sure."

Rumbles of thunder sounded on the far side of the lake. A fisherman in the motorboat was floating in that direction, his line a hazy thread running from a pole stuck between his legs. Too far out to matter, or so Cody hoped. Man, they had to get this show on the road. He wouldn't put it past the government to station a watchdog fisherman out here. In fact, that was their speed.

"You're thinking I'm fucking with you, don't you?" he said to Arly.

"I put hell of a lot of work into this." Arly turned, arms at his side, the veins crawling under the skin of his forearms, his eyes way too bright for breakfast time. The beak on him made him look Jew. His lower neck was a mass of red tissue, scarred up good from whatever the hell it was.

"And I didn't?" asked Cody.

Arly scowled.

"For one thing, Burger didn't have his part."

"Count the fucking money." Arly's neck jerked; those eyes flashed more fiercely.

Cody held up a hand, noticing Rita behind the screen, smoking. Rat was back at his post on the road. He knew that technically he could back out, since Burger didn't hold up his end. Even more important: could Arly handle it, money or no money? He had to do this delicately, probe and find out. He had put a lot of work into his weapon. "Look, Arly. You up to this anymore?"

Arly glared at him. His brow was full of deep lines; his body seemed to pulse with its own thunder.

Cody didn't like the tension. You needed a fine balance of it, but too much and any operation was in grave danger. From the first time they had met in the diner in Detroit, Cody had known Arly was a self-contained dreadnought. He was maybe too bullheaded and his emotions were about as balanced as nitro. But overall he was perfect for the personal sacrifice needed with something like this. If you could keep him just close enough to the edge without going over, you were in fine shape. Question was, how close was he to falling over, if he hadn't already? The further question: did Cody need to nursemaid him any farther? He had hoped to give him directions to Gregor's barn and then be on his way.

"I'm wondering maybe now's not the time to blow the popsicle," Cody said evenly, the open bag at his feet, staring at Arly. "A lot's already gone down."

"No choice." Arly's eyes ranged the far shore. The fisherman was drifting downwind.

Cody felt too damned vulnerable out here. They had to get piping. "You know, Burger could have spilled the whole thing." Which was true. Cody wondered if he saw the fisherman talking into a radio.

Arly shook his head. "I never told the fat bastard nothing."

Cody didn't know what to think of that. He had a pretty good hunch that Arly meant it. But, who knew? No one, absolutely no one, could be trusted after a certain point.

"How much does that prick know?" Arly asked.

"Which prick?"

"Guy by the road."

The grip of Arly's revolver stuck out of the waistband of his pants. Cody checked the doorway again, spotting the whites of Rita's eyes. He suspected she might find killing to be contagious. Or so he hoped, if Arly got any ideas. He knew she was hot to trot out of here, leave the fireworks to Arly. Hop in their station wagon and make hay into Canada with the money until things cooled.

Bending, Cody quickly rifled through the stacks of slick, sloppy bills in the green sack. "Man, Arly, you been wiping your ass on this?"

A grumble, like a sound deep in a sewer.

No sir, Cody wasn't liking this. He always wanted to be on top, and he was definitely feeling poorly about this situation. Arly was like a fat stupid cobra, ready to strike if you farted too loud. He sensed the sick bastard was starting to get ideas about taking back his money. "Rita, you mind picking up the Uzi in there and keeping an eye on Godzilla while I do my banking?"

Arly turned slowly, his arm reaching in his waistband.

"Shoot me, asswipe, and you'll never know where I stashed the truck," said Cody.

Arly's weapon slid out, his eyes flashing, chest heaving. Guy was strung out bad, a tight rope ready to break. Cody believed he remained as committed as ever to the cause. He was just going to need some help, a little hand holding, to pull it off. Or maybe not; maybe this was going into the shitter, whatever happened. "Look, Arly, I'm in this as deep as you." Rita had done as he asked. He saw the silver muzzle behind the screen. Good girl.

Arly saw it, too. But he didn't let his gun drop. "Just hurry the fuck up. Sonofabitch, damnit shit." He started doing that thing with his head.

Cody counted. Paranoia, within reason, was a good thing. It was going to be important to not push Arly so hard that bugs escaped his bird brain. Yup, hot damn, twenty-five grand. With Burger's eight thousand, a worthwhile effort. They could be halfway to Toronto by noon.

"Cody. It's going on five."

He gestured at Rita to zipper it. "Looks like it's all here," said Cody finally.

"What about Burger's share?"

Cody shrugged, looking up. "Told you, he didn't have it."

"I'm screwed?"

"You'll owe me." Which was silly. One way or the other, Arly would go down.

Cody looked at the sky. A few rays hung there, above the trees on the east side of the lake. The air smelled better now, like pine, but the weather was still muggy, a drumbeat of thunder rolling again. He hadn't planned it this way, but Cody suddenly knew what was right. It washed over him like a shower of pure white prayer. The answer. The plan. He knew there was backup in the woods. They would be there for Arly. For a time, Cody had thought of taking him as far as the barn. Not now. Too dangerous. Plus, he had done his job. He had wrapped the stolen C-4 in the beer barrel, bolted it in the truck, crafted a tidy timer. Sure, he'd like to watch it bust loose, but given all that was happening, he doubted it would get that far. His eyes turned to the fisherman. No, it was time to boogie. The rest was up to Fleck. "I'll get you the map." He stood, hefting the bag.

Arly stared at the sack, as if losing it made him depressed. "How far is this place?"

"Not too far. And there's a few of the boys who can meet you on the way and take you in."

Arly didn't like that. "I'm going in alone."

Cody didn't give a rip. By the time the rest of them met up, even if they did, he and the two-timing Rita would be on the road again.

He was starting for the house when Rat huffed up the path. He looked about as squirrely as Arly. Upset over something. "Christ, Cody," he said. "This guy's got a goddamn hostage in his trunk."

CHAPTER 38
CULLY

Deep in the dank place, she had been asleep, locked in a terrible trance. Now awake, if that's what she was, Cully tried to move. Nothing worked. Everything hurt. Curled up in the darkness with a gag stuffed in her mouth, she had been hearing herself moan. Her mind told her to keep quiet, at least until she better understood what Arly had done to her this time. She recalled being shoved down. Him towering over her. Then Arly stooping and a shattering blow blasting her face. That was about it.

She tried to stretch her lower body, which only caused her to groan louder. Her leg muscles were in knots, begging to be stretched and rubbed. Her ankles felt fused into one piece of burning bone. Her hands, twisted behind her, had been wrapped at the wrists. Her mind raced, trying to calculate the damage and figure a way out. But first, where was she? She smelled gas fumes and realized where she was—in the trunk of the geezer's car, maybe. As far as she could tell, they were stopped. Maybe that was good. Maybe not.

Then, for a moment, her attention paused in her crotch . She tried to tell if it hurt, or if it was wet. The thought of Arly raping her, if he had, filled her with revulsion and rage. She felt more than violated—

viciously mauled. If she could get out of wherever he had stuffed her, she would make sure to kill him. She would saw off his ugly peter and ram it down his throat.

For a second the sweet thought of revenge gave Cully hope. It didn't last. It was like too much salt; she wanted to gag. Cully knew he had imprisoned her and would return soon to make things worse, if that was possible. She tried to buck up, jamming her head, smelling rotten eggs and feeling something lumpy and hard digging into the spot between her shoulder blades.

Collapsing back into a fetal crouch, since that was the position he'd tied her in, Cully thought for a few seconds of giving up and just settling into her rabbit hole of pain. Let the huge weariness of what he'd done seep into her totally, like a poisoned sleeping potion. Send her back into her trance. It was so awful. Not just rape, if that had happened, but the whole ordeal: Arly bearhugging her into oblivion, sticking the wire around her neck, taping her legs, chasing her in the graveyard and then slamming that—it was a gun, that's right—into her face. Self pity broke over her. She thought of David, but realized he had died on her. He wouldn't be much help.

On her face, she knew, blood had clotted. It stuck whenever she turned on the floor of the trunk. Cully thought of the meditation period they had in the church she and David went to. How the minister, a slender long-haired woman, would lead them gently, soothingly into green pastures. How she told them to close their eyes, to picture sunny fields alive with sunflowers, to envision a vast clear sky, a rolling ocean, some place that gave comfort. Full of terrible cramps now, Cully tried it. She imagined a field with waving fronds of wheat, a large field that stretched forever. She thought of her mother running in it, her long hair flying, like in some silly romantic flick. Cully tried to put her father there. But he wouldn't show up. She couldn't stick him in that field. Then, another image: gaunt, fierce, notebook in hand. Edna. Cully thought it silly that she felt, even in this place, such weird heroine worship. This writer who took no hostages. A force in the journalism that had shaped her life.

Edna was saying to act, or the image was. Stop your mind short of surrender. Cully wrestled away from the useless airy meditation. She forced herself to think again about reality, about her pain, about this story. She focused on how terribly hot and oppressive it was in this trunk. How sweat mingled with blood in her mouth. As she did, she heard sounds, not her own. Crunching, shuffling. Voices, excited. She thought of making noise to alert them that she was near, but held back.

"You did what?"

Cully tried to listen, to make out who it might be. For a moment she felt hope. Maybe it was her dad. Maybe he had heard something that brought him here. But that expectation popped quickly. "Told you." Arly.

The scraping of boots on sticks and leaves, if that's what it was, stopped. "Told me. Goddamnit. You swore you weren't double dealing us."

"I ain't."

"The hell. This doesn't involve us?"

"Told you, not."

"Open it."

No reply.

"Open the fucking trunk!"

Another voice, male: "There's no latch in the front."

"Why didn't you do it before?"

"Thought I should tell you first I heard someone crying."

Cully's stomach turned inside out. Fear spread like an oil spill in her throat. Had she been whimpering?

"I found the key!"

More twigs snapping. Metal pulling, a pinging, a scratching of some sort and a loud snap, right by her ear. She held her breath, waiting, ready to shit her pants.

Suddenly light poured in. Cully twisted around and peered up at two faces. One Arly's. The wild hair, square face, those turkey gullet scars on his neck. He stepped away as the other one bent toward her. He had a bald head, eggshell glasses, fair skin and a Rottweiler's mouth. His intense green eyes examined her. Then he swung back and faced Arly, or so she figured. "Rat!" he said.

More shuffling. God, Cully thought, they're going to drop rodents on me, like in Edgar Allen Poe. "What?" she heard from the other voice.

"Shoot this bitch. Fuck, Arly, what were you thinking?"

Arly, she thought, are you going to stop this? But, of course, he wasn't. He had probably walked away to let them have at her. He'd brought her here after all, like a lamb to be slaughtered.

"Just leave her. She'll bake by noon anyhow."

"Not with these clouds."

Christ, thought Cully, they're going to debate the weather.

"Rat, do it now!"

Cully wanted to turn away from the gray light, the open space. But she didn't. She wanted this Rat, or whoever, to have to look at her. Let him know that she wasn't going to cringe in her last seconds of life. She called on the spirit of David to help, to accompany her to the other side, if there was another side and not just dust and ashes. Maybe he was in heaven. If anyone was, he was, along with her mother.

Another guy hovered there. Skinny, long-faced, with a dangling jaw. Cully willed her bowels to stay tight. Rat, he looked like one all right, with a nibbly mouth and nose, stepped closer. He held a gun, raised it. His eyes reminded her of tiny black peas. She noticed them narrow as he got ready to shoot. Cully couldn't help it; she winced.

But then there was something. From above, another voice, calling down, like God, commanding. Rat turned. More voices, arguing. Then three sharp cracks filled the air. Rat flung back, dropping into the mouth of the trunk, almost flopping on top of her. Cully did her best this time to turn away and wait for the worst to be over.

CHAPTER 39
SOFTSHOE

Jamming on the crowbar, Donnie Mumberto heaved and tugged with all his might. Rain splattered his face. The woods were filled with drifting fingers of fog. Just down the wood chip path to his right appeared a fawn, its eyes bright and brown, its coat slick from the all-night downpour. It glanced his way, curious, then turned and trotted away. Softshoe wanted to yell for it to go after the two men who had just taken the same path. He had wanted to keep after them but knew he had to get the hostage out of the trunk. It was his job. Inside he now heard muffled noises. As metal tore, the conservation officer stuck the tip of the crowbar in farther, stepped back for better leverage, and yanked.

More mumbling from within. Sounded female. He'd only caught a glimpse from the tower. Maybe the cop's daughter.

Mumberto wiped water from his brow. "It's coming," he said to the hostage inside. He didn't think the men had too much of a lead, a quarter mile at best. After Softshoe had plugged the one with the rodent's face, the other two had climbed in the big Buick and spun mud in all directions as they raced away, luckily down the road that dead-ended at this very spot.

As they had fled the scene, trunk lid flapping, the body of the gunman sprawling, Softshoe had dropped quickly down the side ladder of the tower. In his truck, he aimed through a break in the trees, bounced onto the road and, ignoring for the moment the guy he had shot, blasted off. He called for help on his lousy two-way as he drove.

He had arrived just as the two men—one with a beard, the other bald—were getting out of the car. Mumberto figured by the frantic, angry looks of them that they had had every intention of blasting their guns into the trunk. But spotting him, they slammed the lid and ducked into the trees. Probably figured, rightly, that if they left their captive alive he'd busy himself with the trunk instead of taking off after them. Before leaving his truck, he finally got through on the radio, raised the dispatcher in Gaylord, and gave a quick message to be relayed to any cars available.

"Can you hear me?" asked Mumberto, angling the crowbar higher in the space he had been able to inch open.

More noise.

"Take it easy."

Again, mumbling, a moan.

Softshoe used his thighs for leverage, bending low and shoving up with his chest. The tip of the crowbar scraped and scratched loudly, making something shiver. The back of the car raised with his effort. He had looked inside by the steering wheel for a trunk latch but had found nothing.

Feeling like he had it, or nearly so, he envisioned the nub of the tool cutting into and bending the locking mechanism. He heard what sounded like hinges breaking. Mumberto closed his eyes and gave his best. It seemed he was on the verge when the crowbar came loose, flopping him off balance and landing him on his ass in the muck.

"Shit." He did not like having to do so much at once. His grandfather once said Indians lost much when the whites took over, but the biggest loss was patience, the watchful ability to wait for the right moment, or something like that. Drinking had helped him wait, but often he had waited too long. Softshoe took time now to clear his mind and let the bad energy drop into the ground like the rain water.

Then, as if by magic, the trunk slowly opened. A big mouth, the top part pretending to smile. He hadn't even left the ground.

Softshoe pushed himself up and peered at the bundle of woman. Her eyes, the steely color of northern lakes in autumn, stared at him, more curious than scared. Somehow he liked that, but he didn't know why. "I'm Donnie Mumberto."

Saying that sounded terribly stupid to him, so he got busy without spouting any more moronic words. Eyes flitting to the path, anxious to get after them, he used his knife with the hard rubber handle to cut the tape at her ankles. He moved higher and snipped the bonds at the wrists. Then he started for the rag wrapped around the lower part of her face. As he did, he noticed for the first time an ugly, blood-matted lump a couple inches under her left eye, at the lower base of the cheekbone. Spying that, a hot fist grabbed Softshoe in the place of his anger. He hated it when women got hurt by men. If that is what happened, and it probably had. His mother had been one of them, as had his grandmother. That was one bad thing he hadn't done. "Which one did that?" he asked, gently slicing the rag.

Freed from the tape and gag, the woman lay there, hardly moving. Her reddish hair matted her head. Her mouth, without the cloth, looked full and strong. He could see hurt in her face, and weariness. Softshoe reached to touch the damaged cheek, a stupid gesture he knew as soon as he did it. She winced long before his fingers ever reached the spot.

"You're the police chief's daughter?"

Realization stirred in her eyes. A movement, like wind rippling the water, showed she heard him. "Who're you?" she asked, tonguing her lips, giving them moisture.

"Wait here. I'll be right back."

He had only gone a few yards toward his truck when the woman with the autumn eyes called again: "Who are you?"

Softshoe stopped, his mind already configuring the trail the bearded one and the bald man had run down. He turned to the woman, now sitting up. Her cheek was swollen like a small balloon. Mumberto wondered what else had been done to her. Men who harmed women made him think of the coward poachers who killed elk and then left them to rot in the woods. "I'm a conservation officer, ma'am," he replied and then trotted off for his first aid kit, his backpack, and the rifle that had already had a very busy day.

CHAPTER 40

SMEREAS

The Church of Jesus Christ the Redeeming Savior sat atop a small hill on Black River Road south of Onaway. Years ago, maybe a decade, the stone-sided structure had housed a Free Methodist congregation. Rather than closing up shop and selling out to another group, the former church body slowly, and through attrition, grew and transformed itself into the place of worship that it was on this rainy Sunday before Labor Day. A church for white people who wanted nothing more than to rid the world of everyone but themselves.

A few vehicles, mostly rusty, rattletrap pickups and a couple of older Detroit metal heaps, stood in the gravel lot outside as Herb Smereas pulled in, parked, and rested behind the wheel. His head felt as if someone had carved open his skull, stuck in a pound or two of sawdust, and then stitched it up with peppery thread. With his eyes closed, he recalled the Colonel's body, which sure as shit was no suicide, and the weapons in the barn back at the hunting lodge. Himself in the middle of it, talking to the governor's man, learning about the other pieces. What a mess.

When he had left a while before, the State Police and FBI were holding a press briefing with reporters. John Gambrini, the ATF's special agent for Michigan, was there by now, going along for the time being with the song and dance about the militia leader killing himself. Also in front of the mikes was the governor's flack, the guy through whom he and the others had been working. From the start, this whole thing stank to high heaven. The only good thing had been the chance to snatch the bomb maker and possibly clear up some munitions thefts down south. Now that wasn't looking real good.

Smereas had left the scene of the shooting not long before. He was so nondescript looking, so tall and rangy and low-key, that the journalists assumed he was no one to bother. Which was fine with him. ATF agents liked it that way, demanded it, even.

If he had been effective up here at all in this wilderness area of scattered malcontents, it was because he kept his head down and played quietly in the background. When he was undercover in these parts, that was obviously true. But even in recent times, when he was the agency's clear presence, he avoided limelights of any color.

Before leaving he had a quick meeting with Gambrini. The former prosecuting attorney for a suburb of Chicago, now a rising star in the ATF, heard Smereas out. He didn't exactly seem to like what was said, but he told Herb to go to it. If he thought there was more to be had, and the only way to do that was by going in the back door, do it. But, damnit, do it fast, Gambrini had told him. Once so many cops from so many agencies got involved in a deal like this, nothing could be controlled. The suicide story likely wouldn't hold for long, although everyone was busy fudging the scene to make it look that way for now.

After talking to the State Police dispatch out of Gaylord, he learned about the accident involving Gannon down by West Branch. This only made matters worse. He had thought of racing to Big Swede to try to find Mumberto, but then he got a brainstorm. Hence, his stop here.

Popping the glovebox, the firearms agent reached in and pulled out the videotape. A nice little shot at blackmail, and the reason he'd come here. He was lucky he had this copy with him. He thought this could be the key that turned the lock. He only hoped, if he had to use it, that it didn't backfire. It made him a little sick in the stomach to think maybe he was shooting blanks on any of this. In his experience, the militia was made up of many factions, so many of them fighting among themselves. Whatever larger operation had existed was probably down the drain, what with Burger deep-sixed. If so, this neat little video could be put to better use later on.

But, he thought, Gannon had told him quite a story. Which was partly why Smereas had mentioned to the Indian to include Arly Fleck and a female hostage on his list of faces to look for at Big Swede. He checked his watch; almost seven.

He had just decided to stay put when he heard gravel crunch and saw a newer Corsica pull into the spot next to his. An overweight woman and her short husband got out. Smereas knew them both. She had four kids from a previous marriage; he stole gas from underground tanks and peddled it to mini marts with pumps. "Jim," Smereas said through his open window when the husband got out on the passenger's side.

The petro thief paused, letting his hefty wife forge ahead on fragile-looking black pumps that made her ankles sag. "Thought that was you," Jim Pendergast replied, standing there, his hands in the pockets of his oversized suit coat.

"Ozzie preaching today?"

Pendergast nodded. His wife waited on the steps leading up to church. She looked out of breath and unhappy, ready to whip her hubby's butt for dawdling.

"Maybe I'll go in and listen," said Smereas.

"He'll be talking about the Lord, that's for sure."

"Terrific," Smereas said. He was Greek Orthodox, though he was seldom able to go. His wife and kids were doubtless getting ready to attend services at St. George's this very minute. He wondered what the skinny militia mutt might have heard about Burger and his buddies.

"You thinking of joining up?"

"Hardly."

"Then why the visit?"

"Always interested in hearing a good sermon."

Reverend Ozzie Shavers wore a crisp camouflage uniform with the Wolverine insignia of the Michigan Militia on one shoulder. On the other shoulder was stenciled a cross. Hands on the sides of his pulpit, he looked out on his handful of faithful servants and scowled, making his bloodhound face purse into a series of wrinkles and folds.

Shaking his head from side to side, the insurance salesman turned preacher took in a deep breath of air. If he had recognized Smereas sitting in the back, he didn't let on. The firearms agent patted the videocassette in the side pocket of his jacket.

"Brethren," Shavers intoned. "We are living in terrible times. These are troubled waters flowing in our midst. We must take heed. A hammer is sounding in the heavens. Blood is starting to flow in our rivers."

Smereas had been to services here once, back when he was still undercover. Since then, he had stayed away. Watching the thirty or so worshipers squirm in their seats, he didn't know if it was his presence or the reverend's words making them antsy. He figured Ozzie was referring to Burger's death, without being too specific, given the fact that he had the ATF on hand.

"You see, brothers, once again forces larger than ourselves are threatening what we hold dear. The heavens are trembling. The day is closer at hand."

A stained glass window showing Jesus holding a lamb in his arms let in pale light above the pulpit area. Some of that early light touched the side of Shavers's droopy, jowled puss. Smereas continued to fondle the video on the seat next to him. The brimstone-chewing minister wasn't going to like what the tape had captured. But Smereas wanted to get to it. He needed to drive out to Big Swede. If this place hadn't been right on the way, he wouldn't have stopped. For good measure, he had asked the dispatcher in Gaylord to send a county cruiser, unmarked if at all possible, to circle Big Swede and look for Mumberto. The Indian, he knew, could be unreliable. Maybe he didn't find anything and forgot to call before he went home.

"You see, people, the Lord Jesus was a man of action," Shavers went on, making the cop realize he had missed a sentence or two. The first time he'd been here, in his guise of the traveling truck driver, he had secretly taped the minister's words. Nothing much had come out of it.

In the hard-backed seat, Smereas thought of his own church, of the lengthy, colorful service with the billows of smoke and the ringing of bells punctuated by age-old prayers spoken in unison to a mystery beyond all means. The folks in this hardscrabble backwoods church, with its few leaded windows, would be real uncomfortable at

St. George's. For a second, he felt superior to these people in their drab clothes who came to hear the insurance salesman spew his twisted ideas of the Christian message. But then, as often happened, Smereas felt a little compassion as well. These were a literal-minded lot whose lives had always been on the margin and were even more out there nowadays in an economy and world where computers and other wonders of technology ruled.

But it didn't take long for Smereas to remember what these people, or some of them, were capable of. Just look at the gouges on Burger's feet, or the blasted shoulder or bullet-skewered head. Or the building in Oklahoma. Or the places that Cody Burke had helped destroy, especially the one with the children, the blood on the walls. No, they were scum.

"We cannot forget our place as warriors who have been given a message—a message contained right in the Bible—to confront the world of darkness and to commit ourselves to overthrowing it in order to once again establish purity and balance. We are the rightful rulers of our world, the true heirs of Israel. We follow in the footsteps of our fathers, the true Anglo-Saxon tribe of God."

Smereas recalled once again that they believed not in a God of peace, but in a Lord that demanded blood. The blood of anyone other than their own kind, which was just about everybody else when you came right down to it.

Shavers stood straight as a pole in his starched uniform and ranted on for a few more minutes. Soon enough, despite his best intentions, Smereas drifted off, his head lolling. The music from the piano brought him back.

He checked his beeper and read the short print-out message. "Call Gaylord dispatch. Message from Mumberto."

Crap, he thought. Let's get rolling.

Stretching himself alert, he saw Shavers was winding things up with a few words from another bible, *Mein Kampf,* Hitler's book, the handbook of all full-fledged hate groups. Smereas tuned out the words, not up for any more venom. He had a job to do.

CHAPTER 41
GANNON

Gannon left the Kent County International Airport lot and aimed his rented Chrysler LeBaron toward the expressway that bypassed the northern edge of Grand Rapids. From the hospital he had called his former partner in the MPs to tell him that he had arrived and they were wheeling Pham into surgery. Could Chang head over and try to talk the kid as soon as they brought him out of the OR?

"Can't drive, Gannon. Drunk driving. You get me."

The Chief thought of sending a cab for him, but then decided he needed wheels of his own. So he rode the chopper from the hospital to the airport, where he picked up the rental car. Just before he hung up, Chang said: "Come quick, Gannon. Good news for you. I tell you then."

Heavy clouds hung over Grand Rapids as he skirted the north edge of the city, remembering some of this place. Taking a quick exit off U.S.-131 on Anne Street, he rode three miles north on Coit Avenue, which brought him to the entrance to the gravel pit. This was it.

Gannon navigated the bumpy dusty road that led alongside the pit, where a huge dinosaur of a crane stood in mud, and braked to a stop next to a rusty red Geo Metro. He tried not to think of that other pit, the body by the tree, and the way he had treated his daughter.

When he turned off the ignition, he felt the muggy day suck on him through the window. He was about to get out when first one, then a second, and then a third pit bull trotted from around the side of the two-story house. Chang had always liked canines, particularly the killer kind.

Each dog carried itself with a chesty swagger, square jaws set and ready to chomp. They made a half circle in the front of the car, deceptively quiet, shoulder muscles tense, Vienna sausage tails erect. Gannon had visited Chang about three years before; that time it had been German shepherds. The Chief palmed the horn twice. He didn't have time for messing with mean mutts.

One dog looked back at the house, which had needed painting when Gannon had been here before. Now it was more bare wood than chipped paint. The other dogs glared at the intruder.

Finally, a short man in baggy gray pants, a cut-off sweatshirt, and a Chicago Cubs baseball cap came around the same side of the house from which the killer dogs had appeared. Chang paused, shielding his eyes with one hand while the other held a long, thick walking stick.

One of the pit bulls had risen up on its paws, sticking its snout into the open window, which Gannon buzzed back up with the automatic button. The animal remained where it was, menacing eyes even with the Chief's.

Chang shouted and beat the ground with the stick. The dogs instantly relaxed. One even barked what sounded like a greeting.

"Christ, Chang, I thought you were expecting me," Gannon called out the window as it slid back down with the flick of his finger.

"They got hard-on, Gannon. What's to say?" He pounded the stick and uttered a couple more commands. The trio turned and disappeared behind their master. "Two second, Gannon. Coming right back."

Gannon cracked his door and climbed out. The sky looked used up and saggy, as if it wanted to piss on the world and then go to sleep for a week. Weariness sloshed inside him. From the hospital he had tried to reach Smereas again and couldn't track him down. He had no idea what, if anything, was happening, a couple hundred miles from here.

Gannon took a few deep breaths, recalling the van emerging from

the rain and smacking them into the swamp. A close call. He wondered where his daughter was right this second. He tried to feel her, to
send his mind her way, and immediately realized he was getting desperate. Next thing he'd be looking for a psychic to tell him where she
was.

"Gannon. Want coffee?"

The Chief waved a hand at Chang, who was walking toward him
with a large gas station mug in one hand. The pit bull that had been
peering in his widow strutted at his side. "Sure, Gannon? Little woman
make some quick."

"Last I recall, Chang, little woman wasn't so little anymore."

Chang stuck a fist in his mouth to hide his giggling. He looked
back at his house, as if a little worried his fireplug of a wife, Quang,
would see. When he was finished laughing, he gave the Chief a serious once over and observed: "Big knock on the head, Gannon. You
shipshape?"

Quick images came to the Chief's mind: the two of them arm in
arm in the bar in the Bong Sen Hotel, a fairly upscale dive in Saigon,
both drunk and happy after a long week of MP duty. He remembered
the small room with the red chairs and tapestries on the walls erupting
in gunfire. The start of Tet. Both of them had dove behind the bar. "I
could use a couple aspirin, if you have them."

"No, aspirin. Bad for belly." Chang patted his gut.

Gannon shook his head. He realized he could use some breakfast,
not to mention a nap and some damned better idea where his only
child was. Not to mention Arly, the no-good prick. Gannon wanted
him dead and he wanted to be the one who did it. "Ready?"

"Sure thing," Chang replied.

"You bringing the dog?"

"Brother Ho?"

"Ho?"

"Good name, don't you think, Gannon?"

"I thought you hated communists." The dog stood between them,
hardly moving.

"Brother Ho not communist." The dog twisted its head, as if mildly
disagreeing. "He see one, he rip out their balls."

CHAPTER 42
BONES

Patchy sun threw down long rolling shadows on the cobalt blue shelves of water that heaved below. Several boats, some with sails and others powered by motors, busied themselves down there. Foamy waves churned behind many of them. Flitting above were white gulls, wings flapping as they darted in and out of the massive suspension cables of the bridge.

Leaning over the rail, the wind ruffling his hair, Michigan's governor thought for a second about Rolly Walls, his dead father buried in the concrete. Right about where he had stood ten minutes ago, where the ceremony would be held less than twenty-four hours from now. If he closed his eyes, he could imagine the pilings driven deep into the bedrock bottom of the straits. He recalled a dream he had once: hair and nails growing out of cement, deep in the water, a terrible trapped hell. A dream he had, oddly, before Preston ever told him the true story. He also remembered, as wind battered him and traffic rushed past, that long-ago memory of the baby in the mother's arms, peering at this bridge under construction. A false memory. Bullshit. Wishful thinking brought on by the years.

Franklin Bones had been over the news stories again and again, especially in preparation for the big birthday bash. None of them said much about the true nature of his father or the specifics of his death. But there had been some detail: how Rolly Walls met this woman, a gypsy of some kind in Russia or somewhere, late in World War II, brought her here, and began an itinerant life as an ironworker, sometimes bringing her along, sometimes not. Reporters tried to get more, but there wasn't much to get.

There was one grainy photo of his father, showing a swarthy cuss in a work shirt rolled up at the sleeves, standing on a pillar sticking out of the water. The photo was snapped a week or so before the accident. There was another picture as well: Rolly, his mother, and Preston outside a bar in St. Ignace. Preston had claimed he and Rolly were fine pals.

Bones wondered for a moment why he ever got into this. He should have left well enough alone; he had built a good, successful and lucrative life as a trial lawyer defending the little people, the working stiffs, in product liability and wrongful death suits. He was at the top of his league before the run for the governorship. It was a trial, in fact, a lawsuit against the state of Michigan by the family of a mental patient who died when the former governor closed the institution in which she was living, that propelled Bones into the headlines, then into politics, and then to this bridge.

But here he was now, and he couldn't duck it, on a mid morning trip to the bridge to check on progress of the plaque and to go over a few last-minute party plans with his staff. He only wished things were going as he had hoped. The teamsters were still threatening to strike, and then the other business that had kept him up all night still weighted his mood.

Not long before he'd listened to the workmen blab about the last-minute barriers they faced to bolting down the forest green historic marker that bore an etched likeness, from that same hazy news photo, of his old man. They also whined about the wind playing havoc with the small stage on which he planned to give a short speech tomorrow at about ten. Then they'd complained about the overtime glitch. As they talked, they kept glancing his way, letting him know he was to blame.

The governor had quickly grown weary of their bitching, knowing that they were getting union-scale double time for their efforts. Beyond that, he had more serious things to ponder.

Letting his assistants step in and handle last-minute arrangements, Bones had escaped down the narrow sidewalk to this quieter spot to look at the water and drink in some of the sights, plus to get some grip on it all. He let his eyes sweep the wide vista, feeling the vast span of the bridge rocking slightly under him.

The view from up here, as vehicles whizzed by on the grid roadway, was stupendous. There was a vast vitality in it, with the view of both peninsulas and the island on which his wife was waiting so he could take her and the boys to an art show at the library. The art from all over the state was part of a statewide competition Char helped sponsor. She was going to pin ribbons on the winners.

Scanning the water, the boats, the far horizons, the shores of the two halves of Michigan, the governor felt his mood shift and his chest swell with pride. He thought of the friction between the two parts of the state, the vastly urban lower and magnificently rural upper. A rift between state residents he had promised to heal. A rift symbolized, as it turned out, by the former governor closing the state's last mental institutions and turning the most tortured of souls loose onto the streets. One of them had leaped to her death from an apartment window in Detroit and Bones was eventually called in by the family to get the poor woman her due. Odd, he often thought, how it was a mental case that propelled him into this office, given the fact that his wayward gypsy mother was another one of them. For a second Bones tried to check the state of his own psyche, wondering if it was starting to wobble. But, no, he felt fairly sound, even with what was happening.

"Quite the view."

Piersma had sneaked up and nuzzled right in close. He wore a soft fabric sweatshirt with "Traverse City" woven onto the front. Blotchy spots on his cheeks showed he'd been boozing until late or hadn't stopped. The breeze messed up his hair. An hour or so ago, about eight, Jock had called from the State Police post in Mackinaw City to report on the doings from the previous night. Dim news at best. "Anything new?" asked Bones.

Piersma gazed beyond the governor. His eyes were milky and hard to read. The governor felt more tension twist inside him. Jock was the man who had helped guide so much of his run for office, and who had steered many of the reporters delving into this story of Rolly and Rochelle Walls. "They still aren't sure who the second body is," said Piersma.

"But it's tied to the first?"

"Quite possibly, yes." Piersma coughed into a fist. His eyes watered. He looked pretty well battered.

Bones shook his head, feeling the emotions boil. He thought of the late night talks with his wife, with Jock, and then with others. There was much more here than he had thought. "When the hell are they going to know who this one is?"

"Captain Parker will call as soon as they know."

"Where did this happen again?"

"Outside Gaylord."

A man driving a white car beeped his horn as he drove by on the bridge above them, bound for Mackinaw City. The governor dished up a weak smile and a wave.

Piersma didn't respond.

"How did it happen?" Bones asked.

"Shot."

"By whom?"

"No one is sure yet," Piersma mumbled.

Bones turned to face him full on. "Just what are you sure of, Jock?"

Piersma blinked, looking guilty, and shrugged. The governor wanted to reach out and throttle him. And even in thinking about it, he realized how close he was getting to a place he worked very hard to avoid. Preston had been volatile, to say the least. Frank Bones had vowed, at least in public life, to always keep his cool. He wanted to blame Piersma for this whole thing, for ever getting involved with the man who was found in the woods. But Bones knew now that it was unavoidable.

"Do you want me to go back there, sir, on scene?"

"No. We don't need reporters thinking we're too concerned."

"Even though we are?"

Bones let his head drop back and took a good look at one of the towers that stood above, holding up tons of cable. Down the other way, workers were unrolling several hundred yards of crepe paper.

They were doing it from gondolas attached by pulleys running to the tip of the hovering steel trusses. At any minute the union could put a halt to the work.

"What about the union, Jock? Any more on that?"

Piersma said he had delegated that to two aides of a former Commerce Department bigshot who knew the ins and outs of this union and its players. So far, so good. They weren't going to walk.

That, at least, was good news.

He and Piersma stood silently for a couple minutes, the wind whipping around them, the bridge swaying slightly, the water rolling below. Finally, if only by sheer willpower, Bones's mood lifted an inch or so. He forced himself away from the anxiety, got a grip and, started taking back control.

"Did you know, Jock," said Bones, pointing, "that tower is five hundred and fifty-two feet above the water?" It swelled above them, arching toward the clouds, its steel sculpted crest linking one side of the bridge with the other.

Piersma gave it a glance.

"Or that the total amount of wire in the main cables of this bridge is forty-two thousand miles long?"

His aide gave him a one-eyed once over. The blotches spread, like large measles, across his cheeks. Absolute testimony to the bender. Had he been drinking at the scene of the murders?

"How much do you think this thing weighs?" asked Bones. He had pored over the stats to include in tomorrow's speech.

"No idea, sir."

"Almost 1.1 million tons."

Piersma rubbed those cheeks, as if trying to bring health back, or at least stop the march of redness. "Heavy."

Bones turned to face the traffic, his back against the rail. He could have mentioned more, how some of the world's other great suspension bridges included the Brooklyn Bridge and the Golden Gate. He'd seen both in his time, but neither could beat this. Sure, he could have warbled on about bridges, if that would have helped. But it wouldn't. Not now. He knew that; his mood teetered back. For one thing, with this militia crap, would there be a tomorrow? He and Jock hadn't even touched on that. "You look like shit, by the way," he said to Piersma.

His PR man nodded, his eyes dull with remorse, and yet there was something else there as well. Bones tried to read it. "You know that, Jock?"

Piersma shrugged, his blasted face looking drained. The wind had shifted. Whiskey smell now leaked from his pores.

Bones recalled again his wife's story from the previous night. The man in the mall parking lot. They'd been over that, too. But maybe not enough, he sensed. "Is there more?"

Wind was everywhere. The towers seemed alive above and around them, the cables humming tautly, and the road swaying slightly. Several years ago, a woman driving a Yugo had been blown right off Big Mac and into the waters. It took weeks to find her car and body and bring them to shore. Then last year a guy had committed suicide by driving his truck off and into the water.

"Before coming here, I talked to your father," said Piersma. "He needs to talk to you."

"Now?"

"He's waiting at a bar in Mackinaw City."

Preston and his second wife lived in a condo in Charlevoix. He had not said anything about coming up sooner than tomorrow morning, although on the phone late last night he had been keenly interested in the militia threat. "I've got the art exhibit this morning, Jock."

"I already called. Your wife will give her regrets." Jock shoved his hands into the side pockets of his baggy green boater pants. A small gold chain encircled his neck.

Bones didn't like Piersma upending him. This seemed rehearsed somehow. "What the hell is going on?" The bridge bent and bobbed in the late summer wind.

"There's some things you need to know."

"About these bodies?"

"More than that."

From the shore of the Lower Peninsula, where a restored historic Colonial fort spread along the eastern base of the bridge, came a booming bark, followed by an even louder explosion. Even with the wind blowing, the loud popping sounds reverberated their way. Piersma jumped slightly

"Cannons from the fort, Jock."

Piersma nonetheless looked sorely rattled. "You see, Governor, there's a couple things you were never told."

"About what?"

Another cannon boomed from Fort Michilimackinac. The governor winced a little this time. Even so, he mustered a half-ass laugh. "We're under siege."

Piersma gave him a blank, pink-eyed look. He didn't disagree.

CHAPTER 43
ARLY

Little knives of pain cut into his ribs on both sides, making him realize how weary his body probably was. But his mind, often so ready to crackle with wild energy, felt steady. Catching his breath from the long run through the woods and up this hill, Arly tried to scan the meadow below for movement. He wished he had field glasses.

"See anything?"

"No."

"Good," replied Cody, who sat on the ground with one shoe off, rubbing a blister.

"Who was that?" Arly asked, looking for the guy in the tan uniform, the one who had shot Rat from the tower, the sneaky bastard.

"Government, who else?"

The rain had stopped for now. Clouds lumbered across the sky and birds beat their wings, throwing themselves in circles, at the far edge of the tall grass they had just run through. Still no one. On the way, Cody had said something about a Wolf Pack, the Vipers or somebody, who might be out here to help. Arly wasn't so sure they would be any good to him. Already too many outsiders were screwing with him, messing things up. His Browning .38 in his lap, Arly fingered the trigger to keep himself settled. He wasn't thinking too far ahead for the time being.

He heard paper rattle and looked to see Cody spreading a map across his knees. His head glowed softly in the muted morning light. He had set his Colt Anaconda on the ground by his side. Forefingering the wrinkled paper, he sucked his lips. Arly wanted to shoot him, stick a hot slug in that neatly shaved baby's ass of a skull. "How far?" he asked.

Cody didn't say anything for a few seconds. He studied the map so intently that he made Arly think of the eggheads he'd known in high school. So deadly serious, and so useless in the real world. Only thing, here they were in the real world, and Arly was depending on one. "Looks like ten miles."

They were heading to Gregor Pauls's barn in the woods, off a two-track near some abandoned oil wells, where Cody had done his work. He had told Arly that much as they ran. "Do we have to cross any big roads?"

"Depends on what you call big."

Arly thought he heard twigs snapping to the right, through the trees leading down the other side of the hill. Rain started to drizzle again. Somewhere a plane droned. He wondered about the police chief's daughter. He should have killed her earlier. Except he liked her, and she was supposed to tell his story. He tried to remember how much of it he had mentioned. Then they were going to kill her in the trunk, but the government goon had ended that. That government scum was doubtless out there, probably joined by others because they festered like fleas. He looked for the plane, sure it was looking for them. "We better hit it," he said.

But Cody didn't move. He sat with the map on tented knees, toes wiggling on the one exposed foot. "Why the fuck did you bring that bitch?" he asked

As if the skinhead asshole had been reading his mind. Arly didn't answer. He kept scanning the trees, his lungs still hot. He stood, feeling the weight of his weapon. The serenity was leaking out. He was agitated again: the electricity crackling, the snake angels starting to twist.

"Huh?" asked Cody.

"Shut up!"

Cody smiled and shook his head. "You ever read *Black Sunday*?"

From above, Arly got a clear view of soft blonde stubble. He knew lots of people in the movement thought Cody was the cat's ass. He was smart, no doubt about it. "Why?"

"The hero in there's my mentor."

"Your what?"

"Guy I look up to."

Arly cupped a hand over his eyes to survey the sky. They could easily have planes after them by now. Damn, he thought, it had gotten complicated, thanks as much to him as anyone else. He felt electricity jerk in his head and did his best to will it away. When he was little they thought it was a form of epilepsy, which maybe the swearing disease was to some extent. When he was a kid and it came on, he often ran away from home. His mother left him behind so much that it didn't matter.

Arly felt his neck prickle from dripping sweat. He wondered about the other woman, the one in black. Cody should have wasted her back in the cabin, but instead they left her there. For the first time, Arly wondered if he should let this go and try it again later.

"You got any of those?"

Arly turned, tired of the talk, ready to roll. "What?"

"Mentors?"

Cody looked serious. "No," Arly said.

Cody shook his head, the pale light washing out on the rounded lenses of his glasses. He was laughing. He had the skinny type of face, all bones and sharp lines. The sack with the money sat at his side, the sack that had started so much of this most recent trouble. Arly's finger found the trigger slot of his handgun and he swung the weapon down, toward the ground. He hated anyone laughing at him. It made him think of Bernie, the Jew, one of his foster dads. Or the other one, in their trailer by the bridge, that winter.

"I mean, Arly, you're a goddamned trip."

Arly didn't get it. Maybe he had missed the question. He was wondering what sort of welcome wagon would meet them at the pole barn. "What's so funny?"

Cody stood, folding the map, smile gone. "Forget it."

"No, man, what's so fucking hilarious?"

The bomb maker slowly let his face turn from the map to Arly. His eyes got small, pinpricky behind the glasses, the mouth pinched. "If I pushed you one more inch, you'd blow my ass away, wouldn't you?" Cody asked.

Arly hadn't thought about it, but it was probably true. "Now that I know where the barn is, why not?" Snakes of fire twisted behind his eyes. He was on again. No one would be able to stop him.

Cody's expression didn't change. It was hard and cruel and yet curious at the same time. Arly could see respect in it. "Arly, you can't do this without me. I've got to show you how to use the clicker, show you where I hid the truck key, the whole shooting match. That is, if you didn't already talk your ass off to that bitch so she'll have every fucking cop from here to Milwaukee waiting for us when we get there."

Arly didn't like all this talking. He was ready for more running. But first, he had to ask: "Answer one thing?"

Cody nodded.

"Are you in this, even if we end up like the big shot in your book?"

Cody looked dumb.

"Lender, your teacher."

Cody stared at him with new respect. "I didn't know you could read."

Whips of hot current flashed in his brain. Arly thought of that movie, wasn't it about bombing the Super Bowl? He thought of the knife slicing through the singer's neck and the rich warm smell of her blood. He recalled the first time he had killed—the cat that used to sleep with his mother when he wasn't there. He had shaken out lighter fluid and lit it on fire. It ran through the alley like a firecracker with fur. As for Cody, he was making fun. He thought he was so superior. Arly felt those currents snapping, like a belt on his back. He felt his gun rise and noticed Cody get scared. Arly wasn't sure what he would have done if four uniformed men carrying assorted assault weapons hadn't taken that moment to emerge from the woods.

CHAPTER 44
SMEREAS

Watching the dour-faced militia minister gape at the image of himself going at it with the high school girl from Benzonia, Smereas knew he had him. Now he had to reel him quickly and then rush out to Big Swede, where the county sheriffs had found another body about an hour ago now. Damned if he was the last to know. The county cruiser that Smereas sent had found it and made the report. No sign of Mumberto.

"Where'd you get this?" Shavers turned his head slowly, the dewlaps of flesh sagging, the eyes blurry with what looked to be shame.

They sat in the den of Shavers's house, across from the church. Smereas tried to ignore the white power decor. "Doesn't matter," he said.

Shavers returned his attention to the screen. The video was not of Hollywood quality, or anywhere near it, and the girl was eighteen. Still, there had been enough light in the motel room on the outskirts of Traverse City to capture the dirty details.

"Christ, you would use this against me?"

Smereas wondered if the preacher, still decked out in his uniform and shiny boots, was offering criticism about the level to which they would stoop to catch his kind. "Little like the pot calling the kettle black, Ozzie," he responded.

"Where did you get this?" the minister asked again.

"It wasn't Blockbuster."

They watched the preacher's white ass flop above the girl. "So, you got me having sex with a young woman." Shavers folded his arms over his chest, his face stricken, but a flicker of pride leaking into his eyes. Smereas had felt dirty watching this the first time. He felt worse now. "Wait for the finale."

Once they'd finished their afternoon bout on the bed, Shavers disappeared from view, and returned a minute or so later with a shopping bag. The girl waited on the side of the bed, wearing only a Guns 'n Roses T-shirt. She had a bumpy, pimpled face and knobby elbows. The picture wasn't great, but it showed Shavers dumping the contents of a bag on the floor at her feet. A tumble of bootlegged cigarettes, several cartons of them. The girl kicked at a couple with a bare foot.

"What the hell does this prove?"

"You see, Ozzie, we didn't set up this little film fest."

An inkling of awareness dawned. Shavers twisted all the way around in his easy chair, set in front of a window in which an old air conditioner throttled out a stale chill. His wife and three children had stayed behind for some sort of Labor Day breakfast pot luck. To the say the least, he had not been happy to make the trip down here and had only agreed when Smereas gave him a pretty good idea of what was on the video. "Who did?" he asked.

"You know I'm not going to answer that."

The preacher ran fingers over his jowly cheeks and tugged. The pathetic video had stopped. Only fuzz showed on the screen.

"Like to see it again?" asked Smereas. He was anxious to leave, but he needed Shavers.

The militia minister shook his head. "Why would they do that, send this to you?"

Shavers probably meant the rival militia faction, the one that had been on his case for a year, trying to discredit him and his fairly substantial following from presenting themselves as the vanguard of the movement. Smereas had an idea who had made the movie, although no one had owned up to it. The ATF agent had gotten it in the mail two weeks before. Since then they had located the girl and gotten a statement on her involvement. She had begged them not to tell her father, a mechanic in Benzonia, because he would kill her. She would gladly testify to how this fornicating, cigarette-stealing minister had been supplying her with cigarettes to sell on the cheap to her friends. Friends which included party stores. As for the source of the filming, Smereas had wondered if it was an old boyfriend of hers, now in one of the splinter groups.

"You know, Ozzie, you militia guys are worse than women, the way you fight among yourselves."

"That video proves nothing."

"The statement from your little friend does, though."

Shavers slumped in his seat, staring at the TV.

"Right now, I'll make only one deal," Smereas said.

Shavers was all ears, although he acted like he wasn't.

Smereas stretched his long legs in the hard-backed chair, hating the fact that he couldn't bag the bastard right then and there. Shavers could get a couple years for his involvement in the cigarette heists and sale, given he had a prior felony for possession of unlicensed firearms. But Smereas needed an inside source on what was going down now. Especially now.

"I have to know something, and pronto. If I get it, maybe we lose this flick." It made him a little sick to think the idiot could get off that easy, but info now might be more useful than him putting him away for useless time in the can.

The black and olive-green clad belly rose and fell. A hand idly fell crotchward and fingered for a testicle. Quite a minister. Smereas was sure he got his shingle for preaching through the mail.

"I have any choice?" Shavers said.

"No." The room was furnished in lower middle class, white racist chic. The poster of a saluting Nazi sympathizer hung from one wall. A painting of swastikas, representing books of the New Testament, graced another of the wood-paneled walls. The carpet was dingy; a bookcase held all of the hatemonger classics, *The Turner Diaries* among them. The place smelled like musty dog hair, and the ceiling was painted snot green.

"This has something to do with the murder last night?"

"That's partly correct."

"I know nothing about it."

Smereas was too tired and too busy to argue. "Your friend Huntz Burger was on to something and I want to know what."

"Huntz was no friend."

Smereas wiped his hands on his pants and stood. The closeness of the room, with its testimony to small minds run wild with paranoia, got him close to choking. Burger and Shavers were pals. Shavers had been to Burger's island hideout more than once. "I need my answer by this afternoon, if not sooner."

"What answer?"

"I told you. Why was Burger killed? What did he know? And who offed him?"

"TV says it was suicide."

"You may not believe this, Ozzie, but the TV had it wrong."

The preacher's eyes bugged from their sockets. "What's to keep you from using the tape against me even if I find something?" Despite the twisted ideas of his flock, most of them doubtless would draw the line at fornicating with a former parishioner's high school-aged daughter.

"Who said anything about not using it, one way or the other?"

The militia minister swallowed hard, making the wattles under his chin wag. "Why am I supposed to help you then?"

Smereas leaned down and close, getting level with those alligator eyes. "Get me what I want!"

The eyes blinked, as if in agreement.

"If you do, then we'll talk about shitcanning this movie."

CHAPTER 45
CULLY

Rain dribbled down her neck, sluicing along her shoulder blades and making her shiver. Slogging along the path, Cully felt as if she was in another world, a fog universe where nothing but her own thoughts were real.

She recalled the time in Nicaragua that she and David, by then a journalistic duo, made a grueling trip to the far southern edge of the country to interview rebel leaders who had left two days before they arrived. Besides coming up with zero at the camp, their guide got malaria, their Jeep's crankcase seized, and they had to walk thirty miles through dusty, hilly, unfamiliar terrain to a small town in which they were received with anything but pleasure.

The Indian with the long hair and smooth face had made a big mistake when he picked a couple of pain pills, some sort of high level narcotic, out of his first aid kit. Swallowing them with a chug of water from a bottle he handed her, Cully had felt halfway human within minutes. The drugs were starting to take effect, in fact, when he shouldered his pack and rifle and started off down the path for Arly and the other one. He had given her instructions on what to tell whichever cops soon arrived, but she wanted no part of that. She was going with him, if for no other reason than that she wasn't so sure, nor did he seem to be either, that the police would be first on the scene in this godawful remote place. Cully knew now that Arly had taken her right into the heart of Michigan's militia country. No place for anyone whose political ideas were anything but on the far right side of Ross Perot's.

So she had hobbled after him as he stepped onto the path the two had taken. He stopped and protested. But when it became clear she wasn't budging from her decision, he told her he couldn't slow down for her. He had to get after them. With so much wilderness out there, who knew where they would slip off to? The cops would be there soon, but the two guys who took off wouldn't be.

"If I don't keep up, gut me like a fish and leave me on the path for the fire ants," she had said.

The guy had told her they called him Softshoe. He had shaken his head and turned to begin tracking.

Now, a half hour at least into their wordless trip, Cully still felt the effect of the pills. Surprisingly, her legs continued to do as they were told. Her face ached, but so did her throat, chest, and the ankle she had twisted when trying to escape Arly in the graveyard.

Softshoe, which seemed like a silly name, moved gracefully ahead of her. He stopped every so often to examine footprints in the soft earth, touch twigs, sniff the air, do his Native American outdoorsy thing. Even in her state, Cully saw that he had a strong, wiry body, sort of like David's. But right off, she knew this one was no talker, no philosophizer on the wanton ways of the world. His bearing, every part of him, hinted at well-contained reserve. He wore a brown and forest green uniform, property of the state of Michigan.

He held up a hand and crouched. Rain pelted them. She wore his poncho. The drugs gave everything a hazy yellow glow. Wrapped in the arms of pharmaceutical comfort, she heard birds chattering, water hitting leaves, a soft breeze in branches. "What?" she asked without thinking.

Softshoe looked over his shoulder at her. She noticed the high planes of his cheekbones. She sure as shit hoped he had more of those pills in his pack. He stuck a finger to his lips.

"Sorry," she replied, giggling.

When his brow wrinkled, she knew she was too close to the edge.

All of what had brought her here, coupled with the dope, worked to make her giddy with something beyond fear.

Cully waited. She turned her face to the sky and gazed hard through intertwined trees for clouds. As if wanting to see God. Or maybe her dad. Because he was looking for her. The Indian had told her so.

"This Arly, what's he up to?"

Cully had thought mum was the word. But he must have made some type of woodsman's calculation that told him it was OK to talk.

"He's planning to blow up the Mackinac Bridge."

Softshoe stared at her, as if waiting for the punch line. When he got none, he stood and said softly: "They went through this meadow, probably up that hill. If they're up there now, we're sitting ducks."

"So we go back."

"We go around." Sweat and rain glossed his face. He had a thin nose, a wide firm mouth, and mahogany skin. He looked to be about thirty-five.

"How far is that?"

"Not too far. Through there." He pointed at a bramble of berry bushes. "It's open. Bears take this way."

"Excuse me, bears?"

He nodded, very serious.

"Any in there now?" She touched her cheek, feeling the bump and crusty blood. Once again, rage surged. Arly, in that dark place, standing over her with his gun, looking so awful. But as far as she could tell, he hadn't raped her. It was him hovering and then hitting her that made her seethe.

"No bears." He reached and parted a few branches, beckoning her to start down the tunnel of vegetation.

"If you find any bears, are you going to shoot them, like you did that guy?" she asked, feeling suddenly and inexplicably like a child.

He made a slight motion with his head, urging her on, making no answer.

"You know you saved my life?"

"We need to go."

Aware that the drugs were fading, she wiped drizzle from her brow and stepped into the place where the bears sometimes went.

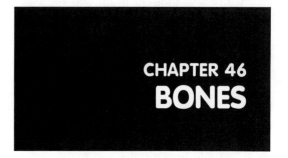

CHAPTER 46
BONES

Preston Bones eyed down the long tip of the cue stick, lining up the striped four ball and calling for the left side pocket. He took his time, hovering there, seeming to give the game his full attention. But his adopted son, the governor, knew better. Pool was one of the diversions Preston used when mulling over important matters.

When he and Piersma had entered the Key Hole Bar in Mackinaw City a few minutes before, the governor immediately spotted his adopted dad in the far corner, circling the green felt, his mane of silver hair aglow in the light flung down by the fake Tiffany lamp. Most likely by choice, Preston Bones was alone, stalking his prey, in this case the hard round balls spread piecemeal atop the slate.

"Jock," Preston said, still scrutinizing the ball, arm extended, cue stick ready.

Piersma leaned against a wooden pillar, his flushed face looking like it had been steamrollered on I-75 and pumped back to life with steroids. It took a couple seconds for him to snap to attention.

"Buy a Coke for Franklin and Manhattan for me," said Preston.

"Make mine a highball," said the governor.

Preston's eyes rose. His son rarely drank liquor during the day.

Getting the picture that he was wanted out of the way for a time, Piersma wiped a hand over his mouth and shuffled off to the bar.

Frank took a seat in a booth next to the pool table. He watched Piersma disappear in a haze of dim smoke in the other room. They had this separate space to themselves, also no doubt by design. The governor watched as the man who had served as his lifelong cheerleader took one last bead on the ball, slid back the stick and gave the cue ball a dead center smack. The four did exactly as predicted. Preston pressed his thin lips together in mild satisfaction.

Folding his hands in front of himself on the Formica table, Michigan's top executive felt as if he was one of those balls about ready to be popped.

"Those union boys still kicking up their heels, Frank?" Preston wondered.

"Jock says they won't walk."

Preston shot him a glance. "Let's hope."

It was funny how diminished Frank felt in the presence of Preston Bones. Always had. And at the same time, he experienced a strong connection to his adoptive dad. He recalled, as a youth, being summoned to Preston's office, entering what seemed like a church, and nearly having to bow before learning what Preston wanted. That had always left Frank feeling a confusing mixture of awe and discomfort.

At the time the Mackinac Bridge went up, Preston was field supervisor for a highway construction company in Manistee. Not long after the bridge opened, he took over the same firm. A few years later he landed a big job in the Michigan Department of Transportation. Eventually that led to him becoming director. In that time, he had eyes on even higher offices but never made it. When Frank had the chance, Preston's blood lust for being near the seat of political power kicked back into high gear. He loved making decisions that affected others.

"You really ought to take up pool, Frank," he said. "It's a helluva way to beat stress."

The governor nodded, aware that a few of the drinkers in the other room kept looking their way. The boozers had been a little startled to see him come in, but they didn't say anything. Preston probably read them some sort of riot act upon arrival. Orchestration of events, along with advice-giving, was his forte. "I've got running to help me relax," he said.

Preston spotted his quarry on the pool table and leaned down to give it a once over. He tilted his long, square, handsome face this way and that, as if mentally measuring the ball's circumference. "Seems to me, son, jogging plays havoc on the knees."

"So far, so good," he replied. His tone carried a hint of sarcasm that he hoped would nudge Preston to get to his point.

Acknowledging the slight petulance in his boy's voice, Preston started the process of taking aim. He wore a lightweight tan jacket of some linen fabric, a button-down collar blue shirt, and comfortable looking jeans. His skin was deeply tanned, softly lined, and his eyes were sharp brown and full of brass-knuckle humor. He had always carried himself like a proud but testy lion, and it was no different in the middle part of his seventh decade.

"I'm anxious to know why I'm here," said the governor.

Preston didn't reply. His attention narrowed on the next shot. "Six ball, side pocket." Almost immediately, the stick pumped back and forward. The ball skittered right, caught the edge of the bumper and spun away from its target. Preston sniffed angrily and shot his adopted son another look, keen, probing and unconsciously arrogant.

"I mean it, Dad."

Preston stood upright, idly chalking the tip of his cue. His hair was piled layer upon layer on his head. An aging but well preserved satyr. There was hardly a time Frank could remember that his adopted father wasn't womanizing. Even with pressing business at hand while his most recent wife shopped along the tourist strip outside, Preston had the air of an animal on the prowl. His gaze drifted off, checking the ample backside of the waitress serving drinks to a table in the other room.

"I know your day is full," he said.

"So, why don't you sit so we can cut through the crap." The governor surprised himself. He rarely spoke to Preston this way.

Preston's gaze registered his son's lousy attitude. He laid the stick on the table and rubbed his hands together. "Jock probably needs to be in on this," he said.

The governor was not used to waiting for anyone anymore. A

perk of the job. But there he was, alone in the booth, as Preston strode away into the smoky bar to retrieve Piersma.

In the few moments he had with himself, Frank Bones felt anxiety swell inside him, like a sail taking on air in churning seas. Piersma didn't say much on their way here, but he didn't have to. His adopted father rarely put in surprise appearances unless something important had to be faced.

When Preston reappeared, Jock showed up right behind. But then a stocky man with a mustache was with them as well. The governor recognized him as a higher-up in the State Police, a man with whom he had dealt on a couple matters in the past. As he remembered it, both times had to do with delicate matters on what the police liked to call potential incidents of terrorism.

The governor stood, extending his hand to the cop. As they shook, he tried to do what he had been able to do hundreds, probably thousands of times in the past, in college, in law school, in courtrooms, when vying for office, and now as governor. He balled an imaginary fist up inside of himself. He forced shut the door on his anxiety. He squared his shoulders, just as you do while playing handball, and got ready to do some downright brass tacks dealing.

Whatever they wanted to dump his way, he had every intention of handling. Come hell or high water, he was ready for it.

Ho Chi Minh, the mutt's full name, sat between Chang and Gannon as they drove across the Grand River and took West River Drive north. They stopped at the Golden Arches for a bag of food for the Chief and Ho. Chang, skinny as a hammer handle, sucked on another cigarette, not hungry.

As Gannon ate, some hope sputtered to life. "This monk, who is he?"

The dog nosed in the bag, ready for another Egg McMuffin. Chang tapped his palm on its head and Ho immediately stopped rooting. "Uncle," he said.

"Whose uncle?"

Chang sucked in smoke and let it swirl out his nose. His compact body took up little space in the car. Ho Chi Minh was much more of a seat hog. "You see," said Chang.

They pulled in front of the Lin Son Buddhist Temple, a blocky former schoolhouse in the industrial district north of Grand Rapids. Graffiti had been scrawled across the Vietnamese characters on the sign. "Even here?" he wondered aloud.

Chang looked at him curiously.

"The graffiti."

"Teenagers, Gannon, big jerks. Hate the Vietnamese." The Chief's friend sniffed out a last curl of smoke. "Let's see monk now."

"Are you sure he'll be able to help?"

Chang smiled, patting Ho's sloping, simian-eyed head. "He very smart."

Three men stood outside the front door smoking, wearing billowy white shirts and equally baggy slacks. "Want me to go with you?"

"Big Bang, Little Chang, sure thing, Gannon."

That's what they'd been known as on the streets of Saigon. A team. In and out of the bars, down the cramped alleys, along the narrow, busy streets. Kicking butt, it was true. Chang, even then, was a tough little mother.

The three of them, Ho in the middle, walked up to the temple. Chang spoke Vietnamese to the men. The dog's body rippled with tense awareness. One man shoved at the pit bull with his leg, a dumb move. Ho grabbed the cuff of the shiny gray sharkskin pant leg and tore off a swatch.

The men on the porch went nuts, arguing and gesturing, eyes bulging. Ho stood serenely, fabric in his mouth.

Chang slipped inside, jerking his head for Gannon to follow. By some unspoken command, Ho remained behind, hunkering down, as if hoping to a catch a few rays of the clouded sun.

Lotus-positioned on the bare floor of a back room, the middle-aged monk had huge empty eyes and a bald head. He wore saffron-colored robes; bare feet showed under the hem. He held a blunt, cloth-tipped stick in his hand. His hand moved, touching a brass gong suspended next to him, sending out a soft, thunking sound.

Behind the monk stood a three-tiered table filled with flowers, a few pictures of Buddhist saints, and bowls of fruit. Gannon was impressed with the monk's straight-backed stature, his body immobile except for the slight hand movement to reach the gong.

When they had come in, an older man had been on the floor talking to the monk. The man, introduced as Kahn, ignored them for a minute or so as he and the monk conferred. Then Chang stepped over and sat between them. A murderous glint in his eye, Kahn stopped jawboning. Chang jabbered at the monk. The monk said a few words back. After that Chang and Kahn rose simultaneously, as if pulled by invisible strings, nodded in unison at the monk and altar, and left through the back door.

The monk hit the gong again. His hairless skull ran in one smooth slope from the crown of his head to the bridge of his eyes. Gannon recalled the crazy-quilt country that had been Vietnam, a land filled with millions of people in constant motion, wiry, talkative peasant folks who fought hard for whichever side they found themselves on. The only ones who seemed to walk and talk at a different pace were these holy men in saffron robes. Gannon could never figure them. He'd been called to the scene in Saigon after a pair of them doused their bodies with gas and lit a match in protest of the war. He and Chang showed up as flames were flickering over two charred and twisted forms. Their arms and legs had stood out like the burned branches of a tree.

The monk laid the blunt stick in his lap. For a moment he let his eyes roll and engage Gannon's, as if he had read the Chief's mind and wanted to acknowledge that it was true—the spirit was stronger, even in a suicide of flames, than any body of bloody politics.

Gannon nodded, feeling his brow pinch with pain, and tried to smile. He wondered if this monk had a daughter. He was tempted to ask, hoping he understood a little English.

But the monk was done trying to make contact. He once again set his attention on some eternal spot in front of him.

Soon afterward the door opened. Kahn came first, eyes on the floor. Chang, bringing up the rear, gave Gannon a big, nicotine-strained grin and a thumbs up over Kahn's shoulder.

The Saigon Market wasn't very busy on a humid Sunday afternoon in August. Muggy heat, combined with the smell of spices and stale cigarette smoke, reminded Gannon of times nearly thirty years before in a city by the same name of this grocery on a busy street in Grand Rapids.

As soon as he stepped in behind Chang and Ho, Gannon felt as if they had moved into a time warp. Cramped aisles, bins of rice, piles of leafy vegetables, and that tinny clanging music native to Vietnam moved him with a great nostalgic force. He had to pause a moment in the doorway, his sweat-soaked shirt plastered to his chest. He felt memories rush toward him, but he shoved them aside as best he could. Gannon was already spending too much time in this city and wasting precious brain power by waxing on about bygone war days. He had told Chang, only half joking, that he would wring his neck if this stop proved useless.

A stocky, dark-haired man behind the counter by the cash register glowered as Chang headed his way, his mouth already in overdrive, yapping out Vietnamese words. Ho Chi trotted at his master's side.

The guy listened for a couple seconds to Chang's chatter before starting his own. More shotgunning of the lips, stuttering out a reply. Or an argument. Or maybe a demand that Chang, his mutt, and his white devil partner hit the road.

But the pair of them were just warming up. They went at it with a vengeance, heads bent close, for a couple minutes. Even Ho drifted off and sat on the floor by a rack of taped music.

Gannon noticed a couple, bent and hobbling, pushing a cart down a far aisle. Just beyond that opened a small archway into what appeared to be a storage area. The door behind him bumped open. He stepped aside to let a large woman in a traditional long-hemmed Vietnamese dress come in. She nodded at him and disappeared down the nearest aisle.

On the drive back into the city, Chang had told him they needed to find someone named Tong. Reluctantly, Kahn had told Chang that this Tong just got out of prison in southern Michigan and worked at his uncle's grocery store.

"Gannon?" Chang was finally done chattering.

Gannon made his way to the counter, noticing the cashier's slug eyes move to the spot underneath the Chief's shirt where he kept his gun in a quick release hip holster.

"He say Tong on vacation. In Florida or somewhere."

"Violating his probation?"

The man behind the counter had oily skin around a large flat nose. He didn't answer.

"He say he give Tong a message." Chang rolled his eyes.

"Does this guy know Pham, in the hospital?"

More jabbering. The place was an oven. Sweat leaked from

Gannon's temples, dribbling behind his ears. "He say, what about Pham?"

"Tell him he's nearly dead. One of Tong's friends put him there."

Chang translated. When he was done, the guy stood there, arms crossed over his white shirt. He shook his head and shrugged. He had turned into a wall. Gannon leaned in and slammed his palms on the counter. "Tell him I'm looking for my daughter!"

The guy didn't flinch. He was ice and stone. But somewhere in there, just as Chang seemed about ready to start doing something more than talking, those black eyes shifted, ever so slightly to the left, toward that archway. The storeroom.

Gannon looked and caught movement. A flash, then gone.

Before any human could do much reacting, Ho Chi was up and at 'em. The dog skittered across the bumpy tile floor, shot through the doorway, and vanished. Meanwhile, Chang had grabbed the guy's shirt and pulled him across the counter. Gannon ignored them and went after the dog.

The back room was dingy, dusty, and piled with sacks of rice, plus boxes of what looked like electronic parts. The store was clearly a front for more than Southeast Asian foodstuffs and music.

Around a small tower of boxes that said Panasonic on the sides he ran. He made the corner with a little wobbling of his right knee and noticed an open back door that led into a fenced alley.

Barking orders to his dog, Chang brought up the rear.

Outside, Gannon stopped and smiled. Fifteen or so feet down the alley, about halfway up the tall fencing, hung a young Vietnamese man with long hair, tight jeans, and a dog's mouth firmly clasping one of his dangling feet.

Ho Chi's blunt tail wagged like a hot dog cooking on a grill. The kid was trying to pull loose, his face a study in stricken lines.

"Bit his ass," called Chang.

"No," said Gannon. "Foot."

Chang stood next to him and pointed. "Check it out. Got his butt first."

Sure enough, the Chief spotted ripped cloth, a whitish circle of flesh and, shortly thereafter, a slick drooling of blood pouring from Tong's rear.

CHAPTER 48
ARLY

Rain swept through the trees in a steady drizzle. It poured from leaves, rivering along the sides of the path. A fairly warm, cleansing rain, if cleansing was what you wanted. In Arly's case, it was just one more damned bother.

Plodding down the far side of the hill, he made himself ignore everything but the effort of marching. One boot in front of the other. Let the toy soldiers protect the hill and keep the enemies, and they were mounting, at bay. He felt like his body was swarming, crawling with the arms of dead people.

Cody, leading the way, hadn't said a word. The coward had wanted to leave this part to Arly. Served him right, having to leave the geezer's car and take them to the barn on foot.

Gregor sloshed next to Arly. He was a big man, full of meaty, muscled fat, wearing a dripping jungle hat, fatigues, and paratrooper boots. He carried a Mossberg Model 500 pump shotgun, the camo series, and a cartridge belt holding bullets was strapped around his large gut. Even in the rain, he was smoking. Gregor owned the barn where Cody had been building the bomb. Right off, Arly knew this

Frankenstein-looking guy and Cody were enemies, which was another bother.

"You know," Gregor said, "you won't be pulling this off now that the whole fuckin' world is interested."

Arly glared at him.

"Are you still going with it?" asked Gregor.

Rain splashed from every direction, drenching him good. But he didn't care. He was beyond comfortable. He tried to quiet his mind and make it a pinprick, focusing on the goal: that bridge crossing the huge blue water. He forgot about the singer and her throat, Gannon and her smart mouth, the chunks of skull that broke apart from the skinny guy's head when they got ambushed by the trunk of the car. Arly didn't allow himself to think about who was out there, who might be after them, about Cody or Gregor or their feud. He was a walking battering ram.

"I mean, the woods will be crawling with federales soon enough, if they aren't already."

Arly picked up his pace to get away from him. So many people were involved; it was all so out of hand.

"Hey, man. I'm on your side."

Cody was thirty yards ahead, sliding along without looking back.

"Truly, I am," said the guy. "Screw Cody."

Arly stopped. He didn't want their fighting to make this harder. "What's your problem?"

"Man, he left Rita."

"Who's she?"

"Long black hair. Great body."

"So what?"

The guy looked upset, almost ready to cry. For such a large lout, he was a sissy. Arly wanted to tell him to shut the fuck up and get them to the farm. But before he could speak, the woods behind them erupted with the sharp crackle of gunfire. It came from that hill where three militia had stationed themselves and vowed to protect the rear.

Arly and Gregor spun and dropped to the ground. Gregor aimed his shotgun toward the hill, but all they could see were trees. More shots popped like a string of firecrackers.

The hill was about a half mile away. After five minutes of tense silence, Gregor stood. "We better haul ass, buddy."

For a second, Arly felt rooted to the ground. He remembered the first foster home. He got left there by his mother's friends, the ones who got money for him. This first foster father owned a dimestore. He made Arly stick his hands on the radiator in the bedroom after he caught him stealing the five out of his wallet. Arly could still feel his palms burning. He couldn't recall why he had wanted the money, but he sure as hell couldn't forget the way his skin smelled after a few minutes on that searing metal. He had scars from that too. Fire and heat had never been his friends.

Then there was that man's skinny daughter. She made Arly smell her underwear and then sniff her bush. What there was of it, since she was only thirteen. Every time she made him stick his nose there, he thought of the radiator. They made him leave that foster home after he bit her, just hauled off and took a big bloody chunk out of her crotch. Still had it in his mouth when she went wailing for her mom. Her mom, also a piece of work.

"Hey?"

Gregor stood above him, water dripping from his nose. "You zoning out, man?"

When the mother came in, he had swallowed that meaty meal, pubics and all. The dad bashed him with his fist when he got called in from the garage. Arly suddenly felt untouchable. In a flash his doubts ebbed, his anger restored. "Who's fighting back there?" he asked.

"Who cares? Let's go." Gregor edged him around and gave him a quick push. Arly was surprised. He didn't mind being shoved at all. Maybe that's what he needed. Together, they started jogging through the mud to the farm.

CHAPTER 49
SOFTSHOE

He knew it was stupid to be thinking about the Little Big Horn at a time like this. A Chippewa and not a Sioux, Softshoe transformed himself into one of those fierce Plains warriors. It was a kind of self-hypnotism when the walls caved in and the floor disappeared. His father sent him once to spend the summer with some Sioux in South Dakota. They were good people, though they liked to drink, which itself wasn't too bad. The woman, Martha Manyfeet, had been there the day they killed Custer, the yellow-haired bastard. She was old and wrinkled and farted every ten seconds. Plus, she didn't like to tell the story; she had related it too many times already.

Still, one night around the campfire outside their mobile home in the Black Hills, she told it to him. In broken English, words came out thick from her mouth. She talked about trapping the soldiers, about the heat, the dust, Custer screaming to his men, the braves shooting and cutting them up. She had been watching with other women on a hill not too far from the slaughter. The last stand that ironically put the final nails in the coffin of the Indians in the West.

Softshoe tried to remember how the shot that wounded him came. The woman, Cully, had been there.

"Hello?"

Softshoe opened his eyes.

"Why don't you take one of these?"

She held out the vial of the narcotic. Three pills left.

He shook his head.

"Why not?"

The woman was soaking wet. The rain had washed the blood from her face but a huge knot swelled under one eye. He thought of the bear and of Cully sliding through that tunnel. His manitou, now gone. He was the one who might need saving. "Don't need them," he said.

"Doesn't it hurt?"

Softshoe looked at his belly, on the right side, at the clot of sticky dark purple blood. It didn't hurt, which surprised him. He had hardly even felt it. More like a wasp sting, a quick, hot pang. As for the pill, it wouldn't a good idea. He had told her to stuff gauze inside his shirt, slowing the blood. He hadn't been able to tell how bad it was. "I'm a drunk," he told her.

She had helped him into this scooped-out cavity in the ground, packed with leaves, a comfortable enough den, after it happened. "What's that got to do with anything?"

Softshoe closed his eyes, saw the young men milling, dabbing on paint, like players before a big game. They joked quietly with one another, pretending not to be scared shitless. The movies, he knew, got it wrong. Indians crapped their pants, too, sometimes before the big showdown. Seemed a book he read somewhere said that. He knew, as he lay there, that it wouldn't be wise to move much right now. He had to wait this out. The bleeding didn't seem too bad.

"Are you going to die on me?" she asked.

In the distance he saw the cloud of dust, the sign of the soldiers. They were out there, ready for massacre, with the long-haired general at their lead. "No," he said, "I don't plan to die just yet."

They had been following the men at a distance when it happened. The shots, coming out of nowhere, surprised him. He had been so keen on what was around them. Besides, he didn't think they, who-ever they were, would actually shoot. Why he thought that, he wasn't sure. But there it was. Sounds slapping out of the trees ahead. He had plunged down, taking her with him, before he knew he'd been hit.

"Then what are we going to do?"

He looked at her again. But he was thinking about himself. He was wondering if he'd been one lucky redskin. Maybe the bullet had cut through without nipping any important organs. Even so, as much as he wanted to move, to get up and test himself, he couldn't. Not to mention the blood. "Do?" he asked.

Softshoe tried to pick up sounds beyond their tiny bunker but only heard rain. He knew they should go, take the deer trail back to the truck and get help. He noticed the steady way she gazed at him, even with the bruised face. "We have to stop them, you know," she said.

"Who?"

"You saw them."

"Too late," he answered. They were whispering. In fact, they had been all along. Why didn't he realize that until now?

"But Arly's going to blow up the bridge."

Softshoe tremendously doubted it. Not with all that had happened. Chances were they'd close it down and test its every nook and cranny for bombs. He was sure this area would be swarming, too, with cops and maybe even National Guard soon. No, this Arly was down the drain. The thing right now was to get her safe and find him some help. Problem was, how to best do that? And then he wondered: Did anyone else know what this Arly was planning? Maybe not. Maybe she had to get out to tell them. Maybe it wasn't as simple as he hoped. "Can you find your way back to my truck?" he asked.

She held her arms close to her, shivering slightly. "I can't leave you."

"Sure you can." She wiped water from her face. He was surprised by her emotions. Very well balanced, she was. Or seemed to be, given what she had been through. "Are you married?" he added.

"What?"

"Are you?"

"Why in the world ask now?" she said.

"Curious."

He was pleased by her small smile. "Are you proposing to me?"

"I'm only wondering," said Softshoe.

"Then, no," she said, sounding suddenly mad, which was just like a woman. "Not any more."

"Divorced?"

"My husband died." Her eyes moved away from him again, to the trees, to the distance of her past, which was likely full of shadows.

"Take my gun," he said. "Follow the path a hundred yards directly behind you and it will take you out to a small road. Walk that for a quarter mile and you're at a trailhead. There's a rustic campground. Someone should be staying there. Ask for help."

"And if it's vacant?"

"Follow the trail on the south side of the camp and it will lead to Clark Road. Flag down the first car." He didn't want her on the path they had walked; he feared the militia jerks would be using it.

He had many questions. How was she kidnapped? Exactly why did this man want to destroy the bridge? Softshoe knew all about rage. But he couldn't ever bring himself to kill innocents just to get his own way. He had to clear his mind of questions, though. He needed to get her out of here; it wasn't safe. He wasn't sure how safe she would be on the trail, either, but he didn't have the strength to go with her. Plus, she had to tell them about the bridge. Even as he thought this, his mind drifted back to the Big Horn. After a while he felt someone rouse him. He opened his eyes.

The woman was shaking her head. Cully, he recalled. That was her name. He should call her that. "And just leave you here for the rats?"

Had she been talking to him all along? He envisioned the blood draining at his side. Maybe the bullet had nicked his liver. "Not many rats in this wilderness. Mice, though."

He closed his eyes, felt himself drawn to the moments before the battle. He had a horse, a chestnut mare, with rippling flanks. He carried a spear with many feathers and wore a pelt of beaver around his loins. Or was it mink, or buffalo? He couldn't make up his mind.

"Even if I go, how do we find this place again?"

"Tell them section thirty-three, one mile west of the left fork of the Grass River."

"That's enough for someone to know?"

"Yes." He wanted to be alone for a little while, to rebuild himself, to assess the real damage. He didn't want her near. He didn't want her to see him when the pain really did start. He realized her best bet now was to go alone. Leave him behind. He wished he had whiskey.

"Can you walk at all?"

He shook his head. "I think the bleeding's stopped for now." A lie. He could feel it pooling.

She touched the mound of gauze packed around the wound, as if stuffing a hole. "Will they come looking for you?"

"Please, Cully, go."

She nodded, the rainfall making her face smooth and glossy. A baptism, he thought. "Are you?" she asked. When he didn't answer, she added: "Married?"

"I told you I'm a drunk. Smart women don't live with drunks."

"But you don't drink any more."

"How do you know?"

She shrugged, eyeing his wound. "Won't it get infected?"

"Least of my worries."

She asked for the directions again. He gave them to her and told her to take the gun. But she refused. She said it would slow her down. Then she sat and waited, not wanting to leave. He told her three more times to get.

Finally, before she stood to leave, she set the pill bottle in his hands. "You might need them." Then she touched his forehead, as if checking for his temperature. When he opened his eyes again, even though he didn't know they were closed, she was gone.

CHAPTER 50
BONES

The amenities of office sometimes bothered him. Governor Franklin Bones knew he didn't need a limo to drive him everywhere. He certainly didn't need the Department of Commerce Lear jet to fly him most places, or the State Police helicopter to haul him to and from cities for meetings. Frequently he shunned those perks when he could, partly to show his constituents that he wasn't going to exploit the privileges of his office, as had his plump Republican predecessor. He was a man for his people, a rolled-up shirtsleeves sort of leader. There was an even more practical reason, too: the rabid media, even though he was still their darling, would use it to tear him a new bunghole as soon as his honeymoon with them was over.

But he was glad now to be seated in the sleek forty-foot U.S. Coast Guard cutter as it carried them across the swelling surface of the straits for a return trip to Mackinac Island. It had been there at the dock waiting, commandeered by Piersma, after the dismal meeting in the bar.

As they boarded, he had told the captain of the boat to take the long way back. Maybe putter around Green Island, the small chunk of land west of the bridge. He needed time to sort through the mess dumped on him by Preston, the cop, and Piersma.

Across the padded rear seat from him, his hair whipped into a frenzy by the wind, good old Jock looked like he'd swallowed a rotten squid. His face was tinged purple, his cheeks puffed out, his eyes swimming with sickness. He wore a V-neck sweater tied loosely around his neck, an Izod noose. He was turned partly away, staring at the water, his stomach moving quickly in and out, as if struggling for air. Bones wanted to dump him overboard. He was a Judas in preppie garb. "Christ, Jock, are you having a heart attack?" the governor asked.

Piersma, his hands cupped in his crotch, turned and shook his head. "Hamburger isn't sitting right."

The four Manhattans you sucked down at the bar probably didn't help either, the governor thought. "If you need to get sick, point it the other way."

Piersma attempted a smile; it came out as a defeated wince. The governor stared at him, as if daring him to puke, then asked over the muted roar of the wind: "What am I to make of what I heard back there?"

Piersma gave him a helpless shrug. "Shit, I wish I'd known."

First Preston and then the state cop with the mustache filled him in. Bones had listened carefully with shock and mounting anger. Goddamnit, he couldn't believe it. They talked with such clipped, antiseptic authority in the back room of that dive. Jock had listened in, ripping up his cocktail napkin. Christ almighty. Bones had done his best to take it deadpan, to let them know this was also something he could handle. But now he wasn't so sure.

He glanced again at Piersma. "You know, Jock," he said, "I feel like the three of you stuck me in the belly with a harpoon."

Piersma made a sick gesture with his mouth. "Frank, I didn't know about this. Shit, think about the press."

Bones sank back into himself for several minutes, realizing he wasn't going to have much time to stew over this. Preston had made that abundantly clear. Here is the bucket of blood. Deal with it.

"Why the fuck didn't you tell me about this crazy bastard before?" he asked, the words blustering out, so unlike him.

"I told you, Frank. Until last night, I didn't put two and two together."

"A man accosts my wife in a mall parking lot and you brush it off!" Bones was surprised by the fine floating feel of his mounting rage.

"How was I to know who that was?"

"This asshole might be my brother!"

"I had no idea, Frank."

Bones took in a deep breath, his head cocked at the sky, filled with heavy gray clouds. He couldn't believe it. Betrayal, but more: how stupid could he be to let this get by him? To have believed Preston's line of bullshit, hook, line and sinker all these years.

Last night the state cop must have told Piersma that Bones's might-be brother, the militia man named Arly, was the suspect in the murders of a man and woman down near Port Huron, and had taken another woman hostage.

Piersma had recognized the name from the investigation after the mall incident and told the cop, Parker, about it. From there a few late night calls were made, one eventually to the nut's parole officer in Mt. Clemens. The parole officer filled them in on prison scuttlebutt about this Arly who had spouted off a couple times about being related to the governor. Of course no one believed him. Bones had no idea why Piersma failed to gather this little bit of personal info before, the lazy cow.

During the conversation in the bar, Preston started out sure of himself, but lost steam as he went. He swirled the amber liquid in his glass, feigning disinterest and looking guilty as hell. Frank had wanted him to give an explanation, this man who used to wait in his study in his silk bathrobe for Frank to come in and be quizzed about one thing or another. This man who drove Frank to be who he was. This man who had lied to him all these years. Or, he seemed to be saying, simply left out a few things. Like a brother, three years older.

"Frank, I think it's all taken care of."

Water sprayed the governor's face. He wanted to reach out and slap Piersma. "What?"

"The media doesn't need to know shit about this."

"That's the least of my worries," Frank replied, although it wasn't.

To the right, hovering over them in a sweeping mass of steel and cable, spread the Mackinac Bridge. From below, the bridge looked even more massive, its foundations sunk in thousands of feet of pre-historic stone. He had planned long and hard for tomorrow. He knew that some important part of who he was, even who he would be as governor, was connected to that structure and to the body buried in there. To the ironworker who, had he lived, would no doubt have given him far less than he received from Preston Bones. To a man who fathered two sons, not one. How could that part get so buried? If Preston had denied it in the bar, he would have believed him.

Preston had not even told Frank about Rolly Walls until he was in his teens, after his adoptive mother, the swimmer, got very sick and nearly died and Frank came across, in her dresser, a birth certificate bearing his name and that of different parents. Preston said it was true; he was adopted. Preston said he had known Rolly and that Rolly's wife gave her son up willingly, just before leaving for New York to basically drink herself to death. A dark-haired gypsy woman, from Romania or someplace.

At no time did Preston ever mention a brother. Even the few press clippings he had seen of the death of Rolly Walls had not said any-thing about another offspring. At the bar, he had wondered if this Arly was an impostor and his rantings in prison were only that. No one had responded to this question. As if saying, no, Arly was his blood. Sitting across from Preston, Frank had said, "Why now? If this guy says we're related, why is it only coming up now?"

Again, dead ass silence from the peanut gallery.

Bones turned back, noticing that the cutter was sliding through the house-sized breakwater rocks into the harbor at Mackinac Island. Already? he thought. Too soon. He wasn't ready to come back.

"Looks like we're in for it, sir."

For a second the governor's eyes ranged across the huge gleam-ing face of the Grand Hotel, a bright white building stationed proudly up there on a forested hill, overlooking the business district below. It was the setting of a movie starring the Superman guy who was now in a wheelchair, paralyzed by a fall from a horse. A handsome man, once in his prime, now a cripple. For all intents and purposes, the star's glory days were behind him. Bones ran a hand over his hair, thinking momentarily about the woman who once went down on him in the back of a pleasure boat as it entered this very harbor. But what was Piersma talking about?

Then he saw.

On the dock where they would land was a small army of reporters. Mini cams gave them away. "How'd they get here?" the governor asked stupidly. Of course, by boat, or plane. Some of the stations in Detroit had their own.

"They'll want to know about tomorrow." Piersma was shaking off his cobwebs, resurfacing his hair with a comb, putting on his media mug. "What should I tell them, Frank?"

Bones sat up straighter, taking one last look at the bridge, its sturdy arms carrying itself over miles of choppy water. Did they know about his psychotic brother? Everyone so far had assured him not. That aside, he was going to have to deal with questions about this militia uprising, perhaps that was too strong a word. And then, the road union. "I'll do the talking."

"Is that wise?"

"You know Jock, I don't even need to have anyone hold my dick when I take a piss these days. Isn't that surprising?"

Piersma shook his head, his face blasted by the wind, bleary eyes hardly registering the governor's words. "Whatever you say. I just don't want this to blow up in our faces."

The governor stood, feeling the wind scrape through his hair. For the briefest second, a strange feeling registered deep in him. At first, he wasn't sure what it was. Then he did. It felt as it he had been raped. Buggered good. By his own adopted father. He suddenly felt very weak and sat down. A brother, flesh and blood of his own. Why hadn't someone told him until now?

"Jock, tell the Coast Guard to back the hell out of here. Go around to the other side. I don't want to talk to them now."

CHAPTER 51
RALPH

Tons of sand stretched before them, a desert dotted with hikers. Literature said they called this place Sleeping Bear because native legend said the humps of dirt, from the air, looked like bears in bed. Ralph Williams didn't know. He was tired. He hadn't been to bed since the call at 4 A.M. from Jock Piersma.

Joy wore sandals, white shorts with cuffs, a large, dark blue T-shirt decorated with a pink tulip on the front, and a safari hat with its brim bent back. She hadn't been to sleep either. In fact since he had found her in the kitchen, she hadn't slept at all. Ralph asked her if she was OK.

"What?" she asked blankly.

"Something bugging you?"

His wife had a round, mushy face with wonderfully shaped lips, eyes that hinted at things that went on in naughty movies, and a lush bosom his hands loved to roam. Boys at the station said he was one of those skinny guys obsessed with chubby women. He couldn't disagree. Ralph loved all of that flesh, both to touch and to view.

"Nothing," she replied.

"Sure?"

"Yes." Snapping at him now.

Ralph admired his wife's spunk, the way she had pushed her way into local politics after she retired from the accounting firm. He had watched with interest and growing respect as Joy battled onto the county board, took on causes, ran and lost for the Michigan House, and now was a bigwig in the state Democratic machine. He supported her all the way. "Piersma's call?" he tried.

Joy swung a hand behind her, as if shooing him away.

Piersma didn't cut any slack when he called. He wanted to know right off from Ralph if he or Joy knew any damned thing about the boy governor having a lost brother from before, from the mother whose husband died on the bridge.

Ralph had cupped the phone and sketched for his wife what Piersma wanted to know. She shoved a hand in the air and told her husband not to tell him a thing. "Joy doesn't know either," he had said.

"Christ!"

"Why, Jock? What's going on?"

Piersma filled him in on part of the picture. The cops were thinking this brother, if there really was one, was on the loose causing trouble, maybe killing, in the Pigeon River area. This sounded crazy, and yet it didn't to Ralph, who knew his wife was far more entangled in Preston's affairs from way back when than she ever let on. "If there is such a person, why would he show up now?" Ralph asked.

Jock didn't answer. "Ralph, put Joy on."

As he turned to call her, she was standing right there and took the phone. By the quick look she gave him, he knew he'd better back out of hearing range. But now he wished he hadn't. Ever since, and that was hours ago, his wife had been in a terrible state. There was something eating at her, and whatever it was, its teeth were still biting.

It took a half hour or so to navigate the swales of sand, edged and scarred by the wind. Ralph stuck his hands in his pockets and shoved on for the ledge of the dune, not too far ahead and lined with people.

He arrived before Joy and let his lungs catch up on breathing while he eyeballed the big lake spread far and wide a thousand or so feet down the dune. Banks of gray-white clouds hunkered in the sky. Patches of blue, higher up, showed through here and there. Boats appeared as white skimming dots far out on the rolling water. More dune trodders specked the beach below. The less hardy stood on the top, taking in the sights in the happy knowledge that they didn't have to climb back up.

"I've got a lot on my mind," Joy said.

Ralph let his expression soften and gave her a quick smile as she stopped next to him. "Sorry if I talked too much to Piersma last night," he said.

She shook her head, as if disagreeing.

"I mean, why call us anyhow?"

"Because," she said, staring at the sky, "I think he finally wants to get at the truth."

He eyed her carefully. "About a brother, you mean?"

Joy laid a hand on his wrist. When he gave her a quick glance, she said, "There's more to this than I ever told you."

He pretended to examine the horizon, where a freighter was in slow motion. He figured by her tone that she was about to lay something heavy on him. He remembered how for a few years, in their early marriage, she worked long nights in Preston's office, the road construction firm. He wondered was she going to admit to some hanky panky? "Like what?" he asked, not wanting to know.

His wife sighed hard. Then she sat slowly on the sand and tucked her legs close to her. Her safari hat shadowed her face.

Ralph thought of staying on his feet. Take this like a man. But he plopped down too, on a spot next to her. He knelt on one knee, watching the way the wind skidded across the water.

Joy eased onto her back, crushing her hat, face turned to the clouds. "Ralph, I was afraid something like this might happen."

"What?"

"That this so-called brother would show up."

"So-called?" He felt relief. This didn't sound like infidelity. Why he would think that about her after all these years wasn't right anyway, he thought.

But then, as she started to talk, he realized that his wife had been holding back quite a bit for a long time. And she hadn't told him a thing about it. Until now.

CHAPTER 52
SMEREAS

Standing on the water tower at Big Swede Lake as more cops than he cared to count milled and poked below, Smereas thought of the woman who had died a couple hours before in the cabin. On the floor of the cottage, Rita Morris, a.k.a. Rita Fonger, a.k.a. Susan Foster, had looked hard, sexy, and yet vaguely innocent. He had seen dead women before, and some had that look. Maybe it was death that did it. Maybe not.

Hands on the railing, Smereas found it surprising how well he was taking this latest debacle. He shook his head at the stupidity of mankind, especially its law enforcement end. Why had the local sheriff's deputy, the first on the scene, found it necessary to shoot without much warning? Sure, he said Rita Morris had a weapon and was brandishing it his way. And quite possibly she would have used it. But maybe not. More than that, why the deputy felt he had to waltz down to the cabin and knock on the door without reinforcements wasn't clear. Common sense and clear-cut police procedures should have told him to wait for backup, to get a much better sense of the scene before tromping into it. But there you had it; she shot at him and he shot back. He got winged in the upper right arm and was now at the hospital in Alpena.

Smereas watched as a group of cops circled the blanketed body on the road down there. Yet another corpse, this one male. Winston Groom, also known as Rat. Hardly twenty-four hours before, Smereas had been eating breakfast at Denny's with him. Now he'd been shot through the skull with what looked like a 30.06. Shells from the slugs that killed him had been found by a couple of crime scene techs who rolled in from Gaylord. Beyond the body below, over the rim of trees, the agent could see movement by the cabin. State Police, getting their hands dirty, checking on Rita.

"Shit," he said to himself. Had Mumberto been up here? The DNR officer's rifle, also a 30.06, had been stashed behind the seat of his truck before he drove away from the hunting lodge last night. With all the commotion, no one had gone searching for him yet. There were fears, probably grounded, that other militia lurked nearby. Everyone was going carefully.

"Agent Smereas?"

He turned and looked down at the fresh-faced young man from some nearby police department standing on the ground. "Captain Parker wants to talk to you, sir, down at the cabin."

The State Police terrorist expert. His sidekick pain in the ass. When had he blown in? "Tell him the view is much nicer from up here."

The officer scowled, not sure how to react.

"I'll be right down," Smereas said, and watched the cop go. He knew Parker would want to pick his brain about the dead woman, shot through the chest and probably still sprawled on the floor next to an easy chair. Smereas recognized her from pictures. An accomplice and off-and-on lover of Cody Burke, a.k.a. Bob Williams, a.k.a. Larry Davidson, the motor city bomber. A member of no known hate group, but a sympathizer with them all. A prize catch; the one he had been wanting to snare. Smereas had heard reports that Burke had been seen in the area of late. With Rita deader than a doorknob, Cody couldn't be too far behind. And that was what frustrated him. If she had been taken alive, she might have led them to Burke. As it was now, the questions were swarming like yellow jackets at a barbecue.

Parker appeared below, hands on his hips. "You find anything interesting up there?" he called up.

"Deep thoughts," the ATF agent replied.

Parker made like he hadn't heard. "We need to talk."

"Has anyone found Don Mumberto's truck yet?"

"Who?"

Smereas didn't care to fill the state cop in on his midnight plan to keep the cabin under watch in case something happened. "DNR officer who probably shot that man down there under the blanket."

Parker turned away and looked at the body. Meanwhile, a tall officer in a crisp blue and gray State Police uniform appeared through an opening in the bushes leading down to the cabin. He gestured Parker over, next to the stiff in the bag, and they started to talk, low-key at first and then more heatedly, but still too muted for Smereas to hear.

Smereas thought he recognized the other cop. It was Henry Brink, second in command of the State Police and fairly new on the job. Come to get his two cents worth of whatever was happening. Pretty soon they were going to have to sell tickets.

Figuring he had a little reprieve, Smereas walked to the other side of the tower and gazed down toward Big Swede Lake. Some complicated violence was unfurling here. Where had Mumberto gone? For a second he wondered if the Indian was in on this somehow. He had a drinking problem; maybe that got him in deeper than he planned. But Smereas didn't think so. It had to be something else.

"Damned fix," Smereas said. His eyes detected a sparkle far away through the trees. Probably the sun on leaves. He dug in his jacket pocket for his field glasses and trained them into the woods.

Through a clearcut area like a bald spot on a man's head, he thought he saw something other than Mother Nature. It looked like a glossy forest green fender, darker than the vegetation. Part of a truck. A state vehicle.

Maybe it was Mumberto's truck. The longer he looked, the more certain he became.

CHAPTER 53
CULLY

One foot in front of the other, Cully plodded forward, up the path, wondering if she was going in the right direction, cursing the pills for her fuzzy brain, not feeling anywhere near the fear and anxiety that she probably should. She knew she should get somewhere safe fast, but her mind kept playing tricks on her, dragging her in different directions. It took effort to pull back from that trance into the present she wanted to escape. Things hurt so much.

Birds exploded out of the trees ahead of her, snapping her out of her lethargy and notching her heart rate up a few beats. She checked ahead of her, then over her shoulder. Arly was still on the loose.

Again, movement. Twigs crackled to her left. She peered through the trees and shafts of sun falling in smoky beam through branches. Sunshine paths to heaven, David had once called them. Cully made her mind go sharp, probably her twentieth comeback in as many hours. She took in the trees, trunks straight as Marines on parade. A pretty place. She felt its peace even as she knew it was a battleground.

As she crested the hill, she ran smack into a trio of uniformed men. At first they seemed as surprised as she; one had just finished peeing. But then another, this one taller, shoved a gun in her direction. "Who the hell are you?" he demanded.

By the snarl on their grubby faces, the tattoos on one of the men's arms, the mismatched quality of their uniforms, their mean eyes, and their cigarettes, Cully immediately took them for militia. Militia wasn't the way to describe, them, she thought. Cowardly Mighty Mouse Commandos was more like it. Real soldiers didn't smoke in the field.

"Huh?" the guy prodded her.

The one who had been pissing played with himself as he finished zipping up. None of them looked older than thirty. They had the same dumb cockiness she had seen in rebels in Central America, gang members in South Philly, union toughs in Newark. Misfit idiots on whom she had done stories. Mostly men, angry, sometimes justifiably so, that they weren't getting their piece of the pudding. And they were going to kick someone's ass about it.

"You deaf and dumb?" asked the pissing guy, shouldering his weapon.

"I'm looking for Arly," she said, rolling the dice, coming up with a plan.

Their faces, as if washed by a medicated rag, took on different expressions. They didn't soften, exactly, but got more curious, less belligerent. This was what she had hoped. Unless she lied and bought herself some time, they would waste her then and there.

"Arly who?" asked the pisser. He had a round red face with a lump under one eye and another in the middle of his forehead. Fatty tumors.

"The one who's going to bomb the bridge."

This took them aback, stunned them for a second. They exchanged looks, as if she'd hit the jackpot. Lumpy spoke first, unshouldering his rifle and shifting it toward her face. "Who're you?"

"He'll tell you."

"What if we don't know Arly from a can of bean farts?" said another, this one with reddish hair under a black baseball cap decorated with a bulldog on the front. He stood between the other two.

All three of them smiled maliciously. But the one farthest from her wasn't as merry as the others. His gaze got serious, taking a measure of her. "Look," she said, "I need to talk to him."

"Why?"

She caught a whiff of them, stale sweat, fumes of beer. The third one, the guy who hadn't talked, had a foot-long flashlight tucked into his field coat. She noticed some sort of stenciling on his knuckles. Probably a missive to his mother. Hi Ma, fuck you. "He's going to want to know this," Cully said.

"Suppose we're looking for him too?" said Lumpy.

"Then that's four of us."

He spat, wiped under his nose, and gave his raunchy companions a hard-to-read look. "You his bitch?"

Cully swallowed hard. She'd been through so much that she hardly cared what happened next. Except that she was tired of being pushed around like some dime store stooge. "Are you going to take me to him or not, asshole?"

The lumpy-faced man stepped forward. The guy with the flashlight grabbed his arm. "Cool it, Milo."

Milo whirled and shoved him back. Flashlight swung up with the barrel of the handgun he'd been holding. It clipped Milo's chin with a thud and made spittle fly. Milo wobbled back, rocking on the heels of his scuffed boots.

"Pardon his manners, miss."

"You broke my fucking jaw, man."

"Your bones are too stupid to break."

Milo shook his head and spat again.

Flashlight let his eyes roll from her head to her feet and back. He shook his head, as if he didn't like what he saw. He had blonde hair, fine features, and a compact body. They all stood on the path.

Finally Flashlight said, "Follow me," turned, and started walking. Cully checked the others. Milo was touching his jaw, giving her a murderous glower.

Red Hair shrugged and gave her a silly grin.

As she fell in behind Flashlight, he looked over his shoulder. "I'm Perry, by the way."

Cully grunted, not giving anything up.

"I probably ought to mention that far as I can tell, Arly's not going to be in any mood for anyone pretending to be his friend."

Hearing the footsteps of the pair a few feet behind her, Cully retorted: "Who said anything about being his friend?"

CHAPTER 54
BONES

The wall-size wooden map of Michigan, crafted out of white pine, hung in the director's office in the Mackinac Bridge Authority building, at the foot of Big Mac. The hand-carved map showed towns and topography from the Indiana border to the shores of Lake Superior. The governor paused for a few seconds, swiveling in his chair, to stare at it. The Great Lakes state. His state, his turf.

He was aware of the activity outside the office, phones ringing, the movement of bodies, of his people. He let his eyes roam across the carved wood to the area south of where he was sitting, Pigeon River, just below the tip of Michigan's Lower Peninsula mitten. A place where oil companies had been fighting for years to grab the rights to drill. The previous governor had let them; Bones was stopping it, environmentalist that he was.

His eyes burning from weariness, Bones tried to piece together all that had happened. A man supplying the State Police with information on a supposed bombing had apparently been killed. The man's partner was dead, killed perhaps by a DNR conservation officer, who was missing. A woman allegedly connected to a bomb maker had been shot by officers storming the cottage in which she was holed up.

And probably related, a state trooper was seriously injured in a head-on collision with a Vietnamese man who was fleeing the police.

To top it off, the militia nut who accosted his wife in the mall parking lot was supposed to be his damned brother. And this lout might or might not be on the loose somewhere. Throw in some screwy information about a police chief from down near Port Huron who was looking for his daughter, who may have been kidnapped by the militia goon, and you had a hell of a mixed-up mess. Oh yes, the Teamsters were striking. State road workers were already setting up picket lines for the morning. Bones had ordered the State Police to send them home, but the police said they couldn't do that without a court order prohibiting them from gathering. Bones knew that, but said the safety of the state was in question. Or was it? Someone had called the Attorney General at his cottage in Munising to find out.

The governor rubbed his temples, turning from the map to the desk he had been using for going on five hours now. Once they had pulled away from the shore of Mackinac Island, in plain sight of the press, he had the Coast Guard take them here to the St. Ignace side of the bridge, to the Authority building, where he set up a kind of emergency headquarters.

Two hours into the deal, after hearing reports come in, he had axed the party for tomorrow. Too much trouble. It would be a political nightmare if anything, and he meant anything, happened while it was going on. It actually surprised him how easily that decision had come to him.

A group of aides and cops now bustled outside the room. Of course the media was camped outside with huge microwave dishes, an array of shoulder cams, and a million questions they wanted to nail into him at the first chance. This thing was going to get national attention now that he had acknowledged it by canceling the bridge ceremony. He had sent Piersma out to make that announcement. He knew they were itching to talk to him. But Jock assured him that no one had asked a thing that connected the governor to one of the militia. He wondered if they would be able to keep that cat in the hat for long. Or forever. If Piersma was good at anything, it was obscuring the truth.

The phone startled him. He snatched it up quickly.

"Frank?" It was Preston. "We're going to need to talk, son."

"I thought we already did."

"There's more."

"What more?"

A long pause. "Maybe now isn't the right time," Preston said.

Bones felt anger flare. Not good. "We've got a lot happening right now."

"Frank?"

He waited.

"Canceling the party was probably wise."

"Call me tomorrow," Bones said and hung up.

What more could there be, he wondered.

Bones could still feel his heart thumping a minute or so later when Piersma emerged from a group sipping coffee by the vending machines in a far corner of the front office. Jock had been pacing the place at breakneck speed all afternoon and into the evening.

"Frank," he said, pausing in the doorway.

The governor folded his hands, hoping he looked calm.

"I'm afraid the news hounds are going to break down the door if we don't give them an update soon."

"What's to tell them?"

"That we've finally got a handle on it?"

"That would be a lie."

The phone on the desk rang again. He winced, hoping it wasn't Preston. He didn't answer and it forwarded to another room.

"As far as I can tell, the worst of it is over," said Piersma.

"Is it?"

"Unless you've got other information."

No, he didn't.

"I mean, let's blow some smoke up their ass. But we've got to tell them something," Piersma said.

Bones nodded to himself, figuring that he probably did need to make an appearance. He should assure the people of Michigan that he had everything under control. But what the hell more did Preston have to say? He should have asked, but he just didn't have the energy for more family revelations.

The governor told Piersma to gather a few of the folks out there for a meeting. He and Jock would put together strategy for a quick press briefing, then call it quits for the night. The State Police commandant had been on the phone with Bones less than a half hour before, informing him that things were more or less in hand. Any threats to the Mackinac area were squelched. Bones had asked what sort of threats. The commandant told the governor not to worry.

The phone rang next to him. Again. His hand went to it. "Let's have the meeting, Jock."

Piersma rolled his neck as he left, an aging warlock in silly golfer clothes. The governor stared at the ringing phone a second before picking it up. "Hello," he barked.

"Frank?"

A tentative but familiar voice. "Joy?"

"Yes."

It was Joy Williams, probably the only woman he had ever trusted, more or less. She had called a couple times earlier; he hadn't gotten back to her. "Sorry I didn't call," he said. "We've been up to our neck in it."

Piersma was rounding up the troops. A few already had started his way, busy little beavers in their wilted summer clothes. Political clones on whom he'd come to rely. He wiped a hand over his face and vaguely wondered how out of place his hair was. He was afraid he looked like a rag doll whose stuffing had come loose.

"Look, Frank. I know it's a terrible time for this."

He caught a tone in her voice, a sharp hint of more trouble. He held a hand up to Peter Francis, a communications specialist in the Department of Consumer and Industry Affairs, who was first in the door. Pete stopped short and backed out, bumping into Kyle Pettibone, a something or another in the DNR. "What is it, Joy?" He turned in the chair, facing the wooden map, displayed over him like a harsh reminder of the geography he had yet to cover.

"Is there any way we can talk?"

"Isn't that what we're doing?"

"In person, if possible."

"That would be pretty hard right now. We're just about . . . "

If he wasn't mistaken, there was snuffling on the other end, as if she was crying. "We're just outside, Ralph and I. He knows the whole story now and he said I need to tell you, right away if possible."

The governor's attention again went to Pigeon River, which showed as bumpy whorls in the grainy wood, a fairly blank, forested area, the hotbed of his undoing. "What story . . . you're where?"

"We just pulled in outside. I didn't want to come in. I'm not sure I could get through all of these media trucks anyway."

Bones waited, still as a skeleton ready to have dirt dropped on it in the grave. "What story, Joy?"

A pause. Some static. Another voice got on. It was her husband. "Governor, it's about your goddamned father, Preston. Joy knows the whole rotten thing. You better hear her out before the newspapers pick it up."

"Pick up what?"

"What he did, Frank, and never told a soul."

CHAPTER 55
SMEREAS

Herb Smereas hung up the phone in the kitchen of the farmhouse out on the far edge of nowhere. Staring at the receiver a moment, he wondered if he should have told Cable Gannon the whole story. But Smereas had no time to think about that. He had a drunk militia nut on his hands. Gregor Pauls was swilling beer in the other room. Smereas heard him crashing around, mumbling to himself, cursing over death of the woman, Rita.

Looking around the kitchen, Smereas saw piles of dirty plates in the sink, empty boxes, soup cans, and lunch meat packages on the counter. The remains of some sort of gathering. He went to the refrigerator and opened the door. Not much in there. A couple apples, wrapped-up chicken, not cooked, and some jars of pickles. Beer. A jug of milk. On a hunch, he checked the freezer. In the back, a square wrapped in tinfoil. Probably pot. More evidence to nail Pauls in case he needed it.

"That's not mine."

The ATF agent turned slowly to see Gregor filling the doorway. He was a massive man, his hairy chest showing under a camo jacket. He had a round raw face, eyes alert even as he slugged on his beer.

"Than whose is it?"

"I told you I'll answer what I can about Burke."

Ozzie Shavers, the good philandering militia preacher, had shown up a couple hours ago back at Big Swede. A group of volunteer firefighters and local police, accompanied by two county tracking dogs, had gone into the forest a while before that, looking for Mumberto and whoever else had disappeared last night. Smereas was thinking of joining the search himself when Shavers arrived to tell him, as they huddled off to the side, that he had a name for him: Gregor Pauls, a militia sympathizer who lived on eighty acres southeast of Onaway. Pauls, he said, would know some things. Smereas had wanted to bring a couple of fellow agents with him, but they were busy helping the feds go over the cabin where the dead woman was found. Anyhow, Shavers said, Gregor wouldn't enjoy too much company.

So the ATF agent decided to take a chance. Things weren't proceeding in any important direction at Big Swede, as far as he could tell. He had a strong suspicion that a ball was rolling downhill and he'd better do what he could to chase it before it reached the bottom. He told his boss Gambrini, now on the scene, where he was headed, gave specific directions, and said to send help if he wasn't back in an hour or so. But his boss wasn't happy about any more freelancing. He told Smereas to stay where he was. They had argued; Smereas finally won Gambrini over, as long as two county patrol units went along as backup.

With Shavers along for introductions, and the county cruisers not far behind, he had driven here. The county guys were parked a mile down the road. Smereas hoped no one saw them. As for Pauls, Smereas had hardly made headway before he got beeped by Gannon.

"You want a beer?" asked his host.

Smereas leaned against the fridge. Shavers was parked in a ratty looking easy chair in the living room, looking nervous, his eyes fluttering around the room. Pauls had been friendly when they arrived, as if he had been waiting for them.

"Who was here earlier?" Smereas asked.

Gregor Pauls dumped more beer down his throat and wiped his mouth with the back of a hammy forearm decorated with the tattoo of a flaming cross. "Remember when you busted me?"

"Four years ago. You and two friends were selling stolen guns, mostly assault weapons and some North American Black Widows, out of the trunk of a yellow Chevy Malibu behind the hobby shop in Onaway. You spent twelve months in prison." Which was nowhere near long enough, Smereas thought.

"Good memory."

"Hard to forget your pretty face."

Gregor scowled. Smereas glanced at the sink and saw a wad of curly hair, a broken hand-held mirror on the counter, some shaving cream, a razor clotted with chunks of black.

"Who was at your party today?" he asked Pauls.

On the way in, Smereas had seen the shadowy hulk of a pole barn out back. He had wondered then, and again now, if they were alone.

Gregor tipped back his bottle. His large square of a face, a sketch of long blunt lines, turned toward Smereas. "Who was it nuked Rita?"

"How do you know she's dead?"

"Heard it on the radio."

"I'm not going to tell you that."

"You're sure it was her?" A mask of pain, the tough edges melting, showed itself to Smereas.

"How well did you know her?"

"She was a friend."

"What was she involved in?" He checked his watch; after eight. To some extent, he wondered if the worst was over. Maybe this Arly was now deep underground. But if so, where?

Gregor turned into the kitchen, ape arms at his sides. "That fuckin' Burke left her there." It was a statement, offered almost calmly but with obvious emotion.

"Was Burke here?" Smereas asked.

Gregor swirled and slammed a fist into the wall by the phone. Shavers blinked and came to life in the other room. A crack appeared as Gregor swung back and gave the plaster another blast. "Cocksucker!" he said, sticking bloody knuckles in his mouth.

Shavers stood, hands in his pockets. He looked ill at ease.

Smereas stepped to the sink, ignoring the mat of hair, and peered out the window down a path to the building out back. A light, throwing down purple-tinted illumination, showed from above a doorway.

He was going to have call in troops and search this place. "Who else was with him?"

"Fleck."

"Who?"

Gregor licked the blood away, his brow wedged with deep lines. "Crazy asshole from Detroit or somewhere."

"Arly Fleck?"

Gregor nodded, just barely, sticking the mashed hand under an arm. At some point he'd ditched his beer bottle. The wall was webbed with cracks.

"Where are they now?"

Shavers came in and stood in the doorway, lazy-eyed. Gregor Pauls turned to the preacher. "Why don't you get the hell out of here!"

The minister's eyes opened, wondering ovals.

"I mean it, man."

Shavers checked over Gregor's shoulder at Smereas, who told him to wait in the car. Once he'd shuffled out, looking hurt, Gregor gestured with his bloody hand at the window over the sink filled with dishes. "Cody and Arly are gone now."

"Where?" The ATF agent's mind was whirling ahead, making plans for this place, hoping they had enough here to build a case. Then, he wondered: did Pauls waste them, out of twisted jealousy? Sure enough, he needed help.

Smereas went to the phone, dialed the dispatcher, and told her to send in the county boys. Gregor watched, hand in his mouth. "We have your permission to search this place?"

Pauls didn't say yes, but he didn't say no. Maybe it was dawning on him what he was admitting to. "Why don't I show you something first?" he said.

"What?"

Gregor shook his head toward the window, outside, toward the pole barn.

Outside, in a moonlit moment that he wished he could have enjoyed more, Herb Smereas tapped his lumbering guide on the shoulder and asked him what was inside. Gregor had insisted that if he was showing anyone anything, Smereas had to go in first. Who knew why? But here they were, and the ATF agent didn't like it.

"I'm showing you where he made it."

Two sharp cracks sounded in the distance. Both men froze. The sound came from off to the south. A rifle, maybe. They waited, but no more shots came. Gannon looked back at the house. He had told Shavers to stand in the road and wave in the cruisers.

"Made what?" asked Smereas.

Pauls scratched the back of his neck. "The bomb."

The night held the soft music of insects. The sky was spread with thousands of stars, their flickering vastness hanging in all directions. A patch of bushes, their branches covered with a skin of whitish dust that glowed dully in the dark, stood to his left. Go carefully, Smereas told himself. "Where's this bomb now?"

"He took it."

"Fleck?"

Pauls didn't reply.

"Where's he going with it?"

"I think the Mackinac Bridge," Pauls answered.

"You're shitting me," Smereas said.

"Nope."

The earth smelled wet and rich; the trees stood around them in tall silent bunches. Smereas had seen a jacket on Arly a while back. He was a marginal player, but all of them were marginal, hovering on the edge, ready to stroll in at any time and add their particular brand of hatred to the mess. Then, there was what Cable Gannon had said. A killing down south; Arly Fleck kidnapping his daughter. And now a bomb.

"Who's driving it, Fleck or Burke?"

"Fleck."

Smereas thought of the hair again. Fleck must have changed his appearance. He also realized how lucky it was that Pauls was letting his heart, strange as it was, overrule his loyalties.

"Was there a girl with him?"

"I didn't see none."

"When'd he leave?"

"Hour ago, maybe."

"Where's Burke?"

Gregor's eyes flipped to the left as someone emerged from the glowing bushes. "Ta da," said the slender, shiny-headed shape.

Eggshell glasses. Sharp features even in the dim light. Well, he had his answer. This one Smereas knew about. He had never met him in person but had heard all about him. He had been the subject of a couple of seminars. The one who left the woman Rita behind. It was odd how Smereas catalogued all of this before having the time to reach into his coat for his gun.

But Cody Burke warned him off with his own weapon. Looked like a Remington Model 700. Long barrel. Twenty-four inches if he remembered right. Satin wood finish, probably weighing in at ten pounds. Again, his mind worked, swerving for information. He left his hands in the open.

"Inside the barn, both of you," said Burke.

Pauls made a low sound in his throat. "You know they killed Rita?"

Burke didn't react, kept his eyes steady.

"You know that?"

"Shut up."

"You shithead."

Burke waved the barrel, warning Pauls and Smereas not to get frisky.

"What the hell are you up to, Burke?" Smereas said.

Burke stepped closer and poked the barrel into the ATF agent's gut, probing for the diaphragm, the easy spot between the ribs. "We've met?" But he stepped back again as Pauls inched closer, his large hands held aloft. "What'd you come back for?" demanded Pauls.

"Told you, zip it."

"I know who you are," said Smereas.

Starlight shone on the bombmaker's skinhead dome and in the moons of his glasses. He had a blade-thing of a face, a pointy jaw. "You invite him here, Gregor?"

"I thought you ran off."

"I came back."

"Where's Fleck?" asked Smereas, feeling wind stir through tree branches.

Without lowering his rifle, Burke checked a watch on his wrist. "Arly's busy right now."

"Busy where?"

"I think our tall stupid friend here just told you."

"That's a big structure to destroy," said Smereas.

"Not if you know what you're doing."

"You know," said Smereas, "I've seen some of your work."

"Oh yeah?"

"You're a disgusting coward." He thought of the bloody walls, a child's foot in the bushes out front.

"I can kill you as soon out here as anywhere." Burke had his legs splayed, his body anchored, weapon ready.

Smereas tried to see those eyes behind the glasses. Maybe peer into the twisted mind of the bomb-making whore. "It's just like you, isn't it? Be far away when things blow."

"Move! Into the barn!"

"That bridge will be swarming with cops. Your man will never get through."

"Not my problem now, pops."

"Gregor?" said Smereas.

The big man faced Burke, his chest taking in large gulps of breath. Smereas wanted to enlist his help, in any way he could. "Tell him more about how Rita ended up after he left her."

Burke stepped in and jammed the barrel under the agent's jaw.

Smereas felt a little loosening in his bowels, but not enough to matter. Let this jerk pull the trigger. It struck him how much he despised this man, and others like him. Especially those who cobbled up the explosives and headed for hills before they did their dirty business. Chickenshit is what he was.

"You know, Mr. Smartass, I don't even know your name," Burke said.

Besides the children in the mobile home, Burke's bombs had killed a family, a black preacher and his wife and three children in Memphis; one of his creations ripped apart a car in a garage in Cedar Rapids, Iowa, maiming a civil rights lawyer forever; another explosive tore a huge hole in the side of a school in Arkansas while a janitor and his son swept the floor. Both were now deaf; the son couldn't walk. There was more. And now this. Cody Burke was top on the ATF's hit list. Scum that had to be swept down the drain. With mild resentment, Smereas realized how stupid he'd been to go it alone.

"You got a name, asshole?" asked Burke.

Pauls stepped closer.

The bald bomb maker shoved hard on the rifle, slamming the steel into Smereas' throat, making him gag and stumble. At the same time, lights flashed; maybe from his pain, but he was sure it came from behind. The front yard, the county.

Then Smereas felt something hard on his shoulder and again on the side of his head. Burke battering him. He spun to the right, trying to grab hold with his feet, suddenly thinking of his family in Lansing, probably fast asleep now. Without him, how would they fare?

If he wasn't mistaken, lights swirled in in front of him. In his mind, as he fell, Smereas planned it. How he would roll onto his side, plant his foot and leap back toward Burke, hoping to forearm the rifle away and then drive into him. From there, who knew? Maybe Gregor would join in. Then again, maybe Gregor was in on this. Whatever the truth, Smereas knew he was as good as dead, even if help had arrived.

But then there was a roar, angry words blasting from Pauls, a surge of fierce, mad energy. And then movement, a flailing of limbs, tumbling on the ground. Smereas knew he had a bloody lump on his head and possibly a huge knot on his shoulder. As best he could, he got to his knees. He was about to join the fray when Pauls suddenly stood and reared up and back, away from Burke sprawled by the bushes.

Before Smereas could say a word, Pauls had aimed down the barrel at Burke and fired as he tried to twist into the refuge of the undergrowth. Once again, sound filled the night.

Pounding through the yard came three deputies.

CHAPTER 56
CULLY

She zeroed in on the story now. No more wishy-washy back and forth debating, trying to escape her strange fate. Cully was locked in, fusing her mind with Arly's. Arly, now clean-shaven, the skin nicked and lightly scabbed, behind the wheel of a Good Humor ice cream truck.

There they were, rolling north the last few miles to the bridge in one of those white-painted vehicles that used to ease through her neighborhood when she was a kid. She remembered bells ringing, calling everyone out to buy fudge bars, toasted almond cakes, rainbow-colored blowpops. A happy time, back then, as they danced around the Good Humor man. But she wasn't doing any dancing now. She was training all of her senses on this violent crackpot in a white uniform.

Arly's new face was pressed close to the wheel, his white outfit a counterpart to the dark night surrounding them. Stuffed next to him was some sort of heavy vest.

"It's in the *Turner Diaries*," he was saying, referring to some manifesto of book that he had already mentioned he all but memorized.

"What is?" She was turned his way. Her door was welded shut. Arly had told her that and made her scoot across from the driver's side when she and her half-baked soldier escorts came across him on the two-track.

They had been walking maybe a half hour when he showed up, rounding a bend in this truck and guiding it up a small hill from a farmhouse below. She gathered that the three soldiers, such as they were, had been guarding the place. Arly had gotten out of the truck, this moving monstrosity, and glared at her. As if jealous, angry she had decided to go to the dance with someone else. Christ, what a cracked mind.

"The Organization," he said.

"Who's that?"

He shot her a glance. His face was strangely vulnerable without the rangy beard. He had oiled his hair and slicked it back. His lips were full, the nose large and fleshy, the cheeks rounded and soft-looking. Still the anger and the clear signs of derangement were there, in the twitching eyelids and neck, in the way his mouth was set. "The ones who do what has to happen," he answered and returned his eyes to the road. "Except, they don't have it either."

They were on F-105, a county two-lane taking them to his destination. Somehow, when he spoke of his plans before, she had dismissed them. She figured it wouldn't happen, that he was just raging in the dark. But here he was. Here she was. In the rolling bomb. He had told her that much.

On the edge of her awareness, lurking there, were images of that horror in Oklahoma City, the mayhem brought on by miserable jackoffs with a cause. It wouldn't take much for those mental pictures, the children being carried out of the day care center, to flip her out. Cause her to lose it, take her back to her fear. And that wouldn't be good. She had to maintain her wits, bludgeoned and embattled as they were. That was key now. They had gotten her this far. She felt as if she had slipped through a doorway, maybe down that bear's berry bush tunnel, and couldn't turn back. She had said a quick prayer for the Indian and was now on her way to wherever.

"What has to happen?" Cully said. She had no pad, no pen, just her brain to keep score. She would write this. She would tell the world Arly's tale of revenge. It was her duty. Busted and bruised as she was, she had risen to the occasion. Here he was to splash blood on the bridge. However it happened, she wanted to live to tell the tale.

The road spun ahead in almost total darkness, the yellow lines swishing underneath. The truck felt sturdy. From the inside, it looked normal. She suspected the explosives were packed where ice cream sandwiches and red, white and blue rocket ship popsicles had once been placed. "Why does this have to happen?" she asked again.

Arly gripped the wheel; she saw his hands tense. "Why did you come after me?"

"I had to tell those shits for brains something."

"They won't let you go easy."

"Meaning what?"

"You saw them."

True. Back on the two-track, once Arly had stopped, they got into an argument. The one called Milo especially. They demanded to know who Cully was and what she was doing out here. Arly had seemed oddly protective of her. He had her climb in and talked them down. Or mostly so. Because when he drove off, they weren't looking mollified. Well, so what? She would deal with that later. If there was a later. Then there was Arly smashing her face on that path and whatever else he'd done. But stop, she told herself. Don't think about it now.

"I mean, you are not truly going to do this?" she said.

Arly blew out his cheeks. The head-jerking was growing more intense. Not a good sign. She didn't want him to blow again. It was just hard to believe his cock and bull about the governor being his brother or whatever it was. And that it was his dad buried in there. And that his dad was killed, that it wasn't an accident. And that some piddly bombing was going to somehow make things better. In his talk, Arly complained that his bomb wasn't as strong as he wanted, that the guy who made it screwed up some, but then he was hard to follow, as always, so maybe she didn't get that straight.

"Why did you want to know?" he asked again.

"You can't blow up the bridge. You'll kill innocent people."

He mumbled, gnawing his lower lip, the neck starting its churn. She didn't care. He was like an oversized kid, too dumb to be a bully. Even so, she figured she wasn't reaching his conscience. She assumed if he had one it was smaller than his pea-size brain. She thought of him as a package of base drives, smelling of shit, reacting to the world, an anarchist without reason. She would pity him, if he deserved it. "I mean it, Arly," she said.

When he did turn, he wasn't a child anymore. Bubbles of rage were in his eyes, a boiling of emotion. "I could have raped you."

The road was still dark and empty. Trees blew past; the sky was high and arched and specked with stars. Worlds away, that milky way of a universe, where the violence of black stars sucking in on themselves was never visible to the naked eye. In Arly, she felt a rumbling volcanic movement. His stability, weak as it was, was starting to slip. He was a black hole, falling in on himself, wanting to take everyone with him.

She knew he could pull off the road and finish it. Why had she asked for this? But, she told herself not to think about that. Pay attention. Don't let go. Stay with the story, an ugly fish she was trying to haul in. Her eyes glanced down at that vest. Enough light came in to show her lumps in the pockets. On top of it, just sitting there, was some sort of TV tuner, a channel changer.

"If I'm going to write this, I don't want to find myself in pieces all over Lake Huron, you know," she said. As for rape, he might as well have done it, even if he hadn't. She knew that now.

"We're all going to die anyway." He said this as his boot stomped the pedal of the ice cream truck and the motor roared, bearing along his payload.

"What is back there?" she asked. "Who made it? You?"

His fists clenched on the wheel. His shaven face shone pale and deadly. "Shut up, just shut the hell up, would you?"

CHAPTER 57
GANNON

Gannon didn't quite understand how Chang had commandeered the monster truck in Grand Rapids. But here they were on the highway, jouncing along at seventy on huge ribbed tires. Chang sat behind the wheel with an intensely happy expression on his face. When Gannon had asked him about the drunk driving charge, he ignored the question.

Ho Chi rested on the lambskin seat between them, his eyes closed, doubtless dreaming of how he took the hunk of flesh out of Tong's ass. Gannon settled back in his seat.

It hadn't taken long after Tong returned to the ground from his quick trip up the fence in the alley for Chang to light into him, demanding information. Gannon had been able to tell by the way Tong went deathly silent, his face losing all expression that the Chief's old Army sidekick had touched a nerve. Chang didn't let up, shoving him into the fence, ready to start punching. Gannon had to step in to back him off.

After that, Tong started complaining about his butt. He stuck a hand back there and brought it up smeared with blood. Chang asked Gannon if maybe they should take him to the hospital for stitches. By the glint in Chang's eyes, Gannon knew he was up to something. They wrapped Tong's backside in a couple of towels and drove to Butterworth, where Pham was still recovering from brain surgery.

At the hospital, Chang ushered Tong through the preliminaries in the ER and waited while he got stitched. Gannon meanwhile tried to ply information out of the detectives still hovering around the hospital, especially about his daughter and the whereabouts of Arly, but no one was talking. Gannon got the definite impression they didn't trust him.

He found a pay phone and got through to a sergeant at the State Police post in Mackinaw City. The sergeant said the governor had canceled tomorrow's birthday celebration on the bridge. The cop said it soon would be all over the news. Gannon had then asked about his daughter and Arly, and the sergeant said he didn't know anything about that. Then he started asking Gannon why he wanted to know.

The Chief hung up and dialed the beeper number Smereas had given him earlier. After ten minutes, Smereas was on the line. He was rushed and couldn't explain anything. He only said, "If I were you, I'd back off. Let us handle it."

"You think he's still going to try something?"

"Truthfully, no," Smereas said.

"Where are you?"

"Doesn't matter. Really it's best if you back off, Chief. There are already too many people involved."

"He has my daughter!"

Another pause.

"Are they checking every car going over the bridge?"

"I don't know."

"Well, I've got to do something. I'm going up there."

Chang returned with the newly stitched Tong, whose sullen expression hadn't changed. The detectives started in on Chang, who got that trapped looked in his eyes. He hadn't expected to be cornered. Tong seemed to like this, but the cops made it clear he was on the hook, too.

Finally a doctor said Pham was stirring. The detectives took Chang with them to interpret. He went reluctantly and came back very sullen. Pham didn't know anything, or wasn't saying. More likely, the drugs and operation had him. He wouldn't be able to talk until tomorrow.

The cops said Tong and Chang were free to go, for now, but they would be in touch. Gannon told the detectives he would walk the pair out. The cops groused but agreed, telling Gannon to hurry back; they wanted his formal statement now. More precious time.

Outside, an oversized Ford pickup, the type Gannon regularly pulled over when they cruised through his town, awaited them in the lot. Motor and parking lights on, no one behind the wheel. Another Vietnamese appeared from around the side. He and Chang talked. The guy strong-armed Tong and took him off through the dark parking lot.

Chang hauled himself aboard and signaled Gannon into the metal monster as well. Ho Chi was already parked in the middle of the seat, ready to roll.

"Who was that?"

"Friend, Gannon, of mine."

"This stolen?"

"No way, Gannon. Hop in. Need big wheels."

"Where're we going?" Gannon had asked.

"You'll see."

Not wanting to get stuck answering more questions, Gannon hoisted himself in. Maybe not wise, but better than the alternative. "Where's he taking Tong?"

"They talk some more."

The truck zoomed out of the lot. It was just after 8 P.M. They had been farting around for way too long.

"Some wheels, right Gannon?"

Gannon wondered when Chang had found the time to order the guy to bring this truck. "Our friends aren't going to be happy when I don't come back."

"Wish for them well."

Gannon didn't like this. But what else could he do? He knew the detectives were only doing their job and would keep after him for another couple hours. "Where the hell are we headed, Chang?"

Chang shot onto the ramp leading to U.S.-131. "Tong say his friend from prison, Mr. Arly, going to blow up Big Mac."

It didn't register for a second. Then it did: "What!"

"What he said."

"You mean, the bridge?"

"Not hamburger." Saying this, Chang busted a gut.

"Why didn't you tell the detectives?"

"Must not remembered, Gannon."

"We have to tell someone."

"We stop. You make a call."

Gannon smiled, even in his frenzy, realizing how far ahead his former partner had been thinking. How he smoothed his way out of the hospital and into a vehicle the detectives couldn't trace. "Chang," he said, "did Pham say anything about Cully?"

"She with Mr. Arly."

"You're sure?"

"Darned shootin'."

The Chief watched the road unroll ahead in a slick dark curve. Stars flickered above. Traffic was sparse. He turned on the radio, got a news station, and heard about the governor's announcement along with speculation as to what it meant.

"Police are asking travelers to avoid using the bridge this evening and at least through tomorrow morning," said the announcer. "A spokesman for Governor Frank Bones assures us that there is no danger, but he wants people to be extra cautious."

"Big strike, right, Gannon?" asked Chang.

"Sounds like."

"They close bridge?"

"I don't think so."

As the monster tires ate up the highway, the Chief fought to stay alert. Kettle drums boomed in his head. Looking out the window through aching eyes, he thought they had to be getting close, but to what, and to whom, he couldn't say. Chang had relayed what he knew. Problem was, Gannon couldn't sort through it. Especially the part about a truck that had bells. He had been twisting the radio knob, searching for more news, but there was nothing he hadn't already heard.

Now scattered images, sharp and compelling, shot through his mind. Himself working with his father in the garage, the mechanic shop on the south side of the river, outside of town. Both of them bent over the open hood of a '46 DeSoto. Then, Sally, his wife, on their first date, spilling Coke on a white skirt. How he laid his varsity jacket on the spill. Of the moment he first saw Cully, her infant, pink, pinched face behind the window at Henry Ford Hospital in Detroit. He was working as a security guard in Romulus at the time, just before he moved them all to East Lansing for college, and he had stood there, wonderstuck, melting in his boots, at the sight of this new life. Never did he think this would be their only child, that a virus would destroy his wife's ability to bear any more.

He saw Cully on the floor of the apartment in East Lansing, playing there with McCabe, their dog. The pet they slipped in and kept under wraps for almost two years. Cully lying in bed between him and his wife, mumbling nonsense words. A spunky kid even then. Cully in her Sunday School class, playing Mary Magdelene in the play and grabbing the boy playing Jesus by the scruff of the neck and throwing him down when he messed up his lines. Even then she had hated it when people changed the script.

Himself in Vietnam, with Chang, marching down the teeming streets, the many vendors, trying to keep the peace amid mounting chaos. His wife near the end, her haunted, hollow, cancer-ravaged face. Cully at her wedding to David, happier than he'd ever seen her. Cully at high school graduation, in jeans and a baggy sweatshirt, coming to the podium as the valedictorian and blasting the school administration for something or other. Got her in the paper. Cully a student at Michigan State University , leading a protest over gay rights. For a time he wondered if she was one. His relief when he learned she wasn't.

His wife on that ship off the shore of Alaska, in his arms, on the deck, love in her eyes, a wincing of pain on her mouth. The cancer was back. Her chest, scarred and pink and torn by the surgeon who could never quite get it all.

Cully's stories, which she sent religiously from far-flung places, the voice of her writing. The sure way she wrote, the anger there, almost always, the passion for the underdog. Cully at David's funeral, the drained, awful expression on her face, the terrible emptiness that his dying brought. Cully back home, helping her mom in the final days. Cully around the house in recent months, full of testiness, wanting to be home, hoping to help her dad but getting in the way. Cully the night he torched the barn, the night he shot Bashful Blue. The way his grief erupted. The flames flying through the air, the barn collapsing, himself by the tall oak, watching with smoldering terror in his heart. How Cully had approached, wanting to help, but started screaming, demanding to know why he had done it. Himself watching the fire, thinking of the burnt carcass of the horse. Of Sally on that bed, the cancer all through her. Gone. His wife. The lifeline he had held on to. Her horse burned to ashes and spread on the ground.

He had listened to Cully yell that night, saw the sorrow etched on her face, but turned away. Let her spew. He and the gas can had spoken. He knew she was probably the one who diverted the attention of the county investigators from him. Everyone had slipped away from him, pretending he hadn't been the arsonist. They had let him be. Which is how he wanted it, liked it, demanded it. Didn't he?

Then the singer's throat, Lonnie's brain matter, the gouges on his back, the smell in Baxter's milk barn.

Suddenly he veered away. Chang was yammering again. They had pulled off the expressway. Up ahead in the dark loomed the bridge. Its first bank of towers showed in a hazy dusting of light. Surrounding the entrance ramp to the bridge were cruisers, lights swirling. The cops were checking cars and talking to drivers. Off to the side, men with picket signs, orange lights from an MDOT truck, a couple of them blocking one of the lanes. A zoo.

"You see it, Gannon? Anywhere, the Humor truck?"

To the left, across an open field and parking lot, spread the grounds of Fort Michilimackinac, the former army garrison that had guarded this important passage through the Great Lakes. To the right, soft yellow lights showed the outline of Mackinaw City. A tourist town now under siege, it looked like. So much traffic, so much activity.

Gannon wondered where they should go first. He was afraid they would get lost in the swirl of this midnight movement. By the clock on the dash of the car he saw it was almost that time. Ho Chi had awakened and stuck his head close to the window, as if he too couldn't quite figure what to make of all the lights and cars and people.

"Huh, Gannon. You see it? The Good Humor man?"

CHAPTER 58
SOFTSHOE

Here he'd been meandering about Custer, imagining himself as a wounded brave, ready to give the last of what he had to help destroy the maggoty Indian hater with the hair of a modern movie star. Slumped in the hole, his body drenched from blood, sweat, rain and, honestly, fear, Mumberto let his brain pull him into a place that could build his courage and diminish the fear. His side still ached, lanced by the bullet.

Almost as soon as the woman had gone, he knew he'd made a mistake. He shouldn't have let her go alone. As best as he could, he had gotten to his feet and started after her. He stumbled through trees and down a path, trying to be quiet, his side on fire, until he couldn't go on and fell to his knees. He tried keep on going but couldn't. He crawled to another spot, a padded place off the path, and rested.

In this new spot he had stayed quiet, maybe sleeping a bit, but mostly letting his thoughts move back in a soft thumping of drum-beats to another fight. Another battle, the seminal one between the whites and the reds. But his mind wouldn't hold it. He had a hard time filling out the edges of that mental picture. It wouldn't get him in the clear.

Instead he began to think about a novel he had read when he was in the jitter joint. A year ago it was, after his world really ripped apart from boozing. Thirty days he spent in the place in Traverse City, drying out, learning about what they called the disease of alcoholism, being taught that he could never really go back to the drink. Not if he wanted to live. The place for juice heads had felt like prison, maybe even worse than that, since he couldn't drift off in his head and put in his time.

They made him read recovery crap, books and pamphlets about getting sober. AA propaganda. But there had been a few ragged paperbacks in a makeshift bookcase. One book, by he couldn't remember who, was about a bad guy, a truly evil character, whose body was able to renew itself after being seriously injured. A science fiction story. A stupid book, but he had read it, or most of it, in his cramped room at night. And what stuck in his brain now, as the rain let up and sun started to sink in the sky, was how that man's busted arms and mashed ribs were able to heal quickly on their own. It was a weird trick of a super-fused metabolism.

Softshoe didn't think that was what was happening to him. No way, José.

But he slowly felt energy seep back into him, his heart pumping blood fully to all parts, as if sending currents of energy through him. Bit by bit this had happened, over a period of a couple hours. He somehow gathered himself; life wouldn't let him go. He was hungry and ate the three candy bars he kept in his jacket, usually for others he found in the woods. He drank from his water bottle.

Maybe it was the sun that helped. Even though it was near dusk, enough of it came down that he felt it on his face. It warmed him and helped him feel less hopeless. Surely he wasn't ready for death, not a brave on the brink of extinction. He began to wonder if the bullet had nicked a small piece of his liver, which would account for the blood. Possibly the wound had clotted, the hemorrhage stopped. The weakness that had been with him for hours didn't get worse.

After a time he stirred, moving his legs, twisting his neck, checking out the crusted mess at his side. It was now dark. He wondered where the woman was.

When he heard rustling in the woods and voices, he sat up, wincing and looked around. He was almost ready to call out, hoping these were rescuers sent here by Cully Gannon. The woman he was supposed to help, whom he had abandoned. Guilt washed into him now, worse than before, for leaving her.

But he didn't make noise. He wanted to see who was out there. Soon enough he was glad he'd kept his mouth shut. The sounds didn't come from anyone who wanted to help. He wasn't sure, but possibly they were the ones who had shot at him hours ago and got lucky. They were militia.

They stopped, not too far from where he lay, so one or a couple of them could piss. He heard the swishing and plashing in the brush. He was afraid that when they stopped leaking, they'd stumble across him. Thinking that, he eased his rifle into a place from which he could shoot. Why hadn't she taken it? He had forgotten. It was strange; he felt as if a fever had broken. Let them peer at him, he thought, and he'd plug whoever wasn't fast enough to get out of his sights.

No one came close enough for him to have to pull the trigger. But they did pause for a bit, maybe twenty yards away, to talk. It sounded like complaining. Softshoe slowly lifted himself further, careful not to crackle the leaves, surprised that his gut, although it ached, didn't feel split open. Through a break in the branches, he spotted movement of bodies.

"Why in the hell you let her go like that, Perry?" one asked.

"What was I supposed to do? Fucking Arly is an animal."

"He lets her go, she'll finger us for sure."

"He won't do that."

"Sonofabitch is unpredictable. You seen him."

"Let's follow them." A third voice. "If she gets away, we'll get her."

"He's long gone by now."

"Bridge ain't far and that thing ain't going off for awhile. Gregor says Burke's got it timed."

"Arly know that?"

"He has to."

"So, they'll stop for a quickie at the motel before?"

"Who knows. They won't be hard to spot. Maybe we can even see the fireworks."

"Man, that's crazy."

"You got any better ideas, numbnuts?"

"Let's dig a hole and hide until Christmas."

As he listened, Softshoe wondered again if one of them had hit him with the bullet earlier. Thinking this, he found himself doing what that guy in the book did. He lifted himself out of his pain, unfolded his broken body, and let it carry him on. Except, as far as he could tell, he was doing it for a good cause. *Mr. Murder*, that was the book, by Dean Koontz. Strange book. About evil crashing into good.

Softshoe rose, feeling like a vapor, not counting the cost of his injury, his rifle ready. He was drawn up by their plans and well aware, without having all the facts, that they were talking about Cully. The one with the smart edge to her, hard planes to her face, a power in her even after she'd been put through the wringer. Obviously she didn't get free. He let her go. Damn. And they mentioned Arly.

Almost without knowing it and certainly without willing it, Softshoe was tiptoeing, doing what his nickname said he did best, through the trees. He was like sifting smoke, his side alive with pain, his senses steady as a laser. Locked in on the voices, he slipped through the trees and came on them just as they were getting ready to haul ass.

All three turned with angry, frightened eyes, lots of white around the rims. They stood there. And suddenly Softshoe had many questions. But it came down to this one named Arly, the one who had the woman.

"All of you, hang your hands high." Shit, he thought, I sound like Clint Eastwood, no Indian's friend.

Almost as one, they did. Holding weapons aloft. Softshoe categorized the hardware. He didn't like what he saw. He should have taken care of this before telling them to hold up their arms. "Let the guns drop," he ordered.

"Who're you?" asked the largest one, a guy with a round face and red hair.

"Someone give you a boo-boo?" asked another.

"Just do it," he said, wincing, feeling a jolt of pain in his side, a stabbing that made him wobble for a second.

The trio used the chance to bring down their arms and swing guns his way. Mumberto stepped to the side, opening up with his rifle, stumbling against a stump, waiting for bullets to smack into him.

As best he could, he got off two shots before landing on the ground. A hurting that was hot and fierce ripped through him. Had they shot him again? He didn't think so. He wasn't sure why they didn't fire back. He heard no other gunfire. From the ground, he glanced up to watch them crashing through brush, disappearing, wanting no part of him.

CHAPTER 59
ARLY

It loomed ahead, spreading itself to him in the night. The towers reached up like arms. Inching forward, trapped in a mass of vehicles, Arly tried to see more. Dancing lights glancing off the cables, marking his goal. But there were a few clouds out there, whiffs of fog, rolling in, stealing the image from him for seconds at a time.

Behind the wheel, he felt hot as an engine about to spill its fluids. But he was in control. The voices told him this was right. They made him think about his father's bones, about the fire that destroyed his mother, about the many ways he had been bent and twisted by the people who should know better. Most of all the governor, not really his full brother, the man claiming more than he possessed, a birthright that wasn't his. His political face, so often in the newspapers, so smug and happy, flashed before Arly, obscuring his vision of what to do next. He saw the man's picture for the first time in the joint. Arly didn't know who his kin was, or where he was, nor did he care, until then.

Someone honked behind him. He jerked the truck forward, rocking the heavy load. He felt for his TV channel changer next to him on the seat, his hedge against the unpredictable.

"This is crazy," the woman said.

Arly ignored her. Exhaust from traffic spread everywhere in the dark, poison fumes, polluting the air. Up ahead he saw a couple of cop cruisers at the entrance to the ramp, talking into cars, checking, checking, checking, nosy bastards. Hands on their guns, waving flashlights, stupid sheep following the directions of politicians who were full of rotten shit.

"You'll never get through," she said.

Not true. He would. The voices came together in one surging current, assuring him of success. He knew he was mumbling, too, the sounds in his head overflowing. But he wasn't letting it get to him. He was planning, sketching his moves, trying to spot the place in the middle, between the towers, his target. The place for his important action. Arly was pissed that he couldn't do this right. He couldn't hold off until tomorrow, when it would be light, when everyone would see, when he could take the bastard governor down with him into the water in a crash of steaming metal. It had been well planned. Burke had somehow gotten him the proper papers, allowing him to take his ice cream truck onto the platform for the party to sell his wares. But that wasn't going to happen now, not after the governor screwed it up. Back at that farm, Arly had not had to wait long to decide: he was going for it tonight. He would make his mark, even if everything wasn't ready. Burke gave him the full metal jacket and directions.

"Christ, Arly, you can't do this."

But he could and would. Real calm, like what he used to get from reading the Bible, started to settle into him finally, the assurance of his purpose. This was the end of the plan he had hatched those many nights in his cell, with Tong overhead egging him on, the chatterbox gook. Then he'd come up here several times and stood on either end of the bridge, using the quarter telescopes to find where the structure was most vulnerable. Arly knew tonight was his best and only chance, and that the diminished payload was ticking inside. The clock was set. Or it damned well better be. Burke better not have lied to him.

"Listen to me!"

She was a hag. Her hair was in strings; her face was swollen, her mouth ugly and twisted purple. Unlike him, she was coming apart. Even so, he knew it was right to have brought her; she would tell the world his story. She would make it right. She was an instrument as much as he was. The voices told him so. He would die in his effort. She would live on. He wished he could wire a bomb to her. Make her blow as soon as she wrote his words.

She said something, too loudly, moving toward him. He held up an arm, which stopped her good. "What?" he asked.

"When we get up there, unless you kill me now, I'm going to scream everything I know to the police."

They were getting close. He saw the cops wave some people on, stopping others. Maybe he would be lucky. "See this?" He slipped the tuner from the seat, all the while thinking of the jacket and its plums. She shook her head.

"I punch the power button and this goes right now."

She was quiet, staring at it. He suddenly knew how he would handle this part, making sure she was around to tell his story. He said: "You talk and I push it. Or we go out. You clear the kill zone and then it goes."

"Kill zone?"

Burke had timed it for 12:40 A.M., less than a half hour away. But with the remote, it would happen sooner. He would give her maybe five minutes to leave, let her warn a few people. Give her the feeling she was saving lives. Keep her from messing it up now. A good plan. He surprised himself at his straight thinking. It was almost as if he got calmer the closer he got. So many hours he had dreamed of this, had plotted it. Staring in his jail room, at Milan, he had imagined it, an idea that started small and grew, hatched after reading those news stories about a politician who took credit for a father who wasn't his.

It had taken so much to get this far. People had double-crossed him, tried to stop him, lied to him. He never thought it would happen as it had. But he knew he had to be flexible. He had to take options when they showed up for him. If he didn't, he would fail. This was another of the unexpected plans he had to make.

To make her see it clearly, he shoved the tuner under her nose. Maybe he was talking, cursing her, he hardly knew. But he did hear himself say: "Decide!"

She looked so scared that he wanted to slam her face with his hand and bash her into the window. Teach her to be afraid. If he wasn't mistaken, she nodded. Just a little. But enough. Which was good. "You say anything and it goes."

Another nod. "But why?" she asked. "I don't understand."

He didn't answer. Only two cars to go before the checkpoint. He glanced at his unfamiliar face in the mirror, the shiny, nicked skin. Smooth. Not him at all. He hated to think he would have to do this not looking like himself.

"Are you that full of hate?"

Arly wished he could answer that. Because it wasn't hate at all that he felt. No, it was something more. A swelling anticipation, enthusiasm was more like it. He was going to give back what he had gotten. And then some.

Before he let her out, Arly suddenly wanted to tell her that he had liked her mother. Back in a grade school, her mother had been a substitute teacher. Once she had come up to him in class and touched his wrist. It was red and bruised from being chained in the basement. The preacher, Lonnie's dad, would get mad, beat him with the Bible stick, call him names, and attach him to the drainage pipe in the basement. Like an animal, filthy in his own rot. Leave him for hours, once or twice overnight. He never did that to Lonnie.

But that time, the teacher, her mother, asked what they were, those bruises. Arly wouldn't say, but she had him go down to the office to be examined. Some man did the checking. Arly never told them anything, knowing what that would bring. Even so, something happened. The preacher never chained him there again. It had stopped, because of the teacher. For that Arly was grateful. And he wanted to tell Cully this. But it was happening too fast. Outside, in the side mirror, he saw swirling lights in the dark. He had easily passed the checkpoint.

Noticing a green truck up ahead, stopped in the right lane, Arly made a quick survey on either side and saw the cable swooping down, the foggy black beyond. He was there. "Out!" he said.

She didn't look to be in any hurry. Suddenly, Arly hated her and her mother. "Right here? In the middle?"

Arly made himself go calm, swallowing a huge gulp of air. She would tell the world; either that, or she would die. "Now!"

"This door's locked."

He rammed his shoulder into his door, jammed down the handle, stood, and reached in for her. She slid over and out. She looked over-heated, her skin on fire, matching her hair. Her mother's color, too. For a second, they locked eyes. Her cheek was swollen, discolored. When he had met her again on the path with the three men, he had almost been happy. He had not been surprised to see her, never asked what brought her to him. He had brought her back, like a revolving door. Now she ran, waving her arms. Arly watched her disappear.

He liked it out here, shreds of fogs flapping in through the dark, the air clean, the bridge sturdy under him. But there was lots of noise, ramming into his ears like fists. And she was yelling, just as he had let her do. Which, he now knew, had been a terrible, terrible mistake. But it didn't matter. Sure, the popsicle was set for twenty minutes from now. So what? He had what he needed to bring the doom and the release much sooner. Crawling in his chest was a swarm of insects, like maggots in meat, and he would break them free as well. Rip away the chain in him. Break open the tomb that kept his father hidden. His father, no one else's.

Cars and trucks had already stopped. Horns honked. He had hoped for better timing, to cut it closer. Somehow it had happened so fast, getting out here, clearing the hurdles. Much quicker than he wanted. But he had slipped onto the bridge and he needed to act. For a moment he was pleased to be here. But the talons of the big bird dug into his head, almost driving him to the ground.

He knew. Best not to wait. He couldn't trust himself. Take the tuner and do it now. She was far enough away. Maybe. He wanted to savor the moment, his final arrival, the thundering wind that was about to roar. But he knew he couldn't waste time on useless thinking. Enough of that had happened already. For a final moment, he recalled that basement, the chains on his wrists, the other foster families, his hand on the radiator, his mother doused in the gas. He would light bigger flames now. Not as he had planned, but good enough. And Cully would explain why.

Arly reached in for the tuner, atop his vest, on the seat inside the truck. Felt for it once, twice, three times. He leaned in and pounded on the fabric, feeling the plums, but not the tuner. Damnit, damnit, assholeshit. She took it. The fucking woman he had tried to help had taken it.

CHAPTER 60
BONES

Standing at the railing behind the Bridge Authority headquarters, Governor Franklin Bones felt as if someone had smashed him in the gut. Twenty feet below and stretching off to far places, the water made him think of dark blood, filling the world, spreading out, away from here. He thought of boats sliding in blood, escaping the Great Lakes, up the St. Lawrence Seaway and beyond. The turgid water, this blood that seemed to be everywhere.

It took effort for him to stand upright, his eyes sweeping across the massive face of the bridge, sprawling out there in its lacy necklace of light a couple hundred feet to the west.

Mighty Mac's vast girders and swooping cables, its huge indifference seemed an affront to him now. Near its top, even in the dark, he saw the curling of vapor. The wind was driving in fog. He wanted to blame the bridge, this highway between the halves of Michigan, for his pain, a pain that went back farther than he had wanted to think. Farther back than he ever knew, until now.

Joy stood next to him. "Can I get you something?"

"A new life."

They had come out here less than a half hour before, slipped out the back door, away from the press, out of earshot of the scurrying bureaucratic mice trying to put a good face on his decision to cancel the ceremony tomorrow. He had been initially pleased at the chance to take a break. But the face of Joy Williams, this woman who had been his surrogate mother, told him she had bad news to share. Which she most damned definitely did. But then again, lately, who didn't?

"I'm sorry. I really, really am." She was spark-plug size, with round, perfect cheeks and hard-looking, overdone hair. She wore a dark pantsuit. Jewelry circled her neck. Her husband had drifted off down the walkway and stood by the rail, smoking, pretending to ignore them. "I'm glad you did," he said. He noticed a freighter rounding the tip of Bois Blanc Island, the getaway from Detroit and everything else downriver.

"I knew it would come out now, and that you had to be prepared," she added needlessly.

He understood this but that didn't mean he had to like it. For that matter, why hadn't she told him earlier, like twenty years ago? Except they had already been over that and had come to this place of silent impasse. The bridge stared down at them like an impervious god. As a child, he had been awestruck any time they crossed it. Preston had talked about helping build it, but never mentioned the other parts. Such as the death of Rolly Walls, who, it turned out . . .

"Are you sure you're all right?" she asked.

"Yes!" he snapped.

Only minutes ago, Joy had told him a missing part of the story. A piece she had known all along, but kept hidden. Now, as this mess unfolded, she had decided she had to tell him. She was sure no one else had, not yet. She just knew, she said, with this business about a brother, that it was long past time for all the cards to be spread on the table. Preston, she had informed him, was his real father.

Again, irritation bordering on rage surged. "Why now, Joy? Why not before?"

She looked remorseful. "Honestly, Frank, I've wanted to tell you for years."

"Why tonight?"

Joy looked away. "I talked to Preston. He told me he told you, about the half-brother. I asked him did he tell you the rest. He said he hadn't and I told him he had to. But he couldn't go that far."

"He didn't say half-brother."

She answered, "I know."

"His father is the one buried in the bridge?"

"It is."

"But, why? Why you, and why now?"

"Frank, I just know that as soon as the press gets hold of this, everything will come out. Or, at the very least, the more you know, the better you can contain it."

Spoken like a true committeewoman. But what he wanted here was not another political operative. Suddenly, Frank Bones felt terribly alone, an odd, disquieting feeling. "There's more?"

Joy shook her head, too quickly.

A boat horn blew on the lake, echoing in the night. Frank Bones looked at the bridge again. He thought of that dream, or was it real, of himself in his mother's arms, with another kid nearby. This one older. In his memory, he saw pilings in the water, tugboats and barges and large dredging machines. Men, small as ants, at work. One of them Rolly Walls, one of them Preston. Both had helped build it. That Preston was having an affair certainly wasn't out of character. But assuming responsibility, namely taking on a child that wasn't his, didn't exactly compute.

"My real mother, Rochelle, you knew her?"

"I met her once." Joy stared at him. In her plump face, made up to show a mask of flawless pancake skin, he saw nuggets of hurt. It had cost her to reveal this, to let him know how much she had held back. She too had lied by omission. As a child he had sat in her ample lap, listening to stories, enjoying her laugh, as Preston and the swimmer frolicked. "It was Ralph's idea," she said. "He said I had to talk to you. That you had been blindsided enough. But even he didn't know, not all of it, until today."

As if aware they were talking about him, Ralph turned toward them. He questioned with his glance, half hidden in the dim lakeside lighting, as if asking were they done. If he was needed. For his wife.

"Preston knows you were going to tell me this?"

"Yes," Joy said.

"He called just before you did."

"Maybe he was going to tell you himself."

"Probably not." Anger shot through him, hot daggers of betrayal. Incredibly, though, he also felt a smudge of relief, as if his character, such as it was, was happier tied genetically to Preston's and not the bridge worker.

To some extent, the governor still wondered: why keep so much hidden, at such a cost? He also asked himself if that half-brother militia man knew this. Then it struck him: he had been planning to commemorate the man he thought was his father, but that would have been a lie. A lie that Preston would doubtless have let him tell if guns hadn't have gone off in Pigeon River. More than that, he realized, he was going to have to do everything humanly possible to keep the whole thing buried. If this came out, he would no longer have the strong connection to the man in the bridge. A political trump card, out the window.

Mixed emotion, he knew, could not prevent him from doing what was right. And that was to keep his hand steady on the helm of his state. To an extent, now knowing what he faced, he was more secure. He could gaze to the future, knowing the challenges it offered. He probably did owe Joy a debt of thanks. Inside once again turned the screws of ambition, which immediately doused his feelings of self-pity and loneliness.

At that moment, as if in answer to his new-found resolve, steps tapped on the sidewalk, coming down from the back door of the Bridge Authority building. Bones swung away from the rail to face the person approaching. Who else but Piersma. His front-line ally. Together they'd spin the story, dodge the bullets, and ride into the off-election year winter with even more of the state on their side. Bones knew he could turn this whole soap opera to his advantage, even if he temporarily had to feed Preston to the dogs.

"Frank, more trouble."

The governor did not reply. Out of the corner of his eye he saw Joy step away. Ralph returned, positioning himself behind her. "Hi, Jock," she said.

Piersma whipped a look at her. "Hello, Joy." Partners in the cover-up at the mall, but that didn't matter now.

"She was telling me the true story of my parentage, Jock."

Piersma's glossy face, swelled by high-octane guzzling, swung between his boss and the hugging, hovering couple. "Pardon?"

"How Preston's my real father. I'm assuming you've been in on that little secret, too?"

Piersma swayed, as if coming to a stop from a road race. He ran a hand over the folds of his face. He looked truly surprised, even stunned. The governor decided to stop dwelling on the sins that had come home to roost.

"Jesus, Frank, I didn't know."

He seemed to be telling the truth. Even if he wasn't in on this one, he was in on many other items. Which made him the perfect spokesman, at least for the next little while. "What trouble, Jock?"

"On the bridge," he finally got out. "Some guy with a bomb."

"Which guy?"

"Him."

"Who said?"

"Press. They're going crazy."

Bones didn't have to ask who was on the bridge. He knew. As if bracing himself for a go at the Supreme Court, the governor turned and started straight for lights of the cameras, gathered by the front of the Bridge Authority office. If they wanted to know what was happening, he'd tell them. If they wanted to see a real governor in action, well, here he went.

CHAPTER 61
CULLY

The first thing she did was fling that TV tuner out over the rails and into the water. She wondered for a second if that would set it off. She probably should have popped it and removed the batteries. But she didn't. She threw it into a waft of fog into the dark and waited to see what would happen. She imagined it falling hundreds of feet to the surface of the water, slapping in, setting off a signal.

When nothing happened after a few seconds, Cully turned and began to scream: "Stay back! Get back! He's got a bomb!"

Already it was a madhouse. Vehicles were stopped everywhere. Arly took up an entire lane of the roadway. The tail lights of the ice cream truck flashed red in the dark. Closer to her, horns blared, the night stinking with fumes. She wondered if Arly had discovered by now that she had grabbed the tuner. She had used what was left of his good nature, maybe even what posed for a conscience, to trick him.

A man rolled down his window. "What the hell is going on, lady?"

"The guy back there has a bomb. Get out of your car and run." She had no idea if this was the best way to handle it or not.

Any second she expected it to erupt, for a terrible ball of flame to break from the ice cream truck. Arly had said the guy who built it set it for twelve-forty, still a few minutes away. The best idea, she suspected, was to clear what he called the kill zone.

The scene reminded her of the time the guy went bonkers at the Liberty Bell. She was sent to cover it. The lunatic had opened up shooting, chasing people onto the street in a screaming rush.

Glancing back again, she saw the truck parked, mostly up on the curb, the rails of the bridge behind, the towers rising above. The cables looped like long arms; the lake lumbered below. She spotted Arly darting around the front of the truck, bending down, searching. Hunched and horrible. Looking for the tuner. Without his beard.

They had gotten past the entry to the bridge without incident. Arly had some sort of fake ID. Also, the cops got distracted, just as she was going to take a chance and call out to them, then grab the tuner away. But the cop had waved them on.

She had huddled by the door, calculating her moves, wishing that she could warn someone about the load in the truck. But apparently someone had, because the place was full of activity now. Someone had said something to someone. She spotted a dark, official-looking truck, a Bronco, with lights flashing on its roof.

"What's going on?" another guy asked from a car.

"Get out, run," she answered. Maybe she should help herd people to safety. Maybe she should go back and help kill Arly. Maybe people should try to back up.

Then Cully spotted a man in a uniform approach through the crowd, headed toward the truck. She recalled that the guy who lost it at the Liberty Bell was Cuban, upset because his girlfriend left him for a Castro sympathizer.

"Stop!" she yelled at the guy in the uniform. But he didn't hear. "Shit." She paused, out of breath, trying to gather her wits.

All around came the dizzy spin of faces, in and outside of vehicles. She knew with a sickness she could taste that it was too damned late. She wondered if Arly had some other way to ignite the bomb. Even if he didn't, the time was close. He had said it didn't have as much explosive as he wanted, but she knew it would still cause havoc.

Cully started running after the man in the uniform and bumped into people fleeing. The Cuban had sprayed gunfire all over the place, tearing down bodies. The uniformed man disappeared up ahead.

Cully stopped, trying to find someone who could help. She felt like a coward. She thought of Arly standing over her on that path. The bastard.

Her legs waited for the concussion of the exploding ice cream truck. On the way, Arly had told her about it. Said the bomb was made out of plastic explosive. That it was supposed to be equal to fifty thousand tons of dynamite but it turned out to be only half that. God, he was crazy.

Cully grabbed at a man running the other way, holding a child on his shoulders. The child was sucking on a sucker, eyes wide. The man stopped, but she didn't know what to say. She waved him on, then ran, stopped, and swung around, her body not working very well right now.

She couldn't believe it; it was surreal. A dark, foggy sky hung above; the bridge itself seemed disinterested, totally unaware that a madman was ready to make it pay. It struck her: escape was silly. Maybe the only choice now was to return and help stop him. Maybe he could be reasoned out of it. Certainly not, but if anyone had his attention, what there was of it left in that rattled brain, it was her. Or she hoped. She had a mental flash of Edna, commanding her to return. Not to abandon this. To help, not run.

But someone was calling to her, a man running in her direction. A stocky man. She recognized him. It was . . .

Then from behind, Cully felt a tug. She twisted and saw the round face, and red beard. The guy from the woods. Milo, wasn't it? He yanked on her, dragging her with him. "Bitch, you're not going to tell anyone a thing."

CHAPTER 62
GANNON

When they saw the Good Humor truck going through the check lane at the south entrance of the bridge, Gannon jumped out of the monster pickup, started running and yelled for it to stop. For a moment he wondered if Chang had been wrong, if he had gotten it garbled. But the Vietnamese had been adamant: Tong told him it was an ice cream truck. Gannon gathered that Chang and his associates had threatened Tong with much more than another trip to prison to encourage him to talk. The Chief was glad they had. But now, standing on the pavement, watching the white vehicle roll farther onto the foggy bridge, he was afraid the knowledge might not do him any good. Not if Arly was at the wheel and ready to make good on his plans.

Watching the white truck with the picture of an ice cream bar disappear into the night and traffic, Gannon stopped his useless pursuit. Out of breath, he had to decide: either find other cops and fill them in or go after it himself.

Chang made it moot. He pulled up in the shiny truck with the amazing tires. Gannon got in and they were gone. After clearing the checklane with the Chief's police ID, they madly pursued the ice cream truck, weaving around vehicles. Behind the wheel, Chang was all business, palming the horn and expertly squeezing between a semi and a huge motor home. Ho Chi sat in the middle, alert. Traffic was heavy, even at this hour, no doubt made worse by the extra security on both ends of the bridge.

Up in his seat, high above the pavement, his head out the window, Gannon tried to peer through the other cars and trucks. He caught a glimpse of the Good Humor sign a half dozen vehicles ahead and yelled for Chang to hit it harder. He had no idea what the plan was. Whatever happened, he had to be there to help his daughter.

They jammed through traffic. Gannon noticed lights flashing behind and in front of them. Someone must have tipped off the police about the truck. More than a mile onto the bridge, near the foundation of the first tower, the Chief spotted the backside of the Good Humor vehicle, parked at the curb, as if pausing for repairs, a little way ahead. How in the hell had Arly hoped to pull this off, the Chief thought, even as he realized the son of a bitch was here and doing something.

People ran from a crisscrossed circus of parked cars. A minor stampede. So many people in flight, a human mass of lava. Floating in, making it even stranger, came wisps of fog reflected eerily in the dark and flashing lights. They knew, then. Word had spread. Traffic was completely snarled.

Gannon shouldered open his door, gazing across the traffic jam toward the truck, and stepped down. Chang had joined him, his arm waving, the dog at their feet.

Suddenly, the Chief caught a jostle of bodies to the left out of the corner of his eyes. More jerking than he detected in the others. A man in army green leaving behind a motorcycle. Gannon wanted to run for the ice cream truck, but something kept him looking at the guy. He had red hair and a loping, lumpy gait. Then, just beyond the guy, wedged between two cars trying to buck through the mob, he saw her. Cully. He could swear she recognized him, even in this frenzied crowd. He saw her mother's eyes, wide and fierce and calm even now.

Gannon leaped forward as the men approached her. He shoved past an elderly man and zigzagged around a parked Nissan with a terrified old woman at the wheel. He had closed half the distance between them when he saw one of the men, this one with a wild bush of hair, grab Cully, forearm around her throat.

Another man in fatigues shoved past Gannon, slamming an elbow into his chest and knocking him to the ground. The Chief fell hard to the pavement, the wind knocked out of him.. From the ground he watched helplessly as the second man joined the first, grabbing his daughter by the arm.

Then he heard Chang's choppy commands, like a drill press, punching out words. As he got his balance, Gannon noticed a burst of speed, low to the ground, zeroing in, sure as a heart pumping. The dog.

Chang kept on, yammering in Vietnamese, or maybe special dog language. The dog wove through a swarm of people, leaving its feet, rising up on piston legs, muscular and springy. Ho Chi answering the call of his keeper, aiming for the throat. Blasting in, jaws open, this animal named after the communist whose trail no one could destroy.

Chang gave him a quick grin, pleased with the lethal weapon that was his pet. Already the one with the ratty hair was on the ground with Ho Chi locked into his skin, likely going for the jugular. The other one had turned, long hair swinging, in search of where this bastard pit bull had hurtled in from. Chang, already there, launched into him with a swing-around kick, clipping him in the chin.

Still on the pavement, Gannon looked up to see his daughter scrambling to her feet. "Cully!" he tried to call out.

But she couldn't hear him. Quickly she disappeared into the crowd.

CHAPTER 63
ARLY

Watching the woman run away, Arly realized he should have kept her with him. Let her feel what it was really like. He wanted to go after her and punish her. But he had to act, now that he was without his clicker.

On his knees, he dug for his flak vest. The special jacket had been fixed up for him by Burke, the dickhead genius. Arly had insisted on the vest and some extra firepower to keep people away. Now he was glad he had. Maybe this way was better. He would go out as a warrior, not a nameless coward who flipped the switch and left the scene.

Arly yanked the vest out of the truck and slung it over the stupid white uniform. He made sure his Colt knife was in its sheath and grabbed the Browning P38 out of his waistband. People ran past him in a panic, their faces blurry. They knew he was here. She had told them.

In a dream he once had of this scene, he had been wearing the flak jacket. It was his dream of the bridge birthday, with the bastard governor well within range of fire. This jackass who thought they had the same father, but they didn't. This man who took credit for something that wasn't his.

Arly felt himself tumbling, unable to stop. He thought of himself outside the post office in Dearborn, dumping IRS forms into a pile, pouring on lighter fluid, striking a match, all to protest an anger he was only now really feeling. "Fuckingshitasshole," he said, wishing he would stop, knowing he couldn't.

He swung the handgun at the crowd. He wanted to drop them like flies, before they buzzed into him. One after the other, he fired shots, first into the air, wanting them to scatter. He didn't want anyone to take him out until the bomb blew. Because he wanted to go out with his popsicle. He didn't want to draw any more attention than he had to. Which he knew was stupid as soon as he had wasted the first shots. Everyone knew who he was; they were coming after him, to stop him.

He suddenly knew he had to hurt these people to keep them away. So he aimed it down and shot. He knew he hit a couple of them because they fell in a flurry. He saw only one face, clean-cut, square-jawed, with a brushcut, piercing eyes, just before it splattered open with blood.

Suddenly he had run out of bullets, and people continued to swarm. He had to clear them out. He reached into his vest filled with plums, M18 colored smoke grenades and M57 frags, jagged metal hiding inside, ready to tear loose. He would use smoke to obscure himself, protect his perimeter, then hunker down and wait for the end. He'd use the frags if he had to. Feeling the fruits bulging in the pockets of his vest, he reached in for a smoke bomb.

But, again, problems.

As he brought out the plum and snapped the lid, he was hit from behind and shoved into the side of the truck. Madly he swung back, slamming something or someone with his arm. He turned to see a cop of some sort sprawled on the pavement, looking up, holding a pistol in one hand. "Stop right there," he said.

Arly dropped the plum in his face. It immediately broke open, spewing purple smoke. The man howled. Furious that none of this was going the way he had planned, Arly stepped over to smash his boot into the man's midsection. He wished the governor was lying where the cop was, under his boot. But once again, he was hit from the side.

His mind seething, he reached to his belt and brought out the Colt knife, the one that had sliced the singer's throat. Whoever had nailed him had slipped away. Arly swung out to his left just as he saw a flash of someone coming after him again through the smoke and darkness. He knew immediately that he caught flesh. He jabbed and ripped and tore. If he had the tuner, he would have pressed it and it would have been over by now. Instead, he was fighting to defend his truck and call the shots on how the end would happen.

Someone slammed something hard into his hand and he lost his grip on the knife. Smoke still poured all around. Arly grabbed inside for another plum. Make this one a flak grenade. Or was it? He struggled to shove heavy weight away from him, blasting out with an elbow, feeling a hot current rip into his neck. Finally he got the fruit in his palm.

He brought it to his mouth and tried to pry out the handle but couldn't quite get his teeth around it. He felt arms yanking at him and dragging him. Pummeling him, the assholes. Who were they? He recalled the girl on the ground, him on top, on that fire road. Then there was the apartment, ablaze in fire. Himself with the gas can. His mother in flames. Her boyfriend, really her pimp, hopping out the window. Then the governor waving at crowds, a hot bullet through his brain. Even as the images jammed the drive-in movie screen in his head, his mouth found the right leverage. He heard voices. Everyone moving in on him. Vultures for the kill.

He surprised them with the grenade, digging out the pin and lifting with his thumb. He let it roll, skidding across the pavement away from the truck. Not smart. He should have stuck it right underneath as a fuse.

An eruption blasted out. He half-expected the big one. What he felt instead was hot searing stink running up his nose and into his eyes. He immediately knew: It had been an M7A3, a riot grenade, filled with tear gas and pepper spray. Not what he had ordered.

But it did the trick. He felt no one around him. They had dropped off, coughing, choking. Jackals. They deserved to die. He waited a few more seconds, wanting to stay, but the envelope of gas was pouring his way, blinding and gagging him. He hatched another plan.

On hands and knees he crawled, his eyes burning with the searing fumes. A stink bomb, blasting smoke, a huge hairy fog. He patted the grating of the deck, his palms scraping metal and bumped into a pipe. The curbing, he knew. He couldn't stay here.

Eyes squeezed shut, Arly took a moment to clear his mind and let the roar leave his ears. It struck him that he was scared. Afraid it wouldn't happen. But it would. It had to. He had defined the kill zone. He would do it again. But he wouldn't do it from here. He had re-played many scenes, night after night, in prison and afterward. Even this was one he had considered. He was going to roll under his truck, take out a plum and light the candle.

But, more trouble. He heard: "Over here. He's by the curb. Shoot the bastard."

Crap. Arly stood. Couldn't see much. Felt for a plum. Dragged it out.

"I got him!"

Arly swung around and his knee shot up into his attacker's groin, the soft spot. He shoved the cop aside as he bent with a painful woof. Then he heard shots.

They were closing in from all sides to kill him before he got all of them. He yanked open another can, quickly popped it, and dropped it into the mess around him. More noise, fumes, guttering smoke, blind-ing stink. If he wasn't mistaken, he heard screams and moans.

He sorted through the inside pocket and felt the ribbed edges. A real one, packed with power. He yanked it out, used his teeth to jack out the pin, and lobbed it out into the crowd. This time, the sound was enormous. A great walloping roar more searing. Except, he didn't feel any flying metal. Were they all tear gas grenades? No huge boom. Nothing to break the bridge and set free the bones of his father. Shit. Goddmanitasswipeshit.

Stumbling away, Arly reached out with his hands and felt some-thing solid. Riveted metal. He had parked in the exact center between the two main towers. His plan was for the bomb to blast downward, rip through the road, and cut the cables, sending the bridge into the lake.

He knew exactly where he was and realized how he could get away and find a ringside seat. Maybe, he thought, he had miscalcu-lated when it would go off. It had to be soon now.

Down below, in the cement, he felt his father stir, demanding release. Arly felt furious that he wouldn't be able to make the right people pay. But he would make his mark. The mark of the beast. He touched the scars at his throat, stepped onto the catwalk, and began to climb.

He heard the slide of shoes rising from below and behind him and knew someone was chasing him. He stopped, grabbed a hard fruit, turned and dropped another plum right down the catwalk that fell all those floors to the ground. He heard it hit twice and then disappear, a dud. Like his truck, like everything else.

Arly kept on trudging, hand over hand, the air rustling against his smooth face. He wondered what had happened below; he expected to be toasted and gone by now. He had only one option: keep climbing. Make it higher, so he could be there when it blew. If it blew. If it didn't, they would have to take him like King Kong, from the roof of the night.

Arly's feet slipped as he climbed, but he held on, suspecting he was closing in on the crown of this creation, this awful steel structure that had haunted him for so long. His lungs were blown-apart sacks, larger than grocery bags full of rotting food. They pumped him along, up and up and up. Hurting, but he didn't care. He thought of stopping to kill whoever was after him, but now he just wanted to get to the top. The slope was steep, the catwalk rounded and ridged, giving only a little traction to his boots. Yanking himself higher by the handrails, he thought of something for the first time in a while.

That night, in his cell, he had read that article in the newspaper, about the man who had just been elected governor. How he took credit for his father in this very bridge. But that was a vile assholesucking lie. His mother, before she died, had told Arly. Someone, he never knew who, had told her who killed him. Or maybe it was the murderer. The man they visited in his office that time.

They had told her that her husband, Rolly, his father, was killed. On this same bridge, at night, by the man whose last name was the same as the governor's. Rolly was pushed in, during a fight, over the baby, the blubbering would-be governor, who was not Arly's real brother. A love spat, starting the lies.

Arly remembered another part. This heathen cocksucker, the ghost, would come at night and slide into bed with his mother. In the mobile home near Lake Michigan. Arly knew it, saw it, smelled it, wanted to talk about it, but his mother made him promise, gave him things and made him swear to keep quiet. She had sent him away when he argued and brought him back when he was better.

But then she had learned the truth. The death was no accident, even though everyone said it was at the same time they tried to hush it up. And his mother tried to use it, he knew that, to get them help. In that man's office, that night. She had asked the man who was called Preston Bones to pay. To help them. But he wouldn't. He pretended he didn't know her. He had ignored her; made her into a whore. Which she was, to tell the truth. His memory felt like grinding teeth.

And then the governor told the newspaper his own story, making it sound like he was the hero, leaving Arly and his dead mother like scum in the ditch. That was when his plan began. A plan that had gone so terribly wrong. A plan that he hoped would lead to peace, for him and his father, and pay the governor back for his lies. But now it was all coming apart: Cody had double-crossed him; that woman had tossed the tuner; the governor was going to take all of the credit. If he knew a better way, Arly would take it now. But there was none. He kept plodding, as if drawn up by a drag chain.

CHAPTER 64
SMEREAS

It was bad. Purple and orange tear gas smoke curled in the air. There was yelling, a crush of vehicles and people. There had been gunfire and a couple of explosions, probably grenades. ATF Agent Herb Smereas took all of this in as he zigzagged through the crowd toward the truck, parked between the two towers of the bridge. He saw sprawled bodies and people with hands over their faces. He wanted to stop and help, but he didn't have time. His own eyes smarted, and he jammed a handkerchief over his nose.

When they got to the bridge and he spotted the ice cream truck, he had Gregor blast ahead and jumped out at the place where everything had clogged. Sidestepping parked, honking cars and trucks, he sprinted toward the vehicle with the painted fudge bar on the side. A picture he recalled from his own teens, the Good Humor man jingling his bell through their neighborhood outside Flint. With all hell breaking lose around him, the ATF agent made a beeline for his target. The key was in his hand, given to him by Gregor, who found a copy in the dead Cody's pocket.

Smereas wondered where the oversized militia farmer had gone. For that matter, what about the Indian? Mumberto had appeared out of the woods as they left Gregor's barn, his belly blasted, and begged a ride. Smereas had wanted to drop him off so he could get someone to drive him to the hospital, but he insisted he was OK. Mumbled something about his dream spirit. Gobbledygook. Because they had no time to do otherwise, Smereas had obliged.

Smereas ran around a car, hopping over a couple people on their knees, peering through billows of smoke caught by the wind toward the truck. Stinking smoke rolled through the air. He stopped, ducked his head, and waited, praying it would pass. Gregor had told him about the grenades, stolen at Fort Bragg along with the C-4 and other goodies. Gregor also said Cody told Arly the bomb would blow at 12:40 A.M. Ten minutes from now.

"Over there! Over there!" someone yelled.

"On the other side. I think he jumped."

Oddly, no one was guarding the truck. The wind came up, whipping colored smoke toward the north end of the bridge, toward the Upper Peninsula, clearing the tear gas away.

Arly was nowhere in sight. Smereas glanced at his watch. Christ, it was close. For a brief a second his lungs seemed to fill with giddy bubbles; rags of doubt caught in his throat. But then he shoved them aside, like a surgeon walking into the OR for a big brain operation.

Giving the truck a quick once over, he stuck the key in the lock that hung from the small storage compartment, exactly where Gregor said it would be. As the lock dropped open and he popped the door, he saw it right in front of him. The clockworks, a bunch of wires leading from the blasting cap to the guts of the bomb.

Gregor said Burke had packed an old beer brewing barrel with the explosive and set it to blast downward and tear a huge hole in the decking of the bridge. Right here in the middle, where the main part hung suspended two hundred feet above the water. Crafty and lethal. The plan was to cause enough reverberation, enough spin-off power, to tear at and cut through a cable, which, if loosed, could topple one of the towers and bring the whole thing down. Smereas doubted it had that much strength, but you never knew.

Smereas searched for what he was told would be there: a green guide wire, the link from the timer to the blasting pad. But, damnit, where was it? It was too dark out here. He had no flashlight. Damnit all to hell. He turned around, ready to call for help, when the air shook and the floor under him moved. At that moment he ran smack into Gregor.

For a full ten seconds, he stood chest to chest with the militia farmer who had found his conscience. They waited for the world to cave in, for the shock waves to rip apart all of their bones. But then he knew that if it hadn't happened immediately, something else was up. Maybe more smoke grenades. By the billowing of the cloudy, rancid smoke, he figured that's what it was.

Gregor shoved him aside. "You get it?"

"I can't find it. It's too dark."

Gregor Pauls stepped over and reached in, as if searching for a push pop, and dug his arm in fairly deep, his face turned away from the door. Doing it by feel, for Christ's sake. Smereas waited, aware of the movement all around, the huge swaying of metal and strength, Big Mac in the wind. Up close, on the deck, the bridge was alive.

"Got it," Pauls said, wiping a forearm across his brow.

"You're sure?"

Pauls held a curled wire in his hand, its ends dangling.

Smereas felt a wave of relief. His nose ran from the chemicals in the smoke. But they'd done it. They were out of the woods. Except for one thing. He looked around through the billowing smoke. Where was the crazy bastard who wanted to set this off?

"Who're you? What the hell are you doing there?"

Smereas felt something hard in his side. He turned to see a state cop pointing a gun, on the edge, his face frantic.

The cop looked puzzled when Smereas identified himself.. He gazed at the open door of the truck to the mess of wiring within, the slumbering explosive.

"The remote," said Pauls, head swinging side to side.

"The what?"

"Just remembered Cody gave him a tuner, too."

Shit. There was a chance the idiot could flick them to hell and back yet. "You disarmed it?" asked the cop.

He was about to answer, when he felt the air move again. The blast broke against his body, followed by the sound of hot metal flying.

CHAPTER 65
SOFTSHOE

Donnie Mumberto looked around at a world filled with a roar of confusion. Someone yelled at him, asking what was going on. But when the person, a woman in a pantsuit, saw Softshoe's rifle and bloody jacket, she disappeared into the mayhem.

Spying ahead through the dark for the girl, Cully, he saw only a mass of people trying to move away from whatever lay ahead. Mumberto had been thinking about her on the way here. He knew he had to follow and not let her go this time.

He saw a man carrying two half-grown children in his arms; a woman wheeling a cart filled with pillows; teenagers shoving at one another; a frightened-looking middle-aged man sitting paralyzed behind the wheel of his car. Softshoe stepped over and slapped his hood, getting a blank stare in return. "Better hit it," Mumberto said.

The guy didn't react. Mumberto left him.

His eyes swept the scene, but he couldn't find Cully through the dark and smoke. His whole body felt light, airy, lifted up. He wondered if she had made it here. The Greek had seemed to think so when he left Gregor's pickup and started running.

Softshoe touched his bullet-gouged side, feeling the crusted blood, and pressed harder, checking for the kind of pain that would force him down for good. But, no, it wasn't there. Back in the woods he had stood up and stumbled onto a road. Saw headlights, thought they were more militia. Collapsed. And got picked up by Smereas.

All around he heard clunking, the sound of tires on the bridge pavement, rattling the girders underneath. Like slipping into a mink's skin, his mind tuned out the junk and he kept on. He ignored the commotion, the smoke, the smell of gunpowder, and trotted toward where he'd seen first Smereas and then the big militia man disappear.

An explosion roared on the roadway ahead of him and he noticed a swirl of smoke guttering up. He winced, waiting for it to tear everything to pieces. Instead, only the smoke came, blending with the darkness and obscuring the bridge in a purple haze. More people pressed his way. He was locked in, unable to move for a moment because of the jostling of bodies. Then it eased, and he popped through. The smoke smarted in his eyes and pinched his nose.

His side began to throb. He heard yelling and a thumping overhead. He stopped to peer up. A helicopter, its blades twisting as the machine hovered. What could they see that he couldn't?

"What is it? What's that smoke?" asked a chubby man in shorts and a plain blue T-shirt.

Mumberto saw a woman hanging close, her head under the man's arm. They stood next to a Winnebego, another misappropriated Indian name. "Get back," Softshoe told them. "Walk out the other way.

Both gave him a nervous look, checking out his sniper special and bloody side, before heading off.

Softshoe picked up his pace into the heaviest cloud of the smoke. His eyes smarted, as if washed by ground glass. Almost immediately he slammed into someone. A cop, it looked like. He had to blink, warding off the pain in his side. They faced off, each examining the other's uniform. "What's out there?" asked Mumberto.

But the cop had no chance to answer before another sound cracked the air. This one was louder, with greater definition. Mumberto turned away, again expecting the worst. When that didn't happen, he looked around for the cop, who had vanished.

The smoke cleared and he saw the ice cream truck. He broke into a run, sprinting along the side of the road, and bumped into a pair of

Bridge Authority officers. One was on a walkie-talkie, apparently clued in on what was happening. Softshoe stood there, listened, and learned that the bomb had probably been disarmed, but the suspect, the ice cream driver, had started climbing the catwalk to the northeast tower. Someone said they saw a womango up after him, but with visibility so bad, no one could see much. Someone suggested sending up a sniper. A State Police SWAT team was at that moment en route via helicopter out of Traverse City.

But then Smereas came on, his voice crackling over the radio, and said they couldn't wait. The bomber had a remote detonator. They had to act now.

That's when Mumberto made it clear he was willing to go up with his rifle. No one argued. Softshoe heard a quick discussion over the hand-held radio, the Greek telling the bridge authority officers that the Indian was a sharpshooter and to let him go up the southeast tower, where there was no chance of spooking the bomber into pushing the detonator button.

One of the bridge officers took Softshoe to the base of the southeast tower. He unlocked a squat metal door with one porthole for a window, told Mumberto to climb through, got in himself, punched a couple of switches, and then they were moving up in a service elevator inside. The dark cramped cage rattled and rumbled up through the inside of the tower. He watched the riveted walls of the structure flash past, the floor under him swaying slightly as he rose.

"Never knew this was here," said Mumberto, his side aching again, wetness starting to leak.

The bridge cop didn't respond. He was grim. Riveted metal rolled past the porthole window.

"How far is it from this tower to the north one?" he asked.

"Half mile."

"How dark is it going to be?"

"Pretty dark."

The enclosed space smelled damp, felt cold and musty. He heard gears and cables grind. The floor swayed under his feet. He thought of Cully, just before she left, the rain shiny and wet on her face. How she used her arm to rub hair from her forehead. He was certain she was still in danger.

"I hope you know how to use that thing."

Mumberto nodded at his rifle. He checked for shells and eased back the bolt action, making sure it sprung. Satisfied, he wondered if he would see anything or anyone out there at all, especially in the dark.

The elevator bumped to a stop, jarring him and sending pain through his side, like a sliver of hot ice, digging deep under the arm. He touched it, sure the wound had opened. Then he tried to get his mind off himself.

The doors slid wide, dumping them into a small alcove. "Got three flights to walk up," said the bridge officer.

He slung the rifle over the shoulder on his good side and followed the guy's ass. Mumberto had to bend his head to clear the ceiling. As best he could, even in this bunched space, he tried to get his mind clear and ready for whatever would come next. Sooner than he expected, they slid through another small porthole doorway, took a ladder another few feet to yet another door and emerged onto a railed roof.

The flat space extended twenty yards across the highway below to the other side of the bridge. It was about thirty feet wide. A quick survey showed no one out here. Only stars above. The wind smelled clean, riffling around him. His eyes adjusted from the pale light of the elevator, a light he hadn't even realized was there, to this. Starkly dark. A vast night, ballooning into the sky and extending far over the lake. The waters of his people, this place that crossed the peninsulas, the avenue for their canoes, for trading, for the final wars that gutted them like bucks nailed to trees.

His feet feeling light, he stepped out further. The wound was a nagging reminder that this, too, was a kind of war. But, it was dark; he wouldn't be able to see anything. His trip here was likely useless.

Softshoe was dimly aware of the elevator leaving, dropping back down. He stepped to the metal railing, about chest high. His eyes became pinpricks of awareness, searching out across the distance to the other tower. Dark, it was dark. But dim light played on it. Enough for him to see. "Anyone out there?" asked the cop.

Mumberto put the Remington to his eye. The weapon had brought down a sick elk at seven hundred yards. He let his eyes narrow in on the other tower, a half mile from where he stood. A long shot. Squinting, he saw little. Maybe the top of a head. Maybe not. Although he was sure something stirred. A slipping, twisting movement.

He placed the barrel of his rifle on the railing, keeping it steady, and leaned back, aiming his attention into the scope. He was vaguely aware of the vast silent sway of the bridge under him and calculated that into his firing range. He made note of the wind, breezing in from the west, slapping the left side of his face, nuzzling him. Fog shifted in; lights from the cables gave everything a yellow aura. Damnit. But he willed away the anxiety. The liquid sopped his side. The wound was open, licking at him.

Even up here, he smelled the acrid smoke wafting from the decking of the bridge, the stink of gunpowder, the sharp tang of hot metal from whatever the crazy man had thrown. "This guy using grenades?" asked Mumberto.

"Sounds like."

"People have been killed?"

"Don't know."

Then, a shape bobbed above the rim of the other tower. Was it him?

"You know that you're bleeding?" said the cop.

Softshoe didn't answer. In his scope he saw a shadow, dark against dark, someone inside the railing.

Suddenly, beams of light fell from the sky, the heavens opening onto the northeast tower. A chopping sound echoed, the spearing lights flung from side to side. A helicopter. The guy on the rail lifted his face toward it. He wore some sort of jacket, a vest. White pants. Beardless with his features caught in the glare of the spotlight.

Voices echoed out of the whirlybird, the machine tilting in but then suddenly banking away as the man waved his hand at them, this one a fist, maybe holding the detonator.

"That's him!" said the cop.

Mumberto kept the barrel steady but made allowances for slight movement as his finger tightened, softly, slowly, firmly and then done. His mind was already ahead of the bullet, the hot compacted metal spewed out by gases and flying along at more than two thousand miles per hour.

CHAPTER 66
CULLY

She had been on the deck of the bridge, just wiggling away from the foul-smelling, red-haired militia jerk who had come up from behind her, when she saw Arly through the thick, rolling smoke. He was down by his truck, running for the edge of the bridge, hopping the curb and disappearing over the side. He left two men on the ground. And he left his truck.

A clear and sudden sense of purpose, mixed with rage, drew Cully to her feet. Looking down, she saw a handgun, dropped by the one they called Milo. As for Milo, he was squirming in the grip of a pit bull, of all things. That seemed appropriate. Saved by a dog.

Hardly thinking beyond that, she grabbed the gun and started after Arly. Crazy, she knew, aware she was in over her head. She hopped the curb by the ice cream truck and at the outer railing of the bridge. Beyond was a long drop into the lake. She wondered if he had jumped.. Behind her she heard voices by the truck. "Did you disarm it?" she thought she heard, hoping to hell someone had.

She looked up a glimpse of him on a two-foot wide cable-encased catwalk, leading up. "He's up here!" she yelled.

"Stop him," someone else called. Or had they?

She could still only see smoke and a bombed-out stillness behind her. More voices rose by the truck. She could see Arly lumbering, his large back swaying, moving up and away, obscured by the fog and smoke and night.

Cully stepped back toward the truck, then stopped. She hesitated only a moment, knowing her next move. She slipped over the railing onto a small platform and turned her attention toward the tower, around whose steel the smoke curled like living hair. She couldn't see him.

She touched the butt of the gun, stuck in the waistband of her jeans. It was a comfort. She would use it if she could. She hovered for a moment, unsure, but only for a moment. Then she yelled, "He's up here!" As her eyes quickly adapted to the foggy dimness on all sides, she started to climb.

The last few feet were awful. She could hardly put one foot in front of the other. Despite herself, she had looked down at the lake slumbering far below in the dark and felt a huge empty gap open in her stomach. But she kept on trudging upward, a slow-footed acrobat in a foggy mess of clouds that ran over her face like wet shreds of paper. Her hands were raw from using the handrails to drag herself up. Her chest felt as if it had been rubbed by jagged shells. Her ankle, sprained and swollen from the jump out of the van in the graveyard, seemed about to tear in two. But now she was almost there. How long it had taken, she had no idea. As for Arly, she had no idea if he was even up here anymore. Much of her ascent had been obscured by the rags of clouds.

Climbing, she had thought about God for a bit; it was hard not to in the stupendous space above the black water. She wondered if He, or she, or it, was out there, up there, in there, wherever. To tell the truth, Cully didn't believe, never could, maybe never would. Jesus was a wonderful story that didn't hold up two thousand years later. The rest, Islam, Buddhism and the flaky caste-crazed Hindus, were well beyond her reckoning. Somehow, with a terrible sense of finality, Cully felt there really was no God watching down on her as she labored her way toward the top. But even so, she found herself praying, calling out for assistance from on high. Somehow, if you're out there, give me a hand, she thought, because I sure as hell need it now.

It was a petition, cast off into the vast, windy night on this steel structure that seemed to live and breathe all around her.

Trudging the final angle of the cable ramp, Cully reached into her waistband and pulled out Milo's gun. She felt its hard, moist metal and wound her finger through the slot, liking the heavy, lethal way it drooped in her hand. She paused a moment, wisps of fog around her, and craned a look at the sky, sharp and glittering with stars. She thought briefly of Edna, driving her on. But, would even Edna have braved this, or, more accurately, have been foolish enough to climb this bridge?

Not sure of that and even more uncertain of what she would find, Cully put her doubts aside and stepped up and onto the top of the tower roof. She was honed to a clear purpose now, well beyond thought. Her body weak and rubbery, she glanced around, weapon ready, and spotted him on the other side of the platform, by the rail, looking down. Twenty feet away. He was turned away from her, digging in his vest for something, maybe more of his hand bombs. Or so it seemed. She thought she heard him singing, a mumbled parody of a child's religious song. "Jesus loves me this I know."

Maybe it was the wind. Or her mind. But it seemed right. At least, Arly thought highly of Christ.

"Because the Bible tells me so."

There you go, she thought. He's blubbering Bible songs. Maybe he just wants someone to save him.

Breathing deeply, she called to him to stop. Or tried to. Her throat wouldn't work. Sounds came out as a croak. If he heard anything, he didn't show it. His mind was aimed hard on the twisted business of pulling a fireball from a pocket.

She tried to get her voice working again, ripping out words, which he didn't hear. He had one of those hand bombs in his palm and was getting ready to rip it open. Even from behind, he looked like a loosed animal.

Thunder boomed above them. A terrible thumping sound. Here and then gone.

"Arly!" she finally got out, waving the hand gun.

Still, he paid her no mind. Cully wondered if she was even talking, if the hard climb up here had sapped her of her voice, of her breath and energy. He leaned closer to the railing, ready to lob the thing, to cause more havoc below. She screamed for him to stop. Squawked out sound. He didn't budge. She took aim and pulled the trigger.

Nothing. Not even a click. She tried again. This time it burst to life, bucking in her hand.

She saw him turn. His rage was so clear she could smell it, heavier than the smoke, even worse than her own anger. She didn't cower. As far as she could tell, she had missed. He held the small bomb in his hand, his thumb pressing down on a lever.

"Throw it the other way, into the lake," she ordered, her hand wavering.

He didn't seemed to understand. She wasn't sure he even recognized her. Most of him was covered by shadow. He looked like a large troll, twisted and humped, yet strangely childish. "Get rid of it." She was on one knee now, bracing the gun, hand under wrist.

Arly's eyes registered something. Then he turned back to the ledge, his arm starting in an arc. She took it a little slower, shutting one eye, trying to get herself steady. She pointed carefully for his left shoulder blade, near where a bullet would rip through and ram his heart. Ready to follow this to the end, her finger pressed for the trigger.

But then the thunder came again and light dropped from the sky. A glaring spotlight, right on him, and Arly turned, irritated, as if wondering who else was trying to block his fun.

This time it was like a curtain had lifted, revealing all of his newly scrubbed face. The folds in it, the lines in the forehead, the thin mouth and large, nondescript nose. The patch of scars on his neck. She saw fear in him, and anger, and something slack and deranged. She knew there was a story here that she'd never write. She wasn't that objective.

Arly was looking up, winding up like a pitcher with his grenade, ready to blot the chopper from the sky. He swore and yelled at the spinning bird. His face was like a blood-engorged eye. His feet were planted on the rail; he hardly teetered. Cully found herself paying attention to every detail. Arly was screaming: "Because the Bible tells me so!"

The helicopter pilot, maybe catching on to what he was dealing with, started to backthrust the motor, trying to rear up and out of range. Arly had them in his sights. His arm moved forward, ready to deliver the grenade and kill them. "Christalmightyfuckingassholes." Same old insane growl. No Bible song now. His body was one mass of terrible intention. The arm finished its arc, the hand about to snap it into the air.

But then, at the final moment, he jerked and swung around, like a puppet, his body growing limp. He did a slow dance on the ledge, his shoulders turning to her, a gush of red, slick with tissue, showing from his forehead. His features registered dull shock, his arms falling. The grenade dropped with a solid bounce onto the floor of the tower. He tipped over the edge of the tower into the darkness.

"Grenade!" The booming, magnified voice.

Cully knew that and wanted to escape it. But her body could hardly move; her legs were cramped from the long climb.

Someone had already gotten to it. He appeared out of nowhere and scrambled across the roof, movement that she barely registered. Someone bent down and reached for the grenade, a broad back, familiar. Her father. It had to be.

Cully ran for him, fearing the thing was going to go off. She wanted to warn him; didn't he know? But of course he did. He was protecting her. That was why he was here.

The explosion came long before she got to him.. It drove her back against a wall and knocked her to her knees. The platform filled with smoke. She heard the piercing wail of someone, her father, in pain. She knelt there stunned for a few moments but then scrambled up.

As best she could, Cully tottered his way, in the enveloping haze, her mouth filled with the taste of hot powder, and fell, face forward, right on her dad. He was curled up, moaning. She swaddled him in her arms. She thought instantaneously of that barn fire, of the dead horse and her father's grief-broken face. That time he had refused to let her hold him. He was in anguish over his dead wife and wanted no comfort at all.

This time he had no choice.

CHAPTER 67
SMEREAS

The shattered body of the militia madman sprawled face down on the hood of a 1993 Acura. No one was in the shiny black car. Smereas saw the end: the cannonball of flesh crashing down, slamming the front of the foreign job and sticking. A horrible sight, a crumbled sack flattening, but best for everyone on this bridge.

Almost as soon as Arly Fleck fell onto the car, cops and bystanders muscled in, Smereas among them. He stood near the dangling legs, not wanting to see what the three hundred-foot fall had done to the man's face.

"Christ almighty," said a tall State Police sergeant. The ice cream truck was still parked in the middle of the bridge, waiting for orders that would never come. After disarming the primary fuse and then absorbing a couple thumps from the grenades, Smereas had slid underneath and found the spot that attached the remote wires to the body of the bomb. They had not been attached, just as Gregor had suspected. Burke had been pressed for time, maybe. Or he may have wondered if Fleck would get anxious too soon and send the deal to kingdom come on the way here. Who the hell knew? Whatever, it wasn't going to blow.

"This is a goddamned mess," said the sergeant.

Several people were lying or sitting or slouching on the bridge and along the curbs in both directions. He had no idea if anyone else had been killed.

As far as he could tell, none had been fragmentation grenades, at least down here. And thank God; if even one had exploded, dozens of people would have been hurt, many of them killed.

Even without that carnage, Smereas knew this would be a terrible mess to clear. Vehicles and people clogged the bridge from one end to the other. Above he heard the thumping of a couple helicopters. He still wasn't sure what had happened up there. He glanced up but saw nothing through the smoke and fog and smudged stark lighting from the choppers. He knew Gannon, along with two county officers, had taken the elevator up.

"We've got to secure this area," Smereas told the state cop.

From above came more whopping of helicopter blades. Smereas saw three men in uniforms slip through the door and into the service elevator for the ride up. One carried a large fire extinguisher. He heard ambulance sirens approaching from each end of the bridge. His nose and eyes still smarted from the tear gas, now cleared. Somewhere nearby he heard moans.

"Are there any more of these maniacs around?" asked the cop, his eyes showing that intense, self-contained look Smereas had seen many times in tight situations. It was probably pasted on his face as well.

"I don't think so," said the ATF agent. But, he knew that with these people, you couldn't count on it. "Let's start getting everyone the hell out of here who doesn't belong."

"Oh for God's sake," the cop said suddenly.

Smereas followed his glance and saw a crowd making its way toward them from the north end of the bridge. He saw bouncing lights and someone in the middle of it, a familiar form: small, square-jawed, blonde hair, wearing a dark parka, coming fast and furiously. If he wasn't mistaken, the frigging governor. What the hell was he doing here now?

More men shoved in from behind. The ATF agent turned. FBI. More state cops. He looked back at the body, twisted and smashed on the hood. Blood drained from where the face lay. Blood dripped from his foot, rivulets on the grating of the bridge. Jesus, what had possessed him?

"C'mon, c'mon, make way," he heard as more people shoved close, like a river running over its banks.

Smereas decided to back off. He wasn't in charge, and he was pretty sure this man Arly was the end of it. There had been a couple of them on motorcycles, but they had been taken care of, and they weren't really part of Arly's show. This disaster. Again, he wondered about the bridge roof, and Gannon, and the girl who had climbed up after Arly. Then there was the Indian. Had he taken Arly out? Even with the mashed flesh, the squashed limbs and upper body, Smereas had seen a hole in the head. Bullseye.

"Hey, what's going on here?" More people, muscling in.

Especially with politicians on the way, Smereas wanted out. He didn't need to handle this part. Let those who wanted the huge profile do it.

But when he tried to turn to slide out, he met a mass of bodies, crowding in, getting a look. He yelled, "Clear out. Step back." He gazed at the swirling searchlights up on the rim of the tower from where this man had dropped. Smoke rose from the roof, curling in large plumes, as if the thing were on fire.

"Governor, governor," he heard.

Unable to slide out for now, the Greek remained and watched the group approaching, the crowd parting as the pint-sized, long-jawed, pretty boy governor appeared. Almost on the other side of the hood.

Smereas recognized some of the bigwigs near him. He also saw the pack of hungry reporters, drawn by the smell of blood. The ATF agent knew the kind of coverage this circus would get. He wondered how this was going to play for his career. After all, he didn't stop Arly, and he was lucky Gregor had stepped in and took care of Burke. People, himself included, were going to take a fall.

"C'mon," Smereas said again, addressing everyone surrounding the car, including the state's chief executive.. Someone had to take charge. He was angry at himself that it ever got this far. "Get back. We need to get this area clear." He faced the crowd, pushing out with his arms. An FBI man whom he vaguely recognized took the hint. He also started to edge people back.

Finally it caught. A couple more cops starting shoving people, demanding they leave. In the distance the ATF agent heard more sirens, whooping in and out, as if in protest of what had happened.

From above the helicopters continued to play their lights through the wafts of smoke. Smereas vaguely realized his body was drenched in sweat. Adrenaline pumped through him like gasoline. "That side too," said Smereas, swinging his arms across the space of the car. "Now, damnit. This isn't a sideshow."

The prying eyes of the cameras, crushing in, seemed to pause and heed his words. More uniforms started the job of spreading the bystanders back and away. The Greek spun his eyes in all directions, taking it all in, seeing three of his fellow ATF agents jogging his way. He waved them toward the ice cream truck. He thought: I'm going to be on national TV.

Within a couple minutes, nearly everyone had cleared. A pack of FBI and state cops gathered to the side, conferring. But one person remained, directly across from Smereas. The deflated, crushed body lay between them.

What in the world was this guy doing out here anyhow? Smereas was about to roar at him to get back too, when the ATF agent realized Franklin Bones had his head bent, as if prayer, his face in a grimace. Even in the madness and confusion, Smereas stopped, surprised.

Without thinking, he had assumed this jerk had strode out here to get in on the action. To stick his fingerprints all over it. After all, his party was nixed; the body of his dad wasn't going to be commemorated. This smashed militia nut had squelched it all. Spoiled the birthday bash because . . . suddenly it dawned. Fleck had a connection here. He wanted to bomb the bridge because the dead worker was his kin, too. The ATF agent had heard that in the last couple hours. Another bit of information he had filed to ponder later. In the chaos, it hadn't registered until now.

"This guy," said Smereas.

The governor, alone, as if on a stage spotlit by the floods from above, now stared at the body. Franklin Bones was shaking his head. He reached out a hand, tentatively, and let it hang above the head. If Smereas wasn't mistaken, water stained the politician's cheeks. A TV camera, like a huge eye, reeled it in from the side.

"Governor," said the ATF agent.

The little man shook his head.

"Sir?" asked Smereas.

Bones raised his face slowly, his expression blank. He shook himself alert, narrowing his eyes at Smereas. The governor snapped back to attention. Maybe he hadn't realized there was an audience. But then, he had to. He brought his peanut gallery with him, didn't he? "Who're you?" the politician asked.

"I'm a federal firearms agent."

"Why didn't you stop him?"

"We tried, sir."

"For God's sake."

Passing the buck. Typical. Smereas made to swing away, to help get the area settled so the hard, tedious business of cleaning up could begin.

"I'm talking to you, agent."

Smereas put his hands, peppered with cuts, into the pockets of his jacket.

A skinny man in a pink sweater showed up behind the governor. Some kind of gold chain around his throat. Piersma. He stuck a hand on the politician's shoulder. Behind him was another glitzy looking man. Older, a mane of gray hair. Smereas recognized him as well, but couldn't place him.

The man with the sweater and chains leaned into the governor's ear. Frank Bones continued to gaze at Smereas as he listened. The talking went on nearly a full minute.

Then, when Piersma stepped back, fading into the swarm of staff people, the governor took another few seconds to examine the corpse. He wrapped his arms around his shoulders, seemed to steady himself, and took a few deep breaths. Apparently swallowing back any more emotion or reflection, he wiped forearms over his cheeks and almost visibly got a grip on himself. Put on a public face.

"You know him?" asked Smereas.

Bones stared, a hard edge in his eyes.

For a second, their eyes engaged in a dance for the truth. In that moment, Smereas got a glimpse of the governor's real story, or part of it. But he also knew he didn't give a shit. There was work to do right now. He was dimly aware of the reporters swarming in and the governor turning to go, raising his hands, refusing to say anything to anyone. The boozer and the other one with the white hair followed..

The ATF agent stepped away and spotted the first of the ambulances arriving from Mackinaw City. If he wasn't mistaken, he also noticed a dog, clamping the end of a man's arm. The man, prostrate on the bridge deck, was crying. One of the militia nuts.

Smereas wanted to smile, but he no time for that either. As the FBI and others now moved in to manage the scene, he decided to head for the tower. He wanted to check on Cable Gannon.

CHAPTER 68
CULLY

The urns were heavier than she could have guessed. Maybe fifteen pounds apiece. Cully brought one from the basement and the other from the trunk of her car. She took the lid off the first, a gray metal job, hefted it, and started to pour, stepping along the edge of the dirt mound on which the barn once sat. An area she had carefully tilled. She turned the open lid and watched thick grainy clumps drop to the ground. What was left of her mother. In many ways, hard to believe.

Circling the edges, Cully then moved in closer, scattering the remains as she went. Walking through soft soil prepared especially for this. Thinking she ought to pray, make more of an occasion out of this. But this rote work, letting ashes meet the ground, muck to muck and so on, was about all she could handle.

She had insisted that she do this part alone. In the last few weeks, as the weather finally started to warm and she put the finishing touches on her book, Cully had come out here. To the back yard, to the scene of the crime, or one of them. To the barn in which her mother's horse, Bashful Blue, had been housed. To this place where her father, in his grief, had shot the animal and torched the structure because he couldn't bear to see the horse suffer from the loss of its mistress, and from the lung sickness that it had come down with. That night, with its fire and her father broken, still stuck with her. That, and other things as well. The bridge and its aftermath.

Out here, she had raked and hauled away debris, some of it bones, she had to believe. Rotten timbers, charred metal, what was left of a small world that had meant so much to her mother, and inadvertently to her dad. She had worked a little at a time, a half hour or maybe an hour a day, often after writing in her upstairs office. Writing the story of Arly and the bridge and the governor, some of whose secrets were finally starting to leak out.

Without realizing it, Cully finished dumping her mother's ashes into the rich topsoil. The urn, carved on one side with a cross, was much lighter now. She took it over to where the other one sat, this one a little fancier and more squat, also bearing what remained of someone she loved. Someone she had loved very much. It sat near the pile of flowers, bulbs, plants and ground cover she would set in later.

Putting down one urn, she brought up the other. As she did, she checked the bright blue May sky. A high, soaring sky this afternoon, seeming endless, full of curiously sketchy clouds. For a second she wondered if she could read her future there, if the book, coming out by a big time publisher in New York, would sell. For that matter, would her editor like what she had written? The story that she had told, this biography of a twisted militia man and his strange relationship with the chief executive of Michigan. To say that Frank Bones had been a reluctant interview was not putting it bluntly enough. Rather, he had tried to keep her from writing it. But when the *Detroit Free Press,* for whom she had written the original stories, got hold of his attempts at roadblocks, he backed off. But he had clammed up, too. Never really told her much. Which was too bad, since it left a more or less one-sided book. A book telling about Rolly and his gypsy wife and Preston's involvement, or part of his involvement, and Arly's awful, awful life. A book about the governor, too, but he had worked hard to discredit her and to put distance between himself and what happened that night at the bridge. Amazingly, he had been able to do it. With flair and grace. Whether he would get reelected a couple years down the road was anybody's guess.

Looking up at those sparse white clouds, Cully had no idea how it would unfold. Maybe she'd get on Oprah; maybe it would be a best seller; maybe her editor would can the manuscript, telling her no one cared anymore about the militia mind. Cully shrugged, to an extent not caring.

The second urn sagged in her arms like a baby, demanding attention. Cradling it, she let her attention skip across the clumps she had already dropped. Later she'd rake it together, then bank it in with living things. A true memorial garden. Later still she might dig a pond behind by the crabapple trees. For a second, she thought of one who wouldn't be buried here. Arly. They'd stuck his remains, after they were done with them, in a pauper's grave outside the burg of Acme in a scrubby graveyard by railroad tracks and a closed grist mill. Cully had made a trip there, once, mostly for the book. She thought of spitting on it, even wondered if she ought to shed a tear over it, and in the end just left, feeling sad and sick and disgusted. Two people had died in his attack on the bridge, and a few others had been hurt.

Smelling some sort of sweetness in the wind, maybe from the honeysuckle she was going to transplant, she started in on the second round of ash strewing. Again, greasy clots, final flesh and gristle. This from the man to whom she dedicated her book. Entitled *Marks on the Beast,* referring to Arly's scars. She never was able to fully determine how he got them. She had the idea from what he had said that they came from a fire in which his mother died. But his mother passed away in a mental institution in upstate New York in 1966, almost ten years after Rolly died on the bridge. Arly had lived in a series of foster homes, one worse than the other. As for his mother, Cully was able to track down a distant cousin who very unwillingly told her that Rochelle had been a prostitute in Poland during the last part of World War II. Rolly, serving in the Army, met her there and somehow brought her back with him. Cully got the strong impression that Rochelle, who actually had a hard to pronounce Polish name, never truly changed her ways once she arrived in America. But that was hard to determine. Cully had tried several times to interview Preston Bones, the man who fathered the governor through her, but he never agreed to talk.

From Joy Williams, a friend of the governor's, Cully learned some things. Actually, early on, she was the one who halfway confirmed a rumor that Preston killed Rolly in a lover's spat, if only by her silence. But then she also got muzzled somewhere down the line and afterward vehemently denied everything, even that Preston was the governor's real father. Without this juicy stuff, her book lost luster and power. She couldn't really reveal the worst dirt. It remained mostly a sorry story about Arly.

For that matter, Cully's editor was making noise about the lawyers not being too sure how much they liked any of this story now. Much of it was unsubstantiated, even though Cully was absolutely sure it was right on the mark. With so many people denying things, she found it tough to nail it down. As for Preston pushing Rolly into the wet concrete, that was the big cheese of a secret that would doubtless make her book a bestseller. But all that remained a rumor. A rumor she mentioned in her book, and which she was afraid the editor would cut.

As she figured these things, she started spreading ashes, imparting them to the soil from one end of the garden to the other, her feet squishing through the wet rich dirt. Her nose took in a symphony of spring smells, new life carrying with it the undercurrent of blood.

Again, sooner that she thought, the urn was played out. She tipped it and tapped the bottom, making sure all of it fell to the ground, mixing in with mulch and some wood chips and the last portions of her mother. Maybe an odd mix, this staunch Methodist mother and a Jewish photographer. Nothing was embossed on the side of David's urn. She had arranged for his ashes to be shipped from the vault in Philadelphia, no family remaining there for him anyway.

Standing in the middle of the soil on which she had worked so lovingly, she gazed across the yard at her home. Three stories, brick and wood sides, with a pitched green roof. A large home, too large even when everyone was around. On the first floor, just behind the window, she caught the reflected shadow of her father watching her from his wheelchair, still healing, his stomach and chest swathed with thin bandages over his burned flesh..

He had spent two months in the burn unit at the University of Michigan hospital. The smoke bomb on which he had fallen had torn through his skin and gone deeper, destroying flesh and, along with the infections, nearly taking his life.

In the hospital, keeping vigil with him, Cully started the book. Before that, even as he was being cared for in the early going, she had written her series for the *Free Press.* It ran in papers all over the country. From it came the book offer, even one proposed movie deal, also squelched by the governor's backroom shenanigans. For a time, Cully had thought the real story was Rochelle, the mother who died insane. This woman who made her way from the ravages of war, only to be ravaged again. Maybe later, in a novel.

Cully raised a hand, waving toward the window at her dad. She had asked if he wanted to come out here for this ceremony, if that's what it was, but he said he'd wait until the ashes were laid out. He must have known that she didn't want him here. But now it was time. She jerked her head in his direction, as if saying get the lead out.

She returned to the burial mound, grabbed up a steel rake and went to work. With quick, long sure strokes, she mixed earth with earth, dust with dust, the debris of two lives with what was left of the barn. Cully knew part of Bashful Blue was in there, too, that sturdy, magnificent horse with muscular flanks and huge eyes that shone every time Cully's mom entered its space.

She heard movement across the grass, coming toward her. She waited, chin on the tip of the rake, her back and arms tingling from the effort, heart thudding, sweat dribbling.

"You're doing one hell of a job covering my tracks," said her father.

"Don't kid yourself. Everyone knows where you've been."

Now, she turned. He was pale and had lost forty pounds, reminding her of an old man with mild palsy. But he was smiling, this man who had wanted to save her life at the cost of his own. Lucky for them that grenade was a smoke bomb. Even if it had caused him terrible and lasting pain. He wore a suit, dressed up for the occasion and sitting in his wheelchair. He was able to walk, but still too weak to use his legs for very long.

Behind him, at the handles, not in a suit, was the Indian. He looked at her with that stern, dark expression, probing her, making her wonder what he saw. He had on a crisp white shirt and string tie; his shiny blue-black hair rested on his shoulders. They stopped at the edge of the mound.

"Who's going to pray?" asked her dad.

"You two decide."

"Well then, him." Her dad craned his head up and twisted around at Donnie Mumberto. Softshoe. Sort of silly, but she liked it, or rather had gotten used to it.

"I guess that's why you're here," she said to him.

He nodded, already knowing that, even if no one had really made plans for it, he was supposed to say the holy words. The men had said they would stay inside while she completed the part that was so important to her, this tender planting. Then they'd come out for the formal part, if this was so formal.

"Before anyone does that," said her dad.

Donnie looked down at her father's head. Cully got down on one knee to get a more even perspective on him in that two-wheeled contraption.

"I was hoping . . . " He gazed beyond her at the mound, eyes watery, skin hanging from his face. "Hoping . . . " Whatever it was, he didn't get it out. Just shook his head, wiped his face with the back of a shaky hand.

It hurt Cully to see him so depleted. She went over to him, knelt at his side. The Indian stood above them. "What, Dad?"

He shook his head, fierce and angry, staring at the dirt, maybe remembering himself with that gas can, the horse at his feet.

The smell of the earth rose up at her. She knew they could all smell its richness, its flavor, the power that it contained. Already she imagined it filled with color, petals and stems and leaves. A living cemetery. She felt her dad reach out to her, hand on her shoulder. "Don," she said. "How about saying that prayer your uncle taught you. The one about the trees?"

She looked at him. He kept his poker face but smiling down in those eyes, he said: "That was my grandfather."

Mumberto had his scars, too, on the side, ones she had touched, but they had healed fast.

Cully smiled. "Whatever."

Softshoe's voice started in, flowed out, almost musical. Telling more a story than praying a prayer. Which was fine. Which was just about right.

It was one of the stories he told her in the hospital, as her dad recovered. Between bouts at her book. A tale about roots and land and people who cared about each other. Yes, it was fine. It was right. It was exactly what she needed to hear.